Pippa Roscoe lives in N
makes daily promises to
she'll leave the computer
countryside. She can't remember a time when she
wasn't dreaming about handsome heroes and innocent
heroines. Totally her mother's fault, of course—she
gave Pippa her first romance to read at the age of
seven! She is inconceivably happy that she gets
to share those daydreams with you. Follow her on
Twitter @PippaRoscoe.

When **Kali Anthony** read her first romance novel at
fourteen she realised two truths: that there can never
be too many happy endings, and that one day she
would write them herself. After marrying her own
tall, dark and handsome hero, in a perfect friends-to-
lovers romance, Kali took the plunge and penned her
first story. Writing has been a love affair ever since.
If she isn't battling her cat for access to the keyboard,
you can find Kali playing dress-up in vintage
clothes, gardening, or bushwalking with her husband
and three children in the rainforests of South-East
Queensland.

FROM ONE NIGHT TO DESERT QUEEN

PIPPA ROSCOE

OFF-LIMITS TO THE CROWN PRINCE

KALI ANTHONY

MILLS & BOON

First Published in Great Britain 2021
by Mills & Boon, an imprint of HarperCollins*Publishers* Ltd,
1 London Bridge Street, London, SE1 9GF

www.harpercollins.co.uk

HarperCollins*Publishers*
1st Floor, Watermarque Building,
Ringsend Road, Dublin 4, Ireland

From One Night to Desert Queen © 2021 Pippa Roscoe

Off-Limits to the Crown Prince © 2021 Kali Anthony

ISBN: 978-0-263-28254-2

07/21

MIX
Paper from
responsible sources
FSC™ C007454

Printed and bound in Spain
by CPI, Barcelona

FROM ONE NIGHT
TO DESERT QUEEN

PIPPA ROSCOE

MILLS & BOON

This was written during the break between Coronavirus lockdowns in the UK when, more than ever, I was reminded of the power of reading romance. The power to escape, the power to hope, to love, and to look to a brighter future with a happy ending.

So, this is for all the incredible romance authors, editors, copy-editors, cover artists, production staff, admin staff, publishers, retailers, bloggers, reviewers… All the individuals who help make romance available to us readers even in the hardest of times.

Thank you.

PROLOGUE

'I'M NOT SURE that I should go.'

'We don't really have much choice.'

'I don't want to leave you with Star and the rest of it…'

Star Soames's heart thudded painfully in her chest. She knew that her sisters would be absolutely mortified if they knew she was listening, but hated the way she had been lumped in with 'the rest of it'. As if she were a duty, a burden, just like the one the grandfather they'd never met—thankfully, as far as Star was concerned—had placed on them.

Star willed back the tears clouding her vision as she tried to concentrate on what Skye, the eldest, was saying.

'It should only be a couple of days. Fly to Costa Rica, get the map from Benoit Chalendar, come home. Simple as that.'

'Except he's not likely to have the map on him, Skye,' came the gently worded reply from Summer, their youngest sister and the peacekeeper of the family.

'Okay, so add in a day to return via France and I'll be back before you know it.'

Star ran her thumb down the length of the thick gold chain of the necklace that they had found only yesterday, along with their great-great-great-grandmother's journals, in a hidden recess tucked behind a section of shelves that swung open at the flick of a notch in Catherine's library. Star preferred that name to the other names the smaller library had come to be known by, like *the women's library* or *the little library*, and she wasn't surprised that none of the male Soames heirs had ever thought to look there.

If anyone had ever suspected Catherine of spiriting away the family diamonds from her evil husband Anthony, it had never been more than a suspicion as generation after generation went half mad trying to solve the mystery of the missing jewels that must be worth a small fortune. It was as if every single subsequent Soames had let the sprawling Norfolk Estate run to ruin in order to chase a myth, including Elias Soames, the man who had rejected and disowned their mother before she'd even left her teens. Star shivered in memory of the image of his portrait hanging in the estate office, where she and her sisters had first heard the terms of his will. As the lawyer had read the fiendish requirements of the inheritance, Elias Soames had stared down at them like a Dickensian villain, for all that the painting could only have been made twenty years before.

Elias had given them only two months to track down the Soames diamonds. And if they failed? The estate would pass to the National Trust. Star nearly laughed. If it hadn't been for their mother, the girls might have given the estate to the Trust with their blessing, none of them wanting anything to do with such a twisted manipulation. But because of their mother...

'In the meantime, please keep an eye on Star. You know how she gets.'

How she gets? Star mouthed to herself, frowning, shifting away from the door, really not wanting to hear any more but unable to get far before hearing Skye carry on.

'I'm worried that she'll try and go after the next clue herself. Especially as it could be so...'

'Romantic?' both of her sisters chimed together, descending into fits of giggles. Star clenched her jaw. She'd read and loved romances for more than half her life, defended them more times than she could count and would continue to do so while she still had breath in her lungs.

'I just worry that she'd get herself into trouble. And we really can't afford to...we don't have the time to get this wrong.'

A stab of hurt cut through her. While she hated what her sisters were saying, they were right. She looked around at the library, through the window where the stars in the night sky blinked over the land that came with the estate. Land that, had Mariam Soames lived there, might have had the right postcode. A postcode that would have meant she'd have had access to the most successful treatment for her stage three cancer. But her small flat in Salisbury, near the New Forest, was about as far as possible from this sprawling estate with two wings and more than forty rooms and was very much in the wrong postcode. Star couldn't help but shake her head at the injustice of it, at the cruelty that meant life or death was based on income, savings or property location.

'We've already lost two weeks getting this far. But now we have the journals, now that you've decoded the secret message written in them, we have our first real start to finding the Soames diamonds. Benoit Chalendar has the map of the secret passageways in the estate, I'm sure of it.'

'Skye, even if you do get the map, then we still need to find out where on the map they are hidden and how to access it when we do find it. They're not going to be just lying in a corner of the secret passageways. And if we find whatever the next clue is while you're still away, then Star will *have* to go. I need to be here to meet with the potential buyer and you know that the clause insists that one of us stay in residence for the two months we have to track down the missing jewels,' Summer reminded Skye.

'Can you believe this is our life right now? On a treasure hunt for diamonds that have been missing for over one hundred and fifty years?'

'No more than I can believe that all this could be for nothing if we don't find the jewels and the entire estate is handed over to the National Trust. And then we wouldn't be able to help Mum.'

Selling the estate was the *only* way that the sisters would be able to pay for their mother's medical treatment.

'You haven't said how you know this mysterious billionaire…'

Star listened for an answer, but none came from Summer.

'You know you can talk to us if you need to.'

'I know.'

Star listened as the footsteps retreated down the corridor away from the library before sinking into the ancient leather chair. Again, her fingers ran up and down the thick bronze twists of the necklace, the action comforting as the heavy rectangular pendant swung like a pendulum back and forth from where it hung. It hurt that her sisters didn't think she could do her part without getting into trouble. That they doubted her. But, instead of wallowing in self-pity, she saw herself like an Arthurian knight, brandishing her sword, battle cry at the ready, determined to fulfil her quest. Gripping the pendant in her fist, she swore that she would follow the next clue wherever it led and she *would* return proving her sisters wrong, she *would* help to save her mother.

CHAPTER ONE

KHALIF INHALED DEEPLY through his nose and out through his mouth. Repeating the action did nothing to dislodge the tension pounding angrily in his temples. He rubbed at his eyes, squinting against his thumb and forefinger.

Five hours.

Five wasted hours he'd sat in that room, while fifteen people stared back at him as coffee grew cold, sweets grew stale and the room had become so stuffy they'd needed to open a window.

Stalking down the corridor, he told himself that he just needed air. Fresh air. He wasn't running. He just needed a minute to himself. Which was why he was taking the staff routes through the palace, not the main ones. He was *not* hiding from Amin, his brother's—no, his *own*—assistant. He was simply ensuring the longevity of the bespectacled man's life.

Through the window, across the courtyard, Khalif could see the tourists leaving the exhibition housed in the public areas of Duratra's palace. The sound of two boys laughing as they were chased affectionately by their mother cut through Khalif like a knife, transporting him back to a time when he and his brother had run rings around the palace guards.

Grief was like a punch to the gut. Swift, harsh, hot

and angry. An emotion he could not allow to be seen now that he was first in line to the throne. Three years on from the terrible accident and he still caught himself noting something to tell his brother, wondering what Faizan would think, would advise. But Khalif wasn't sure what was worse, to do that, or for that to stop.

It was a visceral sense of wrongness. As if that day the world had shifted a few degrees. Grief felt like trying to push the entire world back into place, millimetre by millimetre. And nothing worked. Not even pretending that he didn't feel like an imposter. A substitute for his brother's throne, as if Faizan would just appear from around the corner, laughing at him, telling him it was all a joke and taking back the responsibility that he, unlike Khalif, had been taught to manage. But Khalif knew better than to believe in fairy tales and daydreams.

The urge to find the nearest bar and wash away the acrid taste of resentment and grief with a drink was strong. But he'd not touched alcohol or a woman since he'd received the news about his brother. He might have once been the spare, the Playboy Prince loved internationally and equally by women and newspapers alike, but he was now next in line to the throne. And each and every day had been a battle to prove his worth as he forged himself into a ruler that honoured his brother, his father and his country.

He skirted the corridor that ran parallel to the rooms that housed the large public exhibition on Duratrian history and rounded the corner to where the security suite for the public areas was located and came to a halt. All five security staff, two in uniform and three in plain clothes, were huddled round the monitor as if their lives depended on it. Adrenaline crashed through him, his body preparing for fight.

'What's going on?' he demanded as he entered the room, searching the bank of monitors lining the back wall for any sign of threat or danger to the royal family.

The way the men all started and looked as guilty as schoolboys would have been funny if his heart hadn't still been pounding in his chest, his pulse throbbing painfully in his neck as the adrenaline receded.

'Nothing.'

'Sorry, Your Royal Highness, Sheikh—'

'I know my name, Jamal,' Khalif ground out. 'What is it?'

A few more denials hit the air, too many shaking heads and hands, and even if that hadn't piqued his curiosity a flash of red caught his eye on the central monitor. The one that the men had all been staring at.

'What is…'

A tourist stood in front of one of the large paintings in the Alsayf Hall. Khalif cocked his head to one side as if that would make the image easier to see. The female figure was respectfully dressed, despite the relaxed attitude towards attire in Duratra, with a sage green headscarf that…

Again, there was the flash of red. The scarf had fallen back a little and a long, thick curl of fiery red slipped forward before the woman quickly tucked it back behind the folds of her hair covering. All this was done with an economy of movement and without taking her eyes from the painting. Without the distraction of the bright red hair, Khalif took in the rest of the woman.

The denim jacket she was wearing covered her arms and was folded back at the cuff to reveal a series of gold and bronze bangles that hung around a delicate wrist. The jacket was cropped at the waist so that the white and green striped dress that dropped all the way to the floor should have been perfectly modest had it not hinted at the mouth-watering curves of her—

He forced his eyes from the screen and looked to the men in charge of his family's security.

'Jamal, you're a married man,' he scolded as if he hadn't just been staring at the very same thing. 'I expected more from you.'

'It's not that—' the guard tried to justify.

'No, of course not,' Khalif interrupted with a half laugh, 'because your wife would have your balls if—'

'No, Your Highness, it's really not that... She's been there for an hour.'

'And?' Khalif demanded.

'No, she's been *there*, in front of *that painting*, for an hour,' Jamal clarified.

'Oh.'

Khalif returned his attention to the monitor, where the tourist still stood in front of the painting of Hātem Al Azhar, his great-great-great-grandfather. He frowned, wondering what it was about the painting that had enthralled her for *an hour*. Given that, on average, it took one harassed school teacher to ferry a group of unfocused seven-year-olds a total of fifty-four minutes through the first section of the exhibition on the history of Duratra—a fact he knew only too well since his father had deemed it necessary for him to spend his teenage summers working at the exhibition in an attempt to instil in him a respect for their country's history and an awareness of the importance of tourism. Instead, all it had done was broaden his pick-up lines to include several more international languages. That aside, it *did* seem strange that this tourist had spent so much time in front of one painting.

He felt a prickle of awareness across his skin as he realised that the men had regrouped around the same monitor as if drawn by a siren call. He turned to stare at them until they moved out of his personal space, some clearing throats and others grabbing pens to make useless notes on unnecessary bits of paper.

Khalif gave her one last look, trying to ignore the twinge of disappointment as he took his leave. At one time she would have been just his type.

Star looked up at the large painting of the man who had ruled Duratra over one hundred and fifty years ago and smiled. The patrician nose was broad and noble, the jaw line masterful. Even allowing for artistic integrity, Star was thrilled to see the handsome image of the man Catherine Soames had met after her doomed love affair with Benoit Chalendar.

She felt as if she could get lost staring into the deep penetrating eyes of her great-great-great-grandmother's second love, until the security guard she'd met when she first entered the exhibition that morning cleared his throat. She turned and saw him gesture slightly to the clock on the wall.

'Wahed, I'm so sorry. I had no idea that so much time had passed!' She was shocked and annoyed with herself for being such an imposition. The exhibition should have closed fifteen minutes ago and Wahed had been so helpful showing her around earlier. She smiled her brightest and most sincere smile, leaving the room just before she could catch the blush that rose to his cheeks, and drifted towards the exit.

Her first day hadn't been a failure *exactly*, she thought as she made her way towards the exit. *Yes*, they were short on time, Star admitted to herself, but the ache in her heart from a sadly now familiar panic would help absolutely no one, certainly not her mother.

The day after Skye had flown to Costa Rica, Summer had decoded the second part of the hidden messages Catherine had left in her private journals to reveal a description of a special key that could be found in Duratra. The key would unlock the room where Catherine had hidden the Soames diamonds.

With Skye tracking down the map of the hidden passageways, Star felt with every ounce of her being that finding the key was the final step in finding the jewels. When they did that they would have met the terms of their grandfather's will and they could finally sell the estate and be able to pay for the treatment that would save their mother's life.

On the plane to Duratra, Star had read and reread the stories of Catherine's adventures in the Middle East while travelling with her uncle and his wife. Catherine's father had been convinced that being a companion to her aunt by marriage would keep her out of harm's way until she was ready to marry someone suitable.

Even now, Star smiled at the thought of what Catherine had managed to get up to under the lazy eye of her aunt, of the poignant relationship that had developed between Catherine and Hātem. A smile that slowly fell as she remembered reading of the heartache of the two lovers as they had been forced apart by duty.

But, despite that, after she had returned to England, when Catherine had reached out to Hātem to ask him to make a key of special design, he had created something marvellous: a key that could be separated into two sections that mirrored each other. When joined, they would open a special lock, but when separate they could each be worn on a necklace. He had sent Catherine one half of the key and the lock, and he—as Catherine had requested—had kept the other. To Star, the fact that Hātem would always have a piece of Catherine with him was, as her sisters mocked her constantly for saying, *so romantic*.

Her fingers went to the chain around her neck, patting the thick twist beneath the thin material of her dress, re-assuring herself it was still there. Tomorrow, she would leave it in the safe of her hotel room. But for this first day she'd wanted it with her, as if perhaps somehow it would draw out its other half. She'd had no idea of its sig-nificance when she'd first picked up the necklace from amongst the journals in the hidden recess in the library. Only that she was drawn to it. And now she couldn't help but feel a little as if it had been fate.

As Star made her way down the brightly lit corridors of the exhibition halls, weaving around obstacles with un-seeing eyes, even she had to concede that she might have become a little carried away by the romance of another star-crossed love affair involving her ancestor, but she would never regret coming to Duratra, no matter what.

She had already fallen half in love with the bustling, incredible, beautiful city. In the fifteen-minute walk be-tween her hotel and the palace that morning she had been surrounded by impossibly tall apartment buildings and office complexes and passed sprawling open-air markets before reaching the ancient stone structure of the palace in Duratra's capital, Burami. It was a clash of modern and ancient, as sleek electric cars glided silently down tiny cobbled streets and animals carried food, silks and spices to stalls that also sold the latest mobile phones and music players.

Star marvelled at the feeling that she was walking in both the past and the present—that her steps filled the footprints left behind by Catherine herself. And whether that worked to add a layer of magic and mysticism to the mundane, Star wasn't sure that she minded because of how complete and whole that sense of interconnectivity made her feel. Not that she'd say so out loud, and certainly not to her sisters, who would laugh at her when they didn't think she could hear.

So, despite the fact that she hadn't managed to find any reference to Catherine's necklace, Star wasn't discouraged. Instead, she was looking forward to seeing Burami at night and was even more eager to return tomorrow for the next section of the exhibition.

She was so lost in her train of thought that she walked straight into something tall, broad, not very soft but most definitely clothed. And breathing.

'Oh, I'm so sorry. Really, so—' She started apologising before she looked up, which was probably a good thing because her words were cut short by just one glimpse of the impossibly handsome man staring down at her as if he was more surprised than she was.

Star immediately pulled her eyes from his as if somehow that could stop the searing heat flashing over her skin. She blinked a few times, hoping that would clear whatever had come over her. If she'd been asked in that moment what he looked like, she'd not have been able to answer for all the world. But something instinctual told her that she would have known if he'd been within one hundred feet of her. Even now she felt it, the waves of something more...physical than sight. More visceral.

Still unwilling to meet his gaze, and genuinely concerned about the power he seemed to have over her body, she tried to extract herself from the situation. 'I really am sorry. I genuinely didn't see you there, which does seem a little implausible given...' at this point her hand entered the fray and gestured to the rather large entirety of him '...all that. You see, I get a little lost in my thoughts sometimes,' she tried to explain, finally daring to lift her eyes. 'I'm Star and…' she resisted the need to look away and ignored the burning in her cheeks '… I'm clearly assuming that you speak English, which suddenly feels quite conceited.'

The almost minuscule twitch at the corner of his lips made her think that he might be smiling at her rambling and Star sighed in relief at the indication that he at least seemed to understand what she was saying. 'I hadn't meant to be this late, or get this lost. I was in the exhibition,' she said, looking behind her and frowning, unable to recognise the corridor she was in, 'and time just…' She bit her lip, shrugging, wondering why he hadn't interrupted her yet. Her sisters would have. The teachers she worked with would have smiled vaguely and just pressed on past her. But he was still there. She knew this because she was now staring fixedly at his chest, debating whether Dickens had been onto something with the whole spontaneous combustion thing.

But the longer he stood there, not saying anything, the more aware she became of…*him*. This was silly. Maybe she was overreacting.

'Star…'

Her name on his lips drew her eyes upward like a magnet and she was immediately struck by the sheer force of his gaze.

Nope.

She had *not* been overreacting. He was looking at her as if she had the answer to an unspoken question. She felt as if he were searching for something within her.

She shook her head, severing the strange connection, and slapped him gently on the arm. 'You *do* speak English,' she chided, peering over his shoulder for the exit and missing the look of absolute and complete shock that had entered the man's eyes, which he'd managed to mask by the time she returned her attention to him. 'You had me going there for a moment.'

'Sir—'

Star turned in time to see Wahed, his eyes bright and his cheeks red, rushing towards them, making Star think that she really had overstayed her welcome.

'Wahed, I'm sorry. I took a wrong turn and bumped into…' She turned back towards the man she had bumped into, deciding it was safer to look somewhere around the area of his left shoulder. And then became slightly distracted by the way his suit jacket fitted perfectly to the—

'Kal.'

She jerked her eyes to his briefly, before turning back to Wahed. 'Kal. Yes. Right. As I was saying, I got a bit turned around and couldn't find the exit, but I can see it now,' she said, spotting a green sign with white writing and an arrow that she could only presume to be a sign pointing to the exit.

Looping her arm through the arm of the man mountain she had crashed into, she determinedly dragged him with her as she made her way to the exit. She could *not* afford to get herself barred from the exhibition and, to avoid any more trouble, she was removing herself and this other tourist from the premises ASAP.

'Come on, Kal,' she said, passing Wahed, who looked a little as if he were about to explode.

Khalif was so busy processing the fact that this woman knew the first name of his security guard, whilst simultaneously calculating the number of royal codes of etiquette she had broken simply by touching him, that he did nothing to stop her from marching him halfway towards the fire exit that was for staff use only. But, even if he hadn't been, Khalif could not be one hundred per cent sure that he would have dislodged her tiny pale hand from his elbow. It was so small and delicate he feared he might break it.

He was still staring at it as they drew closer to Wahed, as if by studying the delicate fingers splayed across his forearm a second longer he'd be able to identify just why it was that something so small was sending enough electric currents across his skin to light the city of Burami for a month. And that was when he realised that it was the first physical contact he'd had with another person in nearly six weeks.

Obviously Khalif had not been under the naïve impression that he'd be able to continue his romantic liaisons while being first in line to the throne, but he'd not expected the strange social distancing effect the position would hold. Where once he'd have been able to slap Jamal on the back as he'd mocked him about his wife, now there was the painfully awkward renegotiation of power that still didn't quite sit right with him. And where once he'd have been more than able to remove the tiny pale hand from his elbow, now he seemed entirely incapable.

Wahed hadn't taken his eyes from Khalif, eyes that had grown rounder and wider the closer they came, sweat breaking out on the man's forehead as he clearly tried to figure out how to get his country's Prince out of the hands of this flame-haired pixie-sized bombshell.

'Goodnight, Wahed,' Star said as they drew level. 'I'll see you tomorrow,' she stated.

The look of panic increased on Wahed's features and Khalif had to look away in case he laughed and shamed the man even more.

'Tomorrow?' the guard asked weakly.

'Oh, yes, I've only covered the first part of the exhibition. I have three more parts to explore over the next three days,' she said, throwing the words over her shoulder.

'You're going to explore the exhibition for three more days…?'

Khalif couldn't be sure, but he was half convinced he'd heard an actual whimper from Wahed, who was now staring after them as Star continued to guide him towards the exit.

Unable to help it any more, Khalif allowed the tug on his lips to form a full grin and his chest filled with the need to laugh. It bubbled up, filling his lungs and pushing outwards, and he felt lighter than he had in weeks. Months even. Years… The thought was a pin pressed into a balloon as he realised it was how he had felt before. Before his brother had died.

'Did you like it?' she asked, having turned around, looking up at him and squinting in the late afternoon sun. She'd managed to get them out into the staff courtyard, where he saw Jamal peering at them through the window of the security suite.

'Like what?' he said, shaking his head to Jamal to signal that he didn't need their help.

'The exhibition,' she said, laughing again, as if she were half laughing at him and half with him. That sound, so light, so carefree, caught him like a physical blow. He was almost jealous of it. Her hand was still at the crook of his arm and he knew that he really needed to remove it, but he just couldn't bring himself to yet.

'Well, I don't want to give anything away. You still have quite a bit to cover.'

Rather than being disappointed by his answer, she seemed excited.

'Perfect! Please don't. I like surprises.'

Her face, upturned to the lazy yellow lowering sun,

was a picture. Despite the expectation of green suggested by the red hair that was still just about tucked behind her headscarf, her eyes were blue—the dark blue of dusk.

'Star,' he said, understanding dawning on him.

'Yes?'

'No, sorry. I…'

I am never tongue-tied.

Pull. Yourself. Together.

'It's an unusual name,' he clarified.

She looked at him as if she could tell that wasn't what he'd intended to say. As if she could somehow sense things about him that he didn't want to share. That strange dusky blue of her irises seemed almost prescient. The dusting of freckles across her nose fanned out over her cheeks as if she'd been flecked with gold. He found himself leaning down towards her as if subconsciously trying to take a closer look, as if he was trying to count the freckles, as if there was something he was trying to work out about her but didn't know what.

'Yes. Even in England. And Kal?'

'It's…an old nickname.' It had only been used by his brother and Samira. He'd not said it or heard it for three years.

If she'd noticed that he hadn't answered her implied question and revealed the whole of his name she didn't seem offended by it. She turned to look beyond the railings surrounding the staff exit to the palace and frowned.

'I think perhaps this wasn't the exit,' she said as she finally let go of his arm and took a step towards the road that ran the length of the capital city.

'Do you know where you're going?' he asked. There was no way he could leave her in the middle of Burami— she seemed entirely capable of bringing about some kind of massive accident that would be sure to bring his country to a grinding halt for months.

She raised her hand to her eyes and looked out beyond the railings. He followed the direction of her gaze and clenched his jaw. In the distance he could see his father's sleek black motorcade making its way back to the palace and he felt the tightening of the steel bands of duty around his wrists.

'Yes. I can see the café there on the corner. That's the road my hotel is on. It's a…' She turned to look up at him. 'It's a nice café. If you'd…' She shrugged as if hedging her bets as to whether to finish the sentence or not.

He looked away, hiding just how much he wanted to say yes, from both her and himself. He smiled sadly and by the time his gaze had returned to those eyes understanding had dawned in them. 'Please take a car to your hotel. You are safe in Duratra. But perhaps Duratra is not safe from you,' he said. It was meant to be a tease, a light exchange before he left, but it had come out differently. It had been a warning from a man who was the embodiment of his country.

Dusk descended in her eyes and for a moment it was as if she had understood. And then the smile was back in place, the one that had hypnotised all the palace staff she had encountered—and he could see why.

She nodded and he watched her walk away, just as a gust of wind pressed the white-and-green-striped dress against the back of her legs, causing an explosion of erotic thoughts until Khalif's father's car turned the corner and grim reality intruded.

CHAPTER TWO

FOR WHAT FELT like the hundredth time that day, Star forced herself to reread the English translation of the description of how Duratra had been one of the largest academic centres during the height of the Ottoman Empire. But she just couldn't concentrate. Instead of finding clues or traces of Catherine or the necklace within the paintings and history of this beautiful country, she was hoping to see Kal—despite being aware of how unlikely it was.

She'd gone over and over their encounter in minute detail from the moment she'd left him in the courtyard until her latest breath. Although she'd initially thought him a tourist like her, she now thought that perhaps he worked at the palace. While she'd not wanted to give Wahed a reason to ban her from the palace exhibition, she now wondered if Wahed and Kal knew each other. Not that she'd asked the security guard when she'd seen him that morning.

No, sometimes it was better not to know, because this way she could imagine him as the undercover Prince of a neighbouring kingdom, here on a top-secret mission. Perhaps he was trying to correct some great wrong and he would need her help escaping Burami and together they could ride off into the desert and…

And then she laughed out loud at herself, not noticing how she had startled the other people in the very quiet room. She had never ridden a horse and couldn't imagine that riding bareback would be comfortable. But being in his arms? Once again, Star felt herself flush from head to toe. Looking at him had been like looking at the sun. Heat. All-consuming heat that she'd had absolutely no control over whatsoever.

No one had ever had that effect on her. She'd read about it so many times but had honestly thought it just a metaphor. She'd wondered at it, had brought out the memory of him standing there, searching her face, her eyes and *whoomph!* Head to toe. Every time. Even now she felt that pink heat stain her cheeks and, lost in her own world, fanned her face, nearly taking out a large German tourist with her elbow.

As she moved further into the room, golden glints and rich magentas caught her eye and she came to stand before a tapestry that took up nearly the entire length of the room. It was exquisite in detail, despite the clear effects of age, inscriptions flowing beneath the images, and instead of fighting for space at the explanatory plaque, Star wanted to stand back. Take it in, just as it was.

She wondered whether Catherine had ever seen this, whether she had stood looking at it, searching for meaning the way that Kal seemed to have searched her eyes. She forced her mind away from him and onto the fact that she was on the second day of her search.

Time was running out for Star to prove to her sisters that she could play her part, that she could travel to the other side of the world without needing their support, protection or concern. Why couldn't her sisters trust her when she regularly and successfully managed to take care of a class of thirty seven-year-olds?

She and Summer had decided that if there was no sign of the necklace she would return to Norfolk no matter what. From there, the sisters would decide together what to do next. If any more travel was needed, they would apply to Mr Beamish, the estate's lawyer, and he—as stipulated in the will—would fund whatever expenses were needed during the two-month period. Well, one month and just over one week now, Star thought, doing the maths.

Thirty-eight days. Her heart began to pound in her chest. It was the bass-line that beat beneath the layer of faith and hope she held in her heart. Constant, exhausting. She hated it and needed it. Because while that deep thrum in her heart was there, so was her mother, so was the chance that she'd be able to find the necklace. That she and her sisters would be able to find the diamonds, sell the estate and access the medical treatment Mariam Soames needed…and Star wouldn't lose her only living parent.

A flash went off, slicing through the rising panic in Star's chest, and Wahed crossed the room to speak to the German tourist's wife, who had clearly ignored the sign that said no photography. Before the argument could get heated, Star made her way back out of the room to one of the larger areas, looking for somewhere she could… breathe.

She was trying to find her way out when the hairs on her arms lifted and heat broke out across the back of her neck. She paused, eyes closed, just feeling her way through that moment. Her pulse thudded in her ears for such a different reason than just seconds before, and when she opened her eyes and saw a figure marching down the corridor ahead of her, her heart raced. Instead of continuing down the hallway, he cut to the left and entered the beautiful green courtyard on the other side of the large glass wall that separated the corridor from the exhibition space.

Star placed a hand gently against the glass, the smooth cold surface sucking the heat from her skin. It was one thing to bump into a man and a whole other thing to approach him. She should go back to the public area of the exhibition. She should absolutely do that.

Khalif leaned back against the wooden bench, feeling the sun on his face, eyes closed, remembering the way that Star had done something similar yesterday. Why couldn't he get her out of his head? All the way through the council update with Reza, Duratra's Prime Minister.

'If I didn't know better,' he'd joked, 'I'd ask who she was.'

Khalif's grunted reply had been as non-committal as he got with his oldest friend.

All that morning he'd caught himself looking at his arm where her hand had been, remembering the way that her laugh had cut through him, recalling his last sight of her. It didn't help that he knew she was here. Somewhere in the exhibition. It was as if his body had been in a heightened state ever since he'd reached the lower level of the palace and he bit back a curse. He was worse than an untried schoolboy, lusting over his first crush.

Until the last hour, during a meeting with the Secretary of State for His Majesty Sheikh Abbad Al Jabbal. Samira's father had found fault with nearly every suggestion that the team had put to him. Not that Khalif could blame him. He knew they still hadn't come up with the best way to honour their loss. When it came down to it, there certainly wasn't a *right* way. There was nothing right about the deaths of his brother and sister-in-law, so why should their memorial be? Khalif braced himself against a shockwave of grief that sent out invisible ripples of incomprehension and pain, refusing to bend to it, to go under.

'Funny meeting you here.'

Khalif's eyes shot open and he stared at Star, standing in the centre of the courtyard as if she'd just magically appeared.

'How did you…?' His words trailed off as he saw the commotion gathering on the other side of the glass at the corner of the east wing. Several dark-suited guards were reaching for their weapons, ready to storm the courtyard. He threw a glare their way, wondering how on earth this English girl had slipped undetected past his usually highly efficient bodyguards. He held his hand out to stop them intruding and turned back to Star, who was still looking up at him, thankfully having missed the exchange.

'I hope that's okay… I just… I saw you and you looked…' She shrugged, not quite finishing her sentence.

She looked around the space, giving him time to take in the dark blue cotton headscarf, grey floor-length skirt and white top she was wearing beneath the same denim jacket, so very different to the glitz and glamour he'd seen throughout Europe's most fashionable destinations. But, instinctively, he knew that hers was the face he would remember in years to come. Her bangles clinked slightly as she moved forward to smell one of the plants in the giant urn in the centre of the courtyard.

As he listened to her inhale, he forced his eyes away from her and instead took in the scene he'd been blind to until she'd appeared. Four separate areas were full of thick green foliage and he would always associate this courtyard with the oasis his family used to visit in the desert.

'…hungry.'

'Excuse me?' he asked, dragging his eyes and awareness back to Star.

'You looked hungry,' she replied with a smile.

'Really?' he asked, surprised.

'Aren't you?'

'Well, yes, but…'

Star sat down beside him and began to unpack the large canvas bag she'd had slung over her shoulder. An impressive glass-bottomed lunch box landed between them on the bench. A flask of something was soon propped up against it, while she passed him a smaller box with the instruction, 'Can you open that?'

He found himself once again staring blankly at her before recovering and doing as she'd asked, the traces of yesterday's smile returning to his lips. It had been so long since someone treated him like an equal, he was determined not to break the spell.

He lifted the lid from the box she'd handed him and the smell of parsley and coriander and rich tomato sauce hit him hard, making his mouth water. He stared at the *mahshi* in wonder.

'Where on earth did you get this?'

'Oh, the chef at my hotel,' she replied, reaching over to take one of the courgettes stuffed with rice and vegetables. 'He promised that he didn't mind making it for me.'

'Of course he didn't,' Khalif replied, thinking that she could probably talk the birds down from the sky as easily as getting a chef to make her whatever she wanted. He bit into the courgette he'd helped himself to and groaned. Hats off to the chef. He really hadn't realised how hungry he was until she'd asked.

'We were talking last night and he was telling me about...'

He let her voice trail over him as he cast an eye back to where the security detail had come up against Amin, who seemed almost apoplectic that he'd taken food from a stranger. Khalif didn't really know what he was so angry about. Amin would probably prefer it if there *was* poison in the food. That way he'd be able to fulfil his royal duties without the hindrance he clearly saw Khalif as being.

He cast an eye back to Star, still talking but looking ahead of her and gesturing expressively with her hands, clearly missing the way that the thick tomato sauce was dripping perilously close to his trousers. Khalif supposed that she could be a spy sent to poison him—if it hadn't been for the fact that there had been no threats to either the country or the royal family in over one hundred years. Faizan's helicopter crash had been investigated by both Duratra and an international investigative team and both had confirmed that a mechanical fault was to blame. Accidental death. Somehow the term seemed cruel, especially for the twin daughters he and Samira had left behind.

'And so, after a few failed attempts, it was decided I should probably leave it to the professionals. But it's so delicious I just couldn't refuse,' she said, handing him a piece of flatbread and the little porcelain pot of hummus. She'd managed to convince the chef to make her a packed lunch with breakable china? He stared between the little pot and the redhead, who seemed utterly oblivious to the impact that she had on those around her. And suddenly he envied her that. No second-guessing and doubting the impact of every single move, look, step, decision or indecision. As he scooped some of the hummus topped with beautiful pink pearls of pomegranate and flecks of paprika onto the flatbread, he saw his assistant throw his hands up in the air and as the taste exploded on his tongue Khalif decided that frustrating his particularly sanctimonious assistant was a small victory in an otherwise complete failure of a day.

'That was the best *mahshi* I've ever had,' she sighed, leaning back against the wooden bench.

Khalif laughed. 'Had a lot of *mahshi*, have you?'

Star nodded, her smile lighting up eyes that were a touch lighter than they had been yesterday. 'Yup. My mum, she's…some would call her *alternative*,' she said in a half whisper, as if confessing some great sin. 'But she travelled a lot when she was younger and that influenced her cooking. We're all vegetarian so we do a lot of cooking ourselves. That, and we didn't have a great deal of money growing up,' she announced without the resentment that usually weighed down such a statement.

'What do they do? Your parents,' he clarified, unable to resist going in for one last mouthful of the hummus.

She should have known it was coming. Usually she could feel it building in a conversation, but with Kal it had taken her by surprise so she hadn't been ready for the swift pain that nicked her heart. 'My father died when I was a few months old, but he was a carpenter.' She rubbed her hands unconsciously, as she often did when she thought about her father, imagining the calluses on his hands that her mother had told her about.

'That must have been very hard. I am sorry for the loss you have felt.'

Rather than shy away, this time she wanted to feel the burn, the flame that was lit when Kal looked at her, even if she felt guilty for welcoming it to avoid that ache, but instead what she found in his eyes… Her heartbeat thumped once heavily in sympathy.

'And I am sorry for yours.'

He frowned, his head already beginning to shake, but she stopped him with her hand on his arm.

'I'm sorry if that was intrusive. I don't know who or…' she trailed off '…but I can tell.'

Kal nodded once. It was an acceptance of her offered comfort, but a definite end to the moment. Seizing the threads of the earlier conversation and definitely not ready for him to leave just yet, she pressed on. 'My mother has done lots over the years, but currently she's into candle magic.'

She folded her lips between her teeth, waiting for the inevitable reaction.

'Wait…candle what?'

'Magic. It keeps her happy and there is harm to none, so…'

'Alternative, huh?' he said, wiping his hands on the napkin she'd found tucked beneath the boxes, and she would have replied had she not been distracted by the way he smoothed the cloth across his skin.

'You're the youngest?'

She turned to him, curious as to how he knew that she had siblings.

'You said "we're all" and you don't strike me as an only child,' he explained.

'I'm the middle. Skye is older, and Summer is younger.'

'And do they all have…?' He waved his hand towards a strand of her hair that had come loose from her headscarf.

Laughing, she tucked it back safely behind the stretchy jersey. 'No, just me. Skye's hair is a dark brown and Summer's is cornfield blonde.' She could see his mind working, trying to do the maths, and took pity on him. 'Technically they're my half-sisters. But I'd never call them that.'

'Different fathers?'

She could tell that he was trying to keep his tone neutral and she appreciated it. Not everyone was that considerate. 'It certainly drew a lot of unwanted attention and judgement when we were younger, and a *lot* of stares.' Her sisters thought she hadn't noticed, but she had. Long before her grandparents had made their feelings known, Star had been aware of the way neighbours and some of the school parents and, in turn, their children had treated them, judged them, excluded them.

'Ahh.'

She cocked her head to look at him, as if the different angle would reveal more than he'd done already. 'You know how that feels?'

'A little,' he admitted. 'Different reason though.'

Star looked him up and down, noticing the sharp cut to his clothes, the thick, heavy gold watch at his wrist, the expensive sunglasses sticking out of his pocket and smiled kindly. 'Rich parents?'

'Something like that.'

'Rich *and* powerful. I *am* impressed,' she assumed. He barked out a laugh and she felt as if she'd won something precious. 'Children can be unintentionally cruel,' she said, thinking of the young charges she loved working with.

She sighed heavily, feeling very far away from her teaching assistant's job in the New Forest, and allowed herself a moment to bask in the sun. The warmth of it on her face, the feeling of contentment was tinged with a little something more. She hadn't realised how much of a relief it was to talk to someone. Okay, so she might have been talking *at* him, but still. Without opening her eyes, she drew his image to her mind, surprised how easily it came after the difficulties of yesterday. She mentally reached out to trace the strong jaw line shadowed with a close-cropped beard, imagining the feeling of him releasing the tension that she had seen when talking about loss. Unable to help the way her thumb stretched out to press against the plush lower lip, fire burning her thumb and core. The skin on her cheeks began to tingle, as if she had been stroked, and she leaned her head into the invisible touch, opening her eyes to find Kal staring at her, sending a jolt of pure lightning to her heart.

But, rather than turn away, embarrassed at being caught staring, he seemed to focus only more intently now that her eyes were open. A moment that she would hold to her as more precious than any romance book and she wondered for just a second if he might kiss her. Then he blinked and the haze of desire was banked.

'Where have you reached in the exhibition?'

She took a breath and grounded herself, taking a second to focus enough to remember where she had been. 'The attempted occupation by the Ottomans.'

'Ah. A Particularly violent and difficult period.'

'I should think so too. His Majesty Sheikh Omar could hardly allow the kidnap of his daughter to go unpunished.'

No, he could not, Khalif echoed silently, wondering what Star would think if she knew that, rather than being kidnapped, the family rumour was that Omar's daughter had run off of her own volition to be with a Turkish prince and unwittingly nearly started a war.

'And tomorrow?' He cursed the question that had fallen from his lips before he'd had time to think it through. He really shouldn't care what she had planned for tomorrow.

Star smiled excitedly and it rivalled the sun. 'Tomorrow is the Fatimid period.'

'History interests you?' he asked, unable to curb his curiosity.

'Yes, I like to see how everything comes together. How one generation impacts another,' she said, the blue in her irises deepening.

'What are you looking for?'

'Who said I was looking for something?' she asked a little too quickly and his eyes narrowed at the shift in her tone. He waited her out and, as expected, she clarified. The English were very predictable. 'Research.'

'For?'

'A family thing.'

And then, before he could stop her, she'd leaned over, clasped his wrist, turned it in her hand and read the time on his watch. It was not sensual, no trace of practised flirtation, it was perfunctory and over in a matter of seconds, but those seconds had branded him like molten metal.

'I have to get back. I need to find out what happened to His Majesty Sheikh Omar's daughter before it closes for the day,' and, before he could say goodbye, she'd slipped through the doorway, passed the seven large suited men, none of whom could take their eyes off her, and disappeared into the exhibition.

That night, Star returned to the hotel after discovering that Omar's daughter had been forced to marry a Turkish prince and felt the sting of injustice of a marriage not born from love. She sighed, thinking of Catherine's marriage to her horrible cousin, a man whose sole interest was property and diamonds.

*He has always coveted them. The estate and the
jewels are almost an obsession for him. And though
society deems him worthy of my hand in marriage, I
do not deem him worthy of them. They are the only
part of the estate entailed to the female line and I
will keep it that way.*

She had read Summer's translations of the coded messages over and over again since they had first found them
buried within the pages of her journals. For Catherine,
Omar's daughter and even her own mother, marriage had
been nothing more than a shackle. But…for her? Secretly,
she'd always thought that she'd quite like to be married.
To have a wedding and stand beside someone who told
the world how much she was loved. To be claimed pub-
licly, completely. And though she'd never admit it to her
mother, Star couldn't help but wonder if her life might
have been different had her parents married before he'd
died, whether that might have changed the minds and
attitudes of her grandparents, whether they could have
been a positive part of her life rather than…

Star cut off that train of thought before it could take
hold, turning instead to wonder if she should call Skye
in Costa Rica. She was halfway through her time in Duratra and she was beginning to lose the confidence that
she'd arrived with. She had only two days left and it was
getting harder and harder to ignore the inner voice wanting to know what would happen if she didn't find the
necklace, and what that could mean for her mother. But
if she admitted as much to Skye, she would only tell her
to go home and Star wasn't ready to hear that. She could
call Summer in Norfolk, but she didn't want to hear her
sister's gentle voice reassuring her that it was okay, that

it had always been a long shot to send her to search for the necklace.

Star drew air into her lungs to cover the hurt and turned in the bed onto her side, closing her eyes to see Kal's staring back at her, eyes crinkled with the hint of that enigmatic smile and the light of…interest? Was that what she saw in his gaze? Was that what made her heart beat faster? What made her feel a little sick in her stomach at the thought of seeing him tomorrow, but feel even worse at the thought of not?

Two days, she reminded herself, she had two days. Though this time when she delved into what it was that made her heart beat like specks of sand dropping through an hour glass, it wasn't thoughts of Kal, but the fear of not finding the necklace.

After lunch in the courtyard, and after thoroughly reprimanding a slightly sceptical security detail, Khalif had surprised himself by managing to make some headway in the afternoon. He'd looked for her as he'd left the palace, but Wahed had informed him that Star had already left. Yet knowing that she'd be there the following day made him feel…as if he had something to look forward to.

So it had been a shock to discover that the depth of his reaction to *not* seeing her the next day was nothing short of painful. A sense of panic had risen within him. Panic that he'd never see her again, never find out what she was looking for, never see the accidental chaos that seemed to follow in her wake, never feel that sense of inexplicable peace he'd found in her company… He'd caught himself looking down corridors, purposely walking past the security suite to see if the guards were watching her again. Tempted, so very tempted to ask if they had seen her.

By the time he'd reached the afternoon of what he

knew to be her last day at the exhibition, he'd convinced himself that such an extreme reaction indicated that it could only be a good thing that she was gone from his life. What did he think he could do if he saw her again anyway? Only that thought sent up a cascade of sensual imagery that he shut down before it could cut him off at the knees. He was no longer able to indulge in such whims. There was a plan. In three years, when he had proved himself the steady hand that would provide for his country until his nieces came of age, then a suitable bride would be found. And that suitable bride would *not* have flame-coloured hair and eyes so dark blue they were almost regal.

So as he left his office that evening he was halfway through congratulating himself for having survived a temptation called Star when he came to an abrupt halt. The gods were either laughing or punishing him.

Things might have been different if he had found her anywhere else in the palace. But Star had found the one spot that was sure to pack an emotional punch. The three steps looked deeply insignificant, and probably would have been to anyone else. But to Khalif they were painfully familiar.

He had spent just over seven hundred hours waiting for his father and brother on those steps. Despite having been largely excluded from the lessons Faizan had been required to have from their father on matters ranging from governance and international policy to languages and business studies, he'd thought he could wait them out. And his stubborn streak had lasted for two hours, every day for an entire year.

In that moment he knew what he should do—and what he shouldn't. His Highness Sheikh Khalif Al Azhar walked on, past the security suite, through the exit of the palace and towards his evening appointment with Duratra's council.

Kal, however, stood before a beautiful woman and heaved a sigh of relief.

'You know it all turned out okay in the end,' he said as he stood between her and the sun, her body enshrouded by his shadow. She looked up at him with huge ocean-blue eyes. 'That's the problem with looking at the history of a country backwards. Really you should have started with the Umayyad period, it's especially beautiful, given the metalwork and textiles.'

The smile that spread across her features chased the watery sparkle from her eyes. 'Perhaps you should have been my tour guide.'

'I would have been honoured,' he replied, surprised by the sincerity in his tone. 'You are leaving?'

'Tomorrow.'

'And you don't want to go?' he asked, wondering why that seemed to make her sad.

Her smile wavered. 'I want to see my sisters, and my mother, but… I didn't find what I was looking for.'

'Anything I can help with?'

He would have sworn on his crown that he felt the weight of her sigh. 'No, sadly not.' And he would have given it away to lighten that load.

'So, what are you going to do with your last few hours in Duratra?'

The shrug that barely moved her shoulders an inch was enough to drive him to action. He liked the tumble and roll of her words, the way they wound through his mind, treading down a path to wherever they wanted to go.

All Star could think of was the necklace. She had genuinely thought that she'd find it, and to not have found a trace or clue as to where it might be was devastating. She had let her sisters down. And, worse than that, her mother… She felt a wave of hurt crash over her anew, breaking out in a hot sweat on her neck and down her spine. She'd just got off the phone with Summer. And she'd meant to tell her, intended to explain that she would be coming home empty-handed, but Summer had been full of excitement with the news that Skye had found the map.

Star's phone was full of the pictures Summer had forwarded with promises that she would work on the plans to find where on the map the Soames diamonds were located. And at the end she had asked, hopeful for the first time since Star had got on the plane to Duratra, whether she might have located the necklace. A hope that Star had been unable to respond to. She had proved them right—that she couldn't be trusted to locate the necklace. How silly was she, to think that she could have done this alone?

All she wanted to do was stop for a moment. To not have to think, or fear, or worry. And although Kal had extended an offer of sorts, she'd sensed how torn he was. He probably had something to rush off to. And she certainly didn't want another person having to look out for her.

'Is there anything you haven't seen? That you wanted to?'

'Well, I've spent all my time here, so—'

'Wait, you've not seen anything of Burami?' he demanded, full of not *completely* mock outrage that distracted her heart just a little. Perhaps for the evening, rather than being a daughter hoping to save her mother, she could just be a tourist on her last evening in Duratra?

'Not unless it was between the hotel and the exhibition at the palace,' she replied.

'We can't have that.'

She couldn't help but laugh at his conviction. 'My flight is tomorrow—how much can you show me before then?'

'I can show you it all.'

He held out his hand and while she couldn't explain it, was helpless even to resist, Star felt as if she were Alice about to fall down the rabbit hole.

CHAPTER THREE

HAVING BEEN PROMISED the opportunity to see Burami, Star was surprised when, instead of turning out towards the main road, Kal led her back to the palace. The surprise lasted only a moment. She was distracted by the way sparks flew from where his palm pressed against hers, encompassing it, making her feel comforted in a way just seconds ago she'd not thought possible.

They came to a corner and Kal pulled up short before turning back to her, holding a finger to his lips.

Star folded her own lips between her teeth, but still a smile pulled at the edges of her mouth. 'Are we sneaking into the palace?' she whispered to him.

'Yes,' he replied, peering around the corner to see if the coast was clear.

'You do this often?' She couldn't keep the laugh from her voice this time.

He looked at her, eyes blazing with something a little more than humour. 'More than you'd think,' he replied cryptically and drew her back into the hallway.

They'd made it about four feet towards the staircase Kal seemed to be heading for when they heard the hushed voices of two guards. Eyes wide and heart pounding in her chest, Star didn't know whether to laugh or scream in fright. Either way she was pretty sure that she'd squeaked when Kal spun her round, pressing her back against a wall, arms braced either side of her head, and covered her with his body.

Star wasn't laughing now. They were staring at each other as if that alone would keep them invisible from the palace guards. This close, she could see that there were flecks of gold in the rich espresso depths of his eyes, she could almost taste the smoky sweetness of the breath that fanned gently against her skin. She dared herself to inhale the scent of him, woodsy, masculine, brought to her from the heat of his body. In her peripheral vision she could see the flicker of his pulse just beneath his jaw, and shockingly she wanted to place her palm there, to feel it beat in time with her own.

His head dipped ever so slightly towards her, his nostrils flaring ever so slightly, his inhale expanding to close the space between their chests from inches to millimetres. Beneath the voices, she could hear footsteps coming closer and closer. She pressed into the wall as if that would make her and Kal invisible, adrenaline reaching deeper and deeper into her bloodstream. What would happen if they got caught? Her eyes flew to his, her mouth opening just slightly as if ready to ask the question when she felt the pad of his thumb against her lower lip, just as she'd once imagined doing to him. The gesture she was sure was intended to stop her words, not her heart, but that was the effect.

She wanted to bite down on his thumb, to anchor it there before he could remove it and in an instant any fear was completely consumed by exhilaration. She'd never felt like it before. She could just hear the sound of footsteps over the pounding of her pulse in her ears, and she couldn't resist courting danger.

'Are we going to get into trouble?' she whispered

against the pad of his thumb, instantly gratified when she saw his pupils flare.

'No,' he whispered back with an arrogance that was utterly devastating.

The footsteps receded, and Khalif waited until there was complete silence in the corridor. Not because he couldn't move, he sternly assured himself, but because he was waiting until the coast was clear.

He walked on into the hallway, leading Star by the hand, his heart racing, half hoping someone would stop him, half hoping they wouldn't. This was ridiculous. And certainly the first time he'd sneaked a woman *into* the palace rather than out of it.

Four feet to the staircase. He could still change his mind. Could still turn back.

Three feet. Her fingers tightened within his hold ever so slightly.

Two feet and he cast one last look up and down the long hallway.

One…

They raced up the stairs as if the guards were still behind them, falling through the door and collapsing on the other side in half relief, half surprise as if they'd not actually expected to get that far.

He watched as Star straightened and turned to look around at the room, wondering what she'd make of the large living space, lined with bookshelves on one side and a large television on the other. The sunken seating area was actually an illusion, the rest of the floor having been built up to allow for the cables and security measures fitted retrospectively to the ancient palace.

'Are we in someone's home?' she asked as she looked between the open-plan kitchenette that he couldn't remember using ever and the glass-fronted sliding doors that led to the balcony.

'It's okay, I know the owner,' he replied, watching her walk towards the view he woke up to every morning.

'I hope they'd be okay with this,' she said as she reached the partly opened door.

'They are,' he assured her, but his answer was lost to her as she slipped through the narrow gap and out onto the stone balcony.

He told himself he was giving her time. That it had nothing to do with having to get himself—who was he kidding?—his *libido* under control. He clenched his fists as if it would erase the feeling of her lip beneath his thumb, her between his arms, the ghost trace of her chest against his... Three years without sex might not kill a man, but one night without Star might just do it.

No. This was for her. He'd seen how devastated she'd looked. Whatever had happened, or not happened, this was about ensuring that she didn't leave with that look haunting her eyes. Instead, he reached for his phone, fired off a message to the palace staff asking for refreshments to be brought to his quarters, and another to Reza cancelling their meeting. He then purposefully put his phone on silent so as not to be subjected to the barrage of queries his oldest friend was sure to launch at him.

Clenching his jaw and ordering himself to behave, Khalif made his way out onto the balcony. He loved the large, deep green palms potted either side of the doors. The ornate, detailed carvings in the red stone balcony were almost as familiar to him as his reflection. Off to the left was a cream awning, under which were a table and chairs, but he knew that Star had seen none of it, her gaze instead glued to the whole of the city stretched out before her, beneath a sky that was turning the beautiful deep blue of early night and littered with stars more dazzling than any diamond.

'Burami?' she asked him without looking away from it.

'A very, *very* large part of it, yes.'

It was absolutely the height of insanity to bring a woman to his palace quarters. It was something the old Khalif had never done. Had he deprived himself of so much that he was at risk of recklessness? And then he remembered the look in her eyes as she'd sat on the steps and knew that he'd have done it all over again just to see her eyes sparkle.

He heard the soft click of his door, movement in the kitchen area that seemed to pass unnoticed by Star and the door closing once again. The last thing Khalif felt was hungry, but somehow it seemed fitting to serve Star food, when she had done the same for him. The memory of her basking in the sun sliced through him, competing with the dusk that surrounded them now and haunted his suite.

He retrieved the platter of food and pitcher of the delicious apricot drink he thought Star would enjoy and returned to the balcony, stopping mid-stride. Star was still looking out at the desert, but her shawl had come loose and now hung from her shoulders, leaving her hair…

Thick streams of long, lazily curling fire danced on the wind, a riot of golds, deep reds and every imaginable shade of umber, flooding his tongue with the taste of turmeric, paprika and cinnamon.

She had removed her denim jacket and the long-sleeved top slashed across her neck, leaving her collarbone and delicate neck exposed to his desire. The blue cotton, regal and powerful, strong and bright enough to stand beside the glory of her hair, made him think of an ancient astrological chart he'd once seen, created from the deepest of blues and golds, rich with circles, lines, arrows and stars, all working to prove some mystical assertion.

Mystical. That was what Star made him feel. And it hit him like a hammer, as if this moment was something they'd stolen from ancient gods. Something that was just for them.

Star felt him return to the balcony behind her. As if his presence had the power to pull at her like the tide. He was giving her the time she needed. And she *did* need it. She was in the private rooms of a palace looking out at the desert. She'd had to pinch herself *literally*, she thought as she rubbed the pink flesh on her forearm, to know that this wasn't a dream she'd conjured from her imagination.

She knew that she should feel danger, or at least a very real sense of concern. She barely knew Kal, but that felt wrong. She didn't feel as if he were a stranger. He was physically imposing, that was true, but, rather than making her scared, it made her *want*—want in a way that she'd only ever read about before. She had waited all her adult years to find someone who made her feel the things she'd only ever read about and she was leaving tomorrow.

Star might be very used to daydreams, but she wasn't naïve. She knew in reality that there was nothing past tomorrow for her, for them. But did that mean she should walk away from the possibility of what tonight held? She wanted to laugh at herself for being presumptuous, but… Her tongue ran over her lip, where his thumb had pressed so gently to such great effect. A tremor shivered over her skin and down her spine. Surely she wasn't the only one affected by this?

She turned, expecting to find him looking at her, having felt the burn of his gaze across her shoulders and back, but he was busy removing small plates from a tray, two glasses and a pitcher that was rich with condensation from the warm air, despite the dusk falling around them.

'If you'd like something alcoholic…?'

She smiled. 'No, thank you. I'm afraid the Soames women cannot hold their drink.' She reluctantly moved away from the balcony, fearing that she might search the rest of her life for something as beautiful as that view and never find it again.

She slipped behind the table so that she faced the cityscape edged by golden sand that looked like slashes of an abstract painting. He offered her a small glass of the *amar al din* she was going to miss terribly when she returned to England. Her mouth watered in expectation of the sweet, cooling apricot drink, but that was a mere shadow of the explosion of taste that hit her tongue when she drew it to her lips and she was helpless to prevent the moan of sheer delight that fell into the air between them.

'That is *so* good,' she praised unashamedly when she'd finished it. 'I'm going to have to learn how to make it.'

She chanced a look at Kal and veered back to the cityscape before she could be burned further by the heat in eyes heavy-lidded with desire. It scorched the air she breathed, jolted her heartbeat and pulsed and flared through her body.

By the time Star was ready to risk another glance at him, he had turned towards the desert, staring at the magnificent view as if it were his. Possessively. The way she wanted him to look at her. The way she'd thought, just for a moment, he had.

Blushing, she returned her gaze to the same view, wondering whether Catherine had ever seen it. Star had read over the journals Catherine had written while in Duratra, but she couldn't seem to make the descriptions from then fit with what surrounded her now.

'I wonder what this view would have looked like a hundred years ago,' she half whispered, her voice breaking on the words emerging from a throat half raw from need.

His reply was so long coming she'd begun to wonder whether he'd heard her.

'There was less metal, less chrome and glass, and it was a touch smaller. But one hundred years ago, Burami was still an impressive city.' She watched the way his throat worked as he swallowed, his eyes frowning once again at the view. 'The market you passed on the way to the palace has been there for nearly three hundred years. The skyline would have been not too dissimilar, the silhouette of the minaret and the cross, the turrets of the university. We've always had a mix of cultures, religions—mosques near churches, near synagogues, near temples...all from the very beginning.'

He spoke with a cultural pride that was unfamiliar to her, a sense of personal history she felt that she'd only just begun to experience herself.

'How long has your family been here?'

'Since around then.'

'It must be incredible—that sense of history, that sense of ancestry.'

'That's one way of looking at it. What about you?'

Star sighed. 'We've just discovered a grandfather on our mother's side.'

'And that is what has you upset?'

She resisted the urge to ask how he knew, but it must have been clear on her face. She'd never been very good at hiding her emotions.

'I... I have let my sisters down. My mother,' she said, hating the way that saying it out loud seemed to make it real.

'I know that feeling. With my brother. My father. I wasn't exactly their first choice,' he said before coming to an abrupt halt.

'Choice for what?'

She watched the way his jaw clenched in the darkness of the oncoming night.

'The head of the family business.'

'Really?' she asked, surprised. 'You'd be my choice.'

'You don't know me,' he replied darkly.

It was on the tip of her tongue to deny what he was saying. A half-forgotten song lyric hummed in her head about having loved someone for a thousand years... She shook her head, as if to free the words, but it only sent them scattering. Instead, she caught the words of one of her most loved books.

"'It is not time or opportunity that is to determine intimacy; it is disposition alone. Seven years would be insufficient to make some people acquainted with each other, and seven days are more than enough for others.'"

He barked a laugh, not *at* her but as if *with* her, and she felt the appraisal in his eyes even as he made a joke of it. 'You just happen to have that to hand?'

'It's Austen. She should always be "to hand".'

'Oh, so you're one of those,' he teased.

'If by *"one of those"* you mean someone who reads romance then yes, I am,' she said with pride. 'And there's absolutely nothing wrong with that.'

He held his hands up in surrender. 'I believe you.'

'No, you're humouring me. That's a very different thing,' she said, not unkindly. 'It's very easy to be cynical and sharp-edged in this world. It's harder to have hope, to hold to romance and sentimentality, to allow the enjoyment of them and the sheer optimism, the faith of it all to sink deep into your bones.'

'Faith?'

'The conviction that love in whatever form conquers all.'

'And if I say I don't believe, does it knock a romance reader down dead?'

'No,' she replied, unable to turn to look at him with the smile on her face. 'But it seriously diminishes your chances of finding true love.'

There was a beat—of *something*. Something that passed his eyes and crossed his features before he barked out another laugh that had both traces of the humour she sensed in him but also the weight that pulled at him. And it was that weight she felt partly tied to, as if the deeper it plunged, the more it drew her with it.

She caught herself frowning, not because she was confused by her feelings—she knew what they were, knew that this attraction was something as unique as it was raw. She was confused as to what to do about it. Because, while she didn't need to know the why of it, Kal was holding back and Star just wasn't confident or experienced enough to call it out into the open.

But she didn't want to walk away from it either. She couldn't explain it. But she was sure, more sure than anything she'd ever felt, that if she walked away now, she'd never find this again. This feeling that sank into her skin and delved into her bones, that caught her by the throat and squeezed at her lungs. She wanted to gasp for air, she wanted to gasp for him. Just thinking about the way he made her feel had her pulse quickening, and something deep within her quivering.

The only place he'd ever touched her was the thumb-print he'd left on her bottom lip. She bit down once again, into the soft flesh as if...

'Stop,' he commanded.

'Stop what?' she asked, her words breathless, as she peered at him through the sensual haze that had descended like a fog. The muscle in his clenched jaw flared again and again, as if he was as reluctant as she was to voice this thing between them.

'Stop looking at me like *that*,' he ordered, and she wondered how she looked at him. She'd thought it was just her who experienced the flashover when their gazes met. The thought that he could feel something similar…

'Tell me,' she whispered, hoping he couldn't detect the begging in her tone, the tremor in her voice as she shuddered under the weight of her attraction to him.

'Tell you what?' he asked, his gaze still clinging to the horizon as if his life depended on it.

'What you see when I look at you like that.'

He bit out something in Arabic that sounded hot and heavy, half-prayer, half-curse. She saw him inhale, drawing oxygen deep into his lungs and expanding his chest, the breadth of it making her palms itch and her fingers tingle. He moved his gaze from the horizon to the table between them, as if having to work his way up to looking at her. And when his eyes finally cut across the space, up to her face to meet her eyes, she felt branded.

'It's not what I see but what I feel,' he said, his voice scraping over her nerves with wicked deliciousness. 'A heat that snags on a spark just begging to catch fire. I see a want so pure, so powerful, so…*naïve*…as if it would rush headlong into a burning forest and be happy to die in its blaze.' His eyes interrogated hers, leaving nothing unseen, unexamined. 'I see fuel for a flame that lies deep within me and a fire that I'm too tempted by to not get burned.'

His words caught her heart and drew it upwards into the night sky. Not one book had prepared her for how this felt.

'Which is why you should go,' he said, dragging his gaze from hers, but it was too late. The damage was done. 'You're leaving tomorrow,' he clarified to the question that had yet to leave her lips.

'I know,' she said simply.

'I can't follow you.'

'I didn't ask you to.' She knew that he belonged here as much as she was needed in Norfolk. But she also knew that she would never forgive herself if she walked away from the promise of this night. *One* night.

'Star, you're innocent. You are—'

'A virgin? Yes. I am. Does that mean I don't know what I want?' she replied.

'No, but that doesn't mean I can give you what you need.'

'Oh. Would you not treat me well?' she asked, not thinking for a second that he wouldn't.

'Of course I would.'

'Would you be selfish and only take what you wanted?' She couldn't even imagine it.

'No, I—'

'Would you not be very good?'

The question was a taunt and his response, 'Star...' was a growl on his lips, a warning and an incitement, a call to arms that she felt down to her core, setting her on fire, energising her in a way she could never have imagined.

'So you think I should leave and instead find someone who I'm less attracted to, who might not be good or treat me well and only be selfish in their wants?'

The thought burned the back of his throat and bruised his palms from clenching his fists too tightly. He couldn't argue with her logic. He had spent years cutting a swathe through Europe's most beautiful women and not a single one of them had caused this…arcane chemistry that burned the air between them—and his willpower to dust.

With his unseeing gaze still on the horizon, he felt her eyes like a brand against his skin, waiting for an answer, a response. His mouth ached to say the words, but he held them knowing he needed to be strong. He felt the subtle shift of her body as the fight left it and he closed his eyes, not wanting to see how giving up haunted her eyes.

Wordlessly she stood and approached the balcony as if the silhouette of his city contained answers that he was unable to give. She bowed her head and for a moment looked defeated. He wasn't arrogant enough to believe it was all him.

'I have let my sisters down.'

'You'd be my choice.'

"'It is not time or opportunity that is to determine intimacy…"'

Snippets from their conversation whispered once again in his ear, threatening to pull him under, the word 'intimacy' like a spell drawing him to her. Before his mind could catch up, his body had taken him to her.

He stood behind her, inches from her, his mind on all the reasons why giving in to this desire would be bad and his body itching to touch all the reasons why it wouldn't be. The glorious river of red had fallen over her shoulder, the delicate curve of her neck exposed. But it was when she moved her head slightly to the side, her pale skin gleaming in the light of the moon, willingly exposing her greatest vulnerability, surrendering to him completely, that he was lost.

He placed his hands against the stone balustrade either side of Star's, encircling her without yet touching her. The roar of blood in his veins, the pounding beat of his heart in his ears—something primal, elemental was taking over, and as he placed his lips against that stretch of the palest, smoothest skin he offered his first prayer in over three years.

The shudder that travelled through him rippled through her and he couldn't tell whether it was her legs shaking or his. He pressed his body into hers, leaning them both gently against the balcony, trapping her, holding her still. Her head fell back against his shoulder, her hair streaming over his forearm, offering him access to more of her. Rough stone was replaced by smooth skin as his hands left the balcony and swept around her petite body. He prised his eyes open to see the valley between breasts that were made to be held in his palms. He was torn, wanting to take this slow and wanting to take it all.

'Please,' she whispered.

And the leash on his restraint was lifted.

His hands swept over her breasts, palming the weight of them and feeling complete. His thumbs brushed her nipples into stiff peaks, ringing a shuddered moan that tightened Khalif's arousal. As if feeling it, Star arched back into his groin, pressing against the length of his erection until it was cradled against her bottom. Desire exploded on his tongue and he gently scraped his teeth against the muscle of her neck. She shivered again—and he felt it against his chest, his hands, his thighs and his calf muscles, questioning why they were still standing.

It seemed inconceivable to him that Star was a virgin and, despite feeling all kinds of selfish, he couldn't bring himself to stop. Unless she wanted him to.

'Star, you need to know that if you want me to stop—'

'Don't stop, please, I—'

He bent his head to hers so that his lips were against

her ear. 'Nothing would make me stop. Not the sun falling from the sky, the desert freezing over, floods, locusts, or a third world war. Nothing would make me stop...but one word from you.'

'I don't need—'

'Star. At any point, do you understand? You can stop me at any point.'

CHAPTER FOUR

NOTHING WOULD MAKE me stop. Not the sun falling from the sky... Nothing...but one word from you.

Star couldn't deny that she had been nervous until he'd said those words. Words that had overflowed with the same need, want, *yearning* that she felt deep within her, and the *only* thing she was afraid of was him walking away.

She twisted in his arms, turning to face him, to look up into his eyes so that he knew. So that he believed her when she said, 'Yes. I understand.' She searched his face as if she was seeing it for the first time. Emboldened by his declaration, she was ready to stand in the path of his flame.

'Show me?' she asked, the weight of her desire making her voice shake.

He pulled his gaze from his observation of her face, her body, and dragged—reluctantly, it seemed—his eyes back to hers. 'Show you what?' he asked.

She bit her lip, trying to stop the smile that was ready to burst against her mouth. 'Just how good you are.'

She watched as the rich brown depths of his eyes were eclipsed by the pitch black of his pupils, his response marked in deep red slashes across his cheekbones. He claimed her then, passionately, possessively, his lips crushed against hers, his tongue slipping into her mouth, tangling with her as deeply and completely as she wanted him.

His hands drew her to him, the soft curves of her chest pressed against the hard ridges of his, but it wasn't enough. For either of them. He drew her up and she felt herself lifted from her tiptoes, her legs instinctively wrapping around his slender hips until she was above him, his neck bent back to kiss her, her hair streaming down around them, curtaining them within red velvet tendrils.

Her hands braced against his shoulders, revelling in the flex of his muscles beneath her fingertips, the power as he held her there, restrained and raw—and all for her. He looked up at her as if she were the most incredible thing he'd seen and she felt it. For the first time she really felt it.

He walked them back from the balcony and into the living area and a thought snagged at her mind. 'Is it okay? That we're here? That we…' She didn't quite know how to finish that sentence, but she read the understanding in his eyes.

'It is. This suite…it's mine.'

It was the first time she had seen him look worried, as if concerned what her reaction would be, or what questions she might ask. 'Okay,' she said simply, her faith and trust in him complete. He looked as if he were about to say something, to qualify or justify. 'It's okay,' she said again, before pressing a kiss to his mouth. Then another. And another. Lips brushed against lips until he opened beneath her and this time it was her tongue that led the dance, and raised a dragon within her. One that breathed fire and clawed skin. He had cast a spell over her and she felt transformed.

She lost herself to the feel of him beneath her, eyes drifting closed to savour the moment, and when they opened there was nothing in his gaze but lust. He turned and walked them through a doorway and into a room that faced the same balcony, the same view. Moonlight poured in through the glass doors, casting a silvery glow on a large bed with pure white sheets. Very slowly he drew her downward, his arms and hands cradling her back, so that she was ready when the back of her thighs hit the surprisingly high mattress. She looked up and saw the net canopy hanging from a hook in the ceiling placed at the centre of the bed and stretching out to the four corners. She felt like a princess and almost said as much, until she caught the look in Kal's eyes as he took her in, leaning back on her hands.

She watched as Kal pulled his shirt from the waist of his trousers, slowly undoing each button and revealing inch after inch of impeccable bronzed skin. Only once he had removed the shirt could her eyes roam as freely across his body as she'd wished.

He removed his trousers while she was distracted and on her next inhale she saw him standing before her, black briefs hugging his skin, revealing the contours of his body, the dip of his abs, the flare of his hip bones and the length of his arousal.

'I will stop at *any* time, Star.'

'I know. But thank you for saying it,' she replied sincerely and, no matter what happened that night, she was thankful. Thankful that she was sharing this with Kal.

He came over her on the bed and covered her with his body. It was only then that she realised she was shaking. But the moment his lips touched her skin that shaking became a shiver, became a well of need rising within her.

His hands slid beneath the hem of her top and lifted it

over her head, casting the cotton aside as if the few seconds she was hidden from his sight were too much. Slipping the strap of her bra from her shoulder, he pressed kisses across her shoulder as he slipped his hands beneath her and flicked open the clasp. She gasped into the sudden freedom as he threw her pale pink bra from her body and the bed. The fire in Kal's eyes made her feel glorious as his palms swept up her thighs, rucking the jersey of her skirt into pleats that he bunched in his palms before tugging it gently over her hips and down her legs, from her ankles and onto the floor.

He trailed open-mouthed kisses down her throat, between breasts he cupped, the warmth of his palms reassuring, the thumbs against her nipples sensually unsettling. Her back arched involuntarily, pushing her body upwards against his, wanting more, harder, deeper.

His tongue teased the sensitive skin of her abdomen as his hands moved to her hips, hooking his fingers beneath the small band at her waist and drawing her knickers down, over her thighs, then her knees, gently pushing them away and making room for him between her legs. Her mind was overwhelmed with sensation and she was oblivious to thought or words, but a craving roared to life within her and she felt the echoes of the dragon once again.

She felt herself parted, exposed, but not vulnerable and she relished the groan of pure satisfaction from Kal, just before the world tilted on its axis as he pressed an open-mouthed kiss at her core. She arched against the wild streak of desire that almost lifted her from the bed, thankful for the anchor of his forearms holding her in place as a second sweep of his tongue stole her breath.

And she was lost. To pleasure, to sensation, the sparks of fire racing through her bloodstream that she'd never known before. Kal had set them alight, making her glow from the inside, throb with a pulse of energy that powered both her sense of self and her need.

She heard herself begging for something she couldn't even name and gasped with sheer pleasure as his fingers joined his tongue. The unfamiliar feel of the stretch within her soon gave over to passion which gave over to frustration. It wasn't enough—she wanted *him*.

'Please, Kal,' she begged. 'Please.'

Kal reluctantly drew away from her. He had wanted to feel her come apart on his tongue, to show her the heights of pleasure before any kind of pain she might experience for her first time. But that was *his* want and this was about hers. His tongue swept out across his bottom lip to taste the raw honey and milk of her, not wanting to miss a single drop. She was exquisite, a man's final feast, and the thought that she would be the last thing on his mind before he gasped his dying breath stopped him still.

But then her hands reached for him, pulling gently at his shoulders, and he would have followed her anywhere. Leaning up over her, bracing himself on his forearms, he took in the pink path his rough hands and tongue had traced over such silky skin. The marks would be gone in the morning, but right now the primal animal satisfaction he felt at such a sight made it seem as if she were the royal and he were a beast. He traced his fingers over the outline of her hip, watching her shiver and buck beneath the lightest of touches, across the sweeping hollow of her waist, and tripped them over rib after rib after rib to reach the underside of a breast he couldn't resist cupping in his palm, the weight of it feeling like a lost pound of his own flesh. A missing part of him, one that he'd not known of until now.

He looked up at her face to find her watching him so intently that where he would have smiled, he couldn't. Could barely breathe for the sight of her.

'It may hurt, but I will take that pain away. That, I can give you,' he swore, hoping that she understood all the things that he could not give her. She nodded and he leaned over to his bedside table for a box of condoms that he'd never thought he'd need.

He retrieved the packet, tearing at the foil with his teeth, and felt the searing heat of her gaze as she watched him roll the latex over his length. He felt her shift on the mattress and looked up to find her leaning back on her forearms, her teeth punishing her bottom lip with a bite. He reached out to smooth away a rich red curl that had fallen forward and she leaned into the palm of his hand. Selfishly, he wanted to keep her there. Keep this moment. He could fool himself all he wanted but, while he would do *everything* in his power to make this special for her, he wanted this as much as she did.

'If it gets too much—'

'Then the sun would have fallen from the sky—' she returned his words to him '—the desert would have frozen and I would be myself no more.'

It sounded like a quote from one of her romances, but he didn't recognise it—it felt as if it were just for them. He kissed her back against the mattress and settled between her legs, relishing the way his body covered hers almost completely, fitting together like a puzzle piece.

His pulse began to race, awed by the trust she had placed in him. He leashed himself with more control than he'd thought himself capable of as he cradled her face with his hands and pushed forward gently into her.

Her body tensed, as he knew it would, and she breathed in through the pain he could see she felt. He kissed her neck, the secret spot between her jaw and ear. 'It's okay, Star. Let it go. I've got you,' he whispered, holding himself still, impossibly still, until she was ready. Her deep inhalations pressed her chest into his as he dusted her skin with Arabic, words of comfort, of reassurance, promises that he'd be there to catch her when she fell. Star's body began to relax and he watched as her eyes opened, pain and shock replaced by wonder and desire once again. She nodded at his unspoken question and gently, and so, so slowly, he began to move.

He cursed. He prayed. He'd never felt anything like this. She was everywhere—around him, beneath him. His touch, his tongue, his taste was full of her and the air he breathed was laden with her. As her body undulated beneath him, he moved within her, their bodies joining together as if they were independent of thought and focused solely on pleasure.

Star strained towards him, her hand at the back of his neck pulling him down into a kiss that sent fire racing up from the base of his spine. A fine sheen dusted their skin, slippery and slick, sliding and tantalising, erotic sounds heating the air.

Star moaned into the kiss and he consumed it, the cries of her pleasure feeding his, bringing him closer and closer to orgasm. Each mewl of desire reached a higher pitch than the last and Khalif could tell she was on the brink. And he was torn between drawing out this singularly sublime moment and rushing them headlong into sheer bliss.

But then she tilted her hips downwards, drawing him even deeper within her, to press against a spot that saw Star explode beneath him, thrusting him headlong into an orgasm that stole his breath, his sight and his thought. The moon slipped behind the sun, the ocean poured away, and Khalif was completely and utterly spent.

* * *

When Khalif regained awareness it was to the feel of Star's fingers tracing swirls on his shoulders, her small hands slipping over his skin, as if stealing all the moments she could. Then he felt her lips tracing kisses down his spine, her body reaching over his as he had reached over her. He twisted beneath her and pulled her into a kiss as if the sand in their hourglass had already run dry.

Throughout the night they reached for each other almost endlessly and the sun was a curse on the horizon when Khalif finally made his way to the bathroom, running water from the tap—desperate to quench the thirst that hadn't quit even after the first taste of her. He was about to throw the protection they'd used in the bin when he noticed a small tear. And even had he closed his eyes to block out the image, his mind raced at the speed of light and all the while a voice screamed in his mind over and over and over again.

Pregnant.

Star could be pregnant. She could be carrying his child.

Star woke to the feeling of the sun streaming onto her skin, warming her and reigniting memories of the most incredible night of her life. She ran her hand over the sheets of Kal's bed, marvelling that it was his—the bed, the suite, the room in the palace. Sidestepping what that meant, she indulged in the belief that it had made what they'd shared a little more real, more meaningful than if they had been in a hotel room.

She was so glad that she had waited, that she had saved herself for him. He'd been so gentle, so generous, and her cheeks throbbed with blushes from the memory of what they had done the night before.

She turned onto her back, wondering where he was.

Then, drawing the pale silk sheet around her, she made her way to the door, hearing the sound of voices beyond too late to stop her opening it.

The tableau that met her stopped her in her tracks. Khalif, dressed in suit trousers and a shirt, stood half turned towards her, his hands fisted at his thighs. A look of immense frustration was painted on his features for the second it took to register her standing in the doorway, before his face went blank. He was mid-conversation with another man, also suited, peering angrily at her through his glasses. A shift of weight drew her gaze to a uniformed security guard positioned in front of the door to the rest of the palace and finally a woman stood in the kitchen with a cup in both hands, gently blowing steam across the rim with a look of sympathy in her eyes.

Star shook her head as if trying to clear the image and pushed the door closed, hoping that the next time it was opened all these strangers would have gone and Kal would be there to tell her it was all a dream.

She was still standing there a minute later when he opened the door—through which she could still see the people staring at her.

'We have to talk,' Kal said, shutting the door behind him and walking forward.

'Mmm.' She wasn't so sure she wanted to talk but she was definitely sure she wanted a bit of breathing space between them so, for every step he took towards her, she took one back until the backs of her knees hit the mattress and she half sat, half fell on the mattress.

She clenched her jaw, trying to block everything out, even sound, but it was impossible as her eyes tracked Kal, pacing back and forth before her, his hands sweeping angrily through his hair. His lips, the perfect, sensual, powerful lips that had worshipped her last night, were bringing words Star could barely process into a room where they'd shared such incredible passion. Words that didn't make any sense at all.

In a daze, she tried to assemble what he'd said.

'I'm sorry, can you repeat that last bit? Just one more time.'

'I am Sheikh Khalif Al Azhar. First in line to the Duratrian throne.'

A sheikh. A prince.

He couldn't be.

But then she thought of the way he had looked to the horizon as if he owned it. The way that she now remembered his interaction with Wahed and the other guards, as if they had known each other. At how he had known his way around the palace.

How had she missed that?

She knew how. She'd been caught up in the romantic history of Hātem and the terrible tragedy of Crown Prince Faizan and his wife, and the loss that would be to their two small children. The tragedy had made the headlines of almost every international newspaper, with images of the twin girls being held by their grandparents and a stony-faced half shadowed brother she now knew was Khalif. There had been a subtle aspect of the exhibition that covered it—Samira's wedding dress, pictures, footage. The loss mourned by a nation had been handled well by the exhibition and there were references to an upcoming memorial to the short-lived ruler and his wife, but nothing had yet been confirmed.

He'd lied to her.

'Star,' he said, as if reading her thoughts in the widening of her eyes. 'You didn't recognise me and I…you were the first person to…'

There was a firm knock on the door.

'Not now,' he growled.

Star looked between the door and Kal. No. Not Kal any more. Khalif. His Royal Highness Sheikh Khalif Al Azhar. Hurt, embarrassment and shame flooded her as she realised that he had hidden who he was while she had been absolutely and completely herself. So focused on finding the necklace she hadn't been able to be anything but plain old Star Soames.

Rich and powerful. I am impressed.

Her shaking fingers pressed against her mouth. Oh, God. She'd said that.

It is not time or opportunity that is to determine intimacy.

She'd said that too. Had he laughed at her?

No. While she might not have known he was a prince, she *did* know him well enough that she could tell he hadn't laughed at her.

'But why all this?' she asked, gesturing to the door. 'Why tell me now? Did something happen?' she went on, wondering if it was fanciful to worry that perhaps a war had broken out, or that something had happened to a family member.

He came to sit beside her on the bed, their knees not quite touching, as if something more than his title had put a distance between them that hadn't been there the night before.

'This morning, I noticed that the protection we used had torn.'

She tried to look at him but he was facing straight ahead, as if confronting some unforeseen future head-on. She frowned. Torn protection? She couldn't quite see what he...

'You think I might be...'

'Pregnant.'

A baby.

Could she be?

A flood of pure bright light dipped and soared across her heart, her skin, her mind, before swooping to the floor and scattering like diamonds on marble.

This wasn't how she'd imagined finding out that she might be pregnant. She'd thought that there would be joy and a dizzying happiness as she shared the special moment with her husband, not a sense of confusion and disbelief and the father-to-be looking so...so *forbidding*.

'But it's highly unlikely, isn't it?' she asked him, looking for reassurance.

'That's not really going to work with my advisors.' His voice was heavy and grim in a way she'd not heard before.

'It doesn't have to,' she said, wondering why such a thing would be decided by committee. 'It only has to work with you.' She shrugged. 'I'll catch my flight home and when I can take a test I'll let you know what the results are and we can speak about it then.'

He smiled. It was a firm line of determination. 'There will be no *speaking about it then*, Star.'

She studied him until he finally turned and locked his gaze on hers. 'Oh,' she said, feeling a tremble work its way down her spine.

'What?'

'The sheikh look. Does that actually work on your staff and subjects?' she asked, forcing herself to keep her tone light.

'Usually,' he said, his tone still cold enough to cut stone.

'I spend my days with thirty primary school children who throw much better tantrums than that.'

'That wasn't a tantrum,' he ground out.

'It was about to be,' she said, relishing the heat that

had entered his voice. Heat she could deal with, cold… not so much.

'And that would be at Salisbury Primary?'

'Yes, how did you…?' Her words trailed off as she realised that if he *was* the Sheikh, if she *might* be pregnant, then of course his advisors would have looked into her background. As her heart slowly poked and prodded the idea that she might be pregnant, her mind ran like a stream over cobbles and stones. 'I always wondered what that would feel like,' she babbled. 'You know, in romances, when the hero does a "background check"? He usually gets something horribly wrong and so there's a big misunderstanding between them. I read this one—it was actually pretty funny—where…'

'Can we focus here, Star?'

'Of course,' she replied automatically, wondering how on earth she was supposed to focus when her thoughts had been picked up by the wind and scattered across the desert floor.

She looked up, finding one thread of thought to hold onto. 'Is it that bad?'

'That depends on whether you are pregnant with the heir to the throne of Duratra.'

Khalif left the bedroom while Star showered and dressed. He wished he could ignore the room full of people—the guard, Amin, Maya… No. He'd not ignore Maya. She had made herself as invisible as possible, but the subtle comfort she offered was everything to him right now. He could rely on her confidentiality even if she wasn't married to his best friend.

A best friend who would be calling him every shade of stupid for last night. And he'd be right. What had he been thinking? He'd been selfish. Completely and utterly selfish for wanting her, for acting on it, and now Star was going to pay the price.

This wasn't how it was supposed to be. He was supposed to get to grips with running the throne for a few years and then, after his thirtieth birthday, there would be discreet enquiries as to the availability of a suitable wife who wouldn't challenge him or interfere with his duty. And once the twins were of age, of course, the throne would return to them.

Years ago, he'd imagined something different, *someone* different, to wear his ring and have his children. But then he'd learned. Duty, the throne, family. It all came first.

But this? Star being possibly pregnant? He ran his hand through his hair, ignoring the uneasy glance his assistant sent his way as he stalked through the living area towards the balcony, stopping himself before stepping out onto it, remembering Star in his arms, hair streaming down around them. No one had ever affected him in such a way. Not even the one woman he had loved and lost.

He cursed out loud, uncaring of who heard him, his mind taking him to all the places he didn't want to be that morning.

Pregnant.

Star might be pregnant. And if she was? Then there was no doubt whatsoever. They would marry.

Showered and dressed in the previous day's slightly rumpled clothes, Star was looking out of the window when there was a gentle knock on the door.

The doctor. Star's pulse raced as she realised that she hadn't asked him what kind of examination or questions she was expected to submit to. Expecting a grim-faced old man, she was surprised when a pretty woman a little older than herself came through the door.

'Hello, Star, my name is Maya Mourad,' she said, introducing herself in English lightly flecked with an Arabic accent. Her headscarf was a pretty green and Star was a little distracted by it, which was why it took a moment to connect the name.

'Mourad, like the Prime Minister?'

'Yes, he is my husband,' Maya confirmed, her smile deep and full of the love of a happy wife. 'Khalif has explained that I would be seeing you?'

The gentle way about her was soothing to Star's edgy nerves. 'Perhaps "explained" might be a bit of an exaggeration.'

Maya nodded knowingly. 'I see. So, I am a family doctor,' she explained. 'A little like your GPs, but I specialise in women's health.'

'I didn't think that you could tell if I was pregnant so soon after...' Star's words were replaced by a fierce blush and suddenly she wanted her sisters. She didn't want to be here, no matter how nice Maya was. She should be talking to Skye and Summer about her first time, about how wonderful it was, not how she might be pregnant and how that meant she couldn't come home.

She could almost hear them now. Skye would immediately be making plans about prams and cradles, nappies and booties, Summer would turn to books and have all kinds of information on birthing styles, baby names and vitamins. Both of them would be completely supportive, with all the kind words of encouragement and soothing she could possibly need.

But there would be that silent *I told you so* in Skye and Summer's shared looks. They had expected her to get into trouble and, while they might not have forecasted just how big that trouble was…they'd clearly been right to worry.

'We can't tell whether you are pregnant yet,' Maya said, answering Star's half formed question from moments before. 'But first I want to see if you're okay. Then we'll talk about the options.'

'I won't have a termination.' The words were immediate and determined, natural and instinctive. They came from a place deep within her, and Star almost heard the growl of the dragon that Kal had called forth within her. 'I'm sorry, I—'

'No. It's good for you to know how you feel about this, even at this early stage,' Maya said, her gentle smile soothing a bit of the shock Star was beginning to feel. 'I meant options in terms of the kinds of tests we can do now, the tests you're *happy* to do now, and any medical information you feel comfortable giving me.'

'You mean giving Khalif?' Star asked, more curious than resentful.

'You are my patient. If there is anything you wish for me not to say, then you have my confidentiality.'

Star thought about it for a moment. 'No,' she said finally and resolutely. 'I have nothing to hide.'

Maya smiled and gestured for her to sit. 'So let's start with the easiest question and then work back a little. When was your last period?'

CHAPTER FIVE

THE MOMENT MAYA emerged from his bedroom, Khalif demanded to know how Star was.

'She is fine,' Maya replied. 'Taking a moment, but she is—'

His assistant stood, snaring Maya's attention. 'Any medical conditions we should know about? Family history of—'

'That's enough, Amin,' Khalif said.

'Your Highness, we need to know if there is any—'

'*If* Star is pregnant, we will get to those kinds of questions. Until then I will *not* invade her privacy in such a way,' he warned.

Amin stared at Khalif until Star opened the door to the bedroom and came out, with a smile only he might be able to tell was nervous.

'As I told Star,' Maya said to the room, 'we will need about eleven days before we can be sure a pregnancy test will be completely accurate.'

'That's the day after the memorial event,' Amin said angrily as if somehow that was Star's fault too.

'Yes,' Maya confirmed as Khalif's head began to spin. Everything seemed to be converging on that one event.

'You can't miss it,' Amin said to Khalif.

'Why would you miss it?' Star asked Khalif in confusion and started a little at the glare his assistant sent her way. Khalif was about to say something when she turned to Amin. 'Are you okay?' she asked, peering at him. 'Do you need some water?'

Amin turned an indelicate shade of puce. Khalif couldn't tell whether Star had been purposely oblivious to Amin's obvious anger or simply unseeing of it.

'You cannot leave, Your Highness. There is still too much work to do—'

'Amin…' he warned.

'She can go,' Amin said, waving an arm in her direction as if she were a baggage to be passed around, 'but you are needed here.'

'Enough!' Khalif barked, his hand slicing through the air and any further objection his infuriating assistant might have. He was done. 'Out. Everyone. Now.'

Amin looked as shocked as if he'd just been told categorically that Santa Claus was real and moved only when the security guard in front of the door opened it and gestured to him to leave. Maya ducked her head—quite possibly concealing the ghost of a smile—but left and was followed by the security guard closing the door behind him.

'Did you want me to…?' Star's question fell short, probably at the look on his face which—if it was anywhere close to his feelings right now—would be a sight to behold. He resisted the urge to run his hands through his hair, aware of how much that would give away.

'Do you want a coffee?'

'If I *am* pregnant, probably not, no.'

'Right. Of course. Really? Already?'

Star shrugged her shoulders and stared at him as if he were an unexploded bomb. He certainly felt like one.

'Herbal tea would be lovely, if you have one.'

That he could do. He went to the kitchenette and re-trieved one of the herbal teas he'd always kept for Samira.

His brain stumbled over her name as if, even mentally, he couldn't face it. He glared at the leafy infusion as if it were responsible for creating a link between Star and her at this specific moment.

Pulling himself together, he passed the cup under the heated water tap.

'I know you're a prince and everything, but if you don't know how to boil a kettle…'

He felt a smile soften the grim line of his lips and shifted to the side so that Star could see the steam com-ing from the boiling water.

'Ah… Fancy.'

'Very,' he confirmed. He turned and passed her the tea. 'How do you feel?'

'Not pregnant, if that's what you're wondering,' she said, gently blowing the steam from her tea across the rim of the cup. She looked up at him and shrugged. 'Kal—Your— Oh, please just tell me what to call you?' she pleaded lightly.

He smiled at her evident fluster. 'Kal when it's just you and me, Khalif in front of the people who just left the room, and Your Highness if there is ever anyone else present.'

If there is ever. Not *when*.

Star gripped the cup tighter to disguise the shaking of her hands caused by the realisation that he had no in-tention of introducing her to any more people than was strictly necessary. And while that hurt, could she blame him? She had only intended to share one magical night with him before returning to Norfolk. Something that now seemed impossible.

'I get the feeling you're not letting me on my flight,' she said.

'No.'

A dull thud hit her heart and blood rushed to her cheeks. Eleven days, Maya had said. She couldn't stay here for eleven days! Panic flooded her body, adrenaline effervescent in her blood. What about her mother? Every single minute she stayed with Khalif the necklace remained lost to them, as did the chance to save her mother.

She put down the hot tea before she could spill it and burn herself. 'I can't… I can't be here for eleven days, Kal,' she said, her voice almost a whisper.

'You won't be. In half an hour we'll head into the desert.'

'The desert?' Star asked before realising that he wouldn't want her somewhere she could be found by some unsuspecting staff or family member.

'We have a family residence in the desert.'

'Really?' Star frowned. She'd not heard or seen any reference to it in the exhibition. Maybe, just maybe… She couldn't tell whether the thread of hope winding around her heart at the possibility that she might find the necklace there was fanciful or fated. And then she was horrified at herself for thinking such a thing, for being opportunistic at this time, and her stomach began to hurt as much as her heart.

'I need to call my sisters.' They would know what to do, she thought, rubbing absently at her stomach—a move that Khalif's keen gaze homed in on.

'You can't tell them.'

Her eyes flew to his face.

'You can't,' he repeated. 'If news gets out then…'

'I trust my sisters.'

'I'm glad. But I don't.'

'You are cutting me off from a support that I need right now,' she warned.

'Then allow me to be that support.' His words were at odds with the grim determination on his features.

She turned away from him.

'Star.' She halted without looking back. 'If you are pregnant—'

'We'll cross that bridge when it comes to it,' she interrupted, not wanting to hear the rest of his declaration. Because she knew it would erase all the good that they had shared up to that point, all the moments of connection and how she'd felt *seen* by him.

'I need you to understand that while Duratra is a peaceful, inclusive and diverse country, even we balk at unmarried sheikhs with illegitimate heirs. Family is incredibly important to us. It comes first.'

'I appreciate that,' she said, still facing the door to the bedroom.

'Star. I need you to *understand* that if you are carrying my child, we *will* marry.'

No.

This wasn't how it was supposed to be. She was supposed to come to Duratra, find the necklace and return home to Norfolk, where they could find the jewels, sell the estate and get the treatment their mother needed.

Spinning to face him, 'But I can't be what you'd imagined as a wife?' she said.

'No. You're not.'

She pressed her teeth into her lip to stop the hot ache in her throat from escaping.

'But if you are carrying my child that won't matter.'

'So you'd marry me for the sake of our child?' she demanded.

'Yes.'

'But not love. You'd not *want* to marry me.' Star rubbed at her wrists, trying to soothe away the impression of shackles that her mother—that Catherine—had seen marriage as.

'No royal marries for love, Star.'

'That is very sad indeed.'

'It's just the way it is,' he said as if it were a tenet to live by. 'If you are pregnant, we will marry.'

Less than two hours later the Jeep jerked a little to the right as they skirted the base of another impossibly tall sand dune and he cursed. Usually Khalif was a much better driver than this. He loved this drive. Not that he'd taken it in the last three years. No one had been back here since Faizan and Samira's accident—as if distance alone would help stave off their grief.

Khalif was hit by an overwhelming need to speak to his brother right now.

You're a fool, Faizan would have said.

And Samira would have looked at him with her large, deep brown eyes, accepting, understanding and hopeful that he'd found happiness at last.

He braced himself against the wave of loss that hit as inevitably as the tide. *That* was why he didn't like thinking of them. The pain that always followed was too much to bear.

He gripped the steering wheel and turned to check on Star. She had regained a little of the colour in her face. He resisted the urge to lift his sunglasses and rub his eyes, instead pushing forward with focused determination. As if the distance between them and the palace was something to be beaten into submission.

'I'm sorry about your mother's diagnosis,' he said. It had been burning a hole in his conscience since Maya had told him. He couldn't even begin to imagine what that must feel like.

'Thank you,' she said quietly.

'Is there anything that can be done?'

'We are working on it.'

Star stared at the rich yellow sand, rising and falling as if endless, silently praying for it to distract her. The 'family residence' in the desert was her last hope and she would turn it upside down if she had to.

Because if she didn't find the necklace and they couldn't save their mother then…then…she'd be alone. Her sisters loved her, but her mother *understood* her. And the awful shadow of loss she felt for the father she had never known would be *nothing* in comparison to what life would be like without her mother.

She cleared her throat against the aching burn and Khalif passed her a bottle of water. She refocused her gaze on the miles of golden sand and brilliant blue sky.

'How do you feel?'

'No more pregnant than I did an hour ago,' she said, the concern in his voice a kindness that softened her reply.

If you are carrying my child, we will marry.

It was only now that she might be pregnant that Star realised just how much she'd wanted to marry before having a child. It was in the way her heart quivered at the thought of her baby growing up to experience the same stares and whispers that she and her sisters had. An experience that Khalif had shared in his own way.

'But if I was,' she said hesitantly, picking up the threads of her answer, 'if I *was* pregnant, if we had a child, can you ensure that they wouldn't be judged, or excluded or…?'

'Star, look at me,' he said, removing his sunglasses. Only when she met his gaze did he continue. 'With every ounce of my being I would protect you and our child. Our family has an agreement with the press, both in Duratra and internationally, that protects our children from scrutiny until they turn eighteen. They attend a central city school until they decide whether they want to attend university. We can't protect them from everything, but we do our best.'

Star thought about that for a moment, not immune to the devotion and determination in Khalif's tone. She had grown up sure of her parents' love, even though her father had passed. Their love of her, love of each other, hadn't needed a marriage certificate. But her grandparents' behaviour had made her see through different eyes—ones that were hurt and had caused hurt. And she would never do that to her child.

'If I were pregnant, I would do whatever it took to protect them,' she said, finally turning back to him, knowing that he would understand what she meant.

'As would I.' His words felt like an oath and she felt the stirrings of the connection she'd been drawn to when they'd first met and something tight eased in her heart.

The sound of his phone ringing cut through the Jeep, but he put off answering it until Star returned to look out of the window.

Biting back a curse, he pressed the wireless earbud to his ear and pressed a button on the steering wheel to answer the call. 'Yes?' Khalif answered in Arabic.

'Wow. Okay. Nice to speak to you too,' came the sardonic response from Reza.

'I don't have much time. I'm on the way to Alhafa.'

'Really? Is that…wise?'

Khalif glanced across at Star. Nothing about his decisions had been wise since she'd come crashing into his life.

'There wasn't much choice.'

'The plans for the memorial are barely finalised, let alone—'

'I know, Reza. But what do you want me to do? Abbad will never be happy with the choice of memorial for his youngest daughter. We could have renamed the mountains and it wouldn't be compensation for his loss.'

'If that's what you're trying to achieve, Khalif, then...' Reza's voice trailed off, genuine concern evident.

He cursed. 'I don't know any more, Reza.'

'Well, at this rate, Amin might have a heart attack and be removed from your staff for medical reasons.'

'He's necessary.'

'He was necessary for Faizan. I'm not sure he's necessary for you.'

'Is that what you called me for? To berate me for messing up this memorial *and* my choice of employee?'

'Actually, I called to berate you for possibly impregnating a British tourist, but sure, while we're at it, we might as well—'

'I'm hanging up now.'

'Khalif, it defeats the purpose if you tell me that you're—'

Khalif pulled the earbud from his ear and tossed it into the well near the gearbox, smiling. The moment of relief was, however, quickly dulled by the realisation that Reza was right.

If that's what you're trying to achieve...

'I am sorry,' Star said in the wake of the terminated phone call. He risked a glance towards her. 'For your loss,' she clarified.

He clenched his jaw, only capable of uttering the same

two words she had given to his concern about her mother. 'Thank you.'

'Memorials are hard to choose,' she said, and he wondered if she had somehow understood the one-sided conversation. His anger escaped before his mind could catch up, his response a half growl, half scoff, questioning what she'd know about it, until he remembered the loss of her father.

'My father was cremated,' she said, her eyes ahead on the horizon, but clearly seeing some distant past. 'His ashes were scattered in the Solent but Mum wanted me to have somewhere that I could go to, that I could visit if I wanted to. Somewhere just for me and him. She saved a little bit of his ashes for me, so that when I was old enough I could decide where that would be. I...' She trailed off, as if searching for the words. 'It was hard to decide. I didn't know him, I could barely remember him and I felt this...*pressure* to get it right, like I was being tested somehow on some instinctive connection I should have with the father I had never known.

'And then I realised that it wasn't about him, or Mum, or what people expected. This was for me.' She pressed a hand against her heart and his palm itched as if he felt the beat of her heart there. 'There's a forest near to where we live, and I spent days searching for the oldest tree. It's this beautiful old gnarled oak that's been there for hundreds of years. Mum, Skye and Summer came with me and we lit candles and I buried the little vial of ash in its roots so that he'd always be a part of the wood we both loved so much.'

Khalif remembered that she'd said her father was a carpenter and thought that it was perfect. It must have been a beautiful moment for her. For them. And he was struck by a spark of jealousy. Jealous of the privacy and intimacy of the moment.

'It's not that easy,' he said, his voice shockingly hoarse.

'Easy?' she asked, the tone to her voice making him realise how that had come out.

'I'm sorry, I didn't mean it like that. It's just that this memorial is not just for me, my nieces, my family, my country, but Samira's family, her country... It's...'

'Big.'

'Yes.'

She nodded. 'So all the more reason to find the one that feels *right*?'

He looked at her for a second longer than he needed to, causing the arousal he felt to sneak beneath his defences and grip him low and hard.

'So, tell me about this family residence,' she said, breaking the moment, a brightness to her tone that hadn't been there moments before. And if it felt just a little forced, he could understand why.

He sighed and cast his mind back through the family history and legends of the old fortress. 'It's been there almost as long, if not longer than the city. It was originally a fortress between our land and the neighbouring countries, but it hasn't been used by the military since the fourteenth century. It was barely even used in the last few hundred years, but my father liked it and started to hold family gatherings there, especially since his friendship with His Majesty Sheikh Abbad.'

'Your sister-in-law's father? His country borders yours?'

'Yes. But, before my father, it was mainly known for being used for...'

He trailed off, as if not wanting to finish the sentence.

'For what?' she prodded.

'For the Sheikh's mistresses.'

'How fitting,' she replied drily.

'You are not a mistress,' he announced.

'No, I suppose being a mistress would require more than one night.'

Silence filled the Jeep as they both descended into a mix of memories and fantasies of what had been and what could be. Star wanted to bite her tongue and Khalif clenched the steering wheel.

They rounded the curve of a road that would have been invisible if he hadn't known where to look, and his pulse started to beat a little harder just as Star gasped in astonishment at the incredible medieval structure that was more beautiful to him than the city palace. The ochre stonework stood proudly against the bright blue sky, beside the rich forest-green slash of the palace gardens.

Despite its military exterior, inside smooth functionality gave way to intricate and ornate carved stone and corridors with rooms that opened up like Russian dolls, and mentally Khalif traced a path towards quarters almost as familiar to him as his own.

'Star, before we get to the residence—'

'That's not a residence, Kal. That's a palace.'

'Yes. Sorry, were you expecting—'

'Something smaller, perhaps? As implied by the word *residence*,' she teased. 'Sorry, you were saying…'

Khalif's stomach tightened, hating himself already for what he was about to say. 'Because of the situation, because we can't risk any word getting out, I have to request that you stay in your room for one hour in the morning and one hour in the evening.' She stared at him, those oceanic-blue eyes levelling him with their eerie calm. 'It is so that the staff can get what they need to do done, without seeing you. It's safer for you and them. No matter what happens, I don't want any hint of impropriety linked to either of our futures, no matter what they are.'

'Okay.'

'If you need anything at all, you can just leave a note in your room and they will provide it for you.'

'Okay,' she said again, forcing the word to her lips. Because the sharp sting of rejection was too familiar. Too tainted already with the feelings of shame and being unwanted. And right then she promised herself that if she was pregnant, her child would *never* feel the hurt of that.

He hadn't missed how quiet she'd been since his declaration. Yes, he trusted his staff implicitly and yes, they were all discreet. But he would never put them in a position that would leave them open to questions from the press, or worse—his father. It was vital that he kept them and Star apart. She would understand. One day.

He had shown her the gardens first because they truly were breathtaking. Thanks to the aquifer that fed both the nearby oasis and the palace, there was enough water for the lush greenery that filled the palace gardens and to allow the natural life in the surrounding areas to thrive.

It seemed to have a similar effect on Star as a rosy blush was brought back to features turned stark by the restrictions he had placed on her. He would have wanted to show her more, but he needed to get Star settled so that he could call his father and explain his sudden departure. He drew her back towards the interior of the palace the family affectionately called Alhafa, escaping the searing heat of the desert sun the moment they passed through the doors. The thick outer walls of the palace, deep corridors and open courtyards worked to keep the internal temperature cool and manageable.

'This entire wing has the family suites,' he explained as he led her down the left-hand side of the palace.

'I don't want to take someone's room,' Star announced. It might have been the first thing she'd said since they'd left the Jeep.

'It's just us here.'

She nodded, keeping her head down.

'Thankfully, my father listened to my mother and had the suites fitted with en suite bathrooms when my nieces were born. She refused to have her granddaughters spending time in a military fortress with no decent plumbing.'

As he'd hoped, it drew a gentle laugh from Star and the sound tripped down his back.

'It didn't matter for you and your brother?'

'We were boys. It was different. It was good to toughen us up a little.'

Star looked towards a corridor shrouded in darkness. 'What's down there?'

'Nothing,' he said as icy fingers gripped his heart.

'But—'

'That area is off-limits.'

She turned back without a word and continued in the direction they'd been heading. His gaze was glued to her back because if he looked anywhere else he was terrified of the ghosts he'd see.

By the time they reached the room he'd had prepared for her, Khalif wanted to leave. To return to Burami. He should never have brought her here, where around every corner was a memory of his brother, of Samira. This was where he had first met her...and where he had last seen her. This was where he struggled the most to fit his feelings into a box called grief.

But it was the only place where he and Star would not

be seen. And no one could find out about this. If she was pregnant, they'd deal with how and when the news of their engagement was delivered. If not…then they would go their separate ways and never see each other again.

No royal marries for love.

The words echoed in his mind as he watched her take in the room that would be hers for the next ten nights. She went straight to the balcony. The wooden screens had been pulled back to reveal the majesty of the desert. The bed was freshly made, the scent of jasmine hanging on the air from the beautiful blooms of fresh flowers in vases he'd not seen before. Her fingers trailed over her small suitcase as if in surprise and she turned to him, her hair swept over one shoulder, making him long to touch it.

'Your fairies have been at work.'

'I'm not sure how the staff would feel to be called that.'

'Well, they're invisible and do your bidding and don't you dare say you don't believe in fairies,' she warned, a slight tease to a tone that must cast spells over the children she taught.

'So that would make me Peter Pan?' he asked.

'And me Wendy,' she said, the teasing gone.

And suddenly he couldn't explain it, but his heart hurt at the thought of her returning home while he stayed in Neverland.

They both started when the sound of his phone cut through the moment.

'You can go anywhere you like—apart from that wing. I'll meet you here at seven and we can go for dinner.'

'Oh, taking me to the best restaurant in town?' she joked, as if his father's call wasn't important.

'It's *the* place to be,' he assured her with a quirk of his lips. And as he closed the door behind him, his smile flattened into a grim line and he flexed his hand from fist to open three times before retrieving the phone from his pocket.

This was not going to be fun.

Two hours later and the tension that had built across his shoulders and up his neck was as solid as concrete. The conversation with his father had gone about as well as any interaction they'd had in the last three years—terribly.

Have you forgotten your promise to Nadya and Nayla? You were supposed to spend the evening with them.

He had. He'd completely forgotten—but he couldn't reveal to his father why. Bitterly disappointed in himself, guilt and grief swirling thickly in his stomach, he promised his father he'd make it up to them.

But the words were over-familiar to them both. They had been a constant refrain in the weeks, months and first few years following his brother's death. Khalif had returned to Duratra and, even before the earth had settled on the coffins of his brother and sister-in-law, he had thrown himself into his duty. He'd sat up for nearly three straight nights, consuming every single piece of information needed. He'd made state calls, international calls, presenting himself as the first in line to the Duratrian throne. He'd handed over the running of an international-ally successful business, stopped drinking, womanising, misbehaving and he'd worked. Hard. But he'd also hidden in that work. Hidden from his father, from his mother and most especially from Nadya and Nayla, who had been distraught not only at the loss of their parents, but also their uncle.

He couldn't face them. Any of them. It hurt too much. To see his own grief reflected in their eyes. He hadn't found solace with them, he'd found judgement, he'd found himself wanting.

Raza had intervened. They'd argued and fought until both were a little beaten and bruised, but Khalif had seen the truth of it. In the last year he'd been better, but he knew deep down he'd just been going through the motions.

Until a woman standing before a painting, with flame red hair, had caught his eye.

He almost growled as he stalked along the hallway towards the steam room in the lower level of the palace. His towel low on his hips and his bare feet slapping against the cool stone, diminishing some of the ire-fuelled heat that sparked across his skin.

He'd wanted one night. Just one. With a beautiful woman who made the weight of the crown lighter because it had been invisible to her. He'd wanted the taste of freedom she was unaware she had...and instead he'd quite possibly bound her to him for ever. Trapped her.

He banged the meaty side of his fist against the stone wall as he rounded the corner, welcoming the wet heat that was reaching out to him from the room beyond. He sent a prayer of thanks that Masoud knew him well enough to ensure the steam room was ready for his stay.

He pushed through the door and was hit by a bank of wet white air. He breathed in deeply, welcoming the mandarin and bergamot scented steam into his body, willing the heat to soak into his skin and relieve the stresses of an almost diabolical day.

He grounded himself, mentally drawing power up from deep beneath the ground, letting it fill his feet, his calf muscles, the base of his spine and up his back. He rolled out his powerful shoulders and flexed his neck from side to side. He just needed a moment. One to himself. He inhaled deeply again when he felt something brush past him.

Adrenaline and shock sliced through him as he reached out his hand and his fingers curled around a slender bicep.

'Star?' he asked, surprised and confused.

'Yes. It's me.' She sounded almost guilty. 'I don't want to intrude.'

He willed his heart to recover from the surprise of there being someone else in here, but his pulse didn't slow. Instead, his sight blocked by the steam, his other senses were heightened. He registered the silky sheen to her skin, his thumb smoothing away a drop of moisture, and found himself pulling her towards him. As he drew her closer and closer, she came through the thick vapour into soft focus. His eyes dropped to her chest, straining against a white towel pulled tight beneath her arms, rising and falling with the quickening of her breath and making him want to lose himself in the exquisite pleasure of her all over again and damn the consequences.

With one hand still wrapped around her slender bicep, he raised the other to cup her jaw. She leaned into his touch as if she craved it as much as he did. His thumb traced down her neck and tripped over a gold chain. He followed the loops of precious metal to the pendant that lay beneath her collarbone and stopped.

He took the pendant in his hand, holding it up to his inspection and clenched it in his palm, rocked by fury, shock and a grief as swift and as powerful as the harshest of desert storms.

'Where the hell did you get this?' he demanded.

CHAPTER SIX

THE MOMENT STAR winced as the necklace pulled against her skin, Khalif dropped his hold on the pendant and stepped away from her as if he'd been burned.

'It's mine,' she said past the pulse pounding in her throat.

'I don't believe you.'

The hairs on the back of her neck lifted.

'You recognise it?' she asked, shocked. While she had known that Hātem had kept the other necklace, she had never imagined that Khalif would be familiar with it.

'That necklace belongs to my family and has been with *my family* for over one hundred and fifty years,' he all but growled.

Despite his obvious anger, Star's heart soared. If Khalif recognised it, he knew it. And if he knew it, then perhaps she finally could hope to retrieve it.

'Not this one. Your family have protected its sister necklace, but this one has been with *my* family for over one hundred and fifty years.'

He frowned, searching first her face and then the pendant as if it could reveal the truth of her words. He reached for the pendant again, but drew his hand back, a guilty red slash across his cheekbones.

Star held the pendant between them for him to inspect.

'There's a slight difference,' he said, turning the embellished gold design from side to side. 'As if it's the exact opposite.' There was something like wonder in his voice, until something dawned on him. 'I thought it was just a story,' he said, his eyes gazing over her shoulder on some distant memory.

Star placed her hand over his and brought the necklace back to her. 'I think we have much to talk about,' she said.

'Starting with why you came to Duratra.' His eyes were now firmly fixed on her, assessing her with an almost hostile gleam.

She opened her mouth to speak, but he shook his head.

'We should both be fully dressed for this conversation.'

All trace of the heavy sensuality that had built between them was now gone and in its wake was the horrible feeling that perhaps Star had an ulterior motive for being in Duratra. Perhaps even there had been some kind of plan behind their night together, a seduction maybe? But as Khalif gestured for her to leave the steam room before him, he knew that this was nothing more than paranoia and confusion.

It was simply the shock of seeing the necklace for the first time in three years. In line with their family's tradition, Samira had inherited the necklace on her marriage to Faizan. It had been on her that he'd last seen it. And where once dark skin had embraced and heated the gold, Star's pale skin and red hair brought the gold to life.

Star cast a look at him before she turned down the corridor that would take her to her room. He could barely look at her, the delicate shoulders, the trailing streams of red hair, the way that the thick white towel wrapped around her slender frame made her look vulnerable now. He pulled his gaze from her before he could once again catch sight of the necklace.

He had never wanted a drink more. But he hadn't touched a drop since Faizan died and he wasn't planning to start now. The last time he'd given into temptation…

Star had taken a quick shower, scrubbing the slick citrus-scented steam from her body as if it could rid her of both her unwanted desire for a man she might never again have and the discomfort she felt every time he saw the necklace.

There had been a moment when she'd felt hope. When she'd thought that perhaps she'd been meant to come to Duratra, to find not just the necklace but *him*.

Now she wasn't so sure.

She dressed in a loose-fitting T-shirt over an ankle-length skirt and left her feet bare. For some reason, she wanted to feel the ground beneath her feet—as if it might be the only thing she could be sure of.

When she knocked on his door a few minutes later she didn't hear him ask her to enter, but she was sure that he was there. Gently, she pushed open the door to the most incredible suite she'd ever seen.

She'd thought the room she was staying in was something from a fantasy. It was almost the entire size of the flat she shared with her sisters, and the impossibly large bed had mosquito nets that had become silks fit for a princess in her mind. The view of the desert was something she would take with her until her last breath. The detail of the carvings, the faded plaster and history pouring from every inch of the walls, was so different from the shabby neglect of the estate in Norfolk. It was as if it were full of pride and strength and love from every generation of this family that had ever stepped across the threshold.

She felt that and so much more as she ventured into Khalif's domain.

He was standing with his back to her, hands clasped behind him. Her eyes scanned the room, surreptitiously and quickly. It wasn't obvious wealth, though that was evidenced by the luxurious pieces of furniture, pristine despite their obvious age. By the gold, silver, precious metals and jewels that were scattered across tables, inlaid across tabletops, shelf-edges, doorframes. Everything was exquisite...everything was priceless.

It was that everything spoke of Khalif. The rich dark mahogany that was both weathered and strong, the hard edges and sharp angles opulent and eye-catching. The colours were masculine but there were hints of a playfulness that she sometimes felt he was capable of.

But in the centre of the wall that dominated the room was a shelf that was devoted to his family—photos, trinkets that one would collect, memories. *Family comes first.* It was a sentiment that she could both warm to and be warned by.

On the low slung table between them were trays of food, both sweet and savoury from what she could tell. Steam streamed from the spout of a large silver teapot and she told herself *that* was the cause of her mouth watering, not the power of the man in front of her. Her stomach was hungry, not clenched with desire and need. Her pulse was racing because she was unfit, not hoping for more of the man who had taken her innocence and left in its place a wanton woman whose sole focus was pleasure.

She took a step to close the distance between them and just over his shoulder was able to see what he was looking at that had him so absorbed.

It was a black and white picture of a family of four. Even if she hadn't seen pictures of him in the exhibition, Star would have recognised the good-looking man with the same jaw and nose as Khalif. Faizan had his arm around his two young daughters and was leaning into his wife, Samira, who was smiling at the camera as if there was nowhere else in the entire world she'd ever want to be.

Star's eyes were drawn to the gold necklace hanging just below the neckline of her silk top, almost exactly the same as the one Star had removed the moment she had returned to her suite.

He didn't flinch, noticing her presence, she felt it as if it were more of a tightening within him.

'She was very beautiful,' Star said, shocked by the sudden drop in temperature that followed her declaration.

'Tea?'

His question was such purposeful distraction, it was almost as if it were a challenge, or a warning. She nodded, but walked past him towards the view of the desert. Sand swirled in the distance, like her thoughts, shifting, scattering, only to be swept up by the air and thrown down elsewhere. Khalif, Samira, Faizan. Despite what her sisters might think, she wasn't so clueless as to go blundering into a clearly painful area for Khalif. But there was definitely something there.

She could see it as surely as she could see the sky begin to turn to that purple pre-dusk hue that always reminded her of lavender and salt. And home. She felt a sudden pang of homesickness she'd not yet experienced since arriving in Duratra. Suddenly she didn't want to know how Khalif's family had cared for the necklace, why Samira had worn it and how Star might be able to get it for herself.

She wished she'd never heard of the Soames diamonds, of the estate in Norfolk.

And then a swooping wave of guilt and horror overwhelmed her, knowing that without it her mother would have no hope for recovery. For her mother, for her sisters, she would face Khalif, explain it all and do whatever she had to in order to return to the UK with the key to the missing jewels, whether she was pregnant or not.

She went to sit on the long sofa opposite the chair Khalif had occupied. She took a deep breath and began. 'My grandfather died nearly a month ago.'

'I'm sorry to hear that,' he said, his formality clearly echoing the lack of emotion in her tone.

'We'd never met him. Mum had never spoken about him and I guess we just didn't ask.' There was so much she hadn't asked her mum, so much more she wanted to know. 'We were notified only because he had named us as…sort of beneficiaries of his will.'

'Sort of?'

Star shook her head from side to side. 'His will held a complicated stipulation. If we meet that stipulation, we will inherit his country estate in Norfolk. Which we could then sell.'

Realisation dawned in his tawny eyes. 'And pay for private treatment for your mother?'

Star nodded, breathing a sigh of relief that he understood. That he hadn't immediately assumed she and her sisters were simply out for money. 'It doesn't have to sell for the biggest value—we have no idea what that would even be. It just has to be enough.'

'Star, if you need—'

'We don't,' she said, cutting him off before he could offer her anything. 'Because we're going to meet the stipulation and sell the estate.'

And Mum would get her treatment and be fine.

They had a plan, they would stick to it and everything would be okay, she assured herself. It had become a mantra in the last few weeks. A rhythm in her mind and her heart like a prayer.

'So the stipulation…it has something to do with the necklace?' he asked.

'What do you know of it?' she asked, hoping that might give her some indication of where to start.

'It's been in my family for over five generations and has been worn by the wife of every Sheikh during that time.'

'Really?'

'Yes, why?'

It made her feel strange that Catherine's necklace had been worn by the woman who'd married Hātem. And by the wives that had followed. Perhaps that was why she had not found a trace of it. She had been looking for it with the male heirs. And she suddenly felt a little foolish, remembering the words from the first part of the coded message her sister Summer had translated.

If you have discovered my message then I can assume two things: that you are female, because no man would wade through the private fripperies of my youth, and that you are clever, to have found the journals.

The pieces of Catherine's mystery had remained secret because they had been protected by women. As, even, had this piece.

'I might have been naïve to assume that Hātem would have kept it with him.'

Khalif shook his head. 'The men in our family do not wear jewellery.'

She nodded in understanding. 'And what do you know of where it came from?'

'I thought you were supposed to be telling me,' he said, half impatient, half grumble, his tone completely familiar to her from the little children she taught when they weren't given what they wanted easily.

'Humour me?' she asked.

He sighed and ran a hand absently through his hair. 'Honestly, even now it feels more like a fairy tale than reality or a part of family history. I used to tease Faizan about it when we were children.'

'About what?'

'That his wife would have to wear the *fairy tale* necklace.'

Star threw a hand-woven tapestry pillow at him without realising that the piece was from the seventeenth century and probably hadn't actually been touched for at least two.

He caught it one-handed and put it down with great care.

'I was a child,' he defended. 'Anyway, we knew that it had been worn by our mother, and our grandmother, and our great-grandmother and so on. Every generation was proud and protective of it, always ensuring that the first in line to the throne would present the necklace to his wife.'

Goosebumps pebbled on his skin and the hairs on the back of his neck lifted as he followed his thought to its natural conclusion.

'But you take it seriously now,' she said, unaware of his thoughts.

'Very,' he replied without hesitation. 'We were told

that some day someone would come and claim the necklace. That it would be clear who they were and they would be given it without question or hesitation. Any more than that, I'm afraid I have no idea. My mother might know, but…' He shrugged, his mind still half on the thought that if Star was pregnant it might have found its way to her anyway. Either by becoming his wife, or it being returned to her, Star would end up wearing the same necklace as his grandmother, mother…and Samira.

'My great-great-great-grandmother came here,' Star said, causing Khalif to blink in surprise. 'In the late eighteen-hundreds she was travelling with her uncle as his wife's companion. They were passing through the Middle East and had come to Duratra to meet with His Majesty Sheikh Hātem Al Azhar to discuss Duratra becoming part of the British protectorate. Many other countries in the area had agreed, but Hātem had neither interest or need to do so.'

Khalif raised a sceptical eyebrow. 'And you know this how?' She was right, but it was strange hearing her so certain of the thoughts and feelings of a man who had died over one hundred years before.

'Because Hātem and Catherine grew very close and she wrote about it in her diaries,' she stated, her large blue eyes shining up at him with nothing but sincerity.

'I don't—' He stopped short, his mind incapable of processing what Star was implying. 'This is not possible,' he declared.

Star looked down at the necklace in her hands as if trying to soften the blow of what she was implying. 'Catherine's uncle was called back to Egypt, but his wife refused to travel again so soon. According to Catherine, her aunt had a weak constitution, not suited to the climate, which irritated the husband she was angry with for bringing her to the Middle East in the first place.

'But Catherine was happy to stay behind. She loved it here. She begged Hātem to take her out on horseback so that she could explore as much of the desert as possible.'

'Star, this is all very fanciful but—'

'She spoke of an oasis. Which is what had me confused,' Star said, not noticing the stillness that had come over him. 'I was confused at the palace in Burami because some of her descriptions didn't seem to fit. I just assumed that things had changed in the last hundred years. But when you showed me the gardens here, I realised... *this* is where Catherine met with Hātem. This is where she stayed with her aunt, and spent the night at the oasis with the crossed palms.'

Khalif's mind screeched to a halt. No one outside the family had visited the oasis. So there was no way that Star could have known about the crossed palms. A sudden memory of him and Faizan digging at the base of the huge ancient trees, convinced there was buried treasure to be found, filled his mind and heart, his ears echoing with the sounds of boys' laughter and the feel of sand against his skin.

'What do the diaries say of Hātem?' he ventured, half hoping she was being truthful and half still disbelieving.

'Quite a lot,' Star replied with a smile. 'That he'd seen what had happened in Egypt and the way it was being torn between Britain and the Europeans, the impossible loan rates and finally the political coup. According to Catherine, Hātem insisted that Duratra had been fine without being under the British protectorate and would continue to be so. He'd been surprised when Catherine had agreed with him though.'

'Why did she?'

Star bit down on her lip, distracting him momentarily. 'Because she knew what it was like to live with a gun to her head.' She turned to look at the desert as if needing to gather her thoughts.

'When Hātem and Catherine returned from the oasis, it was to news that her father had died. Everything that Catherine had, all she had known, would be inherited by her cousin—a man who had made it clear he intended marriage. Would it surprise you to know that Hātem asked Catherine to marry him?'

'Yes,' Khalif barked. And then, 'No. At this point, Star, I don't think anything would surprise me,' he said, reaching for his tea to quench both his thirst and his wonder at all of this…information he'd never known about his ancestor.

'Catherine knew that he was betrothed to Alyah. She thought Alyah would be a good bride for Hātem.'

'Really?' Khalif asked, knowing, of course, that Hātem had married Alyah.

Star leaned towards him with one of the little leather journals she had brought with her gently held open and pointed to the top of one of the pages.

He will be happy with Alyah. Kind, loving and patient… We are too similar, too adventurous, too impatient. But he refuses to see that.

'What did she mean by that? That he refuses to see it?'

'Hātem didn't believe that Catherine had to return to England. She said, *Men think women know nothing of duty. Sometimes it is all we've ever known.* He just couldn't see why she wouldn't stay and they parted on not so great terms.'

'But if they left on such bad terms, how did Alyah end up with the necklace?' He felt like an impatient school-boy, desperate to hear the end of the story.

'I thought this was fanciful and...?'

He cut her off mid-taunt with a glare.

'Really?' she demanded. 'Does that stare *really* work on your staff?'

'Yes!' he groused. 'Just not with you,' he said through only half reluctant laughter.

'Catherine wrote to Hātem when she got back to England. Her marriage to her cousin Anthony was much worse than she had expected. He was violent and verbally abusive. The journals really only continued for a few years after the marriage and then she had them packed away, so it's a little hard to say. But she'd reached out to ask a favour of Hātem. She hoped that he would make her a key that could be separated into two parts. One part was to be kept by her, and one to be kept by him, guarded until the day someone came to find it.'

'What is it the key to?'

'Catherine wanted somewhere safe to hide things from Anthony. Her diaries, pictures...and the one thing that Anthony wanted most—the Soames diamonds. Catherine left clues and coded messages in her journals for someone worthy of finding them, but the men in the Soames family dismissed or ignored the signs. Ever since Anthony, the Soames men have been driven mad desperately searching for them.'

'Because none were worthy of it,' Khalif realised. 'So, the necklace is actually a key?'

'When the two are joined, yes. They will open the locked room marked on the map of the secret passageways that Skye found the day we...my last day in Burami,' Star stumbled.

Khalif was too caught up in the story to notice, only now making the connection between how down she had been and her desperate need to help her mother. 'That's why you were so sad? Your sister had found the map, but you hadn't found the key?' He nodded to himself. 'And with the diamonds…'

'If we find the diamonds we can inherit the entire estate and then sell it to fund Mum's treatment.'

'I imagine you could do a lot more than that.'

'We don't want anything more than that. Nor do we need it.'

It was said so simply, as if she was genuinely confused as to why they might want to have more than they needed.

'It's just that…' He tried to find the words to explain. 'It would seem that Catherine went to a lot of trouble to keep those diamonds safe for someone worthy to inherit. And to sell them for less than their value…'

'I think Catherine would understand our duty to our mother over the weight of the past,' she said with a finality and firmness that surprised him a little.

Khalif looked out to the balcony and the night sky beyond, his fingers rubbing at the slight stubble on his jaw and chin as he traced the stars with his gaze. He wondered if it was fanciful to think that the historic link between their families might account for the instant impact Star had made on him.

And then she shifted, her hair cascading over her shoulders, down her back and his gut clenched. No. That was all Star. So Hātem had taken Catherine to the oasis… He couldn't help but wonder whether Catherine was the reason Alhafa was known for hiding royal mistresses. Hātem and Alyah had made Burami their central residence and it had been that way ever since.

'What does it mean, Alhafa?'

His language on her tongue sounded soft and strange but utterly hypnotic. 'I suppose the closest translation in English would be The Edge. You can view the desert from every window and it often feels as if we're at the edge of the world.'

'It's truly beautiful.'

'My brother would have agreed with you. I...don't find it easy being back here,' he admitted. 'Nadya and Nayla loved this palace. Faizan was planning to move them here permanently. When they were younger the twins would run screaming down the corridors, terrifying the staff...' He couldn't help but smile at the memory, but it wobbled as he realised how much he'd cut himself off from them. 'Faizan taught them to swim in the pool, just like our father had taught us. It was where we...we met Samira. Her father's family came to visit one summer.' Samira would have been exactly the same age as the twins were now, the realisation catching him by surprise. 'On the first day, she climbed up the tree in the courtyard and refused to come down.'

'What did it take to bring her down?'

Me.

'Food,' he lied, the word burning his tongue. 'Speaking of which...it's getting late. I'm sorry that wasn't a proper meal, just snacks and—'

'It was perfect. I wasn't hugely hungry,' she said with a smile. 'Though I might be tomorrow,' she warned.

'Then tomorrow we will have a feast,' he assured her.

She stood, but appeared hesitant, worried almost.

'What is it?'

'Khalif, do you know where the necklace is?'

Her large blue eyes were wide with hope. For a selfish moment he wanted to deny that he did. He wanted to refuse her the legacy that was so clearly hers because the necklace was so entangled with his memories. A thread woven through his family that to unpick it, to remove it from them would make Samira the last wearer...

'Yes. I do,' he said gravely.

'Is it here? Can I see it?' For a moment he thought she might clasp his shirt, but instead her hands were entwined before her.

'Star, it's back in Burami, I'm sorry.' She bit her bottom lip again and the sight made him want to soothe away the punishment with his thumb. 'I will speak to my family, but I do believe you, and I believe that it belongs with you.'

'Thank you.'

He gestured for her to go before him and followed her out into the gently lit corridor, realising for the first time that her feet were bare. The sight of them had his fists clenching and he wrestled to get himself under control. He absolutely refused to believe that he had developed a foot fetish in the last twenty-four hours, but he couldn't deny the wicked bent to his thoughts.

He knew that she could feel it too. Hadn't missed the way that her shoulders had tightened, how she'd tilted her head just a little to the side, as she had done only the night before in Burami. He'd pressed his lips and tongue to that spot on her neck...

This time it was he that punished his lip with his teeth, hoping that the short sting would bring him back to his senses. Senses that were almost completely filled with her. She reached the doorway and turned, her hand against the wood, as if anchoring her in place, for which he was thankful. She looked up at him and he was instantly aware of how he towered over her, filled with memories of covering her completely with his body, her pheromones already making him recognise her as his.

She rose onto her tiptoes and he stilled, unsure as to whether he wanted to encourage her or not. Leaning in, she turned her head just slightly and pressed the simplest of kisses against his cheek and it held all the power of a tsunami. While he was trying to navigate his way through the swirling waves, she disappeared into her room and he was left in the dark, clenching his fists, feeling far too much.

CHAPTER SEVEN

KHALIF WOKE FROM a nightmare, heart pounding, skin sweat-soaked, his body tangled in the sheets. The bands of a tension headache pressed against his temple before he'd even opened his eyes, and the cords of his neck ached as if he'd roared his way through the night.

The phone by his bed lit up as it vibrated and he didn't need to check it to see that he had about thirty unread emails and probably at least eight missed calls from his father about the memorial.

He looked at the clock, guessing that it was early as the sun was yet to rise. Five thirty a.m. felt brutal after last night, but there was no way he was going back to bed. The conversations he'd had with Star had felt oppressive and he still hadn't shaken the weight of the past from his shoulders.

He got dressed, choosing loose trousers and shirt, and placed the *kufi* on his head before wrapping the *keffiyeh* into a turban, pressing his palms against the secure familiar material that felt as if it were keeping the pounding in his head contained.

He made his way down dark corridors, not quite ready to let go of his grief, of the images and memories of his brother…of Samira. Of the way she had looked at him just before she'd married his brother.

His heart flared as he stalked towards the stables, looking for his favourite horse. Mavia, a true queen like her namesake was regal, strong, proud and determined, and by far the best in his stable.

She greeted him like a jilted lover and he would have expected nothing less. He really shouldn't have been away from Alhafa for so long. But within moments she was nudging him with her head and demanding the affection he was always willing to give her.

He made short work of her saddle, itching to ride, and he launched himself into the desert just as the sun began to rise and the moon and stars to set. He raced them up a dune and out into the far reaches of the desert—his back to both the oasis, Alhafa and Burami.

He wanted nothing but sand and sky, no past, present or future, just the way his pulse beat to the rhythm set by Mavia. He ignored the sweat on his brow, the fire in his thighs and the ache in his soul as they crested the dune and soared down the other side.

But his mind refused to let up. Doubts, fears, shadows and ghosts rose up around him like a wave of sand before the storm. For three years he'd rode the pain, the grief, the guilt and anger at both Faizan and Samira for their choices, bearing it in silence and in secret. He'd tried to bend and shape himself away from the wanton playboy he'd been and into even half of the leader his brother would have been, and the *one* time he'd slipped, the one weakness he'd given into…

Star.

Her name was like a prayer and a curse.

Only she was the one who would fall fowl of it. That her freedom was the price of his selfishness was nothing short of a tragedy. Everything about her, the bright, effervescent positivity, the gentle soothing babble of

words, her enthusiasm, her hope-filled romantic belief…
he would have to watch all of those things be dimmed by
royal duty and etiquette. He would have to see her denied
the freedoms she so clearly took for granted. He would
have to see her caged.

How would he ever bear the guilt of doing to her what
had been done to him?

As he came to the top of the last dune before returning to the palace he twitched the reins, bringing Mavia
to a halt.

He couldn't.

And in that moment, as the sun crested the horizon,
he swore an oath that if Star wasn't pregnant he would
let her go. No matter what, he would let her go for ever.

Star peered out of her door, holding her breath. Not seeing anyone, she stepped into the corridor and stopped to
laugh at herself quietly. She felt like a naughty school-
girl being caught sneaking out of school grounds. But the
hour she'd been asked to stay in her room had come and
gone, and she couldn't stay locked up in there any longer.

As she trailed a finger gently across the chalky feel
of the corridor wall, she marvelled at how light she felt,
knowing that soon she might have the necklace in her
hands. Her heart felt as if it had swooped upwards last
night and was still soaring high. She'd desperately wanted
to call her sisters to let them know all that she had discovered. But the memory of how low she had felt when
she'd thought she'd never find it…that shocking disappointment had rocked the ground beneath her feet and
she couldn't do that to her sisters. She would wait until
she had the necklace in her hands, rather than getting
their hopes up.

Star turned right, unable to shake the feeling that she

was alone, as if she could sense that Khalif wasn't in the palace.

The silence was rare for her. There was always noise at the school; even outside the classroom children ran down hallways and played in the grounds. There was noise from the busy road she lived on, in the flat she shared with her two sisters. And even when Summer was away at university, Skye was always there, keeping her on track and running like clockwork. Star wondered whether Skye had realised that she'd kept her company almost constantly since the day that Star had met her grandparents.

She wanted to shake that thought off, the low ache she often felt when reminded of them, but there was something in the silence…something about it…that reminded her of Khalif. Not the Kal she had met, though there had been a reservation within him even then. But Khalif the Prince? The man she might have to marry? Unease swirled in her chest and she rubbed her sternum, trying to ease it. She didn't feel as if she knew Khalif as well as Kal who'd she'd spent one magical night with. Because there was hurt and anger that Khalif was holding onto and she couldn't shake the feeling that if she didn't confront it—*him*—then she might never know him completely.

Room after room showed furniture protected by large white sheets, window shutters closed against the damaging rays of the sun. There was not a speck of dust anywhere—unlike the estate in Norfolk. But, despite that, there was the same impenetrable sense of isolation and mourning.

The loss of Faizan and Samira was palpable; it felt as if it were forbidden to utter their names. But that kind of grief could be dangerous. Locked up tight, stoppered, it festered, it wounded, it spread like a poison… And that poison could do very real hurt and damage. She thought of the twin girls, wondered if they were allowed to express their grief, to talk about their parents as her mother had encouraged her to do. Throughout her childhood and into her teens, Star had opened up her feelings, so that difficult became easier and painful became loving. And while there was still an ache, low and constant, deep within her, it was not to be overcome but accepted as evidence of that connection, that love, between her and her father.

Star found her way to the corridor Khalif had specifically declared off-limits and, despite that, she turned down it anyway. There had been nothing particularly different about it yesterday, just a sense she'd had...until she'd seen his reaction.

Passing through a partially opened door, she came to a stop.

Unlike the others, this room looked as if it had only just been left. Drop cloths on the floor, half-painted walls, rollers stuck to trays with dried, cracked paint next to large tins with the same colours spoke of a half-finished decorating project. Moving further into the room, object by object she saw signs of a home, of life she'd not found elsewhere in the palace. A jumper had been thrown across the end of a sofa in the larger living space. Some nail polish on the side table. Toys scattered on the floor, waiting to be put away.

They were signs of a family.

Faizan and Samira's family. She turned back to the room where she'd seen the most decorating equipment and realised that it must have been the twins' room and an overwhelming cascade of sadness drenched her where she stood.

There was something so incredibly tragic about the

half-finished rooms—as if Faizan and Samira's hopes for their children were only half fulfilled. It looked as if the decorators had stopped suddenly, midway through the day. Perhaps to the news of the shocking accident.

She looked at the two tiny beds, now far too small for the twin Princesses, and turned back into the living area, drawn to the warmth and the everydayness of the family photos on the tables and the book lying open at a page.

Star could understand why it had been left, but still... it was such a shame to keep Nadya and Nayla from what was supposed to have been their home, from what their parents had wanted for them. She frowned, looking at the colours chosen for the room, the sweet style of shelving, and she could almost make out how beautiful it would have looked, had it been finished.

She was about to turn back into the corridor when she felt the hairs on her neck lift.

'What are you doing in here?'

She turned to find him full of thunder, heavy dark curls of sweat-soaked hair slicked to his head, his chest heaving as if he'd run here from the desert. His white *thobe* open at the collar, as if he'd been interrupted in the midst of changing it. He looked like an Arabian Darcy having caught her trespassing, but there was no eager welcome in his gaze, no tentative hope in his demeanour. Instead he stood, refusing to cross the threshold, staring at her as if she'd committed a truly heinous crime.

'How dare you?'

Khalif was shaking with rage, grief and shock. He hadn't thought for a minute that Star would betray him in such a way. So when Masoud, awaiting his return in the stables, had informed him where Star was he hadn't believed him.

He tried desperately to keep his eyes only on Star but,

not having been in these rooms for three years, his gaze devoured *everything*. It showed him things he wanted to see and things he didn't. Pictures of his brother and his daughters, himself and his nieces…of Samira. Memories hit him thick and fast and he would have sworn he could smell the perfume Samira used to wear drawing him, against his will, across the threshold.

'I was wondering why the memorial was so difficult for you. And then… I think I understand now,' Star said, her eyes watching his every move.

'You understand nothing,' he bit out angrily. Raw, exposed and vulnerable, he did not want to be here.

'I understand loss,' she said, not once breaking that serene stare of hers. 'Loss that has happened…loss that is yet to happen,' she said.

He hated that. He didn't want that for her.

'Whether it is in the past or the future, they are the same emotions, Kal. Grief, anger, resentment, devastation, helplessness. But this?' She looked about the room. 'It's as if you all stopped breathing the moment they died. Do you even talk about them?'

'Of course we do,' he said, spinning away from her, hoping that she'd just stop.

'When was the last time you said their names out loud?'

'With you,' he growled.

'That's not what I mean, and you know it.'

'It's not important,' he said, unable to stop himself from peering through the doorway to the room that would have been for Nadya and Nayla.

I want the two beds facing each other, and the mosquito netting to be pink, and the nightlight to have stars so that it covers the ceiling with the night sky. It's going to be beautiful, Kal.

Samira had been the only other person to call him that.

'It might not be important to you. Or your parents, who must have many memories of Faizan and Samira's life—'

'Don't!'

In that instant he genuinely wasn't sure if it was because Star used her name, or because of what she was saying, but he really didn't want her to continue.

'It's important to Nadya and Nayla. It will be, if it's not already.'

'What's that supposed to mean?' he said, turning, her words ringing in his heart.

'It means that I know what it's like to grow up in the shadow of grief. I know what it's like to want to know who your parent was before they died. You want to know everything about them. Where they came from, what they were like at every birthday you reach. Whether you're like them, whether they would have liked who you are becoming, whether…whether they would have loved you.'

Everything hurt. For Nadya, Nayla, for Star…for himself.

'And if no one talks about them, it's like a denial. A denial that the person existed. And that makes it feel as if the ache in your heart has no real anchor, cutting you adrift in your grief.'

He opened his mouth to ask, but she pressed on before he could.

'And this?' she said, sweeping her arms out wide and spinning in a circle. 'This suite? This palace? It was going to be their *home*. It meant so much to Faizan and Samira that they wanted to *live* here, they wanted to decorate this suite and make it perfect for their children. It's clear from the photos, the memories, the plans…this was where their heart was and their children haven't been back, their family hasn't been back to it and it's just so sad.'

It was an accusation that cut him to the bone.

'We were trying to do what was best for them,' he defended.

'No. You were trying to do what was easiest.'

'Don't push me on this,' he warned, half growl, half plea.

'Why? Someone has to. You can't stay like this,' she warned. 'You're unhappy with the memorial plans—'

'But they're done!' he yelled, no longer caring what effect it caused. 'Three years on from the accident and at least it's done.'

'Really? Then why are you so dissatisfied with them? You keep changing things to fix it, but it's never going to work if you know in your heart it's wrong.'

'You don't know what you're talking about,' he said, slicing his hand through the air, trying to terminate the conversation.

'At least I'm talking. Really, Kal, is everyone around you so afraid of you that they refuse to tell you what they think?'

'Okay, Star, you tell me. What do you really think?'

'I think you're so afraid of whatever you feel guilty over that it's stopping you from feeling anything real about Faizan and Samira. And because of that you've somehow allowed the memorial to be something not even half worthy of their memory.'

He felt the blood drain from his face. He wanted to fight, to rage, to shout against what she was saying, but he couldn't.

Not even half worthy.

He felt sick. 'It's a disaster,' he admitted through the acidic taste of bile at the back of his throat. 'Everyone knows it. No one wants to admit it. But trying to find something that Samira's father wants, something that my parents would be happy with, not to mention my nieces...'

He felt the weight of her gaze on him, could almost hear the words.

That's not what I mean, and you know it.

He bit the inside of his cheek, torn between wanting to explain everything and wanting to bury it all for ever.

'Samira was six when her family first visited, I was seven and Faizan was eight. We were inseparable, terrorising the palace staff, climbing trees, wreaking havoc...until Faizan had to start taking lessons to prepare for becoming ruler. Then it was just the two of us. It's lonely being royal. Even attending a central city school, it's not that easy to make friends who understand the presence of adult guards, or who don't want to take advantage of who you are or your position. Samira understood it. She understood the constraints of royal life. But where I found it difficult, she seemed to thrive on it. She wanted to use her position to do great things. She would tease me about shirking my responsibilities and I would tease her about taking on too much.'

He missed the sound of her laughter. The way that it had lightened his heart and soothed the ache he felt there. He'd never found it easy being royal, but Samira had borne it with grace and beauty.

'I'd always thought, hoped...' He'd hoped so much. 'Faizan was due to marry the daughter of an ambassador but she ran out just before the announcement, unable to take the weight of public scrutiny. The palace was in an uproar and Abbad... Abbad offered Samira as a replacement. And everyone agreed.'

Without telling him, they had all agreed. Even Samira. Khalif would never forget the moment he'd been told. The sheer incomprehension he'd felt until he'd seen it in her eyes. The sympathy, the silent apology. Even now he felt the wound deep in his heart throb and ache.

'Had you never told them how you felt about her?'

'What do you mean?' he asked.

'That you loved her.' Star's simple words left vibrations in the room that could have cracked the walls.

He could lie and tell her that he hadn't, but it would break something within him, and he wouldn't dishonour either Samira or Star like that.

'I didn't have to tell them,' he replied, like he'd not had to tell Star. 'I did love her—' the words were both bitter and sweet on his tongue '—but the moment she became engaged to Faizan—'

He shook his head, struggling to find the words to describe just how much he'd fought, he'd wrestled and cursed his feelings. 'After she had Nadya and Nayla, my feelings changed completely. Everything changed. She was different…a mother. She had two beautiful babies who were her sole purpose for being and…' Everything really *had* changed.

'It must have been incredibly difficult to watch Faizan and Samira marry,' Star observed.

'She wanted to marry Faizan,' he said, knowing the truth of it. 'She could see how much our parents wanted it. She knew him, *liked* him. He was…better—' Khalif breathed '—he was the better man.'

'He was a *different* man,' Star stated.

'You should have met him,' Khalif replied wryly.

She watched him walk further into the suite, as if somehow dredging up the memories had released the ties holding him back and she was glad. Glad that he'd spoken about Samira. Love should never be something that caused shame or hurt, even if deep down she forced herself to acknowledge a pinprick of jealousy. But it wasn't as much pain as it was sadness for him.

Because he must have felt so incredibly *betrayed*. His family couldn't have missed his feelings for Samira—if *she* could see them still now. She believed him when he said that his feelings had changed towards her when she had Nadya and Nayla. But even so…her heart ached for him and felt now more than ever that he needed this as much as the girls did. They all needed to come home. To where their hearts had once been.

She took a deep breath and crossed her fingers. 'I want to finish what they started.'

He stilled, as if he'd been instantly turned to stone.

'I want to help make this a home for Nadya and Nayla.'

'I'm really not sure about that,' he said, turning to face her. She could see the warring in his eyes.

'I think it would be good for them.'

He nodded reluctantly. 'I'm not sure what you're planning to do,' he said, looking around him as if he wouldn't have a clue where to start.

'That's okay. I have some ideas. Would you like to—?'

'No. Ask for whatever you need from the staff. Just leave the list in your room.'

When Star didn't appear for breakfast the next morning, he had his suspicions. When he reached his brother's suite she was finishing the white undercoat in the hallway that someone had started over three years ago. Her back was to him and every time she reached upward above her head the sleeveless vest she was wearing lifted and he could see a slash of pale skin between the top and the loose linen trousers she wore. And he turned away.

He found an excuse to be at that end of the corridor a few hours later and was surprised by the extent of work she'd achieved. This time he nearly crossed the threshold, but he didn't.

By the time dinner came around, Star looked happy but about to fall asleep in her food. She had tried to keep up with his questions.

'How are you today?' had been met with, *'I still don't feel pregnant,'* which had been delivered with a tired smile. He wondered whether he should just hire a decorator for Star to direct. Even Faizan and Samira had done that. His thoughts flowed with a little more ease than he was used to and he realised then—that had been the first time that he'd thought about them naturally, without that sense of creeping guilt and ache that often accompanied such moments.

The next day he found Masoud hiding in the suite's corridor, looking as if he were about to have a heart attack, periodically peering around the door frame and spinning back to look to the heavens as if in prayer. Khalif was surprised. So far, the staff and Star had managed to stay out of each other's way.

Stepping as quietly as possible up to the man he'd known never to break a sweat under *any* circumstances, Khalif peered over Masoud's shoulder to see what had made him behave in such a way and nearly choked on his own shock.

He clamped his jaw shut firmly.

For there was Star, without a care in the world, humming away as she painted large brushstrokes of admittedly *very* expensive undercoat over a nine-hundred-year-old fresco. Masoud was actually fanning himself and looked almost on the verge of tears.

'We have more, Masoud,' he whispered, reassuring himself as much as the older man.

'I know,' he replied mournfully. 'It's just that this one

was particularly beautiful. I just didn't have the heart to tell her...' He trailed off. 'She's doing such a wonderful thing.'

Khalif could only nod, marvelling at the way the head of the palace staff was willing to sacrifice the ancient fresco for Nadya and Nayla, and even for Star.

'I am a little worried about the drill bits, though.'

'Drill bits?' Khalif whispered harshly.

'She's asked for a drill and several sizes of masonry drill bits.' At this, Khalif could completely understand Masoud's concern. He winced himself at the thought of what she might do.

'We can fix whatever needs fixing...if it *needs* fixing,' he promised, hoping that he was right.

The next day, once again, Star had failed to appear for breakfast and this time Khalif took a small collection of pastries with him when he went to the suite he was beginning to think of as Nadya and Nayla's.

Through the door to what had once been the girls' room, he could see that Star was already painting and yet again her hair was worked up into a large woven cloth turban high on her head. She had finished the hallway and had worked her way around the first corner of the suite and if he wanted to see how she was getting on he would have to cross the threshold.

As if she had been waiting for him to do so, she turned and greeted him with such a beautiful smile that his heart missed a beat.

What would it be like to wake to her each morning?

Not to the blare of an alarm, the flick of the coffee machine or the imperious visage of his brother's acerbic assistant.

'Perfect timing,' she said, looking at him with a gleam in her eye.

'No. Nope,' he said, shaking his head and holding up the pastries.

She looked at the food he was carrying and her eyes rounded with pleasure. 'Thank you! I'm starving. And there's just this little spot…'

He looked over her shoulder to see the stepladder.

'Tell me you weren't just on that,' he demanded, the fury in his tone catching them both by surprise and he bit back a curse.

'Of course. How else was I supposed to—'

'*Khalas!* No. No more,' he said, slashing the air with his hand. 'I'm worried about the paint fumes, I can't trust you not to go up ladders, I'm sure that you'll be trying to move those beds soon enough—'

When her eyes grew wide, he clenched his jaw. 'What did you do?' he bit through clenched teeth.

'I dismantled them before I moved them,' she said, as if that would make it any better.

'How did you—?'

'Well, they're not exactly Ikea, but the principle was the same, and the Allen keys were here, so…'

'Why were Alan's keys here and what does he have to do with…?'

He trailed off because suddenly Star descended into musical peals of laughter. She was almost bent double and sweeping moisture from her eyes.

'I don't understand what is so funny,' he said, trying hard to keep hold of his anger. She made it too easy to breathe sometimes. Too hard not to laugh with her. And for the first time in three years he questioned why that was a bad thing.

'Just take the roller and get into that spot,' she ordered like a military general. He looked down at his clothes. 'Afraid of getting dirty?' she taunted.

'Well, you're clearly not.'

'No,' she said, smiling as she looked down at the splashes of paint across her trousers and forearms. 'They're just clothes that prove how much I'm enjoying myself.'

She had a spatter of paint on her cheek and he itched to smooth it from her skin, but didn't. Instead, he agreed to do the area she indicated, despite the fact that he was already late for a video conference with his staff.

Colour started to appear on the walls over the next few days and Star now had him completely bent to her will. When he'd asked how she knew about dismantling furniture or checking walls for electrics, let alone the mind-boggling range of fillers, sealants, sandpaper sheets and blocks, she'd said something about a man from her sister's job showing them how to fix certain issues in the flat. And when he'd drilled through the wall and taken out a chunk of plaster he'd been half terrified—not that he would have admitted it on pain of death. But she'd only laughed at him and told him that fixing mistakes was the best and only way to learn.

That evening, Star finally managed to get him to open up about the memorial, but instead of questioning his plans, she asked him more about Faizan and Samira. What they were like, what made them laugh, what made them angry. He was recounting a time when Samira had smoothed over ruffled feathers at an embassy ball, when he remembered the nickname they'd given her that night: *jisr*. Because she'd bridged the gap between ideas, people, countries.

'And what do Nadya and Nayla think?'

He looked at her. 'Think of what?'

'The memorial.'

'They're six years old.'

'Yes. Six—not three, not one. Six-year-olds can even generally feed themselves.'

He glared at her teasing, feeling angry and awkward.

She paused, the teasing tone melting away. 'No one asked them?'

He shook his head, not quite sure why he felt so ashamed.

What do Nadya and Nayla think?

It was now almost midnight and he couldn't get those words to stop spinning in his mind. He hated to think that he might have contributed to a sense that his nieces' grief was something to be denied, or ignored. As if his own, his parents' or the nation's grief was somehow more important than theirs. Unable to shake that sense of overwhelming guilt and shame, he knew that he *had* to return to Burami. He needed to see his nieces. And at the same time he just might be able to retrieve the necklace for Star. The need became so overwhelming, he felt as if demons were chasing at his heels. He had to leave—*now*.

CHAPTER EIGHT

THE FIRST TIME that Star had made a list of things she needed and left it in her room for the invisible staff to collect, she'd been surprised to find that it actually worked… That within twenty-four hours, forty-eight at the absolute most, her exact wishes were fulfilled. Out in the middle of the desert.

She tried to stay awake one night to see if she could hear the sounds of Jeeps or even helicopters bringing the materials she needed, but nothing. They just appeared as if by Christmas magic when she needed them. Which wasn't helping Star's determination not to live in her dream world any more. They were human staff, not fairy godmothers, and she was sure that the spontaneously appearing materials had more to do with Khalif being a prince than the staff having any magical powers.

The fact that Khalif was royalty still didn't feel real. Yes, he behaved like a prince and there were as many glimpses of spoilt stubbornness as there were of grief and loss, but in the last few days she'd felt as if they'd been talking. Really talking. Building something, so that perhaps if she was pregnant it might not be so terrible. That perhaps having a child with Khalif could be her own happy-ever-after?

After her morning shower, Star crossed to the living

area, hoping to find the bronze gold paint she wanted to use for the finishing touches across the girls' bathroom ceiling, so when she first saw the note that had been thrust under the door she assumed it was from the staff, apologising for not being able to track it down.

She was already thinking of other ways to achieve the look she was hoping for when she caught sight of the scrawled K at the bottom and her heart leapt.

It was only because she was distracted, she told herself later, that the thought that it might be a love letter crept into her mind. That was where her mind had been so that when she opened the thick cartridge paper she had to read it over three times before she could make out the message.

Which essentially boiled down to a quick apology for having to return to Burami. He'd be back as soon as he could.

Unconsciously she rubbed at the ache in her chest, telling herself that she was silly to have got her hopes up. To be thankful for the reminder that although he was a prince he was made of flesh and blood, not ink and paper and imagination. This wasn't a fairy tale romance. He was important and had been called away, and it wasn't reasonable to expect that he could have woken her up to let her know.

She arrived in Nadya and Nayla's suite to assess what still needed to be done. The bathroom was beautiful. Star knew it was a silly thing to get excited over, but it really was. This was where she had seen the touches Samira had planned most, the bronze gold taps and the antique glass panels. It was a faded beauty, but regal. There was an enormous roll top bath, only marginally outmatched by a shower unit dotted with pale pink tiles that matched the soft natural plaster that ran through the entire palace. But it was the midnight-blue that called to her. The depth and richness of the paint that had been chosen by Samira seemed as endless as the night sky. And when the bronze gold paint arrived she would cover the ceiling in stars. Large, small and everything in between. She sighed, hoping that it would come soon.

Star left the bathroom and walked back into the central living area to the project she had enjoyed almost as much, knowing that she could work on this until the gold paint arrived. She had kept Khalif away from this part of the room, wanting it to be a surprise. Wanting to see the look on his face when he saw the tree. When the girls saw…

She swallowed. It was quite likely that she wouldn't be there when the girls saw all this. Her throat thickened and she blinked back the damp sheen in her eyes.

No matter. It wasn't about her. It was about them. And they would know and see how much love had gone into this. And knowing that their uncle had helped would make it even more special for them.

She ducked under the sheet protecting the special project from view and picked up her paintbrush, trying to lose herself in the rich browns sweeping up the wall. Despite Khalif's instruction, she *definitely* needed a ladder for this, but she had been very careful.

She only had this to finish, and the stars in the bathroom, which was a good thing because in four days they would be returning to Burami for the memorial and to find out if she were pregnant. After one test, she would know whether her life would irrevocably change or go back to how it had been before. For as close as she and Khalif had become in the last few days, she couldn't deny that he had not spoken of what would happen if she wasn't pregnant. And she couldn't shake the feeling that the answer was…nothing. Nothing would happen. She would return to Norfolk as if they had never met.

But, even if that were the case, she knew instinctively that her life would never be the same again. She felt changed. Not just by Khalif, but by Catherine, by Duratra, all of it. It was as if the desert had seeped into her skin and bones and was part of her now.

But, like Catherine, she also knew her duty waited for her back home. She would return to Norfolk with the necklace, they would find the Soames diamonds, sell the estate, her mother would get the treatment she needed and… And then…

For the first time in her life, the thought of returning to the flat she shared with her sisters, and the job she loved so much with the children…it just didn't seem as exciting as travelling through the desert, or seeing what else was out there in the wide world. Meeting so many different people, all with their own stories.

It struck her then that she hadn't spoken to either of her sisters for nearly a week. She knew she was avoiding them because she didn't want to lie to them about the necklace, or about where she was. But she missed them so much. She retrieved her phone and hit the call button, holding it to her ear with one hand while she painted a rich vein of muddy red upwards towards the ceiling.

But as the phone rang and rang she was transported back to a bus stop nearly ten years before. Cold, wet, she shivered even now. An automated voice announced that she had reached Summer's answering service and the tremor that tripped over her body had her hanging up without leaving a message.

Minutes had turned into hours at that bus stop. She'd sat unseeing, facing the road as it rained, stopped and then rained again. Her mother and sisters hadn't come for her. And the entire time her grandparents' voices ran on a loop in her mind.

We want nothing to do with your mother or you. Do not ever come back here.

And that was when Star had realised that reality was a much harder, darker place than stories ever could be.

Khalif hadn't meant to stay overnight, not that he'd slept for more than three hours, or let his staff sleep much more. But he was anything but exhausted.

Star had been right. He should have spoken to Nadya and Nayla months ago. If his mother had been surprised when he'd asked to see his nieces, she didn't show it. And neither did they. They'd run to him as if he hadn't stood them up only days before, they'd run to him as if he hadn't retreated from them emotionally and physically in the last three years.

He'd spent hours playing with them, building forts from cushions and sheets draped over tables and chairs. He'd smuggled in *ma'amoul*, the semolina cookies that had been a favourite of Samira's, and *ghraybeh*, the shortbread that his brother had preferred. And as dusk had fallen and their bellies had filled with the sweet treats, he'd talked to Nadya and Nayla about their parents. He'd always imagined that they would find it sad and difficult but the moment he'd said their names the twins chatted away happily. And while it had taken a little while to get used to, time for his heart to get over the initial jolt of shock and unfamiliarity, the girls had launched into a list of the things they remembered about their parents as if they recited it every day.

Nadya had wanted birds, Nayla had wanted flowers, and Khalif had managed to sidestep World War Three by promising that the memorial would have both. He couldn't believe he'd forgotten how much Samira had loved birds. He had, in the way only adults could, assured himself that the twins couldn't make a contribution that he hadn't already thought of. He felt as if he were see-sawing between a sense of sadness, happiness, relief and regret for so much wasted time.

He'd gathered his team together and informed them of the changes—the *big* changes—he wanted them to implement. He was done trying to please everyone else. There was no way that could be done. Trying to second-guess what his parents, Samira's father and the people of Duratra wanted had only served to dilute all previous ideas and he would not risk that again. And despite the concerned looks that crossed the table from one side to the other about the timeline they had to accomplish those plans, Khalif was finally completely happy with the memorial.

By the time he'd finished the briefing it had been too late, or rather too early in the morning to track down his mother, so he'd returned to his suite, crashed out on his bed fully clothed and woke a few hours later with a thumping headache. He'd showered, dressed in fresh clothes and was a second mouthful of espresso down when he'd watched his father's cavalcade leave the palace from his balcony. Khalif couldn't say for sure that he'd purposely missed connecting with his father, but it had made the visit easier. Because he knew instinctively that he could not stand before his father—his *King*—and keep Star's possible pregnancy from him. Only when he knew for sure…

Unbidden, the image of himself holding a child—*his* child—left him winded. Because in all the scenarios that had run through his mind—the practicalities of what would need to happen were Star pregnant—he'd not allowed himself to think of what it would be like to hold his baby in his arms. A baby with Star's blue eyes and his dark skin. Someone who trusted and loved him implicitly, without question. The weight of that responsibility heavier than a crown or a country.

In that moment, Star's possible pregnancy morphed from something to be feared to something that he might actually want, might look forward to. And in his mind he saw Star, staring at him with the same trust and love and his heart turned.

His mother had sensed it when he'd sought her out. She'd asked if something had happened and he'd forced his thoughts away from Star herself and instead to the reason she had come to Duratra. When he'd finished explaining what he needed, his mother had seemed surprised and curious, but had done as he'd asked without question.

Now that he turned the last corner on the road to Alhafa, he wondered how Star had been in his absence.

Still not pregnant, he imagined her saying and couldn't help the smile that formed on his lips.

Entering the palace, he went straight to Nadya and Nayla's suite. A quick scan told him that she wasn't there. She wasn't in her rooms either and the tendril of concern that he'd been away too long began to root in his stomach. The palace felt empty. He quickened his pace and went straight to the staff area, hoping that they would know.

He knocked on Masoud's office door, surprised to find the man glaring up at him from behind his desk.

'Your Highness.'

Khalif frowned, the shortness of Masoud's tone unusually censorious.

'Have you seen Star?'

'I might have,' he said, looking down at the paperwork on his desk.

'Masoud.' His tone rich with warning, Khalif glared down at one of his most loyal employees, wondering when Star had enticed him over to her side.

'Sir, with all due respect—'

'Masoud, I'm noticing a distinct *lack* of that due respect,' Khalif prodded.

'You should never have left her alone like that, with no company and no word.'

'Where is she?'

'Have you looked for her?'

'Of course.'

'Have you seen the incredible things she's done in the Princesses' suite?'

'Of course,' he said, even though it was a lie. He hadn't had the chance to see it properly as he'd wanted to see *her*.

'Well, then. She is quite likely to be by the stables.'

Unused to being told off by his staff—other than Amin—he made his way towards the stables, hating the fact that Masoud was right. He turned the corner and immediately stepped back into the shadows. Star was with Mavia, stroking the animal's long neck even as the mare nudged for more.

Mavia never did that. Not for anyone other than himself. Not even for Samira. What kind of spell had Star cast over the palace, making everyone fall in...

His thoughts were cut short as Star looked up and straight at him and he felt a punch to his gut.

Although she'd hidden it behind a quick blink of her eyes, he'd seen it. The pain, the loneliness. The hurt. And in an instant he remembered. What it was like to be left behind. To be sidelined. And he'd done it to her without even a second thought. He'd been so lost in his own needs—his own desperate need to plan the memorial properly, to impress his father, the country—that he'd left her behind.

He emerged from the shadows, an apology already on his lips. 'I'm—'

'Did you find what you needed?' Star interrupted. She had chosen those words carefully. Because she didn't want the other words to rush out. Words that would make her sound needy, desperate…lonely. As if she couldn't be left by herself.

Only she couldn't. Not really. Every single minute he'd been away had felt like torture. Her mind had delved into things that hurt, things she hadn't thought of for years and had no desire to think of now.

Perhaps her sisters had been right. She wasn't ready to do this on her own. Either of them would have had the necklace by now, returned to Norfolk, and they quite likely would have found the jewels. She should have stayed behind.

Would she have been as lonely in the estate in Norfolk? No. It was the pain of knowing that there were people she couldn't talk to. People she couldn't be seen by. People who, as kind and amazing as they had been to fulfil her requests each day, could deny they'd ever met her.

Shame. She'd felt shame.

Again.

'Ye—'

'I'm glad,' she said, spinning away before he could either finish the word or stop her.

Tears formed, blinding her to her path, and she dashed them from her eyes. Why couldn't she have cried *be-*

fore he'd returned? she asked herself. Why not at two in the morning when she'd not been able to sleep? Why not when the horrifying realisation had swept over her that she had filled her life with people and distractions to escape from the feeling of loneliness and shame that had scarred her when she'd visited her father's family.

'Star…'

Khalif's hand was heavy on her shoulder and he spun her round to face him.

'Who hurt you?' he asked, staring deep into her eyes.

'You did!'

He flinched, but as if he'd been braced for it. 'I know. And for that I'm sorry. But I meant…who hurt you *first*?'

She almost collapsed under the sudden ache in her stomach and heart—as if the years of pushing it down, desperately ignoring it had given the pain even more power over her.

She tried to pull out of his arms, but he wouldn't let go of her. He searched her eyes, and she let him see. She opened herself up to the hurt so that he would know and was overwhelmed by it too. He cursed and, just as her legs shook, he swept her up in his arms and she felt… protected.

She knew she should tell him to put her down, ask him where he was taking her. Instead she just let go, ignoring the tears seeping into his shirt, the way her throat ached as if she had been screaming. Perhaps she had been, just silently and for far too long.

She closed her eyes as he took her up stairs and down corridors, almost afraid to look. She didn't want to go back to her room. Didn't want him to just leave her there. A hysterical woman out of sight of his staff.

As she felt him push through a door, she inhaled the rich scent of sandalwood and lime that she associated with him and curled more tightly into his body, not embarrassed enough by her neediness to stop.

He bent beneath her and sat, and she couldn't help but tense as she expected to be offloaded, but it never happened. He continued to hold her to his chest, until her tears and breathing slowed. At some point she registered his chin resting on her head, neither heavy nor intrusive. She was encompassed by his arms, as if he'd wrapped himself around her completely, and in that moment she knew that he'd make the perfect father. Just holding her, allowing her to feel what she needed to feel. No questions—not yet anyway—no impatience or sense of frustration or distraction. As if his only purpose here was her. It was almost enough to start her tears again.

'My mum didn't hide my dad from me,' she began, for some reason not wanting him to have the wrong impression of her mother. 'She spoke about him. There were photos of him in the house and always stories—stories of how they'd met, fallen in love so quickly... She would show me the things he'd made from wood, tell me what he'd hoped for his future...for *my* future. So I always felt that he was a part of my life.'

She shrugged against his chest, her eyes unseeing of the room around her. Instead she had been transported back in time, to the little council house they'd lived in when she was younger.

'I thought that's what families were. Just children and parents. Skye didn't see much of her father after he remarried, and Summer's wasn't a part of our lives so... I didn't know to ask about grandparents, about my father's life outside of us, until school, really. That's when I became aware of grandparents. The older I got, the more I would wonder about my father's parents. What they could tell me about him. Who they were. Were they curious about me? Had they been looking for me? Mum was fairly tight-lipped about them. There had been an argument…but she wouldn't go into the details. She just shut the conversation down whenever it came to them.'

Star sniffed a little, pulling her shawl around her and tucking herself against his side as if to ward off what came next.

'By the time I was thirteen, I had convinced myself that there had been a tragic misunderstanding between my mum and his parents. I thought if I just went to see them then somehow they'd just…'

She let out a painful breath, expelling the hope she'd once felt into the room. She shook her head in wonder at her own naivety.

'That they'd just *know*, and we'd all hug each other, and my kind, grey-haired, soft grandparents would welcome my whole family with open arms. I imagined Christmases with stockings—because that's what I thought grandparents did—and perhaps even Sundays at a house with a garden. I'd decided that they had a tiny dachshund. It was called Bobbi and it was half blind and would constantly knock into things, but we would take care of it, me and my sisters, while my grandparents cooked in the kitchen with my mother.'

She huffed out a laugh then. 'I should really have known it was a fantasy, partly because Skye always did the cooking.'

Khalif felt his stomach tighten, instinctively knowing that this story did not end well.

'I'd found their address from some letters my father had written to my mother when he'd still been living with them. There wasn't a telephone number and maybe I didn't want one. It would spoil my plan. I'd saved up enough pocket money for the train ticket, worked out that if I ditched school, I could get the bus to the station and the train from there. I copied out the map from the computer at school. I even took some flowers. Who doesn't like flowers?'

The thought of thirteen-year-old Star with a bunch of flowers travelling to see these people he already didn't like did something to him.

'I was so surprised it worked. No one stopped me, or wanted to know what I was doing out of school. I thought I had been so clever. Then I was standing in front of the red-painted door of number thirty-four College Road. I'd imagined blue, but I quite liked the red. It looked cheery,' she said.

Her voice was laced with a sarcasm he'd never heard from her before.

'I knocked, and the woman who answered looked *almost* like what I'd imagined. There were still traces of the marmalade colour hair she'd given to her son, but faded with streaks of white. Just like the way her eyes faded from an open, pleasant welcome to something almost like disdain. She called for her husband without taking her eyes off me. "I'm your granddaughter," I said. You see, I thought they hadn't realised. But she had. They did. They knew who I was.'

She took a deep breath. 'They said that they didn't have a granddaughter. They said that I was unchristian and unlawful because my parents had never married and they told me never to return.'

Khalif cursed under his breath, not that Star noticed. She seemed to be lost in her memories. 'What did you do?' He was half afraid to ask.

'I found a payphone and called home, but of course my sisters were in school and Mum was away. I left a message asking Mum to come and get me and then I waited by the bus stop.' She shook her head again, the silken strands of her hair brushing against his shirt. 'I felt like I'd let her down,' she said, running her fingers across her lips.

'Who?' Khalif asked, trying to keep the consternation from his voice.

'My mum. I knew why my parents hadn't married. It wasn't because they didn't love each other, but because they did, and they didn't need a piece of paper to prove it. I felt like I'd betrayed that somehow by visiting these people.

'I didn't realise how long I'd been sat there but when a policeman found me it was dark. He explained a bus driver had seen me on his route and been worried. They finally managed to track Mum down and they drove me home.'

It was only when she'd seen her mum and sisters, rushing from the door of their little house and sweeping her up in their arms, that Star had let the tears fall. They'd surrounded her completely with hugs and love and held her while she sobbed, the force of it shaking each and every one of them.

'The only way I was able to stop crying was when Skye began to read me my favourite story. From that day on, almost every night for an entire year, after dinner we would all sit down in the sitting room and take it in turns to read stories of love, hope, happy ever afters.' Until the memories of that awful day at her grandparents' home were buried beneath *Pride and Prejudice*, *Little Women*, *Romeo and Juliet*, *North and South*, *Sense and Sensibility*, *Gone with the Wind*…

'Did it make things better?' he asked, the vibrations from his voice rumbling gently into the side of her body pressed against his.

She wanted to turn her lips to his chest, but instead was content with her cheek resting there.

'It did. Losing myself in romance and happy endings was a much better thing than to lose myself in sadness, hurt and shame.'

She yawned, utterly spent and exhausted. Both the emotions of the last couple of days and the work she'd put in on the suite had drained her completely.

'Thank you,' she said, looking up at him, still encircled in his arms. 'Thank you for just listening.'

'Of course.'

He'd been about to say *Any time*, but he couldn't say it and know it might not be true. 'Shall I take you back to your room?'

She looked almost on the verge of asking a question before she seemed to think better of it, smiled, and said that she knew the way.

Long after she left, he sat in the room with her memories vivid in his imagination. To be so rejected by family was completely alien to him. He might have had a difficult relationship with his parents, but they would never cut him from their lives. They hadn't when he'd run wild through Europe and they wouldn't even if they discovered Star was carrying his child and that he would be marrying her.

He stalked the halls of the palace, returning to the suite that Star had been so consumed by. He knew that it would affect him, being in what had once been his brother's quarters, and he marched towards them, braced and ready for a fight—albeit an emotional one.

First, he opened the door to the bathroom. It had been days since he'd seen it and the breath left his lungs in surprise. All over the ceiling and down the parts of the walls that weren't covered in antique mirrored glass or the shower was an incredible night sky. A deep blue paint was interspersed with thousands of stars, ranging from the smallest dot to an intricate eight-pointed star the size of his palm. It gave the room an infinite depth and he felt as if he were standing in the middle of the cosmos. He knew that it had nothing to do with ego and everything to do with fully realising Samira's dream, and in that moment he knew he'd never forget Star's kindness as long as he lived.

He was reluctant to leave the space, but he was equally curious about what lay beneath the drop cloth covering a large area of the living space wall. His hand shook a little as he pulled it away, as if he sensed that whatever it was would be profound, but as the cloth fell away he had to cover his mouth with his hand to stop his shock from escaping into the room.

A tree wound its way up from the floor to the ceiling. Branches covered the length of the wall, the texture and detail of the bark making him want to reach out and touch it. It was only as he got closer that he saw little hand and foot holds drilled into the walls.

The girls would be able to climb it, just like Samira had climbed the tree in the palace garden. Stepping up to the wall, he felt the floor beneath his feet change to a soft mat that would protect them if they fell. Star had thought of everything. He shook his head in wonder.

'I hope you can see this, brother,' he whispered out loud. 'Samira, I know how much this would mean to you.'

Now it was up to Khalif to try and repair some of the hurt he'd caused and it came to him instantly, knowing the rightness of it by how his chest filled with excitement and his pulse pounded.

He knew just the way.

CHAPTER NINE

STAR GENTLY PADDED down the corridor to the dining room she'd been shown on that first day and never used. She hugged the midnight-blue silk kimono around her, still feeling a little vulnerable from her conversation with Khalif the day before.

'No, that will take too long,' she heard Khalif say before she'd entered the room. The smell of cardamom tea made her mouth water and the sweet pastries she was going to have to learn how to make had her stomach grumbling.

'It will have to be the Jeep… Yes… I don't care about the expense, it's worth it,' he growled. The moment he saw her in the doorway, he ended the call and put his phone on the table.

'Was that Amin?' she asked, coming into the room and sitting down where her place had been set. He poured her a cup of tea as she took a few pastries—she couldn't say which ones because she'd become lost in the way that his powerful hands gripped the thin silver arm of the teapot, and then the tiny porcelain handle of the cup.

She blushed when he actually had to say her name to get her to take the cup he was offering her.

'Yes,' he said. When she looked up at him he frowned. 'It was Amin,' he clarified.

Oh, good God, she had to get a grip of herself.

'Why did you ask?'

'You always get that tone in your voice when you speak to him,' she replied, inhaling the scent of the aromatic tea that tasted so much better here than it ever had in England.

'What tone?'

'Mmm…that *I-don't-care-what-you-think-just-do-it* tone.'

The look on his face told her that her impression had hit home.

'I don't know what you mean,' he evaded.

'Yes, you do. He irritates you,' she stated easily.

'Because he judges me,' Khalif growled.

'Probably because you're clearly irritated with him,' she replied, unable to help the smile pulling at her lips. 'You should either make peace with him or let him go.'

'And that is your professional opinion?'

'Absolutely. If you don't want it to descend into playground taunts of "He started it".'

Star could have sworn she heard him say, *But he did*, under his breath, but by the time she looked up at him he was furiously studying a mark on the table.

'How do you feel today?'

'*Still* not pregnant.'

He smiled, and her heart eased a little.

'I… I spoke to my sisters last night.' She hated the way that his body tensed, but she was thankful that he waited to hear what she had to say. 'I told them only that I might be able to get the necklace.'

'What did they say?'

'They are very happy.' It wasn't exactly a lie. They had been happy, or at least relieved. Star had intended to wait until she had the necklace in her possession, but she'd felt awkward keeping the news of it a secret. So she had told Summer that she knew where it was and hoped to have it soon. Star would have sworn she'd felt her sister's sigh against her skin as if it had whooshed through the phone speaker. Summer had mentioned something about making the meeting with the buyer easier and had then asked some bland questions about Burami, clearly forgetting that Star was now in the desert. It was a bit unlike her. Or had been unlike her three months ago... but ever since she'd returned from her mid-term holiday there had been something almost distracted about her, even though she'd denied it every time Skye or Star had asked her about it.

'And actually, Skye is engaged,' Star announced, thinking of the later conversation with her older sister.

'Congratulations. What's he like?'

'I have *no* idea. I've never met him,' she replied as Khalif blinked in surprise. 'But she's happy, I can tell.' And Skye really had been, happier than Star had ever heard her. It had been strange to hear Skye shine with the romance of her thrilling Costa Rican adventure.

It wasn't that Star wasn't happy for her, it was just that... She rubbed at her sternum, hoping to ease the tightness there. Was she jealous? Star looked at Khalif. Here she was, in the desert with a gorgeous sheikh, literally on a treasure hunt, and while it could look like the perfect romance for all the world, beneath it all, she was only here because she *might* be pregnant.

But as the days had worn on, and as Star grew closer and closer to the man she'd first met and merged that with the complexities of the man before her, as she felt her heart slowly spread and stretch, she began to suspect that she wasn't pregnant and could no longer ignore her fear that she didn't mean to him what he had come to mean to her.

'That's good, right?' Khalif asked, looking at her as if he were worried about her.

The tea nearly jerked over the rim and she had to place the delicate cup down before she lost even more of it. She knew that he was not speaking about her thoughts of him, but his words had still cut through her.

'That she's happy?' he clarified.

'Yes. Yes, of course,' Star replied, forcing a little pastry into her mouth before she could make things worse.

'Eat up,' he pressed. 'We have places to be.'

'Do we?' This really was a confusing morning. 'Where are we going? Don't we have to be back in Burami tomorrow?'

'Yes. But, in the meantime, you're being kidnapped by a handsome prince.'

Her heart soared, loving the way he'd just teased her. 'Oh, really? Where is he?' she asked, looking around the room.

'Funny,' he groused. 'Meet me by the stables. And dress comfortably.'

He probably should have asked her whether she knew how to ride *before* he'd made his plans, but the excitement and determination that had shone in her eyes was worth it. Mavia was so completely under Star's spell that he'd almost had to stop the mare from lowering to the ground for Star to mount.

If he wasn't careful, he would not have any subjects left in the country because they'd have all sworn allegiance to her.

Star had dressed as he'd asked. A long-sleeved white top and cream linen trousers were protected by a pale

gold pashmina that compared unfavourably to the rich
red ropes of hair that curled down her back.

But it was her smile that truly shone.

By the time he had Star on Mavia in front of him,
his pulse was ready to burst. His horse didn't even complain once at the unusual extra weight, instead flicking
a gaze at him from her bent head as if to demand what
he was waiting for.

In truth, he was waiting to regain control of his body.
He'd not counted on the way that having Star in between
his legs and against his chest, or the way his arms felt
wrapped around her would affect him.

She hadn't asked him a single question, he thought as
he flicked Mavia's reins. She launched from the stables as
if as desperate to show Star the magical wonders of the
desert as he. Star's trust in him was complete. As complete as it had been the night they had spent together. It
made him feel like…a king.

As Mavia galloped beneath them he relished the feeling of having Star so close, and he loosened his hold on
the reins, his horse knowing their destination, having
made this journey more than a thousand times, even if
not in the last three years.

He cast his gaze outwards and breathed deep. He felt
alive here. The stretches of endless desert a mirage, a
trick she played on the weary traveller, to test their met-
tle, to see their true worth. There were no lies in the desert. She may not have been cruel or loving, but she was
most definitely capricious.

In the back of his mind he heard his brother's laugh,
urging him on, faster and faster, and it merged with the
laugh from Star. He felt it in his heart, surrounded by
adrenaline, excitement and all the things he hadn't felt for

so long. He could feel it. The rightness of coming here. As if he had always been meant to bring her to this place.

They were so nearly there and Mavia knew it too because she found a sudden spurt of energy. They crested a dune, trails of sand billowing in their wake for no one to see, and at the pinnacle Mavia came to a stop of her own volition as if just as awed by the sight as the humans she carried. Khalif might have known every single inch of this view, but it still struck him as something incredible and precious, known only by a rare few.

He cast his eyes deep into the valley, over the large canvas tent nestled close to the trees that lined the small lake in the middle of the basin and in the distance he looked up to see the palms Star's ancestor had written of.

Star's mouth had dropped open. Her eyes raced across the image before her, sure that it was a dream. A desert mirage. But it wasn't. She could feel the heat of Khalif behind her and the pounding of Mavia's heart beneath her.

At the mouth of the tent, rich, dark red woven rugs stretched out before a large fire pit—one that was already in full flame. Golden glints and bursts of red hinted at sequin-encrusted cushions and rich deep turquoise silks covered the sand. A low-slung table with a dazzling array of drinks and food were kept cool and contained in a glass-fronted fridge. She was sure there must have been a generator somewhere discreet, but she couldn't see it. Nothing spoiled the fantasy.

The richness of what lay in front of her was almost too much to bear, so her eyes drifted to the far side of the crystal-blue water nestled within lush green vegetation to where she saw two palms crossed at the base to form an X.

Her heart missed a beat and she gasped.

She didn't dare turn around because if she looked at Khalif now, he'd know. He'd know that she'd fallen in love with him. And there, wrapped in his arms, his hands loosely holding the reins, and half convinced that he would be able to feel the beat of her heart, she almost started to shake.

Khalif urged the horse forward and they jostled from side to side with the horse's uneven but regal gait as Mavia made her way down into the basin where the oasis flourished. When they came to a stop, Khalif dismounted and she hastily swept at the moisture in her eyes, not wanting him to see how much being here meant to her.

He reached for her and took her into his arms, bringing her down from the horse, and stood her barely an inch from him. He searched her eyes in that way of his and she thought, *I want you to look at me like that for ever.* Finally, she looked away, hiding from his scrutiny, pretending to find the lake fascinating, when all she could think of was him.

'Do you know where you are?' he asked, his voice low but strong.

'This is where Hātem brought Catherine.' *Before she had to leave,* Star concluded silently, trying to surf the wave of sadness that swept over her at the thought that she might soon be leaving too. 'Why did you bring me here?'

He looked over her shoulder, the desert swallowing the sigh that escaped his lips. It was as if he needed a moment to gather himself because when he turned back to her, his eyes were fierce. His hand cupped her cheek, holding her gaze—as if she could or would ever look away from him.

'I brought you here to remind you of the family who

want you. Not just your sisters and your mother. But the family who knew you would come, following in their footsteps. To remind you of the one who trusted in her people, in the women of her blood and the women bound to those she loved. It is they who have kept her secret safe, ready and waiting for you. Not for anyone else. But you.

'You have been waited upon for over one hundred and fifty years, Star Soames. That is no small thing.'

She felt his words in her soul, as if something ancient had been woken beneath the desert and was reaching for her. So when Khalif delved into the bag on his saddle and retrieved a small velvet pouch her heart didn't pulse with surprise, it vibrated with an overwhelming feel of *rightness*. As if something predestined was finally coming to conclusion.

He took a necklace so familiar to Star from the pouch and held it up for her to inspect. She pressed slightly shaking fingers against her lips. This was what they had been looking for. It was the key to so much. To the past, to her mother's future... So much rested on such a small, beautiful thing. Khalif had been right. There were subtle differences, but it could have easily been mistaken for the one that she was wearing around her neck.

'May I?'

'Of course. It is now yours,' he said with a solemnity that felt ceremonial.

Taking it from him, she made her way blindly to the silks and woven rugs. She folded her legs beneath her, and she looped the gold chain over her head and brought the two pendants together.

She knew that they should fit together—Catherine's coded message had said as much—but she didn't quite... She ran her finger over the embossed pattern on the surface of the pendant and felt something shift. Pressing down released an indented piece of silver from the bottom of the pendant. She picked up Hātem's pendant and did the same. Staring at the two pendants, she didn't quite know what to do next. They needed to…

Khalif reached over. 'May I?' He seemed as lost in the task as she and she was happy to pass him the necklaces if it meant she could spend just a moment looking at the man who had given her more than he could ever know.

He turned the pendants in his hands, twisting and turning one piece while holding the other steady, and then, as if suddenly seeing how it could be, hooked one pendant into the other.

'Oh,' Star marvelled. Together the pieces created one key, the thick gold base forming the head and the two thinner silver offshoots forming the blade—the indentations becoming the ridges and notches that would fit into a lock.

Khalif pressed against the head of the key and the silver blade retracted into the body of the pendant. 'There. You can now wear them together.'

She stared at him, shaking her head in wonder.

'You don't like it?' he asked as if confused.

'I *do*! I love it. I just… I don't think I ever imagined actually finding it.'

I don't think I ever imagined actually finding you. *Finding the man I would love for the rest of my life.*

'Are you trying to tell me that you didn't believe your search would have a happy ending? And you call yourself a romantic,' he tsked.

She tried to swallow around the lump in her throat and a smile wobbled on her lips. 'Of course I do.'

He held up the necklace. 'Would you like me to—'

'Actually…' she said, rising quickly. 'I'd like to explore,' she exclaimed brightly, sure that the overly bright response had given her away, but he kindly let her go.

She couldn't take the necklace. Not yet. Because that would be the end of her search in Duratra. She would be done and wearing the necklace, holding it complete as the key would be the end of her time here. Especially as she was almost sure that she wasn't pregnant.

Khalif went to see Mavia, made sure that she had extra treats for carrying them both here. It hadn't been a long journey and she would have all the rest she needed, as he and Star would be driving out of here tomorrow.

He could see that Star had been affected by the necklace. He had been too, not imagining for a moment how it would feel to give away something that had been worn by the women of his family for over one hundred and fifty years. In doing so, it felt as if he'd entrusted part of his family to her.

Something red flashed in his eyeline and he knew that Star had undone the long thick plait of her hair. He clenched his jaw against the need to turn and look. Instead he worked on building a fire, ignoring the way ripples of water lapped against the fertile green border of the pool.

While his imagination painted images of mermaids with flowing red tresses and mystical creatures, he unpacked the food he had brought, placing it in the cool fridges running from the almost silent generator behind the tent.

The staff from Alhafa had worked through the night to make this happen, happy to do a kindness to the woman who had brought life back to the palace. He marvelled at how quickly, readily and easily she had become their Queen. But would it make her happy? Would being royal, being a princess in a foreign land, be right for her? Becoming a spectacle for the world to investigate, judge and find wanting, no matter how perfect she was. Her life would be on display and at risk and he knew that he could not do that to someone as pure and beautiful as her.

The fire took, the crackle and burn mixing with the chirps of the cicadas and the cry of the birds that stopped at the oasis on their journey across the desert. Wind gently rustled the leaves in the trees and water rippled and in his mind's eye he could see Star in the lake, her hair splayed on the surface and her body hidden from his gaze by the distortion of the liquid, no matter how pure.

His pulse pounded in his ears, blocking out the sounds of the desert. He cursed the wood beneath his hands because it wasn't smooth, freckled skin, soft as satin. A swift inhale followed a pinprick and he looked down to find a splinter in his thumb. Frowning, he removed the sliver of wood, watching the tiny bloom of blood before pressing it to his lips.

He'd never wanted a woman like this.

And he never would again.

'What happens if I'm not pregnant?'

Her voice, a little shaky, a lot tentative, came from behind him.

'You've only told me about what happens if I am.'

Because he'd not wanted to let her go.

He cleared his throat from his emotions' tight hold. 'You will return to Norfolk. I will return to the throne.'

'And that's it?'

'That's it.'

'I'll never see you again?'

She had posed it as a question that he chose instead to take as a statement, unable to bring himself to answer. Silently he roared his fury. Everything in him wanted to

reach for her, just one last time. Not damning the consequences, but fully understanding them and facing them.
His mind taunted that it was a gift, this one night, more
than either he or she should have ever expected, but his
heart berated him. Maybe unconsciously he'd known
that coming here wasn't just for her, but for him—to
have this, to have *her*. He was selfish and she deserved
so much more.

'Thank you for bringing me here.' The finality of her
tone ate at him. It was as if she were saying goodbye.

'It was the least I could do.' He paused, knowing that
his next words would open up a path neither should take,
but both seemed powerless to resist. 'It may be the *only*
thing I can do.'

'I understand,' she said quietly.

He spun around and pierced her with his gaze. 'Do
you?' he demanded, furious with her, with himself. There
wasn't anything about this that he understood.

'I do.'

It was then he took her in. Long red tresses soaked
into ropes, lying flat against her skin. The long-sleeved
white top almost transparent, revealing more than it concealed, pressed against her body the way he wanted to be.

His hands itched to reach for her, to take her, to pull
her to him.

He was shaking his head as she took a step forward
and stopped, but he caught the way she masked her hurt
in an instant and he cursed. She turned to walk away,
but he was up and reaching for her before she could take
a second step, turning her in his arms before she could
take another breath, and punishing her with a kiss—
punishing them both—before he could think again.
She gasped into his mouth and he took it within him,
locked it away because that was how she made him feel.

Shocked, awed, thrilled... He wanted her to remember this moment for the rest of her life, because he already knew he would.

Her arms came up to his shirt, her hands fisted the cotton, pulling him to her, their passion frantic, needy and desperate.

His hands flew over her wet T-shirt, lifting and pulling to reach her skin, as if only that would soothe the burning need within him. Hand flat against the base of her spine, he pressed her into him, her taut nipples pebbling into his chest, her neck beneath his tongue and teeth, all the while her nails scratched trails of fire into his skin.

This was madness, utter madness, but neither seemed able or willing to stop.

He pulled back, long enough to let her lust filled gaze clear, having never seen anything more beautiful in his entire life. 'Star,' he warned as he took her in, pupils wide with desire, breath heaving. She looked utterly gorgeous.

Her name felt like an apology on his lips and she wanted to shout at him, yell and scream that she didn't want apologies, she wanted *this*. She wanted him. Needed him almost as much as her next breath. Before he could say another word, she pulled him to her, kissed him with all the passion she was capable of. All the surety she felt that, no matter the reality, no matter what happened tomorrow, he was the man she was supposed to love for the rest of her life.

His hands came around her waist, pressing against her hip and ass, and she lifted herself into them, wrapping her legs around his waist, glorying when she felt his erection at her core.

'Please,' she begged against his lips. 'Please, just tonight. Just this.'

He raised a hand to sweep her hair from her face, holding her there, looking into her heart and soul. 'Of course.'

That night, Star was lost in a sea of pleasure. Fingers tangled, tongues danced, her skin was alive beneath his touch. She felt a fire building deep within her, expanding and filling her until the point where she couldn't contain it any more and an explosion of the most intangible beauty scattered her being across the star-covered desert.

Again and again he broke her into pieces, only to put her back together as something new, something different, and in that moment she knew she would never be the same again.

By the time the sun's rays cut a path through the tent's awning to rest against her skin, Star was aware that Khalif was no longer there. She dressed, her clothes feeling as if they didn't quite fit, and a sense that the morning—and the day—wouldn't quite be right fell against her soul.

She found him looking out across the desert.

'What are you…?' Her voice broke a little, her throat raw from screaming her pleasure through the night-time hours.

'I was making a wish. I—'

'Don't tell me,' she rushed out. 'It won't come true,' she warned.

'I was wishing not to be a prince.'

She swallowed the emotions begging to be released. It was a wish they knew couldn't and shouldn't come true.

'You are a wonderful prince. Conscientious, careful about others and what they think, thoughtful about doing the best thing possible for the greatest number of people. You will make a good ruler. Fair, strong, determined.'

Still looking out into the desert, he quirked his lip into a wry smile. 'Why do I hear a "but"?'

Star hurt for him, shook her head, but determined to

say this to him. *For* him. 'You are not being *you*. You are being the Prince you think they want.'

'I am not my own any more. I am theirs,' he said, as if trying to explain himself to someone who refused to see his truth. When in reality he was simply refusing to see hers.

'You could be the ruler you want to be, if you are willing to stand by the consequences.'

She knew how that sounded, but Star really wasn't thinking of herself. She was thinking of the man who had already begun to lose himself under the weight of the crown. 'I wish I could have seen you before.'

'What,' he scoffed, 'as the disreputable playboy?'

'No. Just the boy.'

Khalif reared back as if she had struck him. He was about to reply when the roar of a Jeep's engine cut through the desert.

They were out of time.

CHAPTER TEN

'So, Star's appointment with Maya is tomorrow?' Amin asked for the hundredth time that day. Even Khalif's other members of staff glared at the bespectacled man.

Reza leaned against the wall of the meeting room, refusing to take his eyes from Khalif, who was spending an unnecessary amount of time trying to ignore that fact.

'And you know she can't attend the event tonight?'

Khalif was going to have to see a dentist before the week was out. And Amin might be paying a visit to the doctor. He opened his mouth to speak when he felt Reza's hand on his shoulder, as if holding him back from the violence he wanted to inflict.

'I think we all understand that. In the meantime, let's take a short break before reconvening for the run-through for tonight's event.'

The quiet authority of Reza's tone had the desired effect on his staff and the opposite effect on Khalif.

'I don't need you to speak for me,' he growled.

'Of course you don't. But you also don't need a mutiny on your hands, which is what will happen if you push your staff any harder.'

'It is no harder than I push myself.'

'You're right. It is considerably less. But that doesn't mean either is manageable.' His best friend let go of the hold on his shoulder as the last staff member left the room. 'What are you more afraid of? That she is pregnant or she isn't?'

'Does it matter? I couldn't do this to her,' he said, finally saying it out loud. 'I know what it is like to have that freedom taken away and I can't...' Khalif shook his head.

'I know the sacrifices you have—'

'Sacrifices? I changed *everything*! I *stopped* everything.' Khalif stared at his best friend in disbelief. Finally, after three years, it poured forth. 'I gave up an international business I had built from scratch, I dropped everything and came home. I buried my brother and Samira in front of the world's press. I made phone calls and shook hands within hours of their funeral... I did what I had to and would do it again. But Reza, I couldn't *breathe*, let alone grieve in the way I wanted.' And for *who* I wanted, he finally admitted to himself. 'This? It's like being in a straitjacket, folded in on yourself, cramped, confined. The expectation of everyone, the watching, the pressure. How on earth can you think I would willingly put that on someone as innocent as Star?'

Reza stared at him with deep understanding and sympathy. He placed his hand on Khalif's shoulder, the weight both comforting and steadying. He nodded once and Khalif knew that his best friend understood.

'Okay,' Reza said simply. 'Then let's talk about how this holographic presentation is going to work, because that is going to blow their minds.'

It felt strange to be back in Khalif's suite. Especially since everything that had happened between then and now had begun to feel like a dream. She was on the balcony, the late afternoon sun sinking into her skin, warming her pleasantly...but not quite enough.

She rolled her shoulders, bracing her hands against the balustrade, eyes searching the horizon. The view of the city looked a little different now that she knew out there, beyond the stretches of golden sand, the sloping dunes and hazy blue skies, was a desert palace seen only by a few and an oasis that would always be in her heart.

She glanced at the rucksack containing everything she had brought with her and one new item. She had returned the connected pendants to the velvet bag and was yet to be able to wear them, putting off the moment until she truly knew that she would be going home. The necklace now had a double chain, as if it would always acknowledge that it had needed two people to come together to make it whole.

She felt a tide of anxiety washing against her soul, back and forth like the sea. She was nervous for Khalif, knowing how much the reveal of his plans for the memorial meant to him. So much so that she'd borne the look of guilt he'd worn as he'd explained why she couldn't come to the event that night with understanding and acceptance. Both of which she truly felt. But it had hurt nonetheless.

Yet it hurt in a different way to how she had felt alone in the palace in the desert. This was not the sense of shame and rejection she had felt because of her grandparents, it was more a sense of inevitable ache. A sense of loss that was down to fate rather than intention. Where once Catherine had been forced to do her duty, now it was Khalif's turn—and Star honestly couldn't have argued against either.

He'd offered her a way that she could still see the presentation, which she would take, because it was his moment and she wouldn't take that away from him. Which was why there, on the balcony, facing the desert, she sent a prayer to Catherine and Hātem, and Faizan and Samira, to look out for him that night.

There was a knock on the door. Star had been expecting it, but it still made her jump. She turned back into the room to find Maya closing the door behind her. She smiled at Star, who braced herself.

'I was hoping you could help me with something. Do you think it's possible to take the test today and for it still to be accurate?'

Khalif flexed his jaw, hoping to relieve the ache in his cheeks from the perfunctory smiles he'd masked himself in.

Samira's father, Abbad, had been casting grim glances his way since the first guests had arrived and his wife's vacant gaze wasn't any better. The only time he'd felt himself relax was when Nadya had winked at him and run off to play hide-and-seek amongst the legs of the guests. His parents were thankfully preoccupied by small talk with dignitaries and international diplomats.

'It is a stunning design,' Reza said quietly, having stuck by his side the entire afternoon.

'I know.'

'You should be proud.'

'And she should be *here*,' he growled, his tone grating his throat.

'There are three hundred people present, the Duratrian press both inside and outside the palace, along with more than a few representatives of the international newspapers. You think that a woman with hair like the sun would go unnoticed in here?' Reza reminded him. 'Tonight is about Faizan, Samira…and you. *After* tonight,' he pressed, 'is another matter entirely.'

You are wrong, my friend, Khalif thought, no matter how much he wished it weren't the case.

Khalif stepped up to the podium and the audience grew quiet and turned to face him. He looked out across the faces he could see beneath the bright powerful glare of lighting trained on the stage. He felt the hairs on the back of his neck lift, his heartbeat stumbled and while he didn't know how, or where, Khalif knew that Star was here. He took a breath.

'Ladies and gentlemen. My family and I are honoured that you could be here tonight. For some, it may have seemed like a long time coming,' he acknowledged to the gentle murmur rippling across the guests. 'However, I truly believe that my brother and Samira deserved such consideration. The...hole they left in the lives of their family and friends is immeasurable and it was important to respect that grief. Faizan and Samira touched so many lives. They didn't just merge two families, but they brought two countries together and two beautiful princesses into this world.

'Growing up with Faizan was no mean feat,' he said, to the slight laughter of the crowd. 'He was focused, driven, bright, intelligent, compassionate. And I can see those qualities already in Nadya and Nayla. Faizan always knew what legacy he wanted to leave behind him. One of peace in the present and hope for the future. Hope not just for his people, but his planet. And Samira? She was always smiling, always ready to be the balance in disagreements, always ready to bridge the gap between her husband the Prince and the man who loved his family and his people above all else. Samira and Faizan were proud, loving and very conscious of their countries.

'She was the bridge and he the river that ran deep beneath it and that is how I, and I hope all of you, will remember them.'

He stepped back from the stage and allowed the lights to dim. The gentle hum of excitement building from the crowd momentarily stopped in awe when they saw the first images from the holographic display.

Khalif heard the words of his pre-recorded voice-over explain about the area between Duratra and Udra that had long since been abandoned. It was a kind of no man's land where the river, coming from the Red Sea, cut between Duratra and Samira's home country.

The hologram showed images of what the country looked like now and slowly how the area would be cleared, cleaned and prepared for what was to come. Over the next few minutes, the graphics showed a bridge being built over the river between the two neighbouring countries. Beautiful plants and lush greenery developed along both sides of the banks as well as each side of the wide bridge. Oohs and aahs came from the audience as they could see the trees grow, healthy and strong and high on top of the bridge.

'There will be no cars or vehicles in the area. It will be completely pedestrianised. Wildlife will be introduced—birds, insects and eventually larger animals—all cared for by specially trained staff who will provide guided free tours for any visitor.

'It will be a sanctuary. A place for people to come and honour the memory of Faizan and Samira, and the investment in the future that was always so very important to them. It is the paradise they would have wanted for their children, and it is what their children wanted to honour and remember their parents.'

His family needed this, his country needed—*deserved*—stability, unity, cohesion and healing and he knew deep down in his bones that this would be the first step.

Khalif looked out into the audience, touched by the overwhelming emotion he felt rising up to meet his own. Goosebumps pebbled his skin and he thought that he saw a flash of red, looking up in time to see the movement of a curtain at the balcony near the private suites on the upper level.

'Uncle Kal... Uncle Kal!'

He turned just in time to catch Nadya, who had thrown herself at him in wild abandon.

'You had the birds!' Nadya's voice was a little muffled from where her face was pressed against his stomach and she gripped his waist like a limpet. Nayla, the shyer of the two, stood with a massive grin and wide eyes showing her delight, standing with one foot tucked behind the other.

'And flowers,' he said to her, and she nodded enthusiastically.

'Will it be bright blue and pink like the hologriff?'

Kal didn't have the heart to correct her. 'Well, maybe we can speak to the designers about that. We have quite a bit to do before we get to that point.'

Over his nieces' heads, he saw his parents making their way towards him. Unease stirred briefly but then he grounded himself. He knew that he had done the right thing—not because it pleased everyone, but because he felt it in his gut. The memorial would be doing the right thing by his nieces and by Faizan and Samira.

'My son,' his mother, Hafsa, greeted him, her eyes crinkling the fine lines at the corners into fans. He wasn't sure whether it was a consequence of losing his brother, or valuing the family he did have and the love he felt for them, but his heart felt torn—between being here with his family and being with the woman upstairs. And he knew that neither deserved half a heart.

It took him an hour to extricate himself from the gala, but he couldn't have said that he'd tried too hard. He had felt it. Something in the air had shifted. A kind of knowledge, or awareness, had begun to creep over him, without him knowing specifically what it was. He just knew that he had to get to Star.

His heart was pounding as he made his way through the private areas of the palace, but his footsteps were slow and purposeful. Something inside him was roaring to get out, but he hardly made a sound. He smiled at the staff and few family members he passed, though in his mind's eye he saw only one thing...one person.

He closed the door to his suite behind him and stopped. He inhaled the scent of her on the air, wondering if that might be the last time he did so. He didn't have to look, to know that she was out on the balcony. She loved that view almost as much as he did.

He took two steps into the room and paused. Letting himself see her. The way her hair twisted in the gentle desert breeze. From this angle she stood at the balcony amongst the stars and he bit his lip to stop himself from saying something, not wanting to spoil the moment—for her or him.

She turned slightly to the side, as if sensing his presence, and wiped at something on her cheek that he didn't quite see, so caught up in the sight of her.

'What are you doing here?' she asked.

'I live here,' he said, but the joke fell flat. 'I was worried.'

'About the presentation?'

'No, that went well. Really well.' He closed the distance between them as she turned to face him fully. 'Everyone loved it.'

'Of course they did.' She smiled and his heart ached at the easy acceptance and surety ringing in her voice. 'You should probably get back,' she insisted, 'it's still early.'

'I was wrong,' he said, offering her all that he could. 'To ask you to stay here.'

'You weren't and you know it,' she replied without malice or anger. This was Star as he'd never seen her before. Regal, poised and absolutely breathtaking. And that was when he saw the necklace, the double strands of the chain on either side of the pendant making it something strangely beautiful. And instinctively he braced himself against something he felt he already knew.

Star searched his features, her eyes running over his head, shoulders, down the length of his body, consuming as much of him as she possibly could. There was no way Kal could have let her be there at the event that evening. She understood a little of that duty now. How the crowd had looked up to him, watched him, hung on every word. How they had cried and sighed their appreciation of his plans for the memorial. He had given them a focal point for their grief and the beginning of the healing process. She supposed in some way she was about to give herself the same.

'I'm—' Khalif started.

'I'm not pregnant,' she interrupted before he could say anything more.

He simply held her gaze as if he had felt it in the same way she had. When Maya had presented her with the results of the test, Star hadn't been surprised by the fact she wasn't carrying Khalif's baby, but by the extent to which she'd actually been wanting to. Not once had she let herself hope or believe because…because, she realised now, she had never wanted anything more in her life.

'Maya assured me the test was accurate.'

He closed the space between them in just two steps, drawing so close to her, only inches really. It was as if he wanted to touch her, reach for her, just as much as she wanted him to…but couldn't. Wouldn't.

In one breath, Star was lost just to the sense of him. His exhale shuddered against her cheek, before he turned to stand beside her, facing the desert. She placed her hands on the stone balcony close to his, their little fingers almost touching, but her heart knew the distance might as well have been a chasm.

Go…go now.

But she couldn't. She forced herself to stay, refusing to turn and run. She was a reader. She was a romantic. And, whether it was foolish or not, she had hope. All the things they'd experienced—an impossible meeting, ancestors torn apart by duty, families brought back together by fate. She had found Catherine's Duratra out there in the desert. Khalif had found her necklace…

'So that's it then.' His voice was rough and dark in the dusk.

She felt as if she'd conjured up the words herself. The first steps of the dance that would see them either spending the rest of their lives together or…

'Is it?'

'Star…' he warned.

'No, Khalif. It's a question I am asking you. *Is* that it then?'

She refused to look at him, even though he was staring at her hard, trying to get her to face him. But she wouldn't. Couldn't. Because he'd see. He'd see all that she wasn't quite ready for him to see.

'It's funny how people behave when they think they don't have a choice,' she said to the desert. 'It traps them, makes them feel helpless, makes them behave in ways that aren't authentic to them. Ways that aren't right for them.'

'You can't consider my life to have choices.'

'Why not?' she demanded. 'Look what you did when you realised that you had a choice for Faizan and Samira's memorial? Look at the incredibly beautiful, amazing thing you have set in motion. Do you not think that we could—'

'It's not the same. *Everyone* in my family, every heir to the throne has been in the same position,' he growled.

'The definition of madness is doing the same thing over and over again and expecting different results.'

'Why do you think I'm expecting different results?' He looked at her, genuinely confused. 'There were no disastrous results for my parents. And Faizan and Samira's marriage was a very happy, fruitful one.'

'But not for you. Not the hurt it caused you,' she half cried. 'Would you force this on your nieces? Would you expect them to marry for duty rather than love?'

'No! I'm doing this so that they can have that option for themselves.'

'Really? You're not doing this because it's easier than being true to yourself?'

His gaze met hers in a fiery clash, the golden flecks in his umber eyes swirling like a sandstorm. 'Star—'

But she couldn't listen to him. She had to press on. This was her last chance. Her only chance. 'Because I suppose you can't really fail if you're always trying to please everyone else. If you're being everything other people need, then it's their need that's failed, not you. And you'll never know.'

'Know what?'

'You'll never know how incredible you could be if you were just yourself.'

Her voice rang with such sincerity, such hope and such optimism he half wanted to believe it himself. It was seductive, what she was saying. Be himself, choose her, be a great ruler. But she was wrong.

'I was myself,' he bit out angrily. 'For three years, I wined and womanised my way around Europe. Is that the kind of ruler Duratra deserves? Is that the kind of man you want?' His voice had become a shout.

'You were hurt. Your entire family condoned a marriage between your brother and your first love. Of course you acted out,' she said, desperately grasping for justifications for his terrible behaviour.

'Acted out? Is that what…?' He ground his teeth together, hating the way that her words ran through his head and heart. Her understanding, her belief in him crucified him, made a mockery of every single choice he'd made since, tearing him in half between what he so desperately wanted and what he felt he needed to do.

And he was furious. In that moment, he wanted to bring down the palace, smash and burn everything— anything to make the questions stop. So he did the only thing he could do.

'I know you think being a prince means that—'

'Don't,' she said, the single word a plea. 'Don't use that—'

'I know you think being a prince means that magical adventures await and love comes with singing birds and talking clocks,' he said, looking away from the tears brimming in her eyes. 'But it's not. It's *not*, Star,' he insisted. 'It's constantly putting the country first. It is making a marriage that is strategic and for the good of this country.'

'And there is nothing strategic about marrying me?'

'No.' He shook his head. 'There just isn't.'

'Your happiness is not strategic? It doesn't count?'

'No. It never has,' he said with the same sense of acceptance that had descended the moment he'd realised he was to take the throne.

'If you allow that feeling, that anger and resentment about Samira marrying Faizan to shape everything you do, the choices you make—'

'Don't say her…' He couldn't finish the sentence so instead he bit off his words, his tongue. It had been cruel, and he knew it. The hurt on Star's features was two red slashes on her cheeks.

'You can attack my dreams but I can't challenge your fears? Is it yourself that you're punishing by refusing to listen to your heart, or someone else? Why would you damn yourself to unhappiness?'

Why wouldn't she stop? Why was she pushing him like this?

'Is it because,' she pressed on, 'if you can have a happy marriage, if *you* can choose who you marry, then so could Faizan? Then it would mean that your wonderful, incredible brother made the wrong choice and it hurt you?'

'Wow, you're really going for it tonight, aren't you?' he scoffed bitterly, wondering what else she was going to drag him through. Because being angry with her was easier than feeling the truth of her words.

'Of course I am. My heart is on the line. My love for you. Can't you see that?'

White-hot pain slashed across his chest, a death blow that wouldn't end his life but could still stop his heart. Because only in the moments when his heart wasn't beating could he find the strength to be cruel enough to force her to go.

'Love? In two weeks?' he taunted. 'That really *is* a romance,' he said, forcing scepticism into his tone that burned all the way down. 'Then again, it's easier to fall in love when the fantasy can never live up to the reality, isn't it? You hide in your romances, preferring them to reality. But I don't have that luxury, Star.'

She looked as if she'd been struck and the only decent thing he could do was bear witness to it. He hated himself more than he ever had done before, but her words had taken hold and weren't letting go. He couldn't follow them, not now, not yet, and he greatly feared what would happen when he did. He felt like a bull, head down and ploughing forward, because anything else meant that he had to confront his feelings, her feelings.

Confront *her.* The way she was always challenging him, demanding of him, expecting him to be better when he couldn't.

'You're right. I do have choices. And I'm sorry that the one I need to make causes you pain.' His words were mechanical, forced. She knew it, he knew it, but there was also, inevitably, a truth beneath them. 'But I would make this choice every time. I choose Duratra.'

She wiped at a large, fat tear that escaped down her cheek, the action reminding him of what he'd seen when he'd first come onto the balcony. And he realised in that moment that she'd been crying before they'd talked. Before he'd said the horrible things, because she'd always known how the conversation would play out. She had known, before she'd even told him that she wasn't pregnant, what his reaction would be.

As she walked from the balcony, out of the suite and the palace, he realised then that he'd got it so terribly wrong. She was not a coward, hiding in romance. She was strong enough and brave enough to face reality. Stronger and braver than him.

The blow to his stomach and heart was doubly hard, physical and emotional, and he collapsed to the floor, his back against the cold, unyielding stone balcony that both held him up and anchored him while everything in him wanted to run after her.

CHAPTER ELEVEN

AT AROUND TWO in the morning Khalif found himself in one of the larger family suites, looking for whisky. He'd not had it in his quarters for three years. He'd not even had a drink in three years. But tonight he needed one.

He opened the door to the alcohol cabinet his father kept for visitors, retrieved the weighty cut glass tumbler and poured himself a satisfyingly large couple of inches of whisky. He swirled it around the glass as he sat, letting the peaty alcoholic scent waft up to meet him, his taste buds exploding with expectation and his conscience delaying the moment of gratification as punishment.

What had he done?

He was about to take a sip when the door to the living room opened and he looked up to find his father surveying him with something like pity.

'I haven't seen you drink since before Faizan died.'

It was on the tip of his tongue to lash out and say he'd not actually had the drink yet, but that felt churlish. Instead, he watched his father go to the cabinet and retrieve the whisky bottle and pour himself an equally large glass. 'I haven't seen you drink since…'

'Faizan's funeral?' his mother asked as she too came into the room. Both men's faces held the same look, as if they'd just been caught with their hands in a cookie jar. Never had they more appeared like father and son. 'Oh, don't be silly. If I was outraged at this, I'd have never survived the first six months as your Queen,' she teased the men in her life, leaning to press a kiss to her husband's cheek.

Bakir grinned conspiratorially at his son and took a seat in the large leather chair opposite Khalif as his wife perched on the arm.

Then the light dimmed from his eyes and Bakir took a breath. 'Faizan and Samira,' he said, raising his glass.

Khalif raised his and blinked back the sudden wetness in his eyes, swallowing his grief with the first powerful mouthful of whisky.

'Khalif, we are—'

He held his hand up to ward off his father's words but, though he paused, Bakir pressed on.

'We are so very proud of you. The memorial is...'

'Perfect,' his mother concluded, her smile watery and her eyes bright with unshed tears. She sniffed and her husband handed her a handkerchief without breaking eye contact with his son. 'Where on earth did you get the idea?' she asked.

Khalif clenched his jaw before prising the words from his conscience. 'A friend. She asked about Faizan and Samira, encouraged me to remember them. She suggested I talk to Nadya and Nayla about what they might like to have in the memorial.'

'She sounds very clever,' his mother observed.

'She is,' Khalif agreed.

'Did she encourage you to do anything else?' his father asked.

Through gritted teeth, he said, 'To be myself. To stop trying to be you or Faizan,' he confessed.

'She really *is* a wise woman,' his mother said, the

smile in her voice evident. His father scoffed and Khalif's head jerked up to stare at his parents. He wanted to yell at them, to say that it wasn't a laughing matter.

'That's only because you said a very similar thing to me many years ago,' Bakir groused.

'*And* you barely listened to me,' his mother complained.

Khalif's head was swimming and it wasn't from the alcohol. 'What are you talking about? I thought you had an arranged marriage?'

Bakir cast a level gaze at his son. 'Well, a lot of work went into making it look that way, so I'm glad it was successful.'

Khalif couldn't work out whether his father was being sarcastic or ironic.

'We had met before,' his mother explained on a slightly flustered, and somewhat guilty, exhale. 'Before the engagement.'

'Your mother told me that if I couldn't orchestrate a good enough reason for us to get married, how would I ever manage to run a country? So I found a way.' Bakir shrugged. 'She challenged me then, and has each day since.'

His father stared at him intently and sighed deeply, as if not looking forward to what he was about to say. 'We all knew that you cared for Samira and she for you.'

'Cared?' Khalif almost choked, anger gripping him almost instantly.

'But we also knew that she wasn't right for you,' his father continued. 'Us, Faizan and even Samira.'

Khalif fisted the glass and clamped his jaw shut. He was furious. Not with his father but because he knew that his father was right.

'You were the younger son, Khalif. The one protected

from the lessons and the rigours of royal instruction. In hindsight, that was a mistake. I…' Bakir seemed to struggle for words for the first time Khalif could remember. Finding his strength, he pressed on. 'My father taught me nothing about ruling a country, for fear that I would try to usurp him. My learning curve was steep. I didn't want… Faizan to have the same difficulties. I never thought—'

Hafsa placed her hand on her husband's and their fingers intertwined.

Khalif put the glass down on the side table, reached forward and placed his hand over theirs, joining them in their grief but also their love. He was ready to hear whatever his father had to say.

'I knew how much you wanted to be part of Faizan's lessons, but I feared the distraction. So you were given every freedom in compensation. And while you didn't want those freedoms, wouldn't have chosen them for yourself, you *did* have them. You were spoilt by that freedom—wholly unintentionally.

'No one challenged you, not even Samira. You had a special bond, no one can deny that, and we all loved her greatly. But she would have let you do anything, and you would have run roughshod over her all the while, never needing to do more, to be more, or better. You wouldn't have been good for each other.'

Khalif had braced for it and his father's words still hurt. But he couldn't deny the truth in them. All this time he had taunted Star for romanticism, but had he not done the same? Had he not fantasised the perfect, but mainly imagined, future with Samira? Had that not been the truest form of romanticism? All the while Star had questioned him, teased him about his preconceptions, challenged him to make better decisions, to follow his gut, encouraged him to make mistakes and learn from fixing them. And with that thought hope bloomed and his heart soared.

'What is that look on your face?'

'I've made a terrible mistake, Father.'

'Then why do you look so happy?'

'Because now I get to fix it,' he said, the smile lifting his lips and his heart soaring for the first time that evening.

'And how are you planning to do that?'

'Romance books. I need romance books.'

'I think he's gone mad,' his father said to his wife, looking deeply concerned. But his mother's eyes were lit with sparkles that only reminded Khalif of Star.

Star plucked at a loose thread on the long end of the pashmina she wore, her eyes sore and finally dry. She had sandwiched the phone between her ear and shoulder to leave both hands free so she could tackle the frayed cotton.

'I can be on a plane in two hours.'

'Mum, you don't drive, your bank account is pretty much empty, you hate carbon emissions more than you hate the Tories, and my plane leaves in three hours, so I'll be back in England before you would even get here.'

'Your sister said exactly the same thing,' Mariam Soames grumbled.

'It's the thought that counts, Mum. Star sounded happy?'

'Yes, she did. I'm looking forward to meeting this Chalendar. And I'm looking forward to having all my girls back in the same country and under the same roof. I don't like the idea of Summer at that house all on her own.'

Star marvelled that her mother had grown up in the

sprawling, dilapidated Norfolk estate and insisted on calling it a 'house', despite the fact it had over thirty bedrooms. Star's fingers left the cotton thread and lifted to the gold ropes of the chain at her neck.

How she and her sisters had thought they would have been able to keep the search for the missing jewels from their mother a secret, she had no idea. It had hurt to reveal Elias's manipulations to their mother, but when Skye had called them from France they'd known that it was time to tell Mariam everything. She had been as angry as much as Mariam Soames was capable of being angry with her daughters, which was about as long as it took to sigh.

'I know what you girls are trying to do—'

'We're so nearly there, Mum,' Star whispered, more of a plea than a promise. 'Skye has the map of the secret passageways, I have the key—we just need to find them now.'

'I know, Star. I just...' There was a pause on the end of the line and Star imagined her mother shifting her shawl around her shoulders. 'I've decided that I'm going to move in with Samantha for a bit.'

'Really? I thought you might want to—'

'Live with my just-beginning-to-find-their-feet, lovely and well-meaning daughters?' Mariam replied and Star couldn't help but smile at the laugh in her mother's voice.

The words *just beginning to find their feet* really struck Star. It was a little too close to what she'd hoped to achieve by coming to Duratra—to prove that she could stand on her own two feet—and Star felt as if she both had and hadn't.

'Samantha has known me for years. She's perfectly capable of putting up with me for a little longer,' Mariam said assuredly but without thought. A sob rose suddenly and shockingly in Star's chest. 'I didn't mean it like that,' her mother said.

'I know,' Star promised.

'We are going to beat this.'

'*I* know,' Star replied, forcing a smile to her lips in the hope that it would be heard in her voice. 'Actually... I was thinking about moving out of the flat and setting up somewhere on my own. Do you think that Skye would be okay with that? I mean—' Star struggled to find the words to explain her sudden need to hold onto that bit of independence she'd discovered in Duratra '—with Summer away at uni most of the year...'

Her mother sighed. 'I think that Skye will worry but, with her engagement, it's more than likely that she'll be relocating to France. If it feels right for you, my love, then we will all support you one hundred per cent.'

'I think it might scare me a little, but it's something I would like very much. I love Skye and Summer but...they need to see that I am capable of being independent.' Star sighed, all the pent-up emotion pouring from her chest in one breath. 'Mum...' she started, nervous as to the answer. 'Do you think Kal was right? Have I been hiding?'

'No, my love,' said her mother, her voice warm and reassuring. 'You haven't hidden in romances. You've been learning. Learning what you like, what you want, and what you will and won't put up with.

'Romances don't warp our expectations, they raise them. And there is nothing wrong with that. They show us that it is okay to put ourselves, our desires, at the forefront of our intentions. They show us not to be ashamed of our wants. Whether that want is emotional, practical or sexual, my love.' While cringing at her mother using words like sexual, because that was *never* going to be okay, Star knew what she meant. 'You should never have been made to feel ashamed or rejected. Not by your grandparents, nor your prince.'

'He's not my prince, Mum.'

'They should be the ones who feel shame, Star,' Mariam carried on as if Star hadn't interrupted. 'You reached out to make a connection with honesty, integrity, love and hope. They are lesser for turning you away. You are worthy of someone who reaches for you.'

Star smiled at the old family joke and she couldn't help the flood of memories overwhelming her. Khalif reaching to take her from his horse...the incredible gift of taking her to the desert, giving her a connection to Catherine that felt fated...making her feel loved and wanted by her ancestors, even if he hadn't been capable of it himself.

She allowed herself to feel that love, for her heart to swell with it as she promised to call her mother the moment she touched down in England. But as she ended the call, clutching the double-chained necklace which she kept interlocked together, she forced herself to face reality.

He had also left her alone without barely a thought and kept her hidden even when he knew he shouldn't. He had pushed her away with cruel words because it was easier than fighting his demons. And he had made her feel just as unwanted as wanted. But, despite the hurt and pain she felt, she knew he had been right.

He couldn't have chosen her any more than Catherine could have chosen Hātem, but she couldn't help but feel that there was a sense of wrongness about repeating the same decisions that had been made by their ancestors.

She glanced at the departures board, frowning when she noticed that there was a delay sign against her flight that hadn't been there two minutes ago. Everything in her wanted to go home, but she couldn't shake the feeling that her home was no longer in England.

Perhaps the desert sand had got into her blood somehow. She shook off the curious notion as she noticed a few heads turn towards the entrance of the airport. There was a rise and fall in murmurs, like the dip and swell of the sea and, while she tried to ignore it, more and more heads were turning and she began to hear audible gasps.

A group turned into a crowd and nearly forty people were now gathered near the entrance, all focusing on one point and then parting like the waves to make way for…for…

Oh, my…

The first thing she saw was Khalif, his eyes blazing with purpose and something she dared not name. Then she saw the horse. Mavia, she recognised, decked out in a saddle that had more gold and jewels on it than Star had thought possible. What on earth was he doing here on a horse?

The gold brocade *bisht* over his *thawb* was immaculate, and the *keffiyeh* around his head picked out the same gold tones, making him impossibly regal and almost too handsome for her to look at. Star focused on as many details as possible, trying to ignore the burst of hope that swelled in her heart.

Mavia lifted her head as if to say hello and Star soon found herself within metres of the incredible animal and her rider. The crowd who had at first held up their phones to capture a picture of their Prince, soon began to lower them one by one, some being nudged by a neighbour, others of their own volition, and Star could have sworn that she'd seen Amin somewhere in the midst of it.

Khalif swung ever so gracefully from Mavia and took

two steps towards her before dropping to his knee, much to the gasped delight of the crowd.

'Kha—' Star clamped her mouth shut, took a moment and tried again. 'Your Highness,' she said—clearly unable to ignore the royal on bended knee right in front of her.

Once again, she felt the familiar search of his eyes across her face, her body, as if trying to take her in all at once and it not being enough. At least that was what she felt she was doing to him. Searching, hoping…waiting.

'Miss Soames,' Khalif said, loudly enough for the entire crowd to hear, 'I stepped down, trying not to look at you, as if you were a Star, yet I saw you, like a Star, without even looking.'

The words were poetic and lovely, but familiar and— She frowned. Wait, was that *Anna Karenina*? If not in full, then near enough. She opened her mouth to ask, but he pressed on.

'Because whatever our souls are made of, yours and mine are the same…' he insisted with a smile, as if confident she would recognise that as Brontë. 'Because I assure you, I was asleep, until I fell in love.'

Star couldn't stop the roll of her eyes. 'I refuse to believe that you read *War and Peace* in the last twenty-four hours, Khalif,' she chided.

'It might have been the crib notes version, but still… A very clever romance novel once said that "It is better to love wisely, no doubt: but to love foolishly is better than not to be able to love at all."'

'Thackeray,' she whispered, the goosebumps spreading from her toes to her shoulders.

'"In vain I have struggled. It will not do. My feelings will *not* be repressed. You must allow me to tell you how ardently I admire and love you."'

She couldn't smile—not yet. In spite of all the hope and all the love she felt in that moment, she needed more. '*Pride and Prejudice*? Really? Is that how you come to me? With the words of others on your tongue?' she demanded.

'No,' he replied, with no hurt or censure in his eyes, as if he'd expected her to challenge him. 'That was just to get your attention.'

'And you didn't think the horse would be enough?' she teased.

The crowds laughed a little, reminding her that they had an audience.

'Do you want to go somewhere a little more private?' she whispered to him.

'I am right where I need to be, Star Soames,' he said, his voice loud, confident and carrying, causing tears to gather in her eyes. 'And no. The horse was not enough,' Khalif said, as if all joking was done and now he wanted her to know the sincerity of his words. Of his love.

'I'm not completely sure that there will ever be enough ways for me to tell you how much I love you and why. But I'm going to try. You exploded into my life, dragging me by the arm and leading me to places I never expected.'

She blushed at the memory of how she had first encountered the Prince of Duratra, not having a single clue that he had been anything other than another tourist.

'You put your trust and faith in me from the first, though I had not earned such a gift. You experienced, in the harshest of ways, the constraints of royal life and bore them without question, without argument or censure. You taught me things I didn't know I still needed to learn and helped me to rediscover the things I knew but had forgotten. And in return I made you doubt your dreams. I will not forgive myself for that. I made you feel unwanted, and I promise never to let you feel that again. I made you feel shame by hiding you away, but *I* was the one who should have felt shame for my actions. So now I vow to you, before the people of my country, that I will spend every day for the rest of my life being worthy of you—even if you choose not to do me the honour of becoming my wife.'

Star looked down at him, bent at the knee on the floor of the airport, and still the most amazing thing she'd ever seen.

'What do you say?' he asked, and the flash of uncertainty nearly broke her heart.

'Well, I'm tempted to say that you should never ask someone to marry you in the negative, but that's only really because you asked me to challenge you.'

A gasp of consternation that sounded very much like Amin caused Khalif to smile. He smiled because it was exactly how he'd hoped Star would reply, loving that she still surprised him and kept him pushing for more, for better. Her smile was a little wobbly, but her eyes were bright, clear and full of love he felt to his very soul.

'Surely,' she said, her voice carrying without effort, 'my faith in my dreams would not have been that strong if it was shaken by one conversation? In as much as my sense of self would have to have been weak if I blamed you for making me feel unwanted or ashamed. And how could that be, when you were the one to show me that I have been looked for all my life, wanted and cared for by my family through centuries? When you were the one who has shown me that reality can be even more romantic and wonderful than fantasy?'

She shook her head as if in wonder that he hadn't,

couldn't see what she saw in him, her love for him. He got to his feet and reached for her, cupping her jaw in his hands, taking what felt like his first breath since the early hours of that morning as she rested her head against his palm.

'Ask me again,' Star whispered, her eyes locked with his, lit with love and a happiness that made his chest burn.

'Will you, Star Soames, be my wife, my love, my partner, my Queen?'

'Yes,' she said as a tear of happiness rolled down her cheek.

'I love you so much,' he whispered so that only she could hear.

'Good,' she replied, with a cheeky smile that made his heart soar. 'Now, please, can you take me home?'

'To England?'

She shook her head and smiled, playing with the strands of the necklace. 'No. To Alhafa…to the desert.'

'As you wish,' he said, his heart full of love and peace.

'*After* we have couriered the necklace to my sisters,' Star said, with light sparkling in her eyes.

'I know just the man to do it… Amin?'

EPILOGUE

Star stood on the balcony of the suite she shared with her husband at Alhafa, gazing out at the view of the desert she would never tire of.

She could hear her husband in the shower, and the scent of eucalyptus oil was heavy on the steam escaping from the bathroom. She inhaled deeply, trying to catch it before it disappeared, loving the scent she always associated with her husband.

She blinked away the jet lag from the time difference between Duratra and the Dordogne, smiling as images from Skye's wedding to Benoit Chalendar filled her mind and heart. Her older sister had looked breathtakingly beautiful, the love she felt for her husband shining so bright it touched each and every guest. Their mother had cried through the entire ceremony, just as she had at Star's wedding, stopping only for a short while to laugh at Summer's daughter Catherine who, despite her mother's intentions, absolutely stole the show. But only for a heartbeat. And none of the sisters would have had it any differently.

The relief following her mother's successful treatment had been both shocking and surprising in its intensity. Khalif had been there and supported her through an aftershock that she had not expected, as all the fear, the hurt and pain she had kept at bay during their search for the jewels had run free only *after* they had accomplished all they had set out to do. Khalif had held her, comforted her, reassured her, soothed her and loved her through it all.

Star absentmindedly smoothed a hand over her stomach as she looked down at the sapphire wedding ring on her fourth finger of her other hand, remembering not only Khalif's proposal but her own magical wedding day six months before.

A smile lit her features and her heart as she thought of how the whole of Duratra had turned out to watch the wedding of Sheikh Khalif and his bride. Celebrations had filled the streets for days and Star had found a welcome and acceptance she could never have imagined. The love that Khalif had shown her in the year since they had first met was something wondrous to her and she thought she'd never have too much of it.

She smiled now as she remembered how protective he had been of her, especially in the first few months of their engagement and marriage. She would never forget the look of shock on Khalif's features as she'd requested Amin as her personal advisor. He had asked her again and again if she was sure, but Star had been determined. Within weeks, Amin and she had become allies and she now considered him one of her most loyal and trusted friends as he guided her through royal etiquette and protocol. And, surprising to almost everyone, she hadn't caused an international incident. *Yet.*

As another wave of tiredness hit, she yawned, despite the excitement thrumming through her veins. They were supposed to be heading into the desert with Nadya, Nayla and Khalif's parents and, although she would absolutely love to go with them, she wasn't sure she was quite up to it.

Star had been there when Khalif had revealed the suite to the twin girls, and been half deafened by their squeals of excitement and squeezed as hard as six-year-old girls could squeeze with their love and thanks. Surprising both their uncle and their grandparents, Nayla had been the first up the tree, while Nadya had had to be bribed away from the bathroom, but both loved their bedroom equally. Hafsa and Bakir's eyes had sparkled with tears of gratitude and love and Khalif had held her hand as if he would never let her go.

She heard the sound of bare feet stepping out onto the balcony and turned to see her husband, her Prince, her King, standing there with nothing but a towel wrapped low around his hips, making her instantly dizzy with desire.

He smirked as if he could read the shockingly intimate, passionate thoughts running through her mind as he walked towards her and pressed a kiss to her forehead.

'I know we're supposed to be going to the oasis, but you look exhausted.'

'Gee, thanks!' She laughed, playfully slapping him against his big broad shoulder, the secret flickering in her chest burning away the tiredness and brightening her with expectation and excitement.

'How are you feeling?' he asked, his hands burning a trail of desire down her back and over her hips. Her pulse picked up and her core throbbed with need, but she pushed that all aside for just a moment.

'Pregnant,' she said, smiling, knowing that Khalif was half distracted and it would take him a moment to—

'Wait, what?'

She looked up at him, a smile wide on her lips, loving the strong connection between them, their gazes locked, hers filled with confidence, his with wonder and disbelief.

'I'm pregnant.'

His hands went to her hips, his fingers gentle against the ever-so-slight bump, but his eyes had not left hers. His gaze searched hers in the same way he'd always done, as if awed and unbelieving that he'd found her, that she had chosen to be his and would always be his.

'I love you,' he whispered against her lips before pulling her to him and kissing her with all the love she could ever want and more. And in all the years to come, all the time they had together, she never felt anything but cherished, wanted and loved.

* * * * *

OFF-LIMITS
TO THE
CROWN PRINCE

KALI ANTHONY

MILLS & BOON

To my beloved editorcat.

Our last book together.

I miss your paws on my keyboard every day.
Nineteen years was not enough.

CHAPTER ONE

HANNAH STOOD IN a shaft of bright sunlight at the rear of her studio. A sickening pulse beat in her chest. The dizzying smell of paint and solvent, usually a reminder of everything she loved, threatened to overpower her. She hurried to the window and threw it wide open onto the rambling tangle of a cottage garden. Gulped in the warm, summer's air.

The hollyhocks were in bloom.

Her mother had loved the hollyhocks best of all the flowers growing here.

'Miss Barrington?' A bodyguard. One of three mountains of men who'd arrived minutes before. Two of whom were now stalking through the place, assessing her home for any risk. The one staying with her frowned, no doubt concerned she might be letting in an assailant to harm their employer, whose arrival was imminent. As if she could organise anything like that with the half-hour's warning of his impending visit her agent had given.

'The smell of paint.' She waved her hand about like she was shooing away any offending scents. 'It might irritate His Highness.'

The man nodded, likely satisfied she was thinking of his employer's comfort. They probably wouldn't care about hers, or that in this moment it was like a hand had grabbed round her throat and squeezed. She took another deep breath. The bodyguard stationed himself at the doorway separating her studio from the rest of the house and crossed his arms as though he were guarding *her*. Did she look as if she were about to run?

Tempting, but there was nowhere else to go.

Her country cottage, the family home. Her safe place and haven was all she had left of her parents. She looked around the bright room she'd made her studio when she'd been old enough to move out on her own. People said she was crazy to come back here, away from the city, to a place tired from nine years of tenants. But people didn't understand. Even though there'd been a fresh lick of paint, no one had covered over the marks on the wall in the laundry where her parents had notched her height over the years. The low-ceilinged kitchen remained unrenovated, a place where they'd sat to eat their meals and laughed. The whole place sang with those memories. The happy and the devastating.

The burn of tears pricked her eyes. Now all this was at risk. Her aunt and uncle had been her guardians. Looked after her inheritance when her parents had died. Taken in the broken teenager she'd become. Sure, they'd been distant rather than cruel, never having wanted children of their own and not knowing how to deal with her. But she'd trusted them, and her uncle's betrayal still cut deep and jagged. An investment she hadn't wanted gone terribly wrong. Almost everything, lost. Her father would be trying to claw his way out of the grave over the way his brother had behaved towards his only niece.

Everything seemed tenuous in this moment. Nothing else had broken her. Not her parents' death in the accident, not the loss of her horse and everything she loved. She'd clambered out of the well of grief on her own. Sure, her fingertips might have been bloody, nails torn, the scars carved into the soul of her waiting to open at any given moment. But to have to sell this, the little farm where she'd lived some of the best days of her life? That would crack her open and no king's horses or men would ever be able to put those pieces back together again.

Perspiration pricked at the back of her head, a droplet sliding beyond the neck of her shirt, itching her skin. She moved closer to the window. Fished a hair tie from her jeans pocket, scraped her hair back and tied it up in a rough topknot.

The bodyguard looked down at her. Crossed his arms. 'You seem nervous.'

How could she tell him that his employer's past and her own were inextricably bound? That his employer was the last person she wanted to see, because he was a reminder of the worst day of her life? Of teenage dreams destroyed?

'I've never met a prince before.' It wasn't *exactly* a lie. 'And I haven't had time to tidy up.'

The bodyguard's gaze roved over her in a disapproving kind of way. She looked down at her hands. Nails short and blunt. Cuticles ingrained with paint. She grabbed an old rag and wet it with solvent, rubbing at her fingers in a vain effort to clean them. Perfect princes probably wouldn't admire commoners with filthy hands. Not that she was seeking admiration, but still. She supposed she had to keep up some kind of an appearance. After a short effort she dropped the now dirty rag on the tabletop and sniffed at her fingers, which smelled like pine.

She held them up. 'Better?'

The bodyguard grunted.

Hannah checked her phone. Still some time. She picked out a slender paintbrush and stood back from her easel. Her art usually calmed her, a way to lose herself in colour and light. Nothing could touch her when she was in the flow of a portrait. She tried to loosen the death grip of her fingers. Dipped her brush into some paint. A swipe of Tasman blue, a touch of titanium white. She frowned. The eyes in this portrait gave her trouble. Too much sadness, not enough twinkle. She reached out her brush to add a dash of colour near the pupil, trying to ignore the tremor in her hand.

The cheery tinkle of a doorbell rang through the room. Hannah's paintbrush slipped from her fingers and clattered to the floor, leaving smudges of blue paint on the old boards.

The burn of bile rose to her throat. He was early. She left the portrait and wiped her damp palms on her jeans.

'Remember to curtsey,' the bodyguard said.

The teeth of anger bit her then, at this man's disdain when she was the one being imposed upon today. She'd said no to this commission when it had first been proposed months ago, before she had had any idea how bad her finances were. His employer had ignored her refusal. It was just like saying no to her uncle when presented with a speculative investment. He'd ignored her too. She gritted her teeth, hating that these people hadn't listened to her, as if her opinion were meaningless. But even though things were bad it didn't mean she had to grin and bear it.

Hannah stalked up to the man guarding the doorway and glared. He towered over her but she didn't care. She wasn't going to be pushed around, by anyone. Looming bodyguard *or* prince.

'I do have a concept of manners. And I understand how to behave around royalty.'

The man didn't move, but his eyes widened a fraction as if in surprise. Good.

A murmur of voices drifted down the hall. The tap of fine leather on floorboards grew louder. She backed further into the room, tried to swallow the knot rising in her throat but her mouth was dry.

A shadow appeared in the hall behind more security.

Grew and grew till it took human shape, striding through the doorway.

'His Royal Highness, Crown Prince of Lasserno,' the bodyguard announced.

Alessio Arcuri.

More beautiful than she'd remembered, though the recollection was coloured by her youth at the time. Then, she'd only caught thrilling glimpses of the handsome, fairy-tale prince, a rider on the showjumping circuit. The young man her teenage heart had crushed over with a terrifying ferocity. Now, she could fully appreciate the height and breadth of him. His severe yet tantalising and lush mouth. The perfection of his aquiline nose. The caramel of his sun-bronzed skin. The shock of his thick, dark hair. She could pretend her admiration was one of an artist surveying his commanding masculine shape. But who was she kidding? This was a distinctly female attraction to a male in his absolute prime.

After nine years, she still felt like that giddy teenager.

It made her prickly all over. Too big for her skin. She wanted to shed parts of herself like a husk, and come out more sparkling, more polished. Just *more*. Because she didn't need a mirror to realise she looked like some ruffian and he looked as if he'd walked straight from a red carpet.

She resented his perfection, when his snap visit with little warning meant she'd had no time to tidy her own appearance. His exquisitely cut suit in the deepest of navy, a pristine white shirt. Red and blue tie in the finest of glowing silk. She was sure she stared before remembering her manners, dipping into a curtsey. 'Your Highness.'

'Signorina Barrington.' He canted his head in a way that suggested she was *adequate*, then motioned to the man standing behind him. 'This is my private secretary, Stefano Moretti. He's been communicating with your agent.'

The other man was almost as perfectly attired and presented as his employer. Attractive, but without the indefinable presence of the Prince. She nodded to him. He smiled back.

'Welcome to my home and studio. It's a surprise and I'm underprepared. I didn't expect royalty to drop by today. Would you like a tea?' She motioned to a battered table in the corner of her studio, the ancient electric kettle, some chipped cups.

Alessio looked to where she'd indicated, gaze sliding over the table as though viewing a sad still life. No one came here—this was her private space—so there was no one to bother about damaged crockery. Personal sittings took place in her public studio on the outskirts of London. The one she'd only recently given up, her uncle's actions meaning it was an extravagance she couldn't afford. Yet seeing the room with Alessio in it reminded her how tattered and worn it seemed. She'd never worried before. This was her home. But all it took was a perfectly pressed prince to bring into screamingly sharp relief how threadbare her life had become.

'Tea? No. I was in the area purchasing some horses, and, since you've been ignoring my secretary's requests...' His voice had the musical lilt of Italian spoken in a glorious baritone. Honeyed tones she could listen to for hours. The voice of a leader that would echo on castle walls. One whose dictates would invariably be followed by most.

Not by her. She wasn't this prince's subject.

'I haven't been ignoring them. My answer was clear.'

He hesitated for a second, cocked his head as if he were thinking. She had the curious sensation of being a specimen under glass.

'Have we met before?'

The high slash of his cheekbones, the strong brows. The sharply etched curve of his tempting lips. Eyes of burnt umber framed by the elegant curl of lamp black lashes.

Hannah had never formally met him, but she'd never forgotten him from the showjumping circuit. Alessio Arcuri was the kind of man to leave you breathless. The fearlessness as he rode. The sheer arrogance that he would make every jump successfully. And he did. Horse and rider the embodiment of perfection.

It was why she and her friend had been chattering away in the back of the car on that terrible day. Gossiping about why he'd retired from competition at the age of twenty-two, much to their teenage devastation. Now, it seemed so young. Back then, he'd been the epitome of an adult and everything a clueless sixteen-year-old craved to be. How he appeared to know, in a way that was absolute, his place in the world. The utter confidence of him, when Hannah was still trying to find her bearings. Then she dropped out of riding too, the deaths of her parents and her horse too much to bear. And she'd tried not to think about Prince Alessio Arcuri since.

At least, until her agent's call a little over half an hour ago, when all the memories she'd bottled up had come flooding back.

'No. We haven't met.' Not exactly. He'd been handing out the first prize at a showjumping event she'd competed in after his retirement had been announced. Her friend had won that day, Hannah a close second. Unusual for her but Beau had been off, as if her horse were foreshadowing the devastating events of only hours later. She'd been so envious of that first-prize ribbon. How she'd coveted the handshake Alessio had given to her friend. Craved for him to acknowledge her. Then their eyes had met. Held. And for one perfect, blinding second her world had stopped turning.

After what had come later in the afternoon, those desires seemed childish. It had taken another terrible moment on that day for the world to stop turning a second time. It hadn't restarted.

His being here brought back too many memories of a split second when all her innocence and faith in the good of the world had ended. Riding passenger in the car driven by her friend's parents. Rounding a corner, littered debris...the...carnage. Car and horsebox destroyed. Everything she'd loved, gone. A freak accident. A tractor in the wrong place on a narrow country road. Hannah flinched. Shut her eyes tight against the horrible vision running like a stuttering film reel in her head.

'Are you all right, Signorina Barrington?'

She opened her eyes again. Nodded. Breathed. Stitched up the pain in her heart where it would stay for ever. Hannah didn't want to go back to that time, and if Alessio truly remembered he might start asking questions. She couldn't deal with them, not now.

Alessio looked at his bodyguards, standing as a brooding presence in the corner. Said something in rapid Italian and they bowed and left the room. The atmosphere relaxed a fraction.

'I'm here to discuss you painting my portrait.'

Hannah clasped her hands behind her back. 'As my agent would have told you, I have a number of commissions...'

Alessio stepped towards her and she was forced to look up because, whilst she wasn't tiny, he dwarfed her. He was even more astonishing up close. Nothing marred his features. It was as if no part of the man would deign to be anything less than polished and perfect. He held her transfixed with those velvety brown eyes of his. Till looking at him any more left her head spinning.

He must have taken her silence as reticence.

'Your fee. I'll double it. And I'm a prince, so...'

She stepped back. It was either that or lean into him and

all his solidity in a moment when she felt a little broken. 'I know what you are.'

What was she doing? Crucifying herself, that was what. She needed this commission, but she couldn't help herself. She'd made a promise when she first started painting, that she'd only take the jobs she wanted. Trying to establish a connection with your subject could prove taxing some days. In the early stages after her parents died she'd drawn them incessantly, terrified that the memory of how they looked would fade. Day and night she sketched, to perfect them so she could never forget. It had exhausted her, the obsession. Made her ill. Sometimes it still did when she became engrossed with a commission. It was why she chose so carefully.

Alessio Arcuri would never be a careful choice. Any connection with him could break her.

'Then I promise if you paint my portrait I'll ensure everyone knows who *you* are. So far those you've painted have been…inconsequential.'

Portraiture had never been about accolades, but about preserving memories. The minutiae, the nuance of a person. Sure, she was paid well for what she did, but it was *never* about simply being paid. It was about ensuring people weren't forgotten.

She looked at the portrait of the older woman currently on her easel. A believer in justice, lover of barley sugar and Yorkshire tea. 'I wouldn't say a judge is *nobody*. The law's important, as is doing the right thing. But I mostly like painting pictures of people the world overlooks. They deserve their moment to be seen, to be remembered. You're seen all the time.'

Alessio shrugged. That movement seemed out of place on a man who appeared only to move when absolutely necessary. 'Is anyone truly seen? The press often tries to paint pictures of me and they're rarely right.'

'What picture do they try to paint?' The cool command? The lack of emotion? She could imagine they'd claim he was more automaton than real and relish finding the tiniest chink in his gleaming armour to take him down.

Alessio raised an eyebrow. 'You haven't looked me up on the internet? I thought you were renowned for knowing your subjects.'

'You're not my subject so I haven't needed to know you.'

'The judge.' He inspected the painting, eyes narrowing as he stared at the woman on the canvas. 'That portrait tells stories. I want you to tell mine. You're the best. No one could see me like you could.'

Part of her wanted to mine the essence of him, because people fascinated her. But doing so had a cost and she wasn't sure she was prepared to pay it when Alessio reminded her of everything she'd lost.

'"The best" is subjective. I have terms for everyone I paint. My agent tells me you refused mine.'

Sue had been clear. You didn't say *no* to a prince. Hannah had to keep her options open… She knew what those ominous words meant. Once her uncle's duplicity had been discovered, this meeting with the Prince had become necessary. Resented, but necessary none the less.

'I'm here now,' Alessio said. The hard, uncompromising set of his jaw told her he might register what she said but he wasn't really listening.

She turned her back on him and walked to a paint-splattered desk on which her palette and scattered half-used tubes of oil paint were strewn in the haphazard way of this whole room. She opened a drawer and pulled out a few papers, then walked back to where he stood and thrust them in his direction. He took them from her paint-ingrained fingers. Flicked through.

'Am I a cat or dog person?' His eyebrows rose in disbelief. 'What is this?'

She took time with her subjects. The questionnaire was one small part. There were personal sittings, the live sketching. She'd been comfortable with each person she'd painted so far. Had liked them and their quirks in their own way. But Alessio Arcuri? She wasn't sure she could. A person's eccentricities, no matter how small, gave them personality. How could she do justice to this man, who didn't seem to have a quirk about him? He dazzled like a flawless gemstone.

'Those questions are the reason I'm so good at what I do. I get to know my subjects. Intimately.'

At the last word his eyes widened a fraction. Surely he wouldn't think… Heat rushed to her cheeks. The corner of his mouth kicked up a minute fraction. The moment counted in milliseconds and then it was gone, before his attention returned to the paper in his hands. But even those seconds had her heart racing in an attempted getaway.

'"*What is your best childhood memory?*" "*Your worst?*"' A frown marred his forehead. He thrust the pages back at her. 'No. If the press got hold of this—'

'They won't.' She ignored his outstretched arm. 'I read it, then destroy it. I also sign non-disclosure agreements for those who want them. No information has *ever* reached any press outlet from me. You could take some time and fill out my questions right here.'

He seemed to stand even taller now, imposing like the prince he was. She could even imagine the gleaming crown on his head.

'All these people you paint. The press has no interest in them. Me? I'm royalty. You know how tabloids clamour for stories. I give them none. But this?' He waved his hands over the offending document as if he were trying to bat away some pestilential bug set on biting him. 'I don't answer twenty questions, for anyone.'

'There are eighteen questions. But the number isn't important. You can *tell* me the answers.'

He dropped the papers on the table next to him. 'You're a stranger.'

And that was the way it would stay for ever, even though there was something about this tussle Hannah began to enjoy. A tiny thrill that his interest still held, no matter how she pushed. It told her he *really* wanted her to paint him, stroking an ego she didn't realise needed attention. What would her sixteen-year-old self think now?

That young girl would think all her dreams had come true.

'Here's the thing. Doing this allows me to paint at my best. The type of picture you seem to desire, seeing as you're still standing in my studio. You want me to paint your portrait, then…double my fee and answer my questions.' She rose up, stiffening her spine to match him. If he was playing the prince card then she'd pull a queen on him, because this studio was *her* domain and she ruled here exclusively. 'You can take it or leave it.'

Alessio hadn't expected a warm welcome, but he'd expected something more polite than this. Certainly, she'd curtseyed as expected. A seemingly respectful bow of the head when he was sure none was meant, because her eyes had flashed a kind of warning, the whole of her bristling like some disapproving hedgehog. Cute, but all spike and prickle. Right now, she stood framed by the light from the windows behind her. Dark hair mussed in an unruly top-knot. Dressed in a blue and white striped men's shirt with a frayed collar, cuffs pushed back on her forearms, smeared and smudged with paint. Loose, ripped jeans. Trainers as paint-spattered as the rest of her.

Dishevelled and all the more enticing for it.

'I tend not to accede to ultimatums,' he said. Though

he admired hers more than he'd admit. She'd hold her own with some of the best of his courtiers, this woman.

She glared at him, no respect meant there at all, and their eyes truly met. Hers were green, perhaps. Arresting. Their depth and swirls of colour transfixed him. She carried the world in that luminous gaze and something drove him to discover what lay behind it, when discovering anything about her other than whether she was prepared to paint his portrait was impossible. He pushed the interest aside.

Ruthlessly.

'I tend not to *give* ultimatums.' Her voice was deeper than he'd expected. Almost…aristocratic in its tone. It feathered his spine the way a stroke of her paint-ingrained fingers might. And in these moments he couldn't avoid the pressing sense of déjà vu, as if he was missing something. Everything about her seemed…strangely familiar.

She claimed not to know him but was as skittish as a colt in spring when he'd first mentioned it. Perhaps it had something to do with his security detail. They tended to suck the air out of the place with their professional brand of malevolence, which was why he'd asked them to leave. Stefano stayed, of course. Alessio didn't spend time alone with women he didn't know, not any more. There would be no ugly rumours. Everyone who surrounded him was carefully vetted and explicitly trusted. He'd learned lessons about putting faith in the wrong person. His father might have courted the press with his outrageous behaviour but Alessio gave them nothing.

'We seem to be at a stalemate,' he said.

She cocked her head. Raised her eyebrows. 'Yet you're *still* here.'

Perhaps there was an answer which could accommodate everybody. His life had been spent trying to find solutions to every problem, mostly regarding his father.

He'd become an expert at it, spending his hours working to silence hints at his father's worst excesses, the rumours about the missing gems from the crown jewels. As for Hannah Barrington—when he'd asked Stefano to find the best portrait artist in the world he hadn't expected it to be a reclusive young woman of twenty-five, whose paintings looked as if they contained the experience and insight of a life long-lived. On viewing her portfolio of work, he knew he'd found the person for his portrait.

He turned to his secretary. As he did so, Hannah seemed to start towards him, then checked herself. Interesting. Did she think he was about to leave? Perhaps she wanted this commission more than she was prepared to admit? If so, everyone had their price. And he was prepared to pay a high price for her. Hannah Barrington was the best, and he'd have nothing less. *'Start as you mean to finish,'* his English nanny had used to say, teaching him her language as a young boy and what it meant to be leader of his principality. Better a foreigner who knew the value of royalty and duty, than his father, who valued none of those things. The lessons Alessio had learned at his knee were all about excess, indulgence and infidelity. Not the qualities of the leader Alessio wished to aspire to be.

Stefano raised an eyebrow as Alessio approached looking far too entertained at developments. His friend, partner in crime in the years gone by and now private secretary remained his most trusted confidant.

'It gives me great satisfaction that there's one woman in the world who's immune to your charms,' Stefano said in their native Italian, presumably so Signorina Barrington couldn't understand. 'Although you're not being charming today.'

Whilst he knew it was rude, Alessio didn't switch to English, and wouldn't until he had his solution. 'I need to know the state of my diary. I've *no* need to charm anyone.'

He'd set aside that reputation years ago. Alessio would admit in his youth he had relished in the position his birth gave him. He wasn't proud of those things now, especially the string of women who had cemented his playboy reputation. *Like father, like son*, the press used to say. A creep of disgust curled inside him. Not now. An advantageous marriage to a perfect princess was next on his agenda. To give Lasserno the stability it had lacked since his mother's death. Some heirs to continue his line. The royalty in Lasserno would soon be feted in its perfection, not mocked for its all too human failings. That was his mission, and he would succeed.

Stefano pulled up Alessio's diary, showed it to him. Busy, but not impossible.

'Your problem is that you don't like people saying "no" to you,' Stefano murmured. In English this time.

How many times had he tried to stop his father? Curb his behaviour? It was what he'd ostensibly been brought home to do, ripped out of his life showjumping and studying in the UK when his mother had fallen ill, because at least when she was well she'd formed some sort of brake on his father's worst excesses. And yet when he'd brought up ideas to reinvigorate the economy and tourism in a country whose beauty and natural riches were equal to anywhere in their close neighbour, Italy, he'd been met with disparaging refusal. No answers as to why his ideas wouldn't work. Nothing at all.

Stefano was correct. Alessio didn't like being told *no* on things he was right about. Not without a sensible reason. Since his father's abdication he'd not heard that cursed word from one of his government or advisors. It was… gratifying in a way he could never have imagined. A vindication of all he'd been trying to achieve over the years.

Alessio turned his attention to Hannah. Checked his

watch. 'I will not write answers to your questionnaire, but I do have some limited time in my schedule.'

Time he could control. Leaking of information he couldn't.

A slight frown creased her brow and he wasn't sure whether the disapproval was back, or whether something else was at play.

'Then I can't—'

'My calendar is free of more onerous engagements. You wish to know me to paint my portrait? You'll travel to Lasserno. Become my official artist for two weeks. Follow me and learn about me. It should be enough.'

He could almost *sense* the weight of Stefano's incredulous stare but he didn't much care what his best friend thought at this moment. The woman in front of him had his complete focus. The plump, perfect peach colour of her mouth. The rockpool-green of her eyes. Eyes which stared deep inside as if they saw the heart of him. Eyes a man could drown in and die happy if he allowed himself, which Alessio could never do. It was no matter. He was used to compartmentalising that side of himself. There would be *no* rumours of improper behaviour on his part. His life was one of supreme control, Lasserno his only mistress.

She planted her paint-stained hands on her hips. 'Now, look. That's—'

'Not your process. I'm aware. This will be better.'

He could get anyone else to paint him. Most people would climb over themselves to take the commission and the accolades it would afford. In coming to his decision he'd been shown the work of many artists who were all superb and could acquit themselves admirably. The minute he saw Hannah Barrington's work, he knew. It was her he must have. No one else would do. And yet here she stood, utterly uncompromising. As if she were still intent on *refusing* him. The challenge of it set his pulse beating hard. He'd not felt anything like it since the last time he'd taken his stallion, Apollo, over the high fence behind the vineyards on the castle grounds.

'I have other clients.' Whilst her hands were still firmly on her hips, her teeth worried furiously at her bottom lip.

'You have an agent. She can tell clients you're painting a portrait of a prince. They'll understand, because my patronage will increase the value of their own pictures. I promise, this commission will be the *making* of you.'

'It's *two weeks* away from my home. You're not the only busy person in the room.' All the glorious fire in her, such a contrast to the cool mint of her eyes. For a moment he wished he were an ordinary man who could explore these ordinary desires, but that was a folly he would not indulge in.

This portrait, the *perfect* portrait, would show the world exactly how he meant to carry on his role as a leader. It would be the best. *He* would be the best prince Lasserno had seen in its long and proud history. He would write over his father's legacy, scratching it out in a neat and perfect script till it disappeared and was forgotten.

Hannah was the first piece in a larger puzzle. Time to sweeten the deal. To make it irresistible.

'I'll offer you *five* times your normal fee for the inconvenience.'

Her nostrils flared, and her eyes sparked at the mention of increasing her fee. Avarice was something he understood, a common currency, and he was happy to fuel it so long as it was legal and he got his way in the end. His former girlfriend, Allegra, was a perfect study in how money won over loyalty. Luckily he had more than the reporter had offered for a story on how his father had been picking gems from the crown jewels and giving them away as favours. Replacing them with paste. He'd never forgotten the lessons learned in that episode about unburdening yourself to the wrong person.

Hannah opened her mouth to speak. Alessio held up his hand, because there was more.

'*But* you accompany me as official palace artist in residence. You won't receive a better offer from any other client,' he said with a smile which felt like victory. 'Take it…or leave it.'

CHAPTER TWO

HANNAH SQUIRMED, TRYING to get comfortable in the chair on which she'd been directed to sit by Alessio's secretary. Who'd have thought something so ornate, with all its carved wood and brocade upholstery, could be so hard and uncompromising? A bit like its owner, and maybe that was the point. Being left like this to await *His Highness* held all the appeal of that one time she'd been sent to the headmaster at her austere boarding school for *'having your head in the clouds rather than in reality, Miss Barrington'*. No sympathy for the plight of a teenager who'd been ripped from everything she knew and loved.

She'd received a detention that day for telling him that reality sucked. After losing her parents, her imagination was a safer place to reside. Drawing obsessively. Trying to remember every line of their faces as the memories faded. The love she saw when they'd looked at her, rather than the feigned interest of her uncle and aunt.

She shut those thoughts down. They had no place here.

Hannah stared at the looming oak doors of what she'd been told was the Prince's office. Everything seemed to loom in an ominous way here, in this imposing castle which rose from a landscape of olive groves and vineyards in turreted glory. Hannah worried at a tiny thread which dared to loosen itself from the chair's rich brocade. Her imagination didn't seem safe now, with Hannah spending far too much time dreading the shape of the next fortnight. Alessio was a reminder of that day, of all she'd lost. She took a deep breath, chased away old memories of her time before the accident when her reality had allowed her to dream of princes who set her heart fluttering complicated rhythms. Of a time when her parents had said she could have anything she wanted if she dared to dream, such as one day riding for her country as Alessio did. Thoughts of a time *before* had started nipping her heels with her arrival in Lasserno polished, primped and plucked. Sue had taken to Prince Arcuri's invitation with an unhealthy enthusiasm, seeing it as her only chance to turn Hannah into something she was not—a woman of the world.

Hannah looked down at her hands. They were almost as unrecognisable as the rest of her with manicured nails, moisturised cuticles and not a stain of paint to be seen. Her hair had been stylishly trimmed, and brows sculpted to perfection. At home in England Hannah never needed much. No fancy dresses or make-up. Simple food on the table. She didn't go out. Her life was paint and canvas, palette and brush. Her art was her work and her work was her life, but Alessio's commission dictated there were some things she required.

New clothes to suit the list of occasions he'd sent were packed in a large suitcase. Well, not exactly new. Her uncle's duplicity meant haunting charity shops, but with a bit of inventive tailoring she'd come up with a wardrobe that would satisfy the eyewatering requirements of His Royal Highness, the proverbial pain in her backside. But, standing in front of a mirror this morning in her jeans and boots, tailored navy jacket with crisp white blouse, she'd been unrecognisable. Hannah didn't know who the person was, staring back at her. She wasn't sure she liked it.

One of the oak doors glided open. Her stomach twisted into sharp, complicated knots as Stefano stepped into the hall. She'd come to know him a little over the past week when she'd been getting everything in order to come here. His missives had been polite, his manner on the phone efficient, sympathetic and kind, but she'd been able to glean nothing about his employer from him. All she'd discovered had been found online.

That the press believed the man's austere demeanour hid greater sins.

'His Highness will see you now.'

She walked through the open door and it thudded shut behind her. She took a few steps over the plush crimson carpet then stopped, overwhelmed by the sheer scale of the room.

Magnificent frescoes covered the ceiling. Adorning the walls were paintings of what must have been former rulers. Uniformed and striking a pose, warriors on horseback with swords drawn, all staring down in their own princely kind of way from their vast gilded frames. But more magnificent than anything else in the opulent space was a man lit up in a shaft of sunlight like a god. Standing behind an expansive antique desk, he outshone any of his forebears, more regal than all of them put together in his dark suit and ultramarine tie.

She almost forgot herself as she stared, Alessio's black hair gleaming, his intense eyes hooded and assessing, the slash of one aristocratic eyebrow raised quizzically. What were all those rules she had to remember again? Sensible thought had fled. Before she made a total fool of herself, she gave a hasty curtsey because it seemed the thing to do, then hurried towards the desk. He made some dismissive waving kind of motion which she took to mean, *Have a seat*, and sank into the armchair opposite. Just in time, because her legs seemed like overcooked noodles in their inability to hold her up. The corner of his mouth threatened an almost smile, and her heart skipped a few beats, its rhythm constantly out of synch in his presence.

'You had a good flight?'

'The royal jet was an extravagance.' With all its buttery leather and plush carpets. She'd been treated like a princess by the efficient flight crew. 'I could have flown commercial.'

'Think of it as a reward for uprooting your life over the next fortnight. I trust your other clients weren't too disappointed about your upcoming absence.'

She noticed it wasn't spoken as a question.

Positively enthusiastic had been the general response. The Prince had been irritatingly right. They all saw the value of their own portraits increasing because she'd agreed to take on the commission. She'd been surprised they hadn't met her at the airport and thrown streamers in a grand farewell as she boarded the aircraft. She shook her head, which earned her another tilt of his mouth in what she suspected was Alessio's version of a smile. Her silly little heart tripped over itself at how the tiny move softened every harsh feature on his face to something more. More handsome, more vital, more…human.

But this man wasn't human, he was a prince. Unattainable. Untouchable. As a young girl she dreamed of princes, but dreams didn't make reality. She could never forget it.

He sat in the leather chair at his desk. Even that move was perfectly executed. 'I thought we would have a brief discussion about expectations whilst you're here.'

'You mean, in addition to the indexed folder I was given on the plane?' There seemed to be so many dizzying rules and requirements, how to address staff, what to wear. An agenda for almost every minute of the day. It was no wonder the man in front of her looked so serious. There didn't seem to be a moment when he sat still, apart from when he was asleep, because the time he 'retired' had been scheduled in as well. When was there ever space to simply *be*? Sit on a comfortable couch, with a warm drink in hand, and stare out of a window at a view. Imagine…a different life.

She looked at him, sitting straight and perfect and still. Not a hair out of place. Not a wrinkle in his shirt. As if he were carved out of painted stone. It seemed he was more statue than flesh and blood.

How exhausting.

'At all times, your behaviour reflects on me. I ask you to recognise that and adjust your manner accordingly.'

She sat up a little straighter in her seat, the heat flaming in her cheeks. A slice of something hot and potent cutting through her. 'I might not be aristocracy but I wasn't brought up in a shoebox. I know how to behave in civilised society.'

He cocked his head. Those umber eyes of his fixed on her with an almost otherworldly intensity. 'How gratifying to hear. When we're in public together, you'll walk behind me. The only woman who will ever walk at my side is my princess.'

'So where is this princess now? Do I get to meet her too?'

'There is no princess yet.'

'Shame. I thought she might be able to give me some tips. Juicy gossip even.'

The perfect Prince's eyes narrowed. His lips tightened.

'There is no *juicy gossip*. My life is my country. My country is my life. That is all you need to know.' His voice was ice. The cold blast of a winter gale. A tremor shuddered through her at the chill of his tone. She almost believed there was nothing more to him than this and didn't know why that thought left an ache deep inside, because it struck her as sad.

'Duly noted,' she said. Her answer seemed to mollify him. He gave a curt nod in reply.

'When we are in public you will refer to me as Your Highness or Sir.'

'I've read the rulebook, though there was one thing it didn't address.' She leaned back into the soft upholstery of the armchair and tried to relax, though nothing about the man sitting opposite encouraged her to do so. 'What about when we're in private?'

'There will be no *"in private".*'

Hannah looked about the vast room, through the windows that gave a view of rolling hills and olive groves beyond. Pencil pines spearing upwards from a garden like dark green sentinels. 'We're alone now.'

'*Stefano.*'

'*Sì?*'

Hannah whipped round. Stefano stood just inside the closed doors of the room. He gave her a wry smile. She turned back to Alessio. Crossed her legs. Clasped her hands over her knee. He followed her every move, almost as if he were cataloguing her.

'Where were you hiding the poor man—in a cupboard?'

'There is a chair, in an alcove, inside the door. However, where Stefano sits is immaterial. What is material is that we will not be alone.'

'Then how am I meant to begin the process of painting your portrait?'

'I would have thought it quite easy. Brush, canvas.'

She shook her head. 'I can't work with strangers… loitering about. Portrait painting is a contract between two people. The artist and the subject. Of its nature it's… intimate. I—'

'So you have said before. You don't get to dictate terms, Signorina Barrington.'

No. There was a way she worked and, although she tried to be a little flexible, the way he spoke to her rankled. She clenched her hands a bit harder round her knees.

'It's a wonder you don't pick up a brush and paint yourself... *Your Highness.*'

Everything about him seemed impassive, inscrutable. Having barely any expression, his face was marked only by a cool, regal kind of presence. She could get the measure of most people, but never the measure of him. Even as a far younger man, there'd been nothing on his face to tell what he might be thinking. Like a blank canvas waiting for the first, defining brushstroke.

'If I could, I would.' Alessio sat back in his leather chair, which creaked as his weight shifted. Steepled his fingers. 'However, there's a reason I engaged you and that's because you're reputedly the best. I will have *nothing* but the best.'

A vice of tightness crushed her chest. Right now, she wasn't at her best. What her uncle had done had floored her. She had thought she could at least trust her family. Now she was being forced to take this commission due to circumstance, which was not the way she'd ever worked. What would her parents have thought of all this? They believed they'd ensured the security and comfort of their only daughter and she'd let it slip away by being too absorbed in her art and not keeping a close enough eye on things, till it was too late and the money gone. The threat of tears burned the back of her nose. Even after nine years the grief still hovered close. All these things had weighed on her and right now her thoughts were not about colour and light, or the gentle tilt of someone's almost smile, but on survival again.

Though that might suit a painting of this man. The expressionless quality. She could try losing herself in that, a simplicity which meant she didn't need to fight the canvas to find the heart of him. Because there was nothing in his face she could grasp, apart from the impact of his sheer masculine beauty. Like the statue of David. Exquisite, perfect, coldly etched. She doubted he had a warm, beating heart. But in the end to do her best, to paint what critics said she was renowned for, she needed *something* curious for her brushstroke to shape. Some expression to show the person before her was man, not marble. Because sadly she was a portrait artist, not a sculptor.

She stood and walked towards a wall on which one portrait hung, of a man sitting on a golden chair. Old. Imposing.

'I didn't invite you to leave your seat.' Alessio's voice was cool as the blast of air-conditioning on a hot summer's day. She wheeled round. He was still seated himself. Was there something in that dossier she'd been given to read about this? She couldn't remember, though the man probably wasn't used to having anyone turn their back on him. Still, whilst he was a prince, she was a grown woman. She'd accord him the respect required because of the quirk of his birth, but asking for permission to stand?

Ridiculous.

'That's going to make things difficult if I need to ask you for permission whenever I have to do something. Your Highness, may I drink my glass of water? Your Highness, may I use the bathroom? Your Highness, may I apply this charcoal to paper?'

He swivelled his chair to face her, gazing at her with an intriguing intensity, as if she were an olive he was about to skewer in the tines of a martini fork.

'There are rules by which the palace and my country is run. Those rules keep chaos away from the door. In this place, you follow mine.'

'That's not going to work when I'm trying to draw or paint you.'

'We'll see.'

'So let me ask.' She swept her hand across the room, taking in all the ancestors hanging on his walls, staring out at them disapprovingly. 'Given you have an opinion on all things, what do you want your portrait to look like?'

He frowned, making the merest of creases in his perfectly smooth forehead, but she saw it none the less. 'Isn't it your job to decide?'

'How about that one?' She pointed to a man on horseback in a grand uniform braided with gold. There was no emotion on his face at all, nor in the way he watched the room impassively, with dark eyes. All the emotion was contained in the wild eyes of the rearing bay on which he sat, as if it were nothing but a plump little pony and he was going for a quiet afternoon ride. 'He looks suitably warrior-like.'

She could imagine Alessio that way. She'd seen him ride, the fearlessness which made everyone hold their breath. The memory was like a stab at her heart, a constant reminder of everything she'd lost. Because she'd loved flying over jumps too. Encouraging herself and her horse to go hard, be better.

'Since we're not at war, no.'

Relief crashed over her like waves in a storm. Not on horseback, then.

'What about him?' She pointed to another grand portrait. The man on the gilded seat. With distant eyes and a hard mouth. His demeanour stern, looking like a disapproving relative. One hand clasping a gleaming sceptre. The other gripping the arm of the chair on which he sat. A large, bejewelled ring adorning his finger. Not a relaxed pose, even though you couldn't tell from his face. The face told her nothing. 'He's sitting on a throne. Very regal and proper.'

'The throne is…no.'

Alessio stood and walked towards her. His flawless grey suit gripping the masculine angles of his body. Every movement long and fluid. It was clear this was his domain and he was comfortable in it. He moved next to her. Not too close, but any distance was not far enough. He had a presence. Not threatening, but overwhelming, as if everything gravitated towards him. She swallowed, her mouth dry, her heart tripping over itself.

'Then who do you want to be? How do you want to be seen?'

He stared down at her. Like a ruler lording over his subject. Except she'd *never* be that. But still, he radiated such authority she almost wanted to prostrate herself in front of him and beg forgiveness for some minor and imagined infraction.

'I *will* be the greatest prince Lasserno has ever had. That is how I will be seen. Nothing less will do.'

As she looked into his coldly beautiful face, Hannah had no doubts he'd achieve it. Her only problem was, how on earth was she going to paint it?

He should have remained seated. He shouldn't be standing anywhere near her, but he was sucked into Hannah's orbit like a galaxy falling to its doom in a black hole. He still couldn't overcome the niggling sensation that he knew her. That alone should have sounded some kind of warning, but he was too enthralled by the way she fought him to worry about a creeping sense of *déjà vu*. Most people bowed or curtseyed. Pandered to his every whim. She didn't seem inclined to do any of those things. She treated him as if he were nobody at all.

It should annoy him, and there was a thread of cool irritation pricking through his veins, but it tangled with something far hotter and more potent. Especially now. When he had last seen her she had been sweetly dishevelled. All mussed up and messy. Somehow completely unattainable because of it. She had looked as if she had no place in his world since there was nothing messy about his life. Not any more. Not since his mother died and he had had to grow up fast, pulling things together because his father had made enough mess for a hundred men.

Yet Hannah today...

Her hair wasn't some tangle of a bird's nest knotted carelessly on top of her head. It swung past her shoulders in a fall of sleek dark chocolate. Soft layers framed her face. Standing this close, he was captivated by her hypnotic green eyes, a wash of deep gold surrounding her pupils, which made them gleam as mysteriously as a cat's. She wasn't paint-spattered, as if that had been some kind of barrier separating them. Her shoes weren't trainers, but polished black knee-high boots which wrapped round her slim calves. Dark jeans hugged her gentle curves. A crisp white shirt was unbuttoned enough to interest, but too high to give anything but a frustrating hint of her cleavage. Somehow, in this moment she looked more woman and less...waif.

What the hell was he doing? It was as if without the paint she'd been stripped of her armour as his artist and become someone attainable. She could never be that. She couldn't be *anything* to him. He was on a quest for his bride, to join him on the throne. A professional matchmaker was putting a list together at this very moment. And now he'd set down that path, his behaviour must be impeccable. No casual liaisons to report to the press in a tell-all that sought to bring him down to his father's level where Alessio would *never* go.

This woman, whilst beautiful and challenging, was effectively his employee. Someone to be afforded appropriate distance and dutiful respect. Not to be the subject of carnal thoughts about her mysterious eyes, or how luscious and kissable her mouth appeared when smoothed with a little gloss...

He stepped away. She'd travelled many hours to be here,

and yet he'd brought her to his office and not even offered her refreshments. No doubt she'd need her room and a rest. He'd ask Stefano to take her there and he'd work to regain his equilibrium.

She took a step towards him, hands on her hips. Eyes intent. A picture of defiance. Nothing like the behaviour dictated to her by the dossier he'd asked Stefano to put together, which was as much about his protection as hers.

'If I'm going to paint the *greatest* prince Lasserno has ever had, I need to see where I'm going to work.'

'Of course, follow me.' He said the words without thinking, before his brain engaged to remind him the less time spent in her presence the better. But it didn't matter as his feet carried him towards the door of his office with her following behind. Past Stefano, who simply looked at him with a quizzically raised brow that had become all too familiar since Hannah had entered his life, rose, and followed as well. Against all better judgement, Alessio almost stood him down. Told him to get back to whatever he was doing on his phone and he would handle this, but his better judgement won.

Nowadays, it always did.

'Your home is beautiful,' Hannah said in a breathless kind of voice better suited to quiet, candlelit dinners aimed at seduction than a stroll through the palace halls, but this place inspired similar reactions in those who'd never seen it before. There was nothing special about her.

'Thank you.' He supposed it was the polite thing to say, but he always felt more of a custodian than anything else. It was all a workplace to him. 'My ancestors built it as a fortress in the Renaissance. However, they refused to eschew comfort and style over practicality on the inside. It was designed to intimidate those who sought to intrude, and delight those invited in.'

Which is what the tour guides parroted, through the

public areas. He'd learned their script. It was easier that way, because his view of the place was tainted by the memories of a childhood where even as a young boy he had recognised the chilly dysfunction between his parents, which had soon descended into a fully blown cold war. Before his innocence and any belief his father could be a good man had been shattered for ever in the throne room he would only sit in once, to take the crown. Then he would never enter it again.

'What was it like living here? In all of this? Did you ever break anything precious?'

The only precious thing broken here was trust. 'Never broken anything, no. I was the perfect child.'

'Of course you were. Striding the halls with purpose, even as a ten-year-old.'

No, he'd been playing hide-and-seek with Stefano in places he should not be, when he'd sneaked into the forbidden throne room. Seen his father, with a woman bent over the arm of the throne. Alessio's stride faltered. Hannah almost crashed into him but pulled up close. He knew. He could almost feel her enticing warmth. He turned to the window overlooking a garden.

'I thought you might enjoy the view. Stefano's ancestors designed the garden in the formal Italian style. I'm sure he'd like to tell you about it.'

Any more quizzical looks from his best friend and Stefano's brows would end with a permanent home in his hairline. Alessio allowed him to tell the story of the famous garden with its clipped hedges and fountains. He stood back, letting the chatter wash over him. Taking slow breaths. *You will not tell your mother. This is our secret.* Both his father's cold eyes and the glassy ones of the woman had been on him that day. He could barely understand why his father's hands twisted into her hair as if it had to hurt, though the look on her face spoke nothing of pain, even to his young brain. He hadn't known why their clothes were in disarray, or why his father's free hand had seemed to be in places it shouldn't on a woman, or so he'd thought as a child.

All he knew was that what he was seeing was *wrong*. He'd come to realise later what had been going on in the throne room. How his father had been defiling it. Each day he felt tainted by the creeping guilt at keeping his father's dirty secrets, because the man had made him party to more than one young boy should know. It was as if he'd been trying to mould Alessio into his own, dissolute image to spite his mother.

Lost in his own thoughts, Alessio had failed to realise Stefano and Hannah were now silent.

'Enough of gardens?' he asked, trying to sound suitably composed and regal. He hadn't been assailed by that memory for years and couldn't fathom why it would creep out of its dark, muddy hole to ambush him now.

'It's very beautiful and…ordered.'

'That's the way I like it.' His own thoughts right now were a messy jumble of memories that should never have seen daylight again.

'Do you ever walk in it? Take time to, I don't know, smell the flowers?'

'I… There are no flowers.' Where was all this uncertainty coming from? His role and what was required of him was *all* about certainty. He straightened, remembered exactly who he was. 'As for aimless wandering, I don't have time.'

Stefano had stepped back to his position three paces behind, but Hannah stood right next to him. Looking up with her entrancing green eyes. Lips slightly parted as though there was something always on the tip of her tongue to say.

He had no doubt she'd say it.

'Important prince and all, I know. That's something I need to talk to you about. The time you've allowed for me.'

He'd asked Stefano to schedule the barest minimum for formal sittings. She was following him about like a shadow for the next fourteen days. What more did she need?

'I'm a busy man.'

'Places to be. Country to run. I've seen your diary, but I need more. And I'm talking hours, not minutes.'

They neared the door of her rooms and the adjoining parlour which he had thought would be the perfect place for her to work. Like her studio in England. He'd searched the palace for somewhere with the same alignment. A similar light to fill the room, although here the sun streamed in a bit more brightly than in her own studio. There was no rambling garden outside, but the view was pleasant enough, he supposed. He never really looked any more, too occupied with briefings from his government to gaze at the horizon and contemplate the landscape.

'I can find more, if it's what you require. Perhaps you could accompany His Highness on some…unofficial engagements.' Stefano this time. It was as if both were conspiring against him. 'There's a hospital visit, to see children.'

Those visits were *private*, never made for accolades. 'The children aren't some circus where you watch them perform.'

Hannah frowned. 'I'd never treat sick children that way. But I need to see all aspects of you, not just the official ones. That's what will make my portrait the best.'

Before he could protest, she turned to Stefano and smiled. Wide, warm, generous. The type of smile which sent a lick of heat right to his core. One you could bask in. It had no agenda or artifice at all to add a chill to the edges of it. 'Thank you. Any extra time you can find me would help my work.'

Better her smile be for his friend than him. There was no place for it in his ordered, planned life. One where everything was cool and clinical. That was the way he preferred things to be. Like the hedge garden, clipped and precise. Even though he now felt inclined to take to the palace gym and hit a punching bag, hours earlier than his normal training session, rather than speak to the finance minister about fiscal policy and Lasserno's deficit.

The doors of the room where Hannah would live loomed large. 'Stefano will show you where everything is. I'll leave you to him.'

A gracious host would escort his personal guest in, ensure she was settled. That she was happy with everything, so she'd gift him some genuine smiles which chased away the cold. Instead Alessio strode down the corridor away from Stefano and Hannah, protocol and graciousness be damned. The temptation snapped at him like a whip and he never gave in to temptation.

Smiles like Hannah's were dangerous, because they chased away common sense.

CHAPTER THREE

HANNAH STOOD IN what was best described as an expansive parlour, in the suite of her rooms. It was if she had been dropped into a fairy tale, except she didn't feel like a princess, but an impostor.

Everything here was too magnificent to touch. Her canopied bed with its silks and embroidery in the palest cerulean blues. Magnificent tapestries of pastoral scenes with shepherdesses and frolicking lambs adorning the golden walls. The deepest of carpets she stood on and wiggled her toes into, as if she were walking on a cloud. It reminded her of how threadbare her life back in England seemed to have become, because there was never a time here that anything would be hard or cold. In this palace, nothing would deign to be anything other than perfect. As perfect as the man who ruled here.

The man she was now waiting for, because her equipment had been unpacked and set up in this room to catch the best light. She'd only brought the bare necessities to Lasserno, pencils and charcoal so she could study and sketch, learn about the Prince who would be taking up her next few months of waking thought. She'd set up what she needed on a small side table next to a chair, ready for when His Highness deigned to grace her with his lofty presence.

A sickening knot tightened in her stomach. As if she needed to run rather than be faced with a blank canvas, her empty sketchbook. Hannah ground her teeth against the rising queasiness. She usually loved the challenge of getting to know a new subject. Finding the key to a person, the one that unlocked every brushstroke she'd put down in the time it took to perfect the essence of them on a canvas. But a lot was riding on this commission. Her future. Her home. It wasn't that she was afraid of doing a job she knew so well, afraid of the thrill of knowing a person, of finding the man Alessio hid. Not at all. It was what she stood to lose if she couldn't fulfil it.

She checked the time on her phone. For a man who wanted his portrait painted, he really didn't want to spend much time anywhere near her. Most people enjoyed their sessions, or so she'd been told. She did. She loved learning someone's nuances, the privilege of being allowed to glimpse a private part of a person that many never saw. Alessio seemed to think she could paint him from memory alone. He probably believed that he was unforgettable, so one glance would be all she needed.

He might not be entirely wrong about that.

Enough. She grabbed her sketch pad and watercolour pencils. There was a pretty desk with a view from large windows, overlooking fields of grapes and olives out towards Lasserno's capital. In a copse of ancient olives there peeked a small, domed structure. Like a chapel, or perhaps a folly, although Hannah didn't think Alessio would allow anything so whimsical as that on the palace grounds. The whole scene shimmered with the warmth of a Mediterranean summer. She sat at the fragile-looking desk and sketched, losing herself in perfecting the cobalt blue of the sky, the ochres, umbers and greens of the landscape glowing in the sunshine.

The muffled noise of a well-oiled door handle and hinges made her turn, spring from her chair as if the seat burned her.

Alessio strode into the room, all of him pressed into hard lines with a flawlessly cut suit and pristine white shirt. A tie of carmine sat at his throat with its fat knot, looking tight enough to strangle. Except she was the one who couldn't get any air, as if he'd sucked it all from the room. He glanced at the gleaming gold watch at his wrist then to her as she wobbled in an uncertain half-dip because she wasn't sure of the protocol if she was going to see him multiple times a day. He flicked his hand in a dismissive kind of way.

'No curtseying unless we are in public.'

'We sort of are, since your secretary's here.' She gave Stefano a little wave. He smiled back in his own handsome kind of way, though it was nothing like the glowering magnificence of his imposing boss.

Alessio looked at her, then to Stefano, and his eyes narrowed. 'You don't strike me as someone who's obtuse, Signorina Barrington.'

'I'm not. You're the one who sent me a volume of rules to follow.'

'So you're prepared.'

'They make me nervous I'm going to get something wrong.' Everything about this made her nervous, particularly him. It was as if all common sense and the need for self-preservation fled in his presence. 'I'm painting your portrait, not stepping out as your significant other. Will you give your princess the same sort of list?'

'No, because, being a princess, she'll know the rules already.'

'Rigidity and protocol don't fit in well with my work. How about we throw away the rules when we're in here?'

He raised one dark, imperious brow. Tugged at the cuffs of his shirt. Checked the time again.

'Who am I to stop you, since it appears you already have?' Alessio stalked towards her where she stood frozen in front of the spindly, gilded desk. She had that sensation again, that she was an insect under a magnifying glass. Alessio loomed close. He wasn't threatening at all. It's that he had a presence. An aura that crammed the space full, till there was no room for anything else. Especially not sensible thought.

'What are you doing there?' He motioned over the sketch she'd started, of the view outside.

'In nine years I've barely gone a day without my art.' There'd been only a few. The anniversaries, where sometimes the grief would steal upon her with a more vicious attack than usual. Sapping her will to do anything but curl up in bed and weep. 'In the last week, I've missed three with all the planning and preparing and I needed to *do* something. It helps me—'

'Relax. I'm like it with horse-riding, yet I rarely get a chance any more.' She froze. The freedom of the ride. Soaring over the jumps in partnership with her horse. She used to revel in that joy too, until the day it represented everything she'd lost. She hadn't ridden since.

Alessio wasn't looking at her unfinished artwork right now, but out of the window, his eyes distant and unfocused. That small offering of something private about himself was a gift and she doubted he realised he'd given it to her. Then the distance in his eyes faded, and they narrowed. As if he'd come back to himself, was pulling himself into reality rather than some faded memories. The whole of him stiffened, and he became the ruler of Lasserno again, rather than a simple man.

'You're drawing with coloured pencils? It seems beneath your reported talents.'

She let out a slow breath, the precious moment lost. 'I use these because they're a challenge for me. Watch.'

She dipped a brush into a small glass of water which was probably crystal and not designed for this task. Alessio didn't seem to mind. He'd probably drunk from crystal since birth. Nothing as common as plain glass would deign to touch his perfect lips. She took the brush and swiped it gently over a part of the sketched scene. The pencil bled to paint in a wash of colour.

'Magic,' he said.

'Oil paints are forgiving. These, not so much. They're unpredictable, and it's harder to cover up your mistakes.'

'Like life,' Alessio murmured, or at least that was what she thought he said as he moved closer, leaning over the picture. She was sure there was something in that fat instruction booklet about not standing too near him, but for the life of her she couldn't remember what it might have said. Not with all the *proximity*. His height, his magnetic presence. The teasing scent of him, something masculine and fresh like the aftermath of a summer's storm. The warmth he radiated, almost better than morning sunshine. She wanted to lean into it and bask. But she was here to do a job. Having poetic thoughts about unattainable princes was not part of it.

She stood back. Put a respectable distance between them. Likewise, he seemed to shake himself out of the fascination for her simple artwork. He straightened, adjusted his tie. Checked his watch *again*.

'I have limited time. We should start. What do you need from me?'

She needed him to stop being so...him. Instead she pointed to a chair she'd manhandled into better light. He looked at it, at the scuffed carpet where she'd half dragged it across the room. Frowned, but said nothing, instead unbuttoning his jacket and lowering himself into the armchair. Watching her as his secretary watched them both.

'I need fewer people in the room. I can't concentrate like this.'

There were too many eyes on her. She took a slow breath to try and ease the weight of expectation in their stares.

'Stefano stays.'

So imperious. Hannah blew out a huff of breath, grabbed a fresh sketch pad and some sharp-as-a-needle pencils, then sat opposite him. His rich brown eyes fixed on her. There was something addictive about all that focus, as if she were the only person on earth.

Yet even though he sat in a comfortable armchair, he didn't look comfortable. There was nothing relaxed about him, as if he were on edge. *Waiting* for something to happen. Which seemed strange because the man ruled a country. She assumed anything that happened to him was entirely his choice and at his whim. Yet, for all the breathtaking perfection of him, he was still a human and she reminded herself that not all the people she painted were relaxed in the beginning.

'Today, I'll be doing a few sketches. All for reference.' He nodded as she opened her sketchbook. Alessio sat upright, not even his legs crossed. Impossibly formal. She didn't want to focus on his face, nor on those eyes which seemed to barely blink. The rest of him was stitched tight into his suit. But his hands… Veins and tendons corded under his golden skin.

She began to lightly sketch the shape. The elegant, blunt-cut nails. Ignored the slight dusting of dark hair over his metacarpals, hinting around the wrist from under the pure and flawless white cuffs of his shirt. She'd leave those details till later, but for now she marvelled in his long, strong fingers, curled tight over the arms of the chair.

'What have you been doing today?' she asked. The sun streamed through the mullioned windows, brightening the room. A light breeze drifted through one she'd opened earlier.

His jaw tightened. 'Ruling my country.'

'And that involves?'

'Making many important decisions.'

Which was no kind of answer at all. She snorted, looked up at him. His fingers flexed a little. Relaxed, but still not enough. 'Okay, you've been very…princely. Let's take a step back. What time did you get out of bed?'

'Four.'

'A morning person, then.'

His eyes narrowed the merest fraction. 'I'm a busy person.'

'No rest for the wicked?'

A muscle in his strong, square jaw ticked. 'You'll have to ask my father about that maxim.'

She hesitated for a second, the pencil no longer slipping so easily over the paper. When researching Alessio, as she did with every client, she'd read about his father. The man who'd abdicated under the cloud of some scandal. It was all a bit murky. As for the man in front of her, apart from his official website and carefully curated online presence, there was really nothing. Alessio Arcuri presented to the world like the perfect prince.

The press wondered whether Alessio was like his father, and only hid it better.

'Can you take a deep breath in and let it out slowly?'

The tips of Alessio's fingers seemed a little whiter on the arms of the chair, his fingertips denting the fine fabric.

'I don't know what you're asking of me.'

'You seem a bit…' she waved her left hand with the pencil in it, as if drawing in thin air '…rigid.'

'Signorina Barrington, I learned protocol and deportment in classes from the time I could speak.'

He leaned forward, his voice low and cool. Eyes flashing tiger-gold in something like a warning. His forearms now resting on his knees, hands in front. Such a compelling picture. She held her breath and waited for more.

'From the age of five, I could sit perfectly still and silent for well over an hour. Never once moving. If I did move, my tutor's dog had a habit of nipping my ankles. I didn't like getting bitten. So this is how I sit.'

She started another sketch of his hands now, with fingers clasped before him as if in some kind of fervent prayer.

'You can't position yourself like that all the time. What about when you're relaxing? Men, they slouch in a…manly kind of way. Lounging with intent.'

Not that she really had much experience in the way men sat, other than those whose portraits she'd painted, but at least they'd looked at home in the chair she'd placed them in. Alessio's secretary seemed to have relaxation down to an art, having perfected a kind of indolence in the back corner of the room. Or her father, who had always looked comfortable in front of the television with her mother, holding hands. She blinked away the tears her memory wrought. All she knew was that the Prince before her looked as if he were about to order someone's execution.

Perhaps her own. He raised a supercilious brow, his normally full and transfixing lips now a tight line. 'Are you accusing me of not being *masculine* enough?'

'No.' Not a single woman on the planet could ever accuse him of that. She stared at the dark shading of stubble on his jaw, even though it was mid-morning and he must have shaved, at the broadness of his shoulders, the narrow taper of his waist. She was almost suffocated by how masculine he was. All that testosterone made her quite giddy. 'You're the epitome of masculinity. That suit. The bold red tie saying *leader*. Does your valet choose the colour based on what duties you have to attend to? Red for ruling, blue for official visits, yellow for meeting children…'

'Now you're questioning my sartorial choices? What makes you assume I keep a valet?'

'I'm sure all princes have them. To…darn your socks if they get holes in?'

'My socks do not require darning.'

'No, they're probably woven from magical thread by some goddess. I imagine that's your style, impeccable as it is.'

Behind Alessio, his secretary jumped from his chair. He might have looked stricken, but instead he appeared to be choking.

Alessio stood too, and she was forced to look up at his imposing form, the energy around him almost palpable. Not so impassive now, with his jaw hard, nostrils flaring. Even if he wasn't a prince, this man could rule any room he entered.

'Stefano. Please attend the oracle and request the goddess weave me more socks whilst I deal with Signorina Barrington's mocking of me.'

'Any particular colour, Your Highness?'

'Black.' He turned and speared Hannah with a hot glare. 'The colour of my righteous anger.'

Alessio began to pace, something blazing and unfamiliar bubbling in his chest. After years of attempting to inject calm and order into the palace and his life, this woman seemed intent on destroying it in the space of a day. He could not allow anyone to witness it, sending Stefano away before the man fell about laughing, which would have led to jokes at his expense for weeks.

'Alizarin Crimson,' Hannah said.

'What?' He didn't understand her, not at all.

'That would be the colour of righteous anger. It's a deeper colour than simple red…solid, less flash. Now, if you were plain angry, the light version of cadmium red would suit better. So I suggest you should have sent Stefano for red socks rather than black.'

Alessio kept up his pacing, unable to sit still. No one questioned him any more, no one mocked him, or disagreed with what he said. After years of chaos in the palace, his rule was absolute. That was by his design, and his demand. People knew what he expected of them and complied. No arguments. Gone was the frustration at ideas cast aside, attempts to thwart his father ignored by those who sought to profit from Lasserno's losses. Graft, corruption and sheer negligence had been rooted out ruthlessly. Stefano argued he should release the reins, relax a little. Allow people to see the man rather than the Crown Prince. But that was the way to chaos, no matter what the press made up about him. The standards he set were highest for himself. His recent life was about calm and control. This? Hannah Barrington seemed designed to torment him.

'I don't want to speak about socks. What's the point of these ridiculous questions?'

All the while she'd sat there in her own chair. Wearing black leggings, and some kind of soft grey top which clung to her slender form, sheer enough so he could see the trace of a bra. No colour on her, yet she was the most vibrant thing in the room, and he couldn't look away. Right now she wasn't looking at him, instead gently sweeping an infernal pencil over the page as he wore a path through the carpet, burning through his frustration. She didn't seem to notice. Nibbling on her plum-coloured bottom lip. A slight frown on her brow. Such focus on a piece of paper, not on him.

'I'm trying to engage in conversation,' she said, 'which would be easier if you participated by conversing back.'

'I am speaking to you.'

She glanced up at him briefly, her gaze searching. Flickering over him as if in a quick and efficient study, then back down at the page in front of her. 'Conversation is a different thing entirely. It's an exchange. You're not exchanging, you're...dictating.'

He stopped behind the armchair in which she'd placed him. Gripped the back till his fingers crushed the exquisite fabric. He'd not sat all day, but had been solving a thousand small problems, and a few large ones, on the move. Reviewed the longlist of candidates for Lasserno's new princess. Whilst he'd wished to be anywhere but here, the thought of stopping for the brief hour he'd allocated to her today had been almost pleasant. Yet she'd kept talking, and those questions had dredged up memories and feelings he hadn't experienced in years. It was as though, if he let her speak any more, he might tell her everything that had plagued him since his mother's death.

'So you converse by asking about a valet? What other staff will you be enquiring about? Whether I have my own personal fingernail-buffer?'

He couldn't see what she was doing, the book in which she drew tilted the wrong way. She looked up again from her page. Cocked her head. Fixed her attention to his hands again. Her lips parted, then she went back to drawing.

'That *would* tell me a lot about you, but you strike me as...assured rather than vain.'

He couldn't help a bitter laugh. At least there he hadn't taken after his father. A man always seeking approval, adoration. Being feted for his looks. Searching out women to worship him. His wife's love had never been enough. In the end coldness and hatred was all that had fuelled their doomed marriage.

'So long as my suits fit, I have little interest. I don't need to appear on best-dressed lists year after year.' Unlike his father, who'd eschewed the court-appointed royal tailor for Savile Row. Almost putting the man and his family out of business, when they'd tended royalty in Lasserno for over a century. Alessio had rectified that slight, supporting locals who had a long and proud tradition rather than looking outside the country for what was easily supplied here.

Anyhow, what did a suit matter when all he wanted to do was spend the limited time available to him on horseback, as if to outride the weight of responsibility that some days seemed as if it could crush him? His suit was a mere costume he wore, the trappings of a leader. It said nothing about the man at all.

Hannah stopped drawing, looked at him again. Long, slow. Her gaze drifting over his face, lower. To his hands. Fixing itself there. The way she studied him took on a life of its own. His heart beat a little faster. An odd sensation stirring in his gut, almost like excitement. He released his grip on the chair in front of him and stood straighter. Was her assessment of him an artist's, or a woman's? Did she like what she saw? He didn't know why that last question was so important to answer, because the answer was meaningless and changed nothing.

'Your suit fits…exquisitely.' Her voice was soft, breathy, almost as if what she said surprised her. The tone of it stroked over his skin, touching him everywhere. Alessio relished the sensation. It was like being handed an unexpected gift.

Hannah placed her sketch pad and pencil face down on the carpet. Stood, pursed her lips. 'And I think that's half the problem. Let's start again. Your Highness, could you please take off your suit jacket and have a seat?'

Your Highness. Said with her perfect rounded vowels. A slight huskiness to it. He hesitated, almost as if being asked to remove his jacket were stripping him naked. As she waited for him she tucked an unruly strand of dark hair, that had escaped her efforts to secure it, behind her ear. Alessio peeled the jacket from his body, the air of the room cooling him as he did.

Hannah walked towards him, left hand outstretched.

He handed her his jacket. She took it and hung it over the back of a small dining chair, running her hands over the shoulders. A stunning flash of heat tore through him as he imagined those hands stroking over his own shoulders. Something that could never, ever happen. He sat in the armchair again. Settling in to get comfortable when all of him was on edge. Tried to *lounge with intent*, whatever that meant.

'You should take off the tie.' Alessio didn't think. He moved his hands to the red silk. Loosened it, and only had a fleeting moment where he could finally breathe before his chest tightened again. He held out his hand with the tie and she took it, the minutest brush of her fingertips on his, and the world could have stopped turning, on the precipice of tempting desires he must ignore.

Was she affected too? Her hands caressed the tie, gently smoothing the fabric, wrapping it round her palm to create a perfect spiral and placing it on a side table. Then she faced him. Perhaps the colour was higher on her cheeks? Or perhaps he was projecting his own torrid desires onto her.

It had been a long time since he'd been with a woman. When he realised the extent of his father's profligate behaviour, he'd seen no choice but for his own to be exemplary. All his waking hours had been taken up with trying to draw attention from his father, hiding his ultimate disgrace, rebuilding Lasserno's reputation. He would not let his people suffer at the hands of his family. These things required him to be better. He shouldn't crave the softness of a touch. He'd inured himself to such things because of the job he must do. It required toughness, no distractions. He'd risen above it before. He would again.

But how for a few bright, blinding moments did he wish he could fall.

She moved closer again, looking down on him. A

strange and discomfiting position to be in. As if for the first time he was at some kind of disadvantage, when his whole life had been full of the advantages of his position. Her eyes were luminous in the late-morning light. A mysterious wash of green and gold, like the ocean close to the shore. Hannah cocked her head. Pointed, waggling her finger at him. He shouldn't have tolerated that. It was a breach of protocol, but protocol be damned. He didn't care.

'The top two buttons as well.'

Dio, in this moment she could have him completely naked if she asked. The thrill of that thought was intoxicating. The whole atmosphere in the room thickened, time slowing to these perfectly innocent words weighted with his illicit imaginings. Alessio didn't even think. He undid the two buttons on his shirt. More slowly than he ought, since she kept her gaze on every move of his fingers, almost as if hoping he didn't stop, that he undid all of them.

Or that was what he imagined. In his fantasies he could allow it. Never in reality.

She moved her hand, as if she were reaching out again. Hesitated. Checking herself. Her lips parted. Then she dropped her arm and stepped back. Shook her head.

'What?' His voice was rough as it ground out of him. Frustrated at the things he could not have.

Hannah went back to her chair. Grabbed her sketch pad and pencil. 'I thought you might run your hands through your hair. Make it a little untidy.'

Their gazes clashed and held. He'd look as if he'd rolled out of bed if he did that. Did she want him messy? As though they'd spent a night together? His hands involuntarily gripped the satiny fabric of the chair again, to hold on to something.

'But then I realise that untidy wouldn't be you... Your Highness.'

He almost shouted to her that yes, it was. He could be

that man. He had been in the past, when life had been freer and he'd thought only of riding for his country, not taking the throne too soon and repairing the disaster wrought by his father. But she'd reminded them both, with his title, that he was born to a job and would not deviate. He clenched his teeth. Swallowed down the bitter taint of disappointment as she began her drawing again, with deft moves of her pencil that felt as if she were inscribing on his skin. He wondered what else she saw of him, with her artist's eyes.

'Could you answer a question for me?' she asked. 'One question, honestly, with no equivocation?'

Alessio gritted his teeth. He'd kept so much of himself private for so long, particularly after Allegra's attempts at courting the press, that agreeing to any question he didn't vet beforehand was unnatural to him. Most respectable journalists in Lasserno knew this and played the game with the rules he'd set. The tabloids made up what they wanted in the absence of a story. He didn't like this stranger, this young, almost guileless woman, demanding parts of him he rarely granted to anyone.

'Yes.' She didn't look up. Showed no reaction to his agreement at all. But he wasn't giving away everything without exacting a price. 'So long as you answer one of mine.'

Her head whipped up from the page. She was paying attention to him now, and something hot and potent thrummed through him. He liked it far too much.

'That's not how this works. It's all about you.'

'You want to know so much of others yet give none of yourself.' She nibbled on her bottom lip again, drawing his attention to her distracting mouth. The way her teeth worked on the soft flesh. He craved to soothe away the sting of her teeth, see if her lips were as soft as they looked.

'It's my job.'

'People might accuse you of having something to hide.'

He wasn't sure she had secrets. She'd been investigated before the commission for his portrait was requested. In his life now, that was a given. But in some perverse way he enjoyed her discomfort, since she was causing him so many inconvenient and uncomfortable thoughts of his own.

'I don't have any secrets. I just find people prefer to talk about themselves. I'm not that interesting. But if you answer my question, you can ask one of yours.'

She shrugged, and the soft shirt she wore sagged a little, exposing the hint of a bra strap before she pushed it back onto her shoulder. But he didn't miss the slice of pale blue, and he firmly shut down imaginings of whether her underwear was lace or something practical. Instead, he checked his watch. Their hour had almost ended, and yet he didn't want to leave. How long could he wait here, sitting in the chair, before someone would come to find him?

'Then ask what you wish.'

'If you want to escape from it all, what do you do?'

He could have laughed, the answer so easy it required no effort at all. 'I ride my horses.'

Her look softened a fraction, or perhaps it was his imagination. The corners of her mouth turning up, her gaze seeming far away. It almost appeared wistful, but the moment was lost as she went back to her drawing. He could have asked her any question at all, but that fleeting look on her face spoke to him in some way.

'Do you ride, Signorina Barrington?'

Her pencil dragged to a stop on the page. Her eyes a little wider as she paled, looking almost...fearful.

'I—I haven't...not for a long time.'

He wondered whether she would answer more questions if he asked them, but a respectful knock sounded at the door. He let out a long, slow breath. The knock reminded Alessio of his real life, not the fantasy that he could do what he wished, without all the responsibilities he had. He rose from his chair as the door opened and Stefano walked inside. Holding a pair of black socks. An eyebrow raised, meaning he would ask questions about what went on in this room whilst he was away, which Alessio would not deign to answer. He needed to go now, but his decision was simple. She wanted to get to know the man? He had the perfect answer.

'Prepare yourself. Tomorrow, meet me at the stables. Then we'll ride.'

CHAPTER FOUR

HANNAH HESITATED AT the door of the magnificent stables on the lower reaches of the palace grounds. Assailed by the earthy scents she'd once loved, of lucerne, hay and straw. In the past that smell had signalled her happiest moments. Spending time with her precious horse, Beau. The hours brushing him, mucking out the stables, never a chore. She'd dreamed of owning stables like this back then. Such fleeting, futile fantasies before everything had turned to dust.

The awe of the space mingled with a heaviness in her chest, making it hard to breathe. She didn't want the memories now. This stable, riding, were symbols of a life lost to her. There was no escaping it here. The glint of crushed metal, the tick of a hot, broken engine. The dread silence from her parents. The terrified whinnies of her mortally injured horse. It all came back with a sickening rush. She faltered for a second. Stood to take it in, work it through. For a moment, the pain of that day was as sharp and bright as if it had just happened. But she had no choice other than to be here. Hannah took a deep breath. This was simply a job. Though it didn't stop the sense of regret and loss almost overwhelming her.

She walked to where she'd been told to go. Where two horses now stood saddled, with a person she assumed was the groom. Their tack was shiny and perfect.

That sick feeling intensified...the roar of blood surging

in her ears, her heart pounding against her ribcage. Everything was swirling in a dizzying attack to her senses of a day when life as she knew it had ended. She'd lost her hopes and dreams in the accident. Her whole life had changed. She'd rebuilt it, but some days the foundations seemed a little unstable. As if everything could fall apart again. Which was more truth than a lie, after what her uncle had done. A sense of betrayal sliced through her again, that the people she should have been able to trust had failed her. It all came down to work in the end, yet right now if she could turn around and flee, leave handsome princes and shattered dreams behind, she would. But her choices ended with her uncle's embezzlement. Hannah faltered, stopped for a second. Took some steadying breaths as her legs trembled.

How was she going to get on a horse's back, when she could barely walk to where they stood?

'Signorina Barrington?'

That voice from behind. Deep, with a lilting accent. Smoothing over her like some balm to her troubled soul. The prickling sensation of someone close. Alessio's presence penetrating the cold grief threatening to overwhelm her.

She turned. He crowded out everything else in the space, not as close as she'd thought, but it didn't matter how far away he stood, she was sure she'd still feel him. It was as if he had an aura a mile wide, obliterating her awareness of anything else. And if she'd been faltering before, right now she was paralysed.

She'd glimpsed him a few times at a distance when she'd been competing, dressed for competition himself. He'd been overwhelming then, to a young girl with hormones making themselves known in confusing ways, like a fairy tale brought to life. But nothing prepared her for this, Alessio in a short-sleeved polo shirt which showed off his tanned skin, the swell of his impressive biceps, the strength of his forearms. His legs, encased in buff breeches and riding boots, caused her mouth to dry. Because, whilst all of him was only hinted at under a suit, this figure before her wasn't the young man she'd pined over, whose riding she'd watched obsessively whenever she could find it. He was a thirty-one year old in his prime and it showed in every inch of him. His broad chest, muscular thighs. Which she probably shouldn't be staring at, and… was her mouth open? She closed it. She was only trying to get air, that was all. Trying to stop her heart pounding. But it wasn't the sickening rhythm of before, instead morphing into something harder, more insistent. The drumbeat of a pulse that spoke of a sultry type of rhythm she tried hard to ignore.

As she looked up from how well his breeches fitted and into his face, he frowned, the merest of creases in his otherwise unmarred forehead. Probably judging the worn old jeans she'd sneaked into her bag almost out of spite, because she was sure nothing that much past their prime would ever grace the palace walls.

'Are you all right?' Something about his question made everything inside her still. It was as if he saw her. 'You look pale. You're not afraid of horses, are you?'

She shook her head. The fear was not of the animals, but of the memories. 'No. Probably a little late to sleep, a little early to wake.' It wasn't exactly a lie. The thought of riding with him today had left her tossing and turning, with dreams of running after things she couldn't catch, of accidents she couldn't prevent. 'As I said, I haven't ridden for a while.'

Still, his gaze searched her. As if he realised she wasn't telling the truth. 'Come. Meet your horse. If you have any fears, she should allay them.'

He walked ahead of her, and for once she was happy to

follow as his rule book dictated. It was no chore to watch his long, assured stride, taking in her fill of the broad shoulders tapering to his narrow waist. She shouldn't look, really, but what woman wouldn't stare at that backside? Her cheeks burned hot at the prickling awareness of him, and how magnificent he was. They arrived at the groom, and Alessio turned, the corner of his mouth quirking in a smile which told her he *knew* she'd been staring and didn't really mind.

Typical.

He reached out and rubbed the silky nose of an impossibly pretty dapple grey. 'This is Kestia. She's a placid mare who knows what she's doing. You'll have no trouble with her. I promise.' Alessio stared at Hannah as he said it, narrowed his eyes. Cocked his head a fraction.

She didn't like that look. It was as if he was contemplating things he didn't want to say. Hannah narrowed her own eyes back at him.

'You're not thinking that I'm a…troublesome mare, are you?'

His full and perfect mouth curled into something of a wry grin. Her breath caught. When he wasn't so stern and forbidding, he was the type of man who could cleave a woman's heart in two if she allowed it. Which was risky, when there were so few pieces of her heart left to break. Alessio placed a hand flat over his chest. 'I'd never think such a thing.'

She needed a distraction from him so she reached out and stroked down her horse's side with her flat hand. The coat was smooth and warm to the touch. Alessio watched the gentle move, before his umber eyes held her gaze for a heartbeat. Then it was as if he came to himself and stepped back, his face cool and impassive again. He moved to his own horse. A dark bay stallion. Tall. Clipped mane. Gleaming coat. His ears were pricked high and his eyes were alert. Nostrils flaring. The sort of horse she would have given anything to ride.

'He's magnificent,' she said, as Alessio took his mount's reins.

'Apollo's special. However, I've been ignoring him lately and if I don't take him out soon he'll punish me. His groom rides him but for some reason he prefers me. It seems we have an affinity.'

'You're both hot-blooded?' She didn't know where those words had come from. They blurted out of her but both Alessio and his horse seemed tense, as if they were bristling to break into a run and never stop.

'He was inclined in the past to be more reckless than is good for him. He's fearless when sometimes he should be cautious.' Alessio stroked his horse's nose. 'He's settled since I've owned him. Is a champion in all ways.'

Alessio had been fearless too, once. She wondered what had happened to him and his showjumping. The reasons he'd stopped had been lost in the annals of history, the internet only briefly mentioning his riding. It was as though that part of him had been scrubbed away. But she remembered him. He'd left her breathless, even then. She had scoured the internet for videos of his events. Watching him over and over. Why give it all away when he was rising to the top of an elite field with everything ahead of him?

'Would you compete again? With Apollo?'

'I have a country to rule. There is no time for anything else.' Alessio's eyes were bleak and distant. He cleared his throat, nodded to the little grey. 'We should ride. We don't have much time, and a dinner tonight to ready ourselves for.'

The dinner. Of course. Though she wondered how much time he thought she needed to get ready, because it was hours away yet.

They mounted their horses with the assistance of the

groom, and she settled herself into the saddle, the warmth of the animal's body seeping into her. Familiar and heart-breaking in so many ways but exhilarating in others. The sensation washed over her again, here, up high. Of being capable of anything. That was how she'd felt once. As if life were full of promise rather than weighed down by reality.

How she wished she could be that sixteen-year-old girl again. To have the freedom and belief that everything would always be okay. To have the hope for life and love, rather than the inevitability that loss was always the risk when you loved another. She had taken years to contemplate dating, at Sue's encouragement. She'd been introduced to someone who might not have made her heart race but seemed kind. Solid and safe. She had thought there was something there, allowed herself the tiniest shred of hope that there was a future worth waiting for. Only to have it crushed when he had said art took up too much of her time. He had wanted some fun, and that it was painting or him. As if she could stop something that was intrinsic to her being. And with his words, any hope had died too. It was an unacceptable risk now. The prickle in her eyes and sting in the back of her nose warned of tears. The grief bubbling close, especially here. Of what she'd lost, sure, but also of what might have been. She took a deep breath, steadied herself. Loosened her grip on the reins and tried to relax a bit.

This fortnight was a job. This moment, a simple ride on a sweet mare with a subject she was supposed to paint. Nothing more. And that subject looked incomparable astride his horse, Apollo prancing in anticipation of leaving the stables, Alessio's control light, brilliant.

'He's impatient to get going,' she said.

'Always.' Hannah wondered if he was talking about his horse or himself—both looked outside the stable doors as if they wanted to bolt and never return. 'Are you ready?'

She nodded, the unsettled queasiness still rumbling around her stomach. Alessio walked them out of the stables and she rode beside him, the rhythm of it all familiar and as comforting as it was heartbreaking.

'I'm surprised Stefano isn't here with us.'

Alessio snorted and his horse flicked and twisted his ears, as attuned to his rider as his rider was to him. 'You'd never see him on the back of a horse. I think he's afraid of them, but he denies it. Are you comfortable riding faster than a walk? Apollo needs to move.'

She nodded and Alessio nudged his horse into a trot. She followed, settling into the rise and fall of it. She pulled in beside him, keeping up easily. He'd been right. She might be a little rusty, taking a while to learn her horse's stride whereas once it would have almost been instinctive, but she hadn't forgotten, even after all these years.

'Where are we going?' she asked. They curved along a path, the sound of the horses' hooves thumping on the ground in a soothing rhythm. If she had her bearings right, they were riding out into the view she saw from her window each day.

'Through the vines, out past the olive grove, then circling back. It should take about an hour and there's space if you feel confident enough to let the horses gallop.'

She felt almost confident enough now, sitting up on her beautiful grey, feeling that familiar thrum of excitement, the desire to take off and be free. But she didn't want Alessio asking questions about her experience. About why she had stopped riding too. It was so hard to hold back, when all she wanted to do was lose herself in the speed of her mount to feel as if she were flying again.

'From the window of my room there's an interesting little domed building amongst some trees. Can we go and see it?'

She didn't miss the slight tightening of his hands on

the reins. The way his horse became restive and tossed his head. Broke his even stride. Alessio murmured softly in Italian. Almost like an apology to Apollo for disturbing him. Then he glanced back at her.

'The pavilion. *Ovviamente*. Of course.'

He led the way past some low fences, towards the grapevines burgeoning with fruit where a few people worked.

'Do you ever jump these?' She nodded to some little gates obstructing the gravel path to the stables. Alessio gave an almost smile. The merest tilt of his lips. Something distant and somehow…wistful.

He turned to her, and her fingers itched for the scratch of pencil on paper, to catch the question in his eyes, the curve of his mouth. The certainty in the way he held himself, that this was his rightful place and destiny. Whilst the idea of a blank canvas had terrified her before, she could see this. How she'd shape the paint to fit him, his body owning the canvas as he owned this land.

'*Sì*. My horses are all able.' The people in the vines ahead of them raised their hands and waved. He waved back. 'I may need to speak to my vigneron later. About the harvest.'

'Everything going well?'

'It looks to be a good vintage. A perfect showpiece for our country's wine industry, and what it can achieve.' He said the words with steel-edged pride, as if it was a personal achievement.

They rode on into the shade of some glorious old olives, gnarled and ancient, the dappled sun warm on her skin, the scent of earth and horse everywhere. She'd forgotten the joy of this, the simple pleasures of riding in nature.

'The countryside is beautiful here,' she said. 'I'm surprised Lasserno's not more popular. There isn't much advertising about its tourism.'

His shoulders stiffened. 'It's a hidden treasure but people think we're a poor cousin of Italy, no matter the natural beauty and riches. We've been undervalued for too long, not enough made of our assets. Industries like winemaking have been left to crumble and waste away. I sought to change that the minute my father left the throne.'

'Was he keen to retire?'

'The only thing he was keen to do was plunder the country's riches for himself. People suffered…the treasury was emptied. I feared nothing would be safe.' Alessio's jaw clenched. 'Had he not abdicated the role I would have taken it from him.'

Even though the temperature was warm, the breeze cool, it was as if she'd been plunged into midwinter. She didn't know what to say. Alessio talked about making war with his own father, and that added another layer to the complex picture he painted for her. This man was the one you'd commit to canvas wielding a sword on horseback, like the imposing portraits of his ancestors.

They rode in silence for a little longer. It was as if he'd said too much and she guessed he had, being normally so self-possessed.

'Are we going to the pavilion?'

He turned to her, his eyes bleak and cold. 'You still wish to see it?'

She nodded. Anything to break the terrible chill that had fallen over them. His shoulders slumped a fraction, and it seemed almost like a defeat. Then he straightened again as if steeling himself.

'Come this way.'

Alessio wheeled his horse around and encouraged him into a canter, as if he'd forgotten she hadn't ridden for years. And all she could do was try to follow in his wake.

Alessio didn't know what it was about Hannah, how when she asked a question it was as if he'd been injected with a truth serum. He said what he wanted, what he'd bottled up, like purging his soul. In that way she was dangerous, non-disclosure agreement aside. People might have tried guessing things about his father, the reasons why he had stepped down, but the truth had been well hidden. Alessio had ensured it. Lasserno's former prince had been all about laziness and destruction. However, *no one* should ever know the extent to which Alessio had investigated removing him. Perhaps his father had had an inkling before his abdication. The palace had been full of spies and sycophants before Alessio had rid the place of them. That could be why his father had jumped before being given an unceremonious push, because Alessio had been ready to give him a final shove if it meant saving the country.

But this was a secret the world could never know, because it signalled instability. Let everyone believe the lie his father had done it for the good of the country. Yet today Alessio had put everything at risk, all because of the gentle questions of the woman riding with him.

Hannah followed close behind him as they approached the pavilion. He wasn't surprised she'd asked to see it, such a quaint building peeking out of the olive grove. A folly to something that would never last. He wondered what Hannah would see here. Whether she'd sense the tragedy or only see the fantasy of the place. Alessio wasn't sure why her opinion on these things mattered.

He pulled up Apollo and dismounted, the curdle of dread filling his stomach. Here sat a tribute by his mother to a love that had burned brightly and exploded in a supernova-like cataclysm, before imploding into darkness, cold and endless. So many hopes and dreams had been built into this little structure. A testament to the dismal failure of relationships. His father, unwilling to be faithful. His mother, unable to forgive. Their country the ultimate loser. Alessio curled his loose reins around an ancient olive tree. Hannah dismounted with a practised ease that belied her supposed inexperience and did the same, her boots crunching in the fallen leaves on the ground as she approached him.

'This is such a beautiful spot.' Her voice was a little breathy as she looked around, her cheeks with a healthy pink glow.

Yes, it was a pretty spot in the dappled sunshine. The whitewashed pavilion with a domed terracotta roof tucked away in the shade. But it had nothing on her. In her worn jeans and buttoned shirt which clung to her elegant curves she glowed as if from the inside out, with something that looked a lot like joy.

'Can we go inside?'

He nodded. 'It's never locked.'

He walked up some small stairs, turned a latch and entered the place he hadn't visited in years. Not since the death of his mother when he had come here and raged at the universe for stealing the wrong parent. But demons needed to be conquered, especially for him now the country was his to rule. There was no place he could fear to tread, not now.

The pavilion had been kept pristine. No leaf or dust dared grace any surface. The floor was an exquisite mosaic of the goddess Venus rising from the waves. Fluted columns against the walls supported the roof, decorated in between with leadlight windows and pantheons of gods staring down at them. A few wooden benches sat inside. Once they'd been covered with plush cushions, this structure designed as an opulent meeting place, away from the strictures and rules of the palace.

Hannah followed him inside, stood in the middle of the room looking up at the ceiling with the painted plaster like a summer's sky. She turned on the spot, her lips parted, face alive as if in wonder.

'What is this place used for? The light's gorgeous. It would be a beautiful space to paint in.'

Alessio shrugged. 'Nothing now. Once it was a retreat. A place to be alone. To contemplate.'

The lies...all the lies. They threatened to choke him even though they needed to be told. He wouldn't betray his mother's memory at the way his parents had debased themselves in their horror of a marriage towards the end.

'It seems almost like it was built for... I don't know. Lovers.'

So close to the truth, this woman. Always probing and finding the right answers. She could be a danger to his equilibrium if he didn't proceed with care.

'It was built by my mother on the second anniversary of her marriage, as a gift to my father.'

'That's so romantic.' Her voice was the merest whisper, the brush of a cool breeze through the olive trees surrounding them.

'Yes, isn't it? Romance is all around us.' His voice in response sounded hard, cynical. Even to his own ears. Echoing in this little space with nothing soft to absorb it.

In truth, this building was a testament to a failed marriage. His parents' relationship had been reported as one of great passion, until his father became bored after Alessio was born. This building hinted at something grand and consuming. Love perhaps. Obsession more likely. Or a desperate, clinging hope of keeping something that was already slipping away. He had no memory of his parents' love, only what cold, black coals were left when the flame had burned out.

'You say that like romance isn't a good thing.'

A slight frown marred her brow, those eyes of hers watching him. Assessing all the time. The sense of it prickled down his spine. A warning that he was transparent as glass and she could see all his cracks and flaws underneath. She was an artist after all. She was programmed to look for those things. He didn't want her to see them. They were secrets he kept from the world. The face he projected was the one he wanted her to paint, not the man he hid.

'If not reciprocated, it's a disaster.' The shouts, the fights. The priceless porcelain hurled across rooms, smashing against walls. His mother's cry. *'You loved me once!'* His father's reply. *'I hate you now.'* That was where romance ended. In rage and recrimination.

'What about you?' he asked. 'Would you build such a lofty monument to romance yourself?'

Hannah looked around the space. Tucked an unruly strand of hair behind her ear. She nibbled at her plump, peach lips. But she wouldn't look at him.

'My art takes up all of my time and emotion.' She appeared to have hunched in on herself, as if she were trying to tuck herself in, fold herself away till she was hidden. 'And that's enough.'

He understood his own attitude all too well. Love was a lie. Romance a folly as real and palpable as the building in which they stood. He wondered what led a young woman like her to reject it, when most had their heads in the clouds.

'So cynical for one so young,' he murmured. And something of a kindred spirit, but he didn't want to think of that. Of the way she stood there. Her cheeks coloured a beautiful pink from the warmth of the day and the mild exertion. How her eyes were the translucent green of Lasserno's coastline, where the water met the rocky shore. How they were alone, where the only thing he could hear were the birds and the whisper of a summer's breeze through the trees outside. The beat of his heart thudding in his ears. Then she looked up at him, a flash in her eyes like sun on the sea. Her gaze casting down his body, then back to meet his. Her lips parted.

This, between them, was nothing about romance but something more primal—though no less destructive. An awareness like a match freshly struck and flaring to life. If he were another man he would have taken the few steps forward to close the space between them, wrapped her in his arms, kissed her and explored this attraction. The heat of desire coursed through his veins, settled down low. Snapping at his heels to prompt him into action. He took a deep breath against the immediacy of this craving. Something he didn't want or need.

The only thing he had to rule his life by was the desire to serve his country. To be better. The best. And nothing else would do, particularly not following this desire running between them when nothing could ever come of it.

'We should move on,' he said. 'The horses need exercise. But if the light appeals, you may come here and paint.'

At least it might help keep her away from him and his incendiary desires with no outlet.

'Thank you.' Hannah's voice was low and husky, the sensation of it scoring over his skin.

They left the small pavilion and he shut the door behind them, on the past. He was all for moving forward, the only direction for him now. They approached the horses, happily nibbling on some grass under the trees, heads lifting and ears pricking as they approached.

'I'll give you assistance to mount Kestia.' He didn't want his horse's back hurt by an inexperienced rider struggling to get on. It had nothing to do with a need to move close, where he could smell the scent of her like the apple trees which graced the sheltered orchards of the palace gardens. It most certainly was not an excuse to touch Hannah in any way, to feel the warmth of her body through her jeans as he assisted her onto the horse, but he needn't have worried. She was graceful, assured. Almost as if she'd been born in the saddle on which she sat. Looking perfect on the horse he'd bought for his future princess, whoever she might ultimately be from the list of candidates now sitting in the top drawer of his desk. After Hannah left, after his coronation, then he'd decide that part of his future. He still had time.

Alessio shoved those thoughts aside. He swung himself onto Apollo's back and led through the olives into the heat of the day, pointing out landmarks as he saw them. Anything to keep his mind off the way her cheeks glowed pink in the warm sunshine, the way soft strands of her dark brown hair escaped the riding helmet, curling round the base of her neck.

He'd rather encourage Apollo into a gallop and keep riding till both were exhausted and covered in sweat, to burn away these sensations that were so foreign to him. And he couldn't sit here any longer, taking this sedate pace. He needed more, to outrun the crushing in his chest. The feeling of being trapped in a way he couldn't explain.

Reprieve came from a man walking through the grapevines in the distance.

'Do you feel confident enough to ride back to the stables yourself? As I said, I need to speak with my vigneron.' It wasn't far and Kestia was quiet and sound.

Hannah hesitated for a second, then nodded. 'I'll be fine. You go ahead.'

It didn't take a moment to encourage Apollo to move. Alessio clicked his tongue and the horse knew what he wanted, accelerating into a gallop and giving them both the freedom they craved.

Hannah watched Alessio ride out. The magnificence of it as he took off over the landscape. She settled Kestia, the little horse becoming impatient seeing the big bay streak away into the distance. Hannah patted her neck as they walked a short way. Out of Alessio's presence it was almost as if she could let out a long-held breath, those moments in the pavilion, built as a tribute to love and romance, filling her with something she barely understood. An awareness that took root and grew unchecked and uncontrolled in that little space, and for the briefest, blinding flash she craved to explore it for herself. But those feelings led nowhere. They were remnants of childish fantasies and nothing more.

Now she was firmly grounded in reality, sitting on the back of a beautiful horse for the first time in nine years. That was a thrill of its own, and with Alessio occupied she could ride as she wanted with no one to ask questions of her.

'Okay, little girl, let's see what you can do.' She encouraged her horse into a trot through the vibrant landscape, the sun high in a cobalt sky, a cool breeze making the afternoon comfortably warm rather than oppressive. They broke out onto the path, towards the castle rising majestically from the landscape. Like a fantasy picture made real.

She spurred her horse on a little faster now, settling into the rhythm, the quiver in her belly all about excitement. How had she forgotten how alive this made her feel? It was as if a switch had been flicked, a light turned on, illuminating all the dark and missing corners in her life. Ahead lay the low gate they'd passed on the way out on their ride and Kestia's ears pricked. Hannah's heart thrummed in her chest, the excited beat of it because this jump was *easy* and she was going to take it. As they approached the obstacle Hannah checked the length of her mount's stride, preparing them for the jump. Adjusted her position and they flew, for the briefest of moments, before safely landing on the other side.

All those things she'd suppressed, forced herself to forget, coalesced into that bright, brilliant moment soaring over the fence. The jump hadn't been difficult for either of them, but still she patted her little horse, whispered words of praise as the tears stung in her eyes. The memories of competition, her parents' pride at her success... There was joy in this moment, but it was also suffused with a deep ache which never really went away.

She rode on, not slowing her horse. They entered the stable area and she dismounted with a smile which might not leave her for hours, rubbing Kestia's mane, smoothing her hands over her soft coat. The thud of hooves in the distance caught her attention and she glanced outside to see Alessio galloping towards them like a warrior. He rode into the stables with a flash and clatter of hooves and pulled up his horse, leaping from Apollo and stalking towards her, reins in hand.

'What the hell do you think you were doing?' His eyes glittered like black diamonds. Jaw clenched hard enough to shatter teeth.

'Riding?' She stroked her horse's velvety nose, trying to ignore the man crackling next to her with the energy of a summer storm. 'She's wonderful. A dream.'

'As she should be,' he hissed, his breathing hard from exertion. 'You could have hurt her by pulling a stunt like that!'

Hannah refused to accept the approbation. She might do many things, but she'd never hurt a horse. 'It was no stunt. I—'

'You said you couldn't ride!'

'I said I hadn't ridden in a long time.' Hannah glared at him, the excitement of the ride still coursing rich and hot through her veins. She stood straight and tall, holding her ground, hands planted on her hips, not caring if this broke every rule in his stupid handbook. Alessio didn't move, vibrating with a furious energy. It was as if both of them were sizing up the other for a fight. She took off her riding helmet and scrubbed her hands through her hair, damp with sweat. 'You told me she could jump and the quality of your horses is obvious. I would *never* have done anything beyond her capabilities. It's not as if I hopped on her back and threw her straight over the fence. We've ridden for an hour already. I had her measure.'

His sensual lips thinned. The merest of frowns creased his brow. 'You've been holding back on me. All morning.'

Something of a warning flashed in his eyes and she knew it was because she hadn't admitted the truth to him earlier in the day. And that was a problem because he'd been holding back for her too, when they both could have ridden like the wind together. But she hadn't wanted him to ask questions about her skills, rusty as they were in the beginning. Questions led to conversations, and conversations brought back memories now bubbling close to the surface, of things which had haunted too many of her days, and some of her nights even still.

'I said I thought we'd met—'

'We haven't...as adults.'

That was why she and her friend had been in the car together and she hadn't travelled with her parents. They'd been giggling and gossiping about *him*.

'I've seen you ride before. I recognise your style and I'll always remember a horse. Who was yours?'

It wasn't really a question but a command. He stood there formidable, with the assurance of a person to whom no one would say no. The type of person who was never unsure. She'd remembered him like that, when she was only sixteen and unsure about everything. His confidence, the certainty about him. Part of her wanted to knock him down now, refuse to answer his questions. But she'd be damned if he thought she'd be reckless on horseback. All she needed to do was withstand the memories that would once again storm over her, leaving her wrung out for days.

She couldn't do that here. There was nowhere to shut herself away and grieve unrestricted.

'His name was Beauchamp... Beau.'

'A palomino?'

She nodded, astounded Alessio could remember. Beau was so beautiful he had looked as if he'd been forged from gold. She might have had no siblings, but he was like her brother, her best friend. His loss in such a terrible way, with her parents, had almost broken her. He might have survived the accident, but he hadn't been able to survive the mortal injuries. She'd wanted everyone to try, because he was all she had left after her parents had died instantly, but the vet said no, and in the end others had made the decision she couldn't make for herself. She'd never shaken the feeling she'd let them both down that day, and in those moments any sliver of hope something might be left to her out of the horror had died with him.

She turned her head, not wanting Alessio to see the vulnerability, the tears that she couldn't prevent.

'You were good. You could make him fly like you both had wings.' Hannah couldn't believe Alessio had noticed her, could remember her horse. She'd always thought he was the type of man who wouldn't notice anyone like her.

'Why did you stop?' he asked.

She couldn't answer that question, not now. 'Why did you?'

Her voice threatened to crack. She reined in the emotion.

'Always with the questions, yet no answers for me,' he said. 'How does someone so young have so much to hide?'

She shrugged. 'I could ask the same.'

He hesitated for a second, which was pronounced because he was a man who hesitated at nothing. 'My country needed me. And you?'

The desire to say it was like a poisoned thing bursting out of her chest and she couldn't contain it any longer.

'There was an accident. My parents. My horse. I lost everything.' Hannah let out a long, slow breath. Closed her eyes. Rested her forehead on Kestia's warm body.

'When I left England, my groom told me of a tragedy but there were few details. I had no idea it was you.' His voice was soft and kind, but it didn't really help. Nothing did. 'I'm sorry.'

'It was a long time ago now, and it's fine. Really.'

Those were the lies she told herself. So many lies. She'd wondered for years what was the purpose of her surviving, till she found she could document the moments of others so precious memories would never be lost. That was her calling now. Photos might fade, but she tried to paint those portraits capturing an essence a photo never could. Her pictures could hang on a wall, there for ever.

'No. It's not.' A brush of heat coursed through her from the soft touch of Alessio's fingers at her elbow. The gentle pressure somehow comforting. She turned around, looked into his darkly handsome face. The tightness of his eyes, the pinch to his mouth. Pain drawn across him, reflecting her own. 'I was called home after my mother fell ill. Then we lost her. The country might have shared the grief but in truth it was all mine, and nothing about that is fine, Hannah. It is as if nothing will ever be fine again.'

He'd moved forward. They stood so close now, the heat from his body warming her cold soul. She wanted to take it all for herself. Wrap herself in it like a blanket and let him comfort her for ever, because in some small way he understood.

'There were days when it was all too hard.'

'And yet here we are today.'

Their bodies were hidden behind the horses, where no one could see. She was so aware of the solidity of him, his broad shoulders holding the weight of grief. The burdens of a prince. How she wished some days she could share hers with another, let them carry the load for a while. Let someone with the strength of this man shoulder them. But that was a vulnerability she couldn't afford because it wouldn't last, a gateway to more pain, and she'd had enough in her twenty-five years to last her a lifetime.

Yet the moment seemed full, teeming with things unsaid, emotions repressed waiting to explode. Hovering between everything, and nothing at all. She could smell him this close, the seaside tang of fresh male sweat from their ride in the sun, and the undertone of something else dark and sweet like treacle she could drown in. One step closer and they'd touch. That was all it would take, a move from either of them.

Alessio cupped her cheek, his palm burning on her flesh. The look in his eyes soft. Sad, as if carrying the weight of the world. Then he slid his hand away, stroking her skin as if wanting to linger. Goosebumps drifted over her as he stepped back. It was as if a tension in the stables had snapped, the release a kind of let-down, almost a disappointment.

'You may come and ride Kestia at any time you wish whilst you're here. Simply let the groom know.'

'What about you?'

The corner of his mouth turned upwards in a wry smile. 'I have a country to rule.'

'Is it enough?'

'It's all I have, and all I was born for. It must be enough.' He called over the groom, who led away his two charges. 'Now I'll leave you. We have the dinner tonight, where you'll accompany Stefano. I have much to do before then.'

He turned and strode out of the stables, as if hell itself were chasing him.

CHAPTER FIVE

ALESSIO STOOD BEFORE a mirror, carefully adjusting the white silk bow tie till it sat stiff and perfect at his throat. He wanted to rip it off, the infernal fabric too tight, the top buttons of his pristine shirt choking him. Instead he turned away, breathing slowly, slipping gold cufflinks adorned with the royal crest into the holes of his turned-back cuffs. Sealing them, and him, into place. He shrugged on his jacket, checked again that the Prince of Lasserno had been buttoned, cuffed and tied into his costume. Trying not to think of the afternoon. Of a woman with dark hair the colour of melted chocolate, flying over a fence on a horse. Her grief that twinned his own. The thrill of her warm skin under his fingers.

In Alessio's experience, women were cool, perfumed, and polished in all ways. Hannah had been none of those things today. Instead she'd been heat and fire and sweat and it was all he could do when the tears had gleamed in her eyes not to crush her to him and burn that grief away with a kiss. To see whether the skin of the rest of her was as soft as her cheek under his palm.

He flexed his fingers. Turned from the mirror and began to pace, his energy restless tonight, even after the ride. He'd held back on Apollo today in deference to what he'd believed was Hannah's lack of skill. That knowledge now pricked at him like an irritation. They'd wasted the afternoon on a sedate ride, when instead they could have challenged each other and their horses. Perhaps he'd go out again tomorrow, alone. But like every day, tomorrow his calendar was full. He supposed if he asked Stefano to find time his friend might suggest dropping the hospital visit, but that was the one thing he'd never cancel. Lasserno's sick children needed him, and he would not give up on them. Alessio dropped his head. Scrubbed his hands over his face. There was no time to rid himself of this sensation of needing to move. Not wanting to stop lest creeping thoughts caught up with him.

He checked his watch as a light tap sounded at the door. Almost time to leave.

'Enter.'

He expected Stefano but as the door cracked open it was as if the breath had been punched from his chest. Hannah stood before him in a floor-length dress in the cool, silver-green of olive leaves, her hair up in some soft, loose style which fell about her face. Lips a perfect plum pout. Eyes a little smoky. She looked up at him and he couldn't breathe, his collar once again too tight, his bow tie choking him.

Alessio tugged at the neck of his shirt as her eyes widened. She was seated with Stefano at the dinner tonight, but, seeing her now, he wanted her with him in a way which defied rational thought. Better still, they could ignore the function and stay at the palace. Have a quiet candlelit dinner for two…

He shut down those errant thoughts. They had no place in his life.

'What are you doing here?' he asked, a little more harshly than he should have, but these were his private rooms. No woman had been in them before.

'Stefano told me to meet you here. Something about running late?'

That was unheard of. Stefano's views on punctuality

were similar to his own. Alessio checked his phone and sure enough there was the message. He'd been so preoccupied he hadn't heard the alert.

Hannah stood, expectant. It wasn't quite time to leave and he couldn't have her waiting in the hall, so he stepped back, inviting her into the sitting room. Her long dress swished against the floor, sparkling at the hemline and part way up the skirt. Apart from that shine, the rest of her was unadorned. He couldn't shake the sense that she shouldn't go to the dinner without armour. Whilst the function was filled with more friends, such as they were, than enemies, even he knew how the worst of them could be. He could take care of himself. As he was Prince of Lasserno, people pandered to him. But any attack on Hannah he might not let go ignored. And he had to ignore her.

Except every fibre of his body rebelled at that knowledge.

'How were you after your ride?' Safer ground. He needed to make conversation rather than entertain thoughts of defending her like a prince from some fairy tale. Life was not a fantasy. Though she didn't appear to be faring much better, the way she looked at him in his suit. There was a prickling in his skin whilst she assessed him as if she were stripping him bare, breaking him down. Sometimes he wanted to know what she saw when she did that. What she was looking for when she cast her eyes over him. Did she find him lacking in any way?

Why the answer to those questions was imperative, he couldn't say.

'I'm a little stiff but that's no surprise, since I haven't ridden for almost nine years. But I had a long bath, which helped.'

Visions of her naked, lazing back in the large tub in her room, flushed with the heat of the water, assailed him and he couldn't get rid of them. What colour her nipples would be. Whether she'd be natural or waxed bare. And now those thoughts were planted in his head, they took root like weeds. This was insanity. Usually with women he had control. Around her his control frayed and shredded like rope being hacked by a knife.

'Excellent.' He could make light conversation. It was one of the things at which he excelled. 'You look…beautiful tonight.'

Not exactly where he wished to head, but he was being polite. Any man would say the same. Although it wasn't mere politeness driving him. She looked like some sprite or will-o'-the-wisp, intent on leading him to his doom.

A soft flush of pink tinted her cheeks at the compliment. Who was there in her life to tell her she was beautiful? Was there anyone at all? The thought that no one might have said this to her recently seemed somehow wrong.

'Thank you.' Her voice was soft. Always that tone which was slightly lower and huskier than he expected, causing a tremor right through him, like fingernails scoring down his spine. And the change in her voice suggested that she was affected too. He grabbed on to that thought as if it were a golden nugget of hope.

He'd never had that hope or insecurity before. Women found him attractive. He had a wealth of experience to back up that certainty. But right now he didn't care about anyone else. He only cared that *this* woman was attracted to him, and Alessio didn't know why it mattered. Certainty was his friend. This sensation, of standing on shifting sands, was not.

She began to move, walking around the room as if inspecting it, her glorious dress glittering under the lights as she did.

'Would you like a seat?' he asked. It was as if she were parading in front of him, and he couldn't take his thoughts from the way her bodice cinched at her slender waist. How her gauzy capped sleeves sat tantalisingly at her shoulders. Half on, half off, as if with the wrong shift they would fall and leave more of her glorious skin exposed, the cool, creamy sweep of her décolletage, which would no doubt haunt his dreams, naked and perfect. It should at least be adorned with some jewels, so they could distract him, rather than cause the near impossible-to-control desire to drop his gaze to the gentle swell of her cleavage.

'No. I'm a bit scared to sit down.' She brushed her hands across the fabric, which seemed to sit in multiple layers. When had the construction of a dress ever held such fascination for him? 'I don't usually wear things like this, and I don't want to crush it.'

His first thought was that she should wear dresses like this every night. The next thought was of him holding her in his arms, kissing her. Crushing her dress in the most satisfying of ways.

'You've no jewellery.'

Hannah cocked her head, as if what he'd said was a kind of slight, when really he was only making conversation to stop the itch in his fingers, which tempted him to reach out and touch, to see how much softer she'd feel after her bath.

'No, *Your Highness*.' Those words contained no deference at all. She wielded them as a weapon. 'I didn't want to outshine you.'

A slight smile touched the corner of her lips. He should be offended, but he liked the way she didn't pander to him.

'I'm afraid you already have. No one will be paying any attention to me with such beauty in the room.'

The colour still ran high on her cheeks, but apart from that blush she seemed unaffected. 'Oh, dear. How does it feel, the risk that the spotlight won't be on you?'

A blessed relief. But it was something he could never admit, for the spotlight would never be turned away. 'I'm sure my fragile ego can handle the assault for one night, especially since I'm accompanied by you. Beauty has a way of outshining the beast.'

She snorted, the sound more cute from her than disdainful. 'You're more Prince Charming tonight than Beast.'

'Perhaps I was a beast this afternoon.'

Her gaze dropped to his mouth and held. Was she recalling his touch in the stables, wishing he'd kissed her? The burn of that recollection, the desire…it ignited and began to flare almost out of control. But he'd had years of practice managing it. No matter how much he might want her right now, it would pass. It always did.

'You obviously love your horses and had no idea of my experience. It was understandable. Anyway, it's well known that a *real* princess can tame the beast, and you'll have one of those soon. Isn't that the way the story goes?'

It should be. His longlist was now slimmed to a shortlist. But Alessio wasn't sure. He didn't care for the map of his life right now, the journey relentless most days, unwelcome on others. Required every day. He had no choices, the needs of his country forgotten too long by his father. His own desire to do better, to repair the damage done to his people, overcame any personal sentiments. But tonight, perhaps *just* for tonight, he could engage in a small moment of folly. Those glimpses of sadness Hannah had exposed this afternoon, the shadows which haunted her face from the loss she'd suffered, they hadn't quite left her. Fleeting happiness was what he could provide, and in his experience, women loved jewels. Though he wasn't sure about anything with Hannah. She didn't fit the familiar moulds. Still, he wanted to make *her* feel like a princess tonight.

'A woman should always outshine the man.'

'That's not the way it is in the animal kingdom.'

'I say that's the way it should be.'

'Are you pulling the prince card here? I'm the ruler… my rules?' Her eyes glittered with mirth under the lights.

He wanted her covered in jewels that shone as much as she did, to keep that smile on her face.

'Wait here.'

He walked through his bedroom, to the dressing room. Behind a panel in the wall, he opened a safe. Drew out a rich purple velvet box. People wanted diamonds, rubies, emeralds, sapphires. The gaudy gems. In his hands was a necklace which matched Hannah's dress to perfection. Matched her, with its understated elegance. It might not have seemed as precious as the crown jewels, but to him it was more beautiful because of how uncommon it was. The stones were awash with the same grey-green as her dress, with swirls of gold like the bleeding colour from the watercolour pencils she'd shown him. The surrounding diamonds were an old mine cut, designed to show their true beauty in candlelight.

He tried not to think too hard about what he was doing as he closed the safe and returned to Hannah. These jewels he'd inherited. They were not part of the crown jewels his father had begun to plunder when needing a bauble to give away or for a bribe. These had been locked in the safe in his room too long. They needed to shine again.

Hannah stood with her back to him, gazing out of the window. Staring at the view into Lasserno's capital, glittering like her in the darkened landscape. As he entered the room she turned, those all-seeing eyes fixed on the box in his hands.

'What's that?'

'Adornments. They match your dress.'

Her eyes widened a fraction, her mouth opened. Shut.

'I'm getting the feeling this is a bit like a movie moment. I'm not sure I like it.'

'I promise you will, and you can always say no. But please look.' He opened the box and turned it to her. The jewels lay on pristine white satin inside.

'Oh.' She reached out and then drew back her fingers. 'What's the stone? The colours… And it looks like there are tiny ferns in it.'

'Dendritic agate. Most people don't appreciate its beauty. But the pattern is made in nature and it would have taken years to put together the complementing pieces. Far harder than matching other gemstones.'

'It looks old.' Her voice was a breathy whisper. The kind you wanted in your ear when making love. The whole of him tensed.

'About two hundred years or so. Everyone seeks out the sparkle of new gemstones, the brilliant cuts, but I prefer this. And the greens match your dress.'

'I can't. It's—'

'Try it on.' It seemed imperative now that she wear it. A drive he couldn't ignore. 'Come here.'

She edged to where he stood, near a gilt mirror. He took the cool, heavy necklace from its box. Reached over Hannah's head and draped it round her neck, settling the gems at her throat and securing the clasp. His breath disturbed fine hairs curling at her nape as they escaped her hairstyle. Goosebumps peppered her skin. He craved to run his hands over them. Feel the evidence of her pleasure under his fingertips.

Alessio looked up at her in the mirror, the moment so profoundly intimate and domestic it zapped through him like an electric shock. Instead of giving in to the desire threatening to overwhelm him, he stepped back.

'Do you like it?'

She reached her hand up, and tentatively touched the central stone. She smelled of the final days of autumn, like apples and the last of the season's roses. Rich and intoxicating.

'It's almost like an underwater scene.'

'It's perfect.'

'I can't wear this.' She shook her head. The diamonds twinkled as she moved. 'They're crown jewels.'

'They're not officially in the royal collection. They're mine to do with what I wish, and my wish is that you leave them on. Every woman should have the opportunity to wear something like this, at least once in her life. To feel like a princess.'

'That might have been Mum's nickname for me, but I'm no princess.'

Alessio wondered whether they had talked of Hannah marrying a prince, and whether her dream had died in the accident. He wasn't sure why it mattered, if it had.

'You look like one.'

It was as though the moment froze, with them standing so close in the room, as if time had paused and was giving them this small slice to cherish before wrenching them back into reality. But Alessio knew reality always intruded.

An alert chimed and here the world caught up with them like some spell had been broken. Then a knock sounded at the door.

'Enter.'

Stefano walked in, gave a brief bow.

'Your car has arrived.' He turned to Hannah. His gaze held at her neck for a heartbeat, that hesitation saying more than words could. Her hand fluttered to touch the necklace again, as if afraid someone would take it away. Stefano gave her a brief smile. 'Signorina Barrington.'

To Alessio, he raised an eyebrow.

'Do you know what you're doing?' The words were spoken in Italian, so Hannah couldn't understand.

Alessio checked the time on his watch. Straightened his bow tie. It was the first time in a *long* time that his friend had questioned him. From the moment he had received the call to say his mother was unwell, he'd known. His course unwelcome but set. Ignoring his needs and desires for the good of the country. He straightened his spine like the prince he was.

'Ovviamente.' Of course.

Stefano responded with nothing more than a curt nod as they left for the cars. And all the while on the journey to the dinner, Alessio's lie stuck like a fishbone in his throat.

They stood outside the doorway of a ballroom in a magnificent villa on the outskirts of the capital. Hannah had been told on the way here that this would be a more intimate function, but it didn't sound like it from the cacophony of voices drifting from the ballroom ahead. She touched the central stone of the magnificent necklace, sitting warm and heavy round her throat in a way that seemed comforting, the piece so beautiful she had almost wept when Alessio had shown it to her.

She'd loved the way he had looked at her tonight, after clasping the gems round her neck. As if she was someone precious. Special. Someone to be revered. The intensity of his gaze had left her tight and shivery, hot and cold all at once. It was how she felt about him, watching Alessio now in his black dinner suit, snowy white waistcoat and bow tie. Dressed so formally he looked…more. In control, in charge, masterful. For the tiniest of moments she allowed temptation to whisper that she'd love him to master her.

Hannah's cheeks heated with the illicit thought, but at least the lights were lower out here in the hall. She wouldn't look so much like a vividly toned root vegetable. No one paid her any attention anyway. Right now, Alessio and Stefano were in discussion with what appeared to be a master of ceremonies, who alternated between wringing his hands and bowing as if in apology as Stefano gesticulated.

Alessio stood back a little, his disapproval obvious in the way he held himself, his jaw hard as he checked his watch. Stiff, as if he were retreating into himself and rebuilding another persona by degrees. He glanced over at her, and she decided not to hang back as if this weren't her place. She'd been invited here. She had the dress, the heels, the jewels, and for one night she could be the princess in a story of her own making.

She walked over to the two men. 'Is there a problem?'

Alessio smiled, but the smile didn't touch his eyes. Fake. A mask and nothing more.

'There appears to have been an error. You've been seated next to me.'

She was supposed to sit with Stefano tonight, but a beat of something a lot like anticipation thrummed through her at the thought of being by Alessio's side. Still, she understood the impossibility of her desire and what was *not* being said. Alessio appearing with a woman would invite speculation which a deeply private man like him would despise.

Hannah pasted on her own fake smile. 'I'll change tables, then.'

'Changing tables means changing place cards and will invite more gossip.'

He turned and spoke in Italian to the worried-looking man still hovering in the doorway between the hall and where the dinner would be held. When Alessio finished, the man sagged a fraction and bowed a final time, before hurrying inside the ballroom.

'Come,' Alessio said to her. 'People know we're here. It's time to go in.'

'What did you say to him?'

'That wherever we're placed is suitable, but Stefano would miss your presence at his table.'

'Will he?'

There was something inscrutable about the way he looked at her.

'Any man would.'

The pleasure at those words slid through her with the potency of a shot of spirits. A sensation all too intoxicating to be good for her, so she tried to ignore it. Hannah moved into position and Stefano took her arm, given he'd walk her inside, but Alessio in front held all her attention. He was entirely changed, the metamorphosis into Lasserno's ruler complete. Strength and stability radiated from him like a beacon. Solid. Uncompromising. And yet behind the mask of his public persona, she still glimpsed the true man simmering underneath. He carried himself with an unnatural stiffness, and a tightness around the eyes suggested he wasn't entirely happy in this new skin.

The master of ceremonies announced something to the assembled guests she couldn't understand. The noise of chairs scraping back interrupted the murmurs from the room. A hush descended as everyone waited. Alessio's shoulders rose then fell as if he took a deep breath, then with a straightening of his spine he stepped forward through the doorway as she and Stefano followed. Her eyes adjusted to the brighter lights of the room and she gasped at the sparkling chandeliers, towering floral decorations and gleaming silver candelabras adorning the opulent ballroom. About fifty people stood round tables scattered through the space and every face was turned to Alessio as he waited at the top of the stairs, allowing the assembled guests to take their fill of him, their Crown Prince, and his most honoured guest. It was a dizzying sensation to realise there were a hundred eyes on them as he made his way down the sweeping marble staircase into the room, a leader of his nation in all ways. Arresting and intoxicating.

As they walked through the room Hannah touched her necklace again, almost as a reflex. The curdle of something like fear slithered in her belly but the jewels reminded her that she had a place here tonight. They moved through tables to their seat and people stared and whispered as she passed. When they reached their table, Stefano pulled out her chair.

'I'll see you later, Hannah,' he murmured. It was said quietly enough to seem private, loud enough to pique people's interest. The game of deflection had begun. She merely smiled. Ignored everyone's curious stares as she sat and accepted a glass of champagne from the waiter, thanking the man who poured it for her.

'Ladies, gentlemen.' The table descended into silence as Alessio spoke. 'I'm pleased to introduce Signorina Hannah Barrington. My portrait artist, who has taken two weeks from her hectic schedule to be here before returning to England.'

It was a statement of intent. One she understood, but something about it left her feeling deflated, like a leftover balloon from a long-forgotten party. Alessio named the people at the table for her benefit. Counts, countesses, the Prime Minister and his wife. Lasserno's aristocracy. The country's *Who's Who*.

A few people nodded with interest or stared as if in disbelief at the position she held, sitting to Alessio's left. She could understand why. He was a man in his prime. Available, a prince. Who wouldn't want to be her? They must know he was looking for a bride. Did they assume she was in the running? Her throat tightened and she took a sip of her champagne, the bright bubbles sparkling on her tongue and slipping too easily down her throat. Surely everyone here knew he was looking for a princess? And yet as she watched the other guests' open looks of avarice, she realised this dinner held all the danger of picking her way through a room filled with broken glass in bare feet.

She steeled her spine. Whatever these people might think, they were all wrong and she'd show them. Alessio had to deal with this every day and Hannah couldn't imagine how wearing it must be. She glanced at him now, making easy conversation with the Prime Minister.

'How do you find His Highness's hospitality?' asked a man in a uniform festooned with medals. She didn't like the supercilious way his brow rose when he spoke to her.

Still, her place at this table wasn't to make trouble but to smooth it over. Hannah smiled. 'His Highness is a gracious host, as one would expect.'

'Are you spending much time in his presence?' The corner of the man's mouth turned up in a smirk. 'For research purposes, of course.'

People near them began to watch the exchange, whilst Alessio seemed engrossed in his own conversation. Around the table the air vibrated with tension, a warning. This question was a kind of trap, but she wouldn't fall into it, because no matter how strong and uncompromising he seemed, Hannah realised that Alessio needed shielding. All these people were vultures waiting for others to hunt down their prey and then pick over the carcass left.

She refused to be their victim.

'He's managed to fit me into his hectic schedule.'

The man's smile in response appeared knowing, when he really had no clue. 'I'm *sure* he has.'

Those words carried a weight and meaning everyone sitting at the table would understand. She pretended to be oblivious. To rise above it, since innocence was her weapon.

'Enough to sketch and make the studies I need for the coronation portrait.'

'You're young to receive such an illustrious commission,' said a countess wearing a shimmering gold dress of liquid satin and diamonds round her neck the size of pigeon eggs. 'You must have quite prodigious…talents.'

Hannah swallowed. She couldn't stop the fire igniting in her belly at these insinuations. She knew her worth, the work and the sacrifice she put into her art. Her achievements. She didn't care what the guests here thought of her. Alessio was the one getting the portrait. She'd never paint any of these people, no matter how much they offered. Even if they *begged*, because she didn't want to know them.

Not the way she was coming to know Alessio.

'I'll leave that judgement to others. My job's to paint. To find the essence of a person.'

'And have you found the essence of His Highness?' Those words were delivered with a venomous smile. One which appeared friendly but carried a sting.

'Not yet. But I've never painted a prince before.'

A few people murmured at her response, but she couldn't understand what was being said. They seemed friendly enough, so she suspected it wasn't a criticism. She hardly cared. They could think what they wanted. She knew the truth. Then next to her, Alessio straightened. She could almost feel the electric crackle of him from his seat.

'I suggest, Contessa, that you do your research. Signorina Barrington has won some of the most prestigious portrait competitions in the world. She is the best. There is *no one* more qualified to paint my coronation portrait than her.'

His voice bristled with warning, sharp and cold. Now everyone at the table stared at them. Whilst his chill was meant to give a clear message, to her his voice was like being immersed in a warm bath. She basked in his defence, even though it would likely cost him. For a man whose private life was deliberately opaque, he'd allowed the door to crack open a chink, showing in the tiniest of ways that she mattered.

She couldn't thank him in public, so she smiled benevolently as if praise like this were given to her every day. But, since they sat next to each other, she moved her thigh towards his until their knees touched. A tiny gesture to say thank you in a way she couldn't immediately vocalise. Hannah applied the smallest amount of pressure, to let Alessio know her move wasn't accidental. The fingers of his left hand flexed on the tablecloth and he pressed back. The thrill of that secret acknowledgement bubbled through her like the sparkle of champagne. They sat knee to knee, calf to calf, ankle to ankle, and even through the layers of her dress it was as if she could sense the heat burning between them.

The conversation changed after his intervention, the flow of it around the table broken by the royal toast. Hannah stood with everyone else and the sense of loss she suffered at the lack of that supportive touch seemed almost visceral, as if something magical had been broken. She watched Alessio, who managed to look utterly alone even when surrounded by this host of people. There was a blankness about him which showed that any emotion had been well and truly shuttered and locked down. She didn't know how he managed to eat, other than out of politeness. She sampled the beautiful-looking food and, whilst delicious, it held no appeal. This crowd would likely poison your meal as anything else. It was almost a surprise that Alessio didn't have an official food taster, they were all so toxic.

'Have you ridden with His Highness?' the Countess asked, after they'd resumed their seats. She was surprised the woman hadn't accepted Alessio's put-down, but she was young enough to be interested in him for herself and there was a determined gleam in her eye. 'He's known as a passionate horseman.'

She decided to tell the truth because enough people had seen her ride with Alessio to make a lie far worse.

'Yes. Have you?'

Even though she wasn't looking at him, she was aware

as Alessio stiffened, so attuned to him now that she could sense the slow freeze again. He shifted as she pressed her leg to his once more. Letting him know she had this. That he'd protected her, but it was okay for him to accept her help too.

The Countess's mouth thinned. If looks were daggers, Hannah would be properly skewered. 'No, I have never been invited to ride by His Highness, but it would be my *extreme* pleasure to do so.'

Hannah raised an eyebrow in a way she hoped looked imperious. 'Perhaps one day, if you're a good enough rider, you'll be lucky and get your chance.'

She didn't think the woman had the care, intuition or skill to be allowed anywhere near Alessio's beloved horses. Hannah only realised now the privilege she'd been afforded being allowed to ride Kestia whenever she wished.

The Countess turned her attention to Alessio. 'Your Highness, it's an uncommon honour you invited Signorina Barrington to sit at your table.'

He fixed the woman with a cold glare. 'It's you who should be honoured, to have such a prestigious artist in your company.'

'The sad truth,' Hannah said, no doubt breaking protocol with her interruption but not caring less, 'is there was a terrible mix-up in the beginning. I was meant to sit with Stefano.'

She was coming to realise gossip was the currency of value fuelling these people, so she'd give them something to talk about. She glanced over to where Stefano sat at a distant table and gave a little wave. He raised his champagne flute and toasted her in response.

'You were looking forward to sitting with His Highness's private secretary?'

'Oh, yes. Very much,' Hannah said. 'But there's always tomorrow.'

This could have been a pleasant evening in a magnificent room, with exquisite food and wine. Her fantasy for just one night. She resented the people here intent on ruining it. Some of them were trying to goad Alessio's responses, to play a game in which there could be no winners.

The thing was, they hadn't counted on her.

Alessio adjusted the napkin on his lap. As he did so his hand brushed hers, feather-light. So fleeting it could have been a mistake, but she knew it hadn't been. Her breathing hitched, a shiver of pleasure running through her, settling low and heavy.

Tonight, she and Alessio were a team. None of the people here could touch them. She ate some more food, sipped more champagne. All the time exquisitely aware of the man sitting next to her. And as their legs touched under the table once more, their secret, she prayed this dinner was over soon and that she'd done enough.

CHAPTER SIX

THE JOURNEY BACK to the palace had been in near silence. There was too much going through Alessio's head for him to say anything at all. The sly comments, the innuendos, all directed at one woman.

A woman who'd seen fit to defend him in the face of obvious attacks.

'Do you need to discuss this evening's events?' Stefano asked as they walked towards the royal suite. Hannah remained silent. Alessio wanted to know how she felt, given everything that had passed. 'And would you like me to take Signorina Barrington on a very public sightseeing tour tomorrow? A quiet word in the right news organisation's ear and—'

'No, and no press.'

'If we used them properly, it could be to your advantage. They fabricate news about you, since they get none. Why not feed the beast a different story?'

This old argument between them could wait for another day. He didn't want Hannah used to deflect attention from his own errors. Inviting her into the hornet's nest was his mistake. She'd done enough tonight by tolerating the dinner. For that alone he must thank her.

'I need to place the necklace in the safe,' he said. Hannah stood there with her head held high, looking more like royalty than he felt after tonight's efforts. Lasserno's aristocracy had not crowned themselves in glory.

Hannah reached behind her neck to undo the clasp and he shook his head.

'You can remove it in my room,' he said, then added to Stefano, 'We can speak tomorrow if there's a need.'

Stefano gave Hannah a lingering look, nodded, then left.

Alessio opened the door of his suite and walked inside with Hannah following. The burn in his gut overtook him now, raging close to the surface over the way she'd been treated. All the while his emotions mingled with something softer, more tempting. She'd defended him, worked to ensure there were no rumours about them. Pretended *for* him. That protectiveness was unfamiliar in his experience. Its allure potent. The memory of their knees pressing together, the hidden support…he couldn't put it out of his mind. In his role as Prince of Lasserno he was tasked as protector of a nation. The weight of all decisions fell on his shoulders. Tonight, Hannah had relieved some of his burden and he could never thank her enough.

'Would you like a drink?' He rarely resorted to alcohol, avoiding any kind of excess, but he needed something to dull the immediacy of his anger.

She shook her head. Standing under the soft lights, glittering and perfect. As if this were her place. But it couldn't be, no matter the temptation.

'No, I think I've had more than enough wine. But feel free.'

He smiled at the audacity of her giving him permission in his own rooms. She was a constant challenge to his position, and he feared he was enjoying the challenge far too much.

'I will.' He poured a slug of amber fluid into a glass.

'You are the Prince and all. You can do what you like.'

The weight of responsibility sometimes threatened to

crush him, and yet he couldn't yield to it. He took a swig of his drink, the burn of the spirit doing nothing to ease the emotions sliding through his veins. Anger, desire. A dangerous mix when coupled with a beautiful, uncompromising woman.

A woman who seemed to be shifting from foot to foot, as if she were in discomfort.

'Are you all right?'

She winced. 'Do you mind if I take off these heels? They're like a torture device.'

'Feel free.' He lifted his glass to take another swig of Scotch but stopped as Hannah grabbed on to the corner of a chair, kicked off the heels and wiggled her toes in the carpet, closing her eyes and sighing as she did so. 'Heaven.'

Alessio couldn't tear his gaze from her toes, peeking out from under the hem of her dress. Red. He swallowed. Bright. Vibrant. Red. For some reason that bold colour was unlike one he thought she might wear. It surprised him. As if he were being allowed to glimpse some secret about her. He didn't know why a need pounded through him now, his heart like an anvil being struck by the blacksmith's hammer. They were only feet. But that intimacy again almost undid him.

'I'm sorry,' Alessio said.

She shrugged. 'For formal occasions I know they're expected. Beauty is pain and all that. I just don't have any need to wear heels around the farm.'

'Not about the shoes.' Alessio couldn't look at her right now. Instead he turned to the mirror and tugged his bow tie undone. Wrenched the top button of his shirt open, crushing the perfectly pressed cotton under his fingers. Even then his clothes choked him. 'The people.'

She came into view, reflected behind him. Picked up a small porcelain figurine of a horse that decorated a side table, inspecting it, running her fingers over the smooth surface. What he wouldn't give right now to have those fingers running over his skin instead. He took another sip of his drink. No good would come of those thoughts. His responsibility was to look after her as an employee, not dream of Hannah undressing him with her gentle, stroking fingers.

Yet it was this last thought he couldn't get out of his head.

'I'm used to the mean girls,' she said. 'You meet a few.'

Alessio wheeled around. She was precious. She shouldn't have to deal with anyone cruel. 'Where would you meet people like *that*? Your clients?'

'No, my clients are nice...' she skewered him with her insightful gaze and smiled sweetly '...in the main. I came across them at boarding school after my parents died. Girls could be cruel to an orphan like me.'

'Oh, *bella*.' Her eyes widened a fraction as the term of endearment slipped out unchecked. He started forward, wanting to comfort her, but that wasn't his role. It never could be. Though the reasons for that seemed to be getting a little hazy. 'Why were you at a boarding school?'

She walked to a portrait on the wall, another glowering ancestor, all a reminder of the job he had to do for Lasserno. He ensured they stared down on him from every private wall in the palace so he would never falter.

'My aunt and uncle were my guardians. They didn't have children of their own and said it would give me stability.'

'Did it?'

'No. It was awful. I didn't...cope. So they brought me home and sent me to the local school. Not prestigious, but small and familiar.'

He could barely imagine the pain she had suffered, both parents lost. Being sent away from everything she'd known. The unfairness tore at him. At least when his mother had died he'd had some sympathetic courtiers, given his father was of no use.

'I enjoyed boarding school. Away from the constraints of the palace. Away from my parents' cold war.' The open battles over his father's infidelity. 'It seemed like bliss in comparison, even though boys can be brutal.'

There was a softness in the way she looked at him now, like sympathy, when he was owed none from her. 'Being a prince, you would have been top of the tree.'

He threw back the last of his drink. Tempting to have more, but not sensible in the circumstances. 'That's not always the best position to be in. It brings with it a certain entitlement which I needed to unlearn.'

She had an uncanny way of getting him to speak the truth of everything. He put his glass down on a side table. The *domesticity* of this scene assailed him once more. As if she should be here. As if this was her rightful place. A delectable sense of inevitability slid through him.

As if there was no other place she should *ever* be.

'You learned that at least. If you had one wish, what would it be?'

Her questions. Funny how she'd stopped asking the ones on her infernal list. However, this one seemed appropriate. He had so many wishes. That he had a sibling, so he was not all alone. That his parents had had a happy marriage like some of those he'd witnessed with his school friends. That his mother had not died. But there was one wish, above all. It came to the fore on nights like tonight, when he realised every choice was taken away by duty. *That* wish pricked at him like a dagger between the ribs, sliding true to his heart. His deepest secret, and some days his greatest shame.

'Not being the Prince of Lasserno.' Being an ordinary man with ordinary choices. He looked over at the decanter of Scotch sitting on the sideboard. He'd never drowned his regrets in alcohol before, but tonight he wanted to down the whole bottle. 'And you?'

Hannah paled, her skin translucent in the lights. The antique diamonds glittering at her throat. She should always be in diamonds, this woman. Draped in jewels to frame her beauty. Her head dropped. She scuffed at the carpet with her pretty painted toes.

'I wish I'd been in the car with my parents.' Her voice was so soft he almost didn't hear it, but the force of what she said struck him like a blow. His whole body rebelled at the thought she might not be here, that if she'd been in that car the world would be without her brilliance.

'No!' He cut through the air with his hand as her eyes widened. He was surprised by his own vehemence. The visceral horror that this was how she might feel. 'You do *not* wish that.'

He strode towards her, the hectic glitter in her eyes telling him tears were close. He wasn't good with tears. His mother had spilled enough of them in his presence, railing against his father. He'd been inured to most of them in the end, learning to comfort without feeling the pain himself.

The threat of Hannah's ripped at the fabric of his being.

'It's my wish. It can be what I want.'

'Survivor's guilt.' As if those two words could ease her dark thoughts. Had she had counselling after her parents had passed? Her aunt and uncle had sent her away to boarding school. Perhaps they'd expected her to get over things without the help a teenager might need after such a loss. 'If this is the way you feel then you should—'

'You don't understand.' She turned away from him, wrapped her arms round her waist. 'If I hadn't travelled with my friend that afternoon, we'd have gone a different way home. We wouldn't have been on that road. The tractor wouldn't have been on the bend. They might...'

They might be alive.

Alessio went to her, placed his hands gently on her shoulders. Her skin was warm, soft as satin. He circled his thumbs on her exposed flesh. She leaned back into him. As if taking, for a moment, the meagre solace he could provide.

'We both want things we can't have,' he murmured.

'You could give up the throne. I can't turn back time.'

He let out a long, slow breath. Occasionally in his fantasies he'd allow himself to simply be a man, but he had the luxury of being able to think that way. 'No. I can't. I have a duty to my people and that duty is more important than anything. More important than a man's desires.'

She disengaged from him and he mourned the loss of his hands on her skin, the warmth of her. 'At least you can change things.'

'I'll always be the leader of Lasserno.'

'Not everything has to be for duty. You talk about finding the perfect princess. Is that duty as well?'

'All that I do is for my country.'

'Then what feeds the man's soul?'

He walked to the windows of the palace overlooking his capital. The city, glittering in the late evening like a bright jewel. One entirely in his care. 'The man doesn't exist in isolation from the Prince. They're one and the same.'

'What about love?'

'What about it?'

'You could marry for that. Love's not about duty.'

Alessio wheeled around. He knew this story, an age-old one. Love had no place in his life. He'd seen how it ate away, destroyed when one party stopped loving the other, or perhaps had never loved them in the first place. His parents' relationship had been the best evidence of that. It inured him to ever seeking anything more for himself. If duty it was to be, then that would extend to his princess, who'd understand the constraints of royalty, the expectations of her role.

Sure he'd had promises before…of love, of adoration… all so a woman could get a crown on her head too. He could never be sure of anyone, whether they wanted the man, the money or his family's name, especially after Allegra's efforts. Better he found someone who knew what this was, a dynastic endeavour. Protecting his country from a vacuum, nothing more. In many ways Hannah was the same as others, accepting the exorbitant fee he'd offered her to paint his portrait. The suspicion overran him, needy and unfamiliar. Had he not been the Prince of Lasserno, would she have agreed to paint him with no complaints? Probably. And that was something he should never forget. Even though tonight, she had seen fit to protect him at her own expense.

'And who would I find to love? You?'

Hannah's eyes widened, and then she laughed in a mocking kind of way, as if what he'd said was ridiculous. 'Me? That's absurd.'

Which was not the answer he'd been expecting. He'd expected a shy glance, some fluttering of eyelids. A woman playing coy at the hint something more might be on offer. Any reaction other than suggestions of foolishness on his part.

'Many women want to be a princess.'

'When they're little girls, perhaps. But I'm all grown up, and those kinds of dreams die when you realise that's all they are. Silly, glitter-covered fantasies which tarnish as soon as you expose them to reality. I'm an artist. A commoner. We don't marry princes.'

Had her dreams died with her parents? He wanted to rail against it. She should be allowed to have the fantasy she could be whatever she wanted. He couldn't have that dream, but that didn't mean the same was unavailable to her.

'What feeds the woman's soul?'

The flush ran over her cheeks. 'My art consumes me. When I paint, nothing else exists. It's all I've wanted for a long time. It's enough.'

It sounded like an excuse.

'You look like a princess. And tonight, at the table, you acted like a queen. No royalty I know would have done better.'

It was as if she'd protected one of her own, when no one apart from Stefano ever leapt to his defence, only tried to tear him down. The warm kernel of something lit in his chest. Bright, perfect. Overlaid with an intoxicating drumbeat down low. Desire that was dark, tempting and forbidden. Something to be taken care of by himself, on the rare occasion it afflicted him, or with a willing partner who knew what this was. A few hours of passion, nothing more.

Not with a woman he'd begun to crave with a kind of obsession. *Never* that.

A slow stain of colour crept up her throat. A gentle smile on her lips. The obvious pleasure in a compliment letting him know she was still a woman underneath all her talk otherwise.

'Thank you. I'll let you in on a secret. For a little while, I felt like one. The make-up, a pretty dress. Some exquisite jewellery that isn't mine. It's all smoke and mirrors really. But for one night, I'll admit it was fun.'

She didn't understand. It wasn't the trappings that had her competing with royalty, but her demeanour. The way she had stood up to those who tried to cut her down. The way she had stood up for him...

'What if for one night, it's what we could have?' The urgency of his need gripped him. The fantasy that he could have her for this moment. Every part of him began to prickle with anticipation, the hum of pleasure coursing through his blood. 'If we could pretend that I'm simply a man, and you're simply a woman.'

'That you're not the Prince of Lasserno? Are you asking me to grant your wish?'

A pulse beat at the base of her throat, an excited kind of fluttering that told him she wanted this too.

'And I'd treat you like the princess that you are.'

Her pupils expanded, drowning the rockpool green of her eyes till the colour was a mere sliver. Her lips parted, as if the oxygen had been sucked from the room, and he sensed it too. The tightening of his chest as if he couldn't fill his lungs.

She stood in front of him, glowing, beautiful in a way which evoked physical pain. He wanted her so badly he would drop to his knees and beg her like some supplicant so long as she granted him one evening, for both of them to lose themselves in the pretence they could be something other than who they were.

Bella?' Her blood-red toes curled into the carpet. He clenched his hands to fists so he wouldn't reach out, touch. Take. 'I will do nothing unless you say yes. The choice, it is yours alone. Stay, or go.'

He had the power here. An imbalance she must never feel beholden to. He needed her to crave him as much as he craved her, to a kind of distraction.

She licked her lips. The mere peek of her tongue almost undid him. How he wanted to plunder that mouth. Tear the clothes from her body. Rip apart the fabric of both their lives for a night of pleasure, lost in her arms.

'If I'm a princess tonight, then who are you?'

The fantasy wove around him. Something which allowed them to forget who they were and what they were doing here.

'I'm the frog you're about to kiss.'

'But that means you'll turn into a prince.'

'I won't be Prince of Lasserno. I'll be *your* prince.'
Hers alone.

Hannah's lips curled into a wicked smile. 'For only one night.'

It wasn't a question, and in a strange way that gave him some comfort. But the thought laced him with a kind of pain, that when the sun rose in the morning this blissful, illicit fantasy would be over.

'That's all it can ever be. Sex has a way of changing things, but it can't change this,' he said, as much of a warning to him as it was to her. Though the fantasy wove into a reality, where she could turn him into someone else for a few hours, because they both willed it.

'And what about duty?'

'Tonight?' It could only be one night and nothing else. That was all he would allow himself. And for him, that would be enough. 'Duty can go to hell.'

Duty can go to hell.

The words rang through her like some clarion call. He stood there, jaw hard. Hands clenched to fists at his sides. His bow tie hanging loose, and the top of his shirt unbuttoned to show the dark hair at his throat. Yet he wouldn't come to her. She knew it. She saw it in the tense set of his body. He wanted her to decide. And she craved him, with a zeal that made little sense to her. She'd never been particularly interested in sex, or so she had always thought, the idea of getting too close to someone, letting anyone in, crushing the breath right out of her. Caring was dangerous. Loving, even more so. But around Alessio, there was no common sense. As if he were all the oxygen in the room, as if to breathe she had to have him.

She wanted to walk into his arms, into all that strength. Bury her nose to the hollow at the base of his throat. Let every part of him overwhelm her. She took a step. The first. It wasn't so hard because this was a moment of fantasy where they could pretend to be other people. Alessio flexed his fingers as she took another step, and another. And only when she stood so close that his warmth seeped into her, did he wrap his arms round her, as strong as she'd imagined them to be. He dropped his head as if in slow motion. She rose on her toes and their lips touched. The warm press of skin to skin. Gentle, strangely innocent in a way that almost broke her heart. She dropped back, looked into his all-dark eyes, the pupils drowning out the velvet brown.

'Look,' she whispered, her voice cracking. A hesitation between them as if everything was tentative and the universe waited. 'I've made a prince.'

And then it was as if the world exploded around them. Alessio groaned and took her face in his hands, crushing his lips to hers. She met him, her hands on his chest, fingers curling into the strong muscles there. She had no experience, but this seemed to lack all finesse, drawn from pure need. Their tongues touched, battled, as if each were trying to win over the other. Her body was all heat and fire, her exquisite dress of fine fabric a scraping interruption to his fingers on her overheated skin. She slipped her hands under his jacket, over the shoulders, tugging because every piece of clothing between them was a travesty. He let her face go, tore the jacket from his body. Tossed it to the floor.

'Your dress. I don't trust myself.'

She barely did her *own* self. But she reached round with trembling fingers and slid the zip down, slowly. As if this were a kind of performance, because she was transfixed by the hooded rapture in his eyes as he watched. There was no time for nerves, no time for doubts. Not here, not now. Tonight she *was* a princess, and she could do and have anything she wanted.

And how she wanted Alessio.

The dress slumped from her shoulders as she shrugged out of the bodice. The fabric slid over her body, fell to the floor. She stepped out of it, as if it were a sea of foam on the ground and she was leaving the ocean, reborn, in only the exquisite lace bra and panties which she'd purchased to match the dress. The single extravagance she'd allowed when preparing her trip to Lasserno. Her skin seemed too tight, as if she were a butterfly ready to burst from the chrysalis. It was as if for the past nine years she'd been in stasis, waiting. And now she'd been changed on a cellular level.

Hannah began to walk forward towards Alessio and he held up a hand.

'Wait. I want to look at you. To always remember your beauty.'

There were so many things that would be left unsaid tonight, but how precious these moments were would not be one of them. Now wasn't the time to be shy, but to be brave.

'I need to see you too,' she whispered, unsure as to whether her voice was loud enough with all the emotion trembling through it. Alessio's throat convulsed with a swallow which told her all she needed to know, that he'd heard her plea. He grabbed his bow tie, dragged it from round his neck and dropped it on the floor. Undid a button on his shirt, then another and another. Tugged the zinc-white fabric from the waist of his trousers, tossing it aside the way of his coat and bow tie. She inhaled sharply at the sight before her, his broad shoulders, the muscles of his arms all sculpted and bronzed. The hair at his chest, dusting the muscles there, trailing down, darkening and disappearing at his trouser waistband. Her fingers became restless to run them through the crisp hair. To touch. He undid his belt, drew it slowly from his trousers before tossing it aside. Her eyes dropped as he gripped the top of his trousers. Even though they were black, the evidence of his arousal was bold and obvious.

She'd done that to him.

'Like what you see?'

'I'd like to see more.'

He chuckled and the ripple of it rolled through her, like a promise for something she didn't know she'd been waiting for. Anticipation at its finest.

'Your wish is my command, *Principessa.*'

A thrill shivered through her, that she had any sway over this man. That he stood there, tense with his physical masculine beauty, waiting for her next word.

'Slowly.'

The corner of his mouth kicked up and he did exactly as she demanded. It was as if each notch on the zip took an age. Almost as if time were standing still. The leisurely, deliberate tease all for her as he hooked his hands into the waistband of his trousers and his underwear. The heat of this moment flamed in her cheeks. The boldness of it, all because of what she desired. It could career out of control at any second, but for now this was hers. Alessio bent at the waist as his trousers passed his thighs, everything hidden, then they slipped to the floor and he rose. Stepped out of the superfine black wool and kicked them and his underwear away.

He stood straight, allowing her eyes to take their fill. She might be inexperienced, but she'd seen naked men before. In art, on the internet, in life-drawing classes. This, however, was more than she had ever experienced. A perfect man, drawn by the hand of angels. Too real to be human, yet undoubtedly flesh and blood. His arousal, because of her, intoxicating.

'I need to touch you. For you to touch me.' His voice was tight, as if he were in pain, and she understood. The ache inside her built and built. She felt she might double over with need, self-combust if their hands were not on one another soon.

'Yes. *Please.*'

He made it to her in a few strides, hands hot and hard on her hips, slipping round to her buttocks, pulling her close and against him. Burying his face in her neck and breathing her in. His lips kissing and skimming the sensitive skin there till she moaned. He slid his hands up her back as she shivered and quaked under his exquisite touch. Unhooked her bra. Slipped it over her arms and let it fall to the floor. He moved his hands to cup her breasts, stood back a mere fraction to look, brushed his thumbs to her nipples and they tightened with a burning pleasure. He looked down at her with reverence, as if she were a kind of revelation.

'Touch me,' he groaned and released one breast, taking her hand in his. Guiding it between them. Clasping it tight around his hard length. He hissed in a breath as he thrust into her palm, dropping his head back, and the tendons on his neck stood out, tense and as if he were in agony. She marvelled at the feel of him, silk over steel, and at his size, which she knew on a biological level should fit her, yet on a pure female level an uncertain niggle like fear began to seed and grow.

Fear had no place here, not tonight on her one evening allowing herself to be the princess in this fantasy. A night to give, take, indulge, before going back to real life, or her new version of it.

His grip on her hand loosened. He left her to stroke him up and down in the rhythm he'd set, returning his attention to her nipples, which were tight and aching. She shifted under his ministrations, *needing* him. It would be easy to ignore the obvious, not tell him about her inexperience, but this would do a disservice to them both, and she'd allow *nothing* to interfere with tonight.

She let him go and he opened his eyes, his lips apart. Eyes glazed and unfocused with pleasure.

'Alessio, I…' She hesitated when this was not the time for it. Now was the time to be bold. To take what she wanted for herself. He stopped teasing her nipples, rested his hands gently on her hips. Looked down at her with the slightest of frowns, of concern, she thought, and the warmth of realisation flooded her. She traced her hands up his body, to rest on the firm swell of his pectoral muscles, as the dark hair on his chest pricked and teased under her fingertips.

'You have something to say, *bella*?'

'I—I've never done this before.'

His grip on her hips tightened and released. 'This?'

'Sex. Any of it.'

His eyes widened a fraction. Then he wrapped his strong arms round her and drew her close into his embrace. The tears pricked at her eyes. Her virginity wasn't something she'd ever thought much of. It simply *was*. A fact. A reality. She'd never believed it merited much thought, until now.

'I'm your first.' The words were muffled and hot, murmured into her hair.

In everything.

'Yes.'

He stroked a hand up and down her spine. Light, tender brushes, and goosebumps sprinkled over her skin, as soft and warm as a spring shower.

'A better man would send you to bed on your own.'

'A better man wouldn't leave me feeling like this.' She pulled back and his arms fell loose. Hannah looked up at him. His pupils were drowning out the colour of his eyes till they were almost black. He was still hard and hot against her belly.

'Like what?' he ground out, all gravel and darkness.

'Empty. Like I'm going to die if you're not inside me. I *hurt* for wanting you so badly.'

His nostrils flared, lips parted a fraction. 'I won't leave you. I'll make it good for you. I promise.'

He slipped his hand to her left nipple again. Toying with it. Harder now. A light pinch.

'Do you like that?' he murmured.

She arched her back into him with the bright spark of pleasure rushing straight between her legs. Not so gentle then, and the slow burn between them became hotter and hotter.

'*Yes.*' Her voice was a sigh, nothing more.

'I can take the pain away,' he said as he eased her panties from her body till they slipped down her legs. 'You'll be screaming tonight from pleasure.'

Alessio slipped his hand between their bodies, between her thighs. Gentle strokes where she needed him most. It was too much and not enough all at the same time. She moved against him, desperate for more. Desperate to be filled, to be overwhelmed by him. She couldn't look at him now. Closed her eyes as if to hold on to the sensation so it would never end.

Then he slowed. Slid a finger inside her. Her fingers clawed into the hard muscles of his chest as he stroked something deep in her body, making Hannah quiver and quake with a flood of heat between her legs. 'I'll take care of you,' he murmured gently into her ear, kissing feather-light where his breath had stroked at her skin.

She clung round his neck because she'd fall if she didn't. Riding his hand like a woman who was a stranger to her.

Her head tipped back, and his lips were on hers. Soft, passionate. She opened and let him in. Their tongues touched, tangled together. She craved for him to invade every part of her. His fingers brushing her nipple, the sense of him deep inside, thrusting with one finger, then another.

'Let go, *bella*.' He whispered the words against her lips before crushing them to his again, adding a thumb to brush over her clitoris in soft, insistent strokes. He was everywhere, her world. She was burning like the hottest flame, till she was sure her skin would blister with it.

Then she came, cracked in two as if Alessio had torn her apart with pleasure. Screaming as he'd promised, in a rush of perfect, blinding heat.

Alessio breathed in the scent of her, the brightness of her perfume, the dark musk of her arousal, as she clenched hot and wet round his fingers. Then the weight of her arms round his neck intensified, as if her knees were giving out underneath her. He swept Hannah into his arms, her body soft and limp, her eyes glazed with arousal, a flush of colour tinting her cheeks, her chest. So beautiful in that dying blush of pleasure it almost caused him physical pain. He dropped his mouth to hers, her lips soft and yielding like the rest of her. All slick and hot and wet.

The privilege of being granted her trust flared inside him. He silently vowed it would be good for her, *better* than good. He wanted these hours with her to transcend mere sex. Something to be remembered, treasured, especially given it was her first time.

There would be no disappointing Hannah tonight. On the contrary, he feared she would be a revelation to shake the foundations of his being. He laid her gently on the covers of his bed, his body trembling with the desire to be inside her, where his fingers had been. But he would make sure tonight was about her. Her pleasure first and foremost.

Her eyes lay closed, the beautiful lashes feathering on her cheeks. He allowed her the bliss of the comedown from her orgasm. Perhaps her first at the hands of another. Marvelled at her body, splayed with abandon on the bed before him. Settled himself between her thighs where he could smell the sweet scent of arousal, the necklace at her throat like a jewelled symbol of his possession, making this all the more erotic. He dropped his head and licked, the taste of her like a drug shooting straight into his veins, and she groaned as he toyed with her. Worshipping her in the best way he knew how.

Her back arched from the bed as she gripped and released the covers.

'Alessio… I…it's too much.'

He ceased his ministrations. Stroked his thumbs gently on the insides of her thighs. As much as she said it was too much, her back arched, bringing her body closer to his mouth.

'Relax. You have no idea how much your body can take but I can show you. I can show you it all. Let me pleasure you,' he murmured against her, so close to where he wanted his mouth to be it almost watered.

'*Yes.*' The word came like the softest of exhales, the sweetest capitulation, and he began his gentle ministrations again, the light flicking of his tongue, till she thrashed on the bed, her words indecipherable. She thrust her hand into his hair and gripped tight, the bright needles of pain causing the heat of passion to roar through him like lava in his blood. He slipped his hands under her buttocks, the whole of her trembling. Held her in place as he sucked on the tight little nub at the centre of her and relished her second scream of the evening, this time his name sung to the room.

There was no time now for him to wait, every part of him frayed and overheating. He had to be inside her. He'd spill himself on the sheets like a teenager if he wasn't, and soon. He reached for his bedside drawer, the condoms there. Sheathed himself with difficulty because he was affected by it too, this thing between them. Climbed over her and she wrapped her arms round him tight.

'Do you want me inside you?'

'Never more than now.'

'I'll go slowly,' he said, a promise voiced so he'd be forced to keep it, because all he wanted was to take. Ease his own agony. But tonight was for her. He kissed her, their tongues twining together, hot, erotic, as he slid against the folds of her, testing her wetness to ensure his entry would be easy enough, even though he wished he could promise her no pain. He notched himself at Hannah's centre, slid a bit further, a little way inside, and shut his eyes at the overwhelming pleasure of her heat enveloping only the tip of him. Worked gentle thrusts, a little deeper, deeper still, till Hannah's kisses became harder, more insistent. Bruising. She tilted her hips and he slid all the way inside, the hitch of her breath catching as he did so. He pulled his head back to look at her, to breathe through the pleasure to ensure her own, almost losing himself to his own orgasm right there.

'Good?' Sentences were beyond him, but he needed to check on her, the desire to make sure she wasn't hurting, that she was enjoying this, clasping at something deep inside him.

She opened her eyes and stared deep into his. Alessio's muscles trembled as she clenched tight and hot round him. Gripping him like the warmest silken glove, so tight it was almost his undoing.

'Perfect.' Her voice was a sigh shivering right through him. The pleasure threaded in her voice, like a plea.

'Should I move?'

'Move? Yes.'

His arms rested either side of her head. He stroked his thumbs to her temples, the necklace glittering in the soft light of the room, winding the blissful fantasy of the night round him once more.

'It would be my greatest pleasure.'

He rocked into her again and her eyes fluttered shut

for a moment before opening. Holding his gaze. He said it would be his greatest pleasure, but all he craved was hers. She wrapped her legs tight round him, moving with him. He lost himself in her gaze, the flush of her skin, her lips, parted as if she couldn't take in enough air. Head thrown back and eyes glazed and far away with ecstasy. The heat of her, the scent of her around him. The sound of their bodies coming together wound him tighter and tighter. And the words left his mouth in his own language. Murmurings of ecstasy, of thanks, of truth.

'I don't understand,' she whispered, her blinks long and slow, her body tightening even harder round his. The tingle at the base of his spine heralded that he was close, so close.

And against all his better judgement he told her.

'You are so beautiful. It is too much. The privilege of being inside you.'

He changed his angle, went deeper. Ground his hips against her body. Her eyes widened as the bright spill of tears gleamed and threatened. Then her gaze became unfocused as she stiffened, gasped and cried out his name as she came. He plunged over the edge with her, the ecstasy tearing up his spine as if he were being struck by lightning. A blinding white flash in his head almost obliterated his consciousness. Then, as he came back to himself once the spasms subsided, all he could see was her. Tears now tracking from the corners of her eyes. The sparkling necklace at her throat. For tonight he'd allow them both the fantasy.

'La mia principessa.'

My princess.

Reality would come soon enough.

CHAPTER SEVEN

HANNAH SAT IN an armchair opposite Alessio's desk as he paced the rich crimson carpet of his office, checking his watch. He was dressed today in a crisp white shirt with a vibrant lemon-yellow tie. No jacket, which she suspected counted almost as casual with him. His body was tense, every part of him bristling as he almost wore a path through the plush flooring. She wanted to put her arm on him. To tell him it was okay to simply stop. She knew he could. That he could channel his restless energy elsewhere. How she craved a repeat performance. To spend her days and nights learning about him in every way. A slide of heat wound through her, hot and tempting. She didn't know how he could be so immune to it all, when she wanted to melt into a human-shaped puddle in her seat.

His gaze rested on her, cool and hard. So unlike the loose, relaxed, passionate man from the night before she was almost forced to wonder whether she'd dreamt what had happened between them. Today all she saw was the ruler of Lasserno, as if the man, Alessio Arcuri, had ceased to exist.

'The hospital visit is private. No press have been alerted. I hope you recognise the privilege of this invitation. The children—'

'*The children are not in some circus where you can watch them perform.* I'm aware how vulnerable children can be.'

She'd never use sick children as fodder, he had to realise that. Or perhaps he didn't really know her at all. But
it wasn't about his comment. No, he was distancing himself from her. Pulling away from the night they'd shared.
This morning, waking to a cold and empty bed. The loss
something almost palpable, drawing tears to her eyes when
she'd wanted to portray herself as a sophisticate who understood they'd had one night together and that was all it
could ever be.

'Sex has a way of changing things...'

He'd warned her and he'd been right. She understood
passion now, the bruising agony of it, whereas once it had
been an abstract concept experienced by others. Now, to
her, Alessio sprang to life in glorious colour. She knew
how his body worked in ways more than the cold anatomy
of him. How his muscles bunched as he moved over her.
The way the cords of his neck tensed as he was close, the
blissful lack of focus in his eyes as he lost himself in her
body. His care *for* her and her pleasure. All these things
she could see even now, as his back was to her. They ran
through her head, causing the whole of her to run hot, as
if on fire. Things which showed he was a human and not
the myth he tried so hard to portray to the world.

Yet something about the way she was being dismissed
slashed at her deep inside. Though she supposed Alessio
could hardly ask *are you okay?* if he wanted to keep what
they'd done secret, given Stefano was sitting in the corner with one eyebrow cocked, watching them both. Did
he know what had happened? Was it painted all over her
face in the heat rising there? How was she going to keep
things together at the hospital?

She took a deep breath. She was an adult, a grown
woman. Last night had been a blissful, incredible, earth-
shattering experience which could never be repeated. *One*

night. One night. She'd say that mantra till it sank in and wove itself into the fibre of her being.

Stefano announced the cars were ready and they left, Alessio travelling alone. He always seemed alone, she realised, and perhaps that was the way it had to be as a ruler, a solitary journey. The ache of that burned in her chest as they arrived at the hospital to a back entrance with no fanfare. Hannah was introduced and welcomed as the official portrait artist, reminding her that this was her *job*, so she pulled out her sketch pad and her pencils from a satchel, the familiar weight of them in her hands spreading a calm through her.

Most people at the hospital seemed to be nonplussed with a prince in their midst, as if he did this often. Maybe he did, though it surprised her that the children's ward was such a dour place. White walls, grey floors. A few faded pictures on the wall. All the children tucked neatly into the beds, though a few brightened up when Alessio arrived, grinning at him, waving as if he were an old friend. He grinned back, greeted some by name. She turned to the doctor who'd brought them here.

'They seem to know him.'

The doctor smiled. 'Yes. A few of the children have serious health problems and have been here for some time. His Highness is popular with them. He visits as often as his schedule allows. He's planning works on the children's ward soon and likes to hear their ideas.'

Alessio talked to a sad-looking little boy wearing a cast. The soft concern on his face made him seem unrecognisable from the stern Prince in the palace he'd shown to her earlier.

'Have you thought about art on the walls?'

'We have hopes for many things. A complete refurbishment. So little money has been spent for so long. But the children would benefit if this were a happier place.'

Alessio now seemed to be having an intense conversation with another child's bear. It could have been a political discussion the way he gesticulated, whilst the little girl who owned the bear giggled, brightening the mood of the room. Hannah's heart melted at the scene, a small shred of joy in this joyless place.

'The corridor on the way in would be a wonderful place for a mural. If the children were being brought into the ward, it could make them less fearful to have something fun to look at. And then in here—' Hannah gestured to another blank wall, the ideas flowing as to the scenes she'd like to paint, the cartoon characters, the animals '—even bright paint colours would be a simple solution. I could jot down some colour schemes and ideas that don't cost much money if murals won't fit into the budget.'

'Please do.' The doctor smiled. 'Now I should introduce His Highness to some of the newest patients here. *Scusi.*'

Hannah sat in a plastic chair, far enough away so she had a perfect view of the whole room. She opened her sketch pad, lingering for a few moments on the drawing of Alessio's hands. His questing fingers, the way they drifted across her skin. But those were thoughts she wasn't allowed to have because there'd be no repeat of the night before. She ignored the ember glowing deep inside, one she couldn't stoke to life again. Instead, she turned to a fresh page and began another drawing. This picture was of Alessio, holding an animated conversation with the little girl's bear.

As she sketched the scene she became aware of movement nearby. She turned to a young boy who'd crept up beside her as she drew. Hannah smiled.

'Hello. What's your name?'

The boy's eyes widened, and she realised he might not be able to speak English. She pulled out her phone and searched for a translation app. *'Come ti chiami?'*

He laughed, probably at her parlous pronunciation. 'Giulio.'

'Hello, Giulio. My name is Hannah.' She patted her chest.

He gave a tentative smile, then pointed to the page where she'd sketched Alessio. She didn't know what to say. Their barrier was language, but her art spoke a language all of its own. Hannah turned to another fresh page and considered the blank wall and what kind of mural she'd put there, then began sketching.

'Watch,' she said to the dark-eyed waif, who'd now pulled up a little plastic child's chair to sit beside her. And she drew a field of grass and flowers. A teddy bear's picnic, with all the kinds of fairy-tale foods the children might love. Ice cream, incredible towers of jelly, cakes. Not a vegetable to be seen. Bears playing, flying kites, including one which had been blown away on a strong gust of wind, and the bear holding it sailing into the sky with others trying to pull it down.

The little boy next to her laughed, and the sound spurred her on. She began mapping out a few ideas, losing herself in the fun of creating a joyous space, something better than this, something to make the children less fearful. Soon she had a small audience watching her. Children with wide eyes and wider smiles. What more could she draw for them? She didn't really watch television, didn't go to see movies, and had no nieces and nephews, being an only child, so wasn't sure what children liked. That sense of isolation pricked at her. Most of the time she didn't really feel lonely, not with her art. It was as if she were always in the presence of the person whose portrait she painted. Immersed in them, kept company by their picture and her understanding of them as a person. Today, she was overwhelmed by the knowledge there was only her. She looked up at Alessio, talking to some of the nurses. He was alone too. Did he ever have the sense of it, a kind of emptiness, or did duty fill the spaces?

He glanced over in her direction, almost like he knew she was watching him. As he took in the children surrounding her, a look crossed his face. Something intense, not implacable at all. The potency of that moment ignited those flickering embers deep inside. Then a child touched her arm and pointed at the page. She laughed because she knew they wanted her to keep drawing, so she turned her attention to the sketch pad once more. Alessio wasn't safe. The children were. Looking at the boy who'd first come to her, with his dark curls and eyes, Hannah began to sketch him, a little caricature. It was how she had first started with her art. Doodling in class, drawing friends, till her parents had died and the obsession overtook her, that her memory of their faces might fade. So she'd drawn them incessantly, etching them into her brain so she would never forget.

A shadow crossed her page as she was almost done. A shiver of awareness shimmied down her spine. There was only one person it could be.

'You have a crowd.' Alessio's voice was as warm as the summer's day outside, heating her as if she'd stepped into the midday sunshine.

She tore herself from her drawings and their gazes caught and held. Her pulse took off at a gallop, the wild beat only for him. 'Is your ego coping with the lack of attention?'

He did nothing for a heartbeat, then burst out laughing. It was as if happiness had exploded into the room. Everyone stared at him. The princely Alessio was a foreboding force. The passionate man in bed a study in absolute focus. But *this* man, laughing and real, showing his human side for the first time since she'd known him—this man was a danger. The type of man who could break a woman's heart.

Except there was nothing left to break. She'd lost her

heart years ago on the day she'd lost everything. She'd encased it in a protective cage and now nothing could get through to harm it ever again. Hannah ignored those musings, and simply took in the man smiling at her in his own blinding way.

'You're a woman who's hard for my ego every day. But I'm sensible enough to know who the real talent is here. It's not me.'

'It's not me either—it's the health professionals.'

The burnt umber of his eyes smouldered like brown coal on fire as the look on his face softened, darkened. She knew it well, having seen it in his bedroom the night before. A shiver of longing coursed through her. Her cheeks heated as she remembered the pleasure, the delicious aches which remained. The memory of Alessio and his body over her. Inside her. Did it show on her face? Because naked desire was written all over his. But it had only been for one night. They'd agreed, and, as much as she craved more of him, she knew she'd only take what life gave her rather than ask for more. Since in the main, if she wanted more, life slapped her down in the cruellest possible ways.

'They are indeed. What are you doing there?' He nodded to the pages on which she'd drawn.

'I had some ideas to brighten up the ward, make it a more welcoming place for the children.'

The doctor who'd spoken to her earlier approached. 'Signorina Barrington suggested some murals. As you know, Your Highness, we talked of the ward becoming more welcoming. Less clinical.'

Alessio glanced at his watch, at Stefano, who began to approach. 'That's an excellent idea. I'll ensure there's a place in the budget. Anything for the children.'

He crouched down on his haunches. Said something to the children surrounding her. A slightly older boy answered back.

'Do you know any superheroes?' Alessio asked.

Hannah smiled. 'I'm sure I can think of a few. Does he want me to draw some?'

Alessio nodded. Even in this position, he ruled the room like the Prince he was. His gaze dropped to her mouth and lingered there. His lips parted as if he was going to say something more, but no words came. Those perfectly drawn lips of his had spent the night exploring her body in the most exquisite of ways, finding places she didn't know could give her pleasure. Yet Alessio had seemed to find them all.

'I—I should get started, then.'

She scribbled on the page with shaky fingers. The children seemed enthralled, and she was too, but by the man blazing in front of her. His nostrils flared. Did he know what she was thinking about? Was he thinking the same? It couldn't go anywhere, so better not to dwell on it at all.

They held each other like that for a few moments, their gazes clashing. Then Stefano approached and cleared his throat. Alessio stood, the break between them almost more painful than waking this morning to find herself alone.

'We should go. You have a meeting with the Health Minister.'

It was said in English for her benefit, she was sure. The children clamoured around Alessio as he moved to leave, making obvious noises of disappointment as they were ushered back to bed by the staff. All Hannah could do was watch his back as he walked away from her, as if she'd ceased to exist.

Alessio walked through the maze-like corridors of the hospital exquisitely aware of the woman trailing behind him, whom he could feel as if she were touching him. The flush on her cheeks. Her wide eyes. Those lips of hers a cherry blush. She had the look of a woman well-loved, as if she'd suddenly come into herself.

It had been all he could do to leave his bed this morning. To gather his clothes, the evidence they'd been together. To shower, scrub his body and try to wash her away. Yet he had failed. Nothing could wash away the memory of her sighs, her skin, so soft under his fingers.

Then with the children… How they'd flocked to her, her natural charm and grace drawing them in like the sunshine on a spring day, something beautiful and warm, welcoming. In a pretty blue dress with dark hair spilling unrestrained over her shoulders, she looked like every fantasy drawn to life. For those fleeting moments in her presence he didn't see problems, but possibilities, where his life only had one course. Right now he should let her join Stefano in the car behind his and travel to the palace by himself. Yet he was tired. Tired of the feeling his journey was one which should always be taken alone, with no one to share it with. For a moment he allowed himself to want without guilt.

'Signorina Barrington comes with me. I wish to know more about her ideas for the children's ward.'

'Do I need to ask again?' Stefano murmured.

Do you know what you're doing?

Alessio cut him off. 'No.'

The word left his mouth with barely a thought, and once uttered he would not take it back. He never did. Yet the truth screamed loud in his head. He didn't know what he was doing. He should be far away from her. Travelling with her was a breach of a self-imposed protocol.

And right now, he didn't care.

Stefano gave a small bow, the merest of smiles on his face. His eyebrow rose a fraction once more, the expression of amusement seeming to have become almost a permanent fixture Alessio had seen it so often over the past days.

He wouldn't explain because none of this was explicable. His driver opened the door of the car and Hannah slipped into the back seat with him. Clipped on her seatbelt and looked out of the window. The car slid away from the rear of the hospital, starting the journey towards the palace.

'You were wonderful with the kids,' Hannah said, her voice soft and almost wistful.

'So were you.' They'd flocked to her, with her drawings of them, cartoon characters and everything in between. Those unwell children giggling with delight at the things she drew.

'They're an easy audience.'

Her smile lit up the interior of the car. Something in his chest clenched, the whole of him too hot and tight. They'd agreed on one night, that it was enough, yet he hadn't realised one night with her could *never* be enough. There was nothing experienced about her, but Hannah's innocence and naked enthusiasm were like a drug that had him craving. He might never erase the memories from his room, which seemed ridiculous, yet no other woman had ever graced his bed at the palace. He dreaded the anticipation of lonely nights when she left. Craving to take his fill now, whilst he could.

His palms itched, wanting to touch, determined not to. Yet his resolve failed as she kept speaking. All he thought about was her natural beauty and how the children clambered over her as if she were a pied piper. As if she were some kind of saviour.

'There are so many ways you could help them. A mural would be a beautiful addition to the ward. It would brighten their lives, especially the little ones who need to stay there a long time. I have so many ideas.'

The cabin of the vehicle closed in on him, compressing to a pinpoint that was only them, as if the rest of the world didn't exist. He loosened his tie, now too tight round his neck. He needed to get out of this small space so he could breathe, so he could think. Even the journey back to the palace felt too long. And, since there was a driver up front, there was nothing he could do here. Yet he kept a small office in the capital, a well-guarded secret, and they were only minutes away from it.

'Manuel, please take us to the city office.'

'Of course, Your Highness.'

A few deviations and they arrived, driving through a gated archway and into an internal courtyard. The car stopped and Alessio didn't wait for his driver. He opened the door himself and stepped out into the baking summer's heat.

Hannah frowned. 'Are you leaving?'

He peered into the cabin where she sat, her teeth biting into her bottom lip. 'No. We have things to discuss. I have an office. It's private.'

Her mouth opened but she didn't reply. Merely nodded and followed him from the car. The few staff who ran the premises in his absence scrambled as he entered unannounced. He smiled at them, but it felt more rictus than genuine, each second not alone with Hannah a moment wasted. With introductions over he flung back the door of his office, and she followed him inside. He closed it behind her. Stood in the cool silence and could breathe again.

'What do you want to discuss, Your Highness?'

He wheeled around, hating that this formality had returned. He'd been wrong in the way he'd treated her this morning. Especially when the desire still ran rich and hot through his veins, calling him out as a liar for pretending what had happened between them was nothing. And, whilst he might lie to himself, he couldn't lie to her.

'Is once enough for you?'

Hannah's eyes darkened, pupils black in the oceanic green. He'd seen them look the same as she'd come apart underneath him in his bed, beautiful and wide with desire matching his own. Her lips parted as a flush crept from her throat. 'Never.'

'Good, because I want more.' His voice was a hiss through clenched teeth at the agony of need unfulfilled. More a command than a request. Harsh and low. Clotted with desire.

Who stepped first, he couldn't have said. They fell into each other, his hands thrust into her silken locks of hair. Lips on hers, hard and fast. She clung to his shoulders, their tongues touching, and he moved back to a large sofa in the corner. Dropped into it with her straddling his hips, rocking forward on the hardness of him as he groaned into her mouth. He slid his hands to her buttocks, drawing her even closer, hiking up the skirt of her dress till he could grab at the soft, pale skin of her thighs. She quivered under his palms as he moved back in the seat a little and slid a finger between them, her underwear damp with evidence of her arousal. He rubbed over her most sensitive spot. Light touches that had her panting and squirming against him, holding her on a cruel edge. Tormenting her in the way she had unknowingly tormented him by merely existing, the noises she made increasingly desperate. He didn't care. He wanted her to beg for her pleasure, here in his office, where they could both lose their minds.

He was agonisingly hard now. Her heat was against him, relentless and brutal. He'd been unprepared. He had no protection. The pulse of need drove him on, but as much as he craved to release himself and slide into the wet heat of her, he wouldn't. The risk to her as much as to him was too great. This journey could lead nowhere permanent. But pleasure was something they could give one another. He had nothing on this afternoon he couldn't cancel. They could spend it in his rooms once back at the palace, or in hers. It didn't matter, so long as he was inside her.

Hannah let out a groan. A curse. A *plea*.

'Ah, *bella*. Am I neglecting you?' The words were said against her gasping mouth. He slid two fingers inside her, curled them to reach the sensitive spot he knew drove her wild. Worked his thumb over the tight bundle of nerves at the juncture of her thighs as her breath held, the whole of her drawn tight as a bow till she broke apart around him, her shuddering body letting him know she'd tumbled over the edge, moaning his name as her spasms went on and on, clenching round his fingers. With a final flutter she sagged into him. He withdrew from her, wrapped Hannah tight in his arms. His own body, so hard and aching, objected to the way she nestled into him, screaming for its own release. Yet he did nothing, giving her this time. After a few moments relaxed in his arms she stirred, rocked against him again. He gasped as a bright burst of pleasure exploded through him.

'What about you?' Her voice was a sigh against his neck, feathering over his skin. She pulled back, her eyes soft, dreamy. Skin flushed a delicate pink. Mouth plump and well-kissed.

What he wouldn't give to forget being a prince, forget the consequences, take for himself and be damned. But that would make him like his father, and he was not that man.

'I didn't come prepared for this.'

'You wouldn't make a very good boy scout, then, would you?'

He chuckled, even though the ache in his groin intensified as she voiced her need to give him pleasure as well. Too often people had been prepared to take from him. Someone considering his true desires seemed like hedonism at its finest.

'It's something I've never considered. Being Prince of Lasserno, others tend to prepare for me.'

The corners of her plush, kiss-reddened lips curled into

a wicked smile. She leaned forward, her voice a whisper in his ear. 'Luckily I have a few ideas for how I can help, *Your Highness*.'

A quake ran through him at the sound of his title spoken with her low, intent voice. It was almost a taunt but he didn't care. She pulled back, and with trembling fingers Hannah worked at his belt buckle, the closure on his trousers, the zip. Then her cool hand reached into his underwear and took him out. He stifled a groan. Almost lost control in that moment, unable to tear his gaze away as she tightened her grip and worked him the way he'd shown her the night before. Damn, if they weren't going to make a mess here and right now, but he didn't care. Gone mad with a feverish desire that nothing bar her would satisfy. Then Hannah moved from his lap, dropped to her knees on the floor before him. Loosened the relentless grip and stroking which had him close to the edge and almost tumbling over.

'I don't really know what I'm doing—you'll have to guide me.'

Alessio frowned, not sure what she was talking about until she dropped her head, and the warmth of her breath caressed a sliver of flesh at his stomach. He jerked in her hand as the knowledge of what she was about to do coursed through him like an electric current.

'Devour me like you've never been hungrier in your life,' he groaned.

She looked up at him, eyes that intense rockpool green, dark and still. With depths he could never fathom. A wicked smile played at the corners of her perfect mouth. 'Just remember, I'm not going to stop.'

She took him into the heat of her mouth. His brain blanked with white noise roaring in his ears. Hannah was tentative till he moaned, and her efforts became intense. Determined. His hand tangled into her hair, guiding her, but there was no need. She followed his instructions to a perfection belying her inexperience. He was close, so close, feeling the tingling at the base of his spine, the heaviness, the tightening in his groin. He held on but the vision of her worshipping him like this, because that was how it seemed, drove him to the edge of control. She wanted him as much as he wanted her. Of that, he had no doubt. And her words, *'I'm not going to stop...'* ran on repeat. Like an endless loop in his head, winding him tighter and higher.

'Hannah... I'm going to... Hannah...'

He tugged at her hair in warning, but she didn't let up on the relentless rhythm. For once in his life he allowed the scorching fire of his orgasm tear through his body with no thought or care for the consequences.

Letting the burn set him free.

CHAPTER EIGHT

ALESSIO SAT BEHIND his desk, trying and failing to make sense of some financial reports. The numbers on the page swirled and blurred into one another. Yesterday had been an exercise in hedonism. Something he'd never indulged in. He and Hannah in his city office. Cancelling his appointments. Spending the afternoon in bed, repaying her a thousand-fold, making her scream. That filled his thoughts. Not these dry figures and graphs about tourism which should be holding his interest.

Yet he couldn't see what he and Hannah were doing as a mistake. Not now. It might be a glorious folly, like the pavilion on the palace grounds. Built to a love that was all an illusion. But they had set an end: the date Hannah left Lasserno. Then he could choose his princess, establish his throne. Renew the glory of his country.

Still, what had once driven him now held no excitement. He rubbed his hands over his face. Took another long draught of his coffee. Today it was as if his bones were made of lead. Strange that around Hannah he seemed... lighter. More energised, invigorated, as if plugged straight into a power source. Not bowed by this weight, as if the expectations of the world sat on his shoulders.

He checked the time, then his diary. More meetings. Soon Stefano would walk in and they'd go. Instead of preparing, all he could think about was another evening in bed with Hannah. Driving away his worries for Lasserno in the warmth of her body. The way her hands stroked tenderly over his skin. A shred of softness at the end of a hard day…

'Sir, His Highness is busy… Sir! You can't go—'

'My abdication does not mean this has ceased to be my palace. I go where I choose. I choose to see my son.'

Alessio's blood froze, then his repressed rage heated it till it was near boiling. That voice sent a jagged spear through the heart of him. His father. Since his abdication he'd barely been near the palace, holed up in his personal villa on the outskirts of the capital, where few people paid any attention to his exploits and greater excesses. The double doors of his office were flung open and the former Prince himself strode in as if he still owned the room. To some people in this country he still did, but that was a problem for another day. Stefano followed, fists clenched.

'I'm sorry—'

Alessio held up his hand. If he'd not been able to curb his father, then his best friend had no chance. 'It's okay. I'm sure he'll leave soon.'

The man in question looked around the room as Stefano backed out and closed the doors behind him. The corner of his father's top lip curled in a sneer. 'I don't favour what you've done with the place.'

'I don't care. Your taste isn't mine.' In *anything*. He'd happily rid the space of the more garish furniture and installed less frivolous antique pieces, more solid and befitting the future ruler of Lasserno.

Alessio gritted his teeth so hard he could almost taste blood. This was the man who'd left his wife and Lasserno's beloved Princess to die alone. The man who'd plundered the crown jewels as he'd seen fit, as if it wasn't bad enough in days long past that the royal family had lost the coronation ring present in so many portraits here, never to be recovered. A reminder to Alessio of responsibility and all he was tasked to protect.

'All your talk of austerity and yet you decide to redecorate. I wonder, is this what hypocrisy looks like?'

'This furniture was already in the palace. None of it's new. At least I didn't raid the crown jewels, the *country's* treasures, to fund my lifestyle or provide baubles to sycophants.'

His father threw back his head and laughed. Dressed in a favoured Savile Row suit, he remained a handsome man, although his hair was greying, and he carried a little thickness around the middle. To Alessio's disgust, he looked more like this man than he did his beautiful mother, with her pale hair and eyes. His father's genes had erased everything of his mother from him...almost. Not her inherent goodness, he hoped. Alessio strove to carry that always.

'The country's? No. We're an absolute monarchy. Everything in Lasserno is *ours*, to take as we see fit. Or have you forgotten? Next, you'll be talking constitutions and presidents. Save me from a straw crown. I want none of it.'

Alessio sat still in his seat, the lessons of his childhood coming to the fore, when all he wanted was to stand and rage. But he refused to give this man the satisfaction of showing any emotion. Anyhow, toddler tantrums were his father's specialty. He had more control. Alessio gripped the arms of his chair a little tighter, to prevent himself from leaping from it.

'A ruler can be absolute, and still do the right thing by the country and its people.'

'Doing what's right for oneself is much more entertaining. Yet, despite your efforts, *the people* don't seem to think you're doing a good job. What are the press saying again?'

That he was cold. Autocratic. Opaque. Those words might have stung if his path weren't clear. The people would see, once Lasserno took its rightful place on the world stage rather than being a forgotten backwater.

'I don't care, and that's where our core difference lies. Since I'm a busy man fixing the messes you left, get to the point. Why did you come here? I suspect it wasn't to criticise my decorating style.'

His father took a seat in the chair opposite Alessio's desk, lounging in an indolent kind of way that was the man's specialty.

'I've come to congratulate you.' His father's gloating tone sounded a warning. 'You're not a lost cause yet, when for some time I thought you were all work and no play. She really is a masterstroke.'

Alessio froze. It couldn't be. He *couldn't* know about Hannah. Everyone in the palace was faithful to him. No one would say a thing. He'd learned a hard lesson about misplaced trust and had rid himself of his father's cronies and hangers-on the minute the man had walked away from the throne. Any whispers could only be rumour because he'd been seen with a woman, whose presence had been well reported before she'd even arrived in Lasserno. It was one of the few things he'd allowed Stefano to tell the press, the coup of his coronation portrait being painted by the world's finest young artist, something to be celebrated rather than hidden.

'Who are you talking about?'

His father waved his hand theatrically, twisting that spear even harder. His disdain for his son and only child had seemed to increase over the years. Alessio had long ceased trying to impress the man. He'd given up around the time he'd been called home from England, leaving behind his dreams of riding for his country any more. Arriving home to find Lasserno in disarray.

'The artist. I should have done the same.'

Alessio's veins turned to ice. 'Stop talking in riddles.'

Yet even as he said the words his voice was like dust in his mouth, dry and lacking conviction. His father was a master of playing vicious, wicked games. He enjoyed them, and Alessio wondered whether the 'mistake' in Hannah's placement at his table for dinner hadn't been a mistake at all but a move designed to create gossip.

'Installed my mistress before marriage. What did that prim little English nanny of yours always say? Something about beginning as you mean to end things.'

Start as you mean to finish.

'I have no mistress.' That was not what was happening here. Hannah would be leaving soon. But the denial caught in his throat, threatening to throttle him.

His father was only guessing, assuming his son would debauch any beautiful young woman the same as he would. The bile rose in Alessio's throat. He tried not to think that was exactly what he was doing. This was different. He didn't have a wife; he didn't have a child. There was nothing currently tying him to any person. He was as free as he could be.

'You can keep telling that to your conscience. Marry the perfect ice-cold princess and have your passionate piece already installed. You're setting the expectations of your wife early. Perfect.'

'I have nothing to trouble my conscience. Unlike you, I'll be a faithful husband and I would never leave my wife to die alone.'

'Your mother wanted me nowhere near her, especially not at the end. If she had I might have spent more time with her. Let's say she was satisfied with having an heir. She was never going to give me a spare. Trust me when I say a lack of passion makes for a very cold bed to lie in for eternity.'

Alessio stood then, began pacing the carpet.

'Perhaps if you'd been faithful, she might have been

inclined to like you rather than despise you. Take care. This is my *mother* whose memory you're disparaging.'

'Whose necklace you allowed your little artist to wear. Which was sensible. They form no part of the crown jewels. Sets the girl's expectations, wearing secondary gems. She'll always know her place.'

'She is not my anything.'

'Lie to yourself all you want but say it with more conviction next time. Or better, admit to your failings. You have me as a father after all. One day you'll awaken a lonely old man and only then, when it's too late, you'll see I was right.'

'Is that all you have to say?' Alessio gritted his teeth, tried to maintain his temper. Swept his hands over the paperwork sitting on the desk. 'Because I have work, and no time for your ravings. You chose to abdicate this responsibility. Now leave me be.'

'Of course, *Your Highness*.' His father's voice was a cold sneer. 'Just remember, the work is always there. As the English like to say, *All work and no play makes Alessio a dull boy.* My suggestion? Keep your artist and find your royal wife. What use is being a prince if you can't have what you want?'

His father rose with the presence of a ruler, stalked to the study doors and flung them back. They smacked into the walls on either side with unnecessary force as he left the room. Alessio couldn't stop moving, the anger burning in his gut as he paced. His father didn't really know what was going on—he was fishing for information. But this, the palace, all the intrigue…it would sully what he had with Hannah, their last precious days spent together. He wanted perfect memories for them both. Had to get her away from here, but everywhere was fraught. Any of the other royal homes, the royal yacht, had bigger problems.

Whilst he'd rid the palace in the capital of his father's sycophants, he couldn't be sure of elsewhere.

Where to go? Somewhere close enough to the capital to be able to return easily, but far enough away to avoid prying eyes.

Stefano entered the room, brow furrowed in concern. 'All okay?'

In those days after his father's abdication, only his best friend knew the true extent of the trouble his father had caused. Alessio stilled. The solution stood in front of him. One he'd used a few times before when riding his horses had ceased to be enough. 'I need to escape for a few days. The usual way.'

Stefano nodded, yet his eyebrows rose again. 'Will Hannah be joining you?'

'Yes.' Alessio clenched his jaw. He would have no judgement on this, not from his friend. 'Are you going to ask whether I know what I'm doing?'

Stefano gave him a wry smile. This man was one of his closest supporters. Like a brother. He placed a hand on Alessio's shoulder and gave a brief squeeze of solidarity.

'I don't have to, my friend. I think you know exactly what you're doing. And for once it's what you want to do, rather than what you believe you should. That's a *good* thing.'

Stefano released him and left the room, phone to his ear. In his office, all alone with the weight of his ancestors' portraits around him, Alessio wasn't sure he could take any comfort from his friend's parting words.

CHAPTER NINE

HANNAH WALKED DOWN a gangplank to the harbour at dawn. The whole journey had been cloaked in secrecy. She had been told to pack for the beach for two days, and that was it. Not that she'd come to Lasserno prepared for needing beachwear. When she'd told Alessio, a host of bags had arrived in her room. Clothes with tags from designers who left her breathless, so she simply stuffed it all into a duffel bag she'd brought with her. In the pale morning light Alessio looked nothing like his usual self, unrecognisable in shorts showing off his strong calves, a T-shirt, cap jammed on his head, like a disguise. The whole episode was all subterfuge. He'd even driven them here through a back exit of the palace, with no entourage. Something cloak and dagger about it thrilled her.

They arrived at a magnificent yacht that looked as if it had come straight out of a classic movie, with three soaring masts and gleaming, honeyed wood. Alessio helped her aboard, where they were met by the crew. He shook their hands. Introduced her.

'Remember, the same rules as last time,' Alessio said.

The captain nodded. 'Of course, sir. We'll be underway immediately.'

'Thank you.'

No *Your Highness*…no bowing. Little ceremony at all, as someone spirited away their bags. Alessio slid a hand to the small of her back and they traversed the expansive deck to the bow. As they reached the rail, Alessio checked his watch. She placed her hand over his wrist.

'You do that constantly.'

'I want to see if we're leaving in good time.'

He'd told her this weekend was for them, to get away. It seemed as if he never could, always managing his day to the last second. She turned his wrist over, unclipped the burnished gold band and slid the timepiece from his wrist. Rubbed a thumb over his pulse-point. Over the mark the clasp had left. Relishing the feel of his smooth, golden skin under her fingers.

'You need to stop sometimes.' She clasped the watch in her fist as Alessio let out a slow breath, his shoulders relaxing as if some weight had been removed. 'I'd like to pitch it into the sea to make sure you do, but it's probably valuable.'

'My maternal grandfather gave it to me.'

'Did you like him?'

The corner of Alessio's mouth kicked up into a smile. 'I did.'

'Then I'll keep it safe.' She slipped it into the pocket of her skirt, its weight against her thigh. A reminder of how little time they had, which was something she shouldn't even be thinking about. She should be living in the now, because her time here had always had an end date. Hannah tipped her head back to look up into the complicated rigging.

'This is an amazing boat.'

'*Il Delfino*. A schooner built in 1910. One hundred and seventy feet long, if you're interested.'

'It's beautiful.'

'So are you.'

She smiled, breath catching in her throat. 'Thank you.' Since her parents had died, there'd been no one to tell her she was beautiful. Her dad had said those words to her, to her mother, all the time. Back then her parents had made sure she felt as attractive as an awkward teen could, with pimples and hormones causing trouble. On the other hand, her aunt and uncle hadn't realised what she'd needed. Or hadn't cared. Maybe the only thing they'd ever been interested in was the money her parents had left.

Tears burned at her eyes. There was no time for them here. Instead she stared out over the horizon. Ribbons of pink and gold threaded through the sky. The cool breeze brushed her face.

Alessio moved behind her, wrapping strong arms round her body. She leaned into him, tried to relax. To make the most of every second here.

'This feels like another movie moment,' she said.

'Is that a bad thing this time?'

'Only if the boat sinks.'

'She's had a complete refit, if you're worried.'

Hannah wasn't. Around Alessio she almost felt more secure than with anyone else, apart from the way she had as a child with her mother and father. 'I'm sure you'll keep me safe.'

His arms tightened a fraction. She closed her eyes to savour the moment. He'd keep her safe physically. Emotionally though…it was as if she stood in a crowded room, naked. But this, between them, was *all* physical. An attraction. Nothing more.

'You mentioned something to the crew about rules,' she said. 'What are they?'

'This is Stefano's yacht. Here, I'm not the Prince of Lasserno, I'm him.'

He played Stefano, so he could hide her. Part of that made sense. He was protecting them both from the press. Another part of it stung like a bee ruining a barefoot walk in the grass.

'Stefano? This isn't just any old boat. Where did he get it?'

'Family. Stefano's the Conte di Varno. The Moretti family and mine have a long history. Each count has served the royal family in their own way. Stefano's way is as my private secretary, since I trust him implicitly.'

'It's nice that you have so much trust in someone.'

Alessio loosened his arms and turned her, a slight frown forming on his brow, the look concerned and earnest. 'And you don't?'

It was as if she were standing on a precipice. This between them was supposed to be casual. That meant light banter and fun. But she was driven to unburden herself, as if telling Alessio might set herself free.

'My uncle was a financial advisor. He looked after my inheritance. Six months ago, he ignored my wishes. Invested in something I didn't want. That investment failed. My parents didn't have much, but my dad had an insurance policy. It's all gone now. I'm hanging on to the cottage.'

Barely. Hannah didn't know if it felt any better, having told Alessio. It was a terrible admission, her failure to keep an eye on things.

Alessio's jaw hardened. His mouth a tight, thin line.

'Are the police involved? Surely by law, your uncle wasn't allowed to do such a thing?'

She hated this. Hated that the people who should have been looking after her interests had let her down so badly. Whilst they hadn't been her parents, they'd been her last link to one of them. But she'd learned a powerful lesson from the experience. All she really had was herself.

'He used a few people's money, and he shouldn't have.' He'd been so sure that everything would be okay, and that in the end she'd thank him for ignoring her wishes. The arrogance of it. 'And yes, the police are involved. But that won't get my funds back. Everything my parents left me, I lost.'

'Ah, *bella*. It's not your fault.' Alessio stepped forward and bundled her in his arms. She rested her head on his chest as he held her tight. As if he were holding her together. And all of it was dangerous. They weren't meant to share, not like this.

'Would you have taken this commission if your uncle hadn't done what he did?'

'No.' She pulled back. Shook her head, honesty all she had left. 'You. Horse riding. The showjumping circuit. It brings back memories I'd do anything to avoid. But now I'm here, I'm glad I agreed.'

'I'm…glad too.'

She noticed it, the slightest of hesitations in a man she suspected hesitated over nothing. He tightened his arms around her.

'Do you trust me?' he asked.

Hannah was lost in the deep, warm brown of his eyes. She didn't know if she trusted anyone, and that caused her gut to clench like a hard fist inside. She had to remind herself what this truly was. It had an end date marching up faster and faster. She'd pack her bags, her art equipment and leave. Paint his portrait. Throw all her emotion into it, then set it free and let him go. Alessio would find and marry his perfect princess, and all would once again be right with the world.

'With my body? I trust you implicitly.'

Alessio's smile in answer to her comment was sultry and slow.

'I'll always look after you.'

That sounded as if this had a permanence to it, which she knew to be untrue. But then, words were easy. It was actions which were harder. And she knew he wouldn't stop her winging away from here. He'd put her on the plane himself. But it was fine. She'd known the day her parents died that the picture of her own life would be different from what she'd imagined it would be as a child. In her wildest dreams, she'd never believed a fortnight like this could happen to her. And the memory of it would be enough. Would carry her through the years.

It *would*.

Enough of this introspective mood. The glorious sun rose in the sky, filling her with a lazy warmth. The tang of salt hung invigoratingly in the air. They had time and she'd take her fill of every second. She needed to lighten the mood, since it had become far too serious.

'So, this is Stefano's yacht. Don't you have one of your own?'

'Of course. Mine's a modern yacht. Some might say… better,' Alessio said with a smirk.

'And I bet it has a crown embossed on the bow.' She gave him a smile of her own. She liked him like this, the man relaxed, unlike the Prince he showed to the world every day.

He held out his arms. Even in casual clothes he had an intoxicating presence. As if he owned the world. 'What's being a prince if one doesn't have the crown?'

'Is your ego taking a bit of a battering that I might like Stefano's better than yours?'

'My ego remains intact, despite your best and most constant efforts.' Those wide arms of his wrapped round her again. Pulled her close. Dropped his head to her ear. 'Let me show you.'

His body pressed into hers, his arousal, bold and obvious, stoking the fire of her own. She flexed her hips against his hardness. Ran her hands down his back, relishing the strength of his muscles as they flexed under her fingers.

'I think there are a few things I need to know whilst I'm here,' she said.

'Port is left. Starboard is right.'

'Thank you, Your Highness.' Hannah laughed. 'No. Your talk of the rules before. Are there any I should know?'

Alessio looked up at the golden sky, brow furrowed as if in thought. 'The first rule is that I'm always right.'

'Oh, really? Any others?'

'Hmm… The second…' He tapped at his chin then looked down at her, the colour of his eyes swallowed by his pupils, the dawn painting him golden as well. 'When we're alone together you should always be naked. Clothes are a travesty on you.'

Heat rose to her cheeks. 'And is that rule reciprocated?'

'*Ovviamente*. Now we're heading out on water, rule two is invoked. You're wearing too many clothes.'

'Are you sure about that?' she asked as Alessio inched his fingers under her shirt, stroking the sensitive skin of her side. A shiver of goosebumps skittered down her arms. He began unbuttoning the soft cotton shirt she wore, his eyes glowing and intent. Always fierce. Always in a hurry, or at least where she was concerned. He dropped his head and began kissing her shoulder, light brushes that made her liquid in his arms.

'I refer you to rule number one,' he murmured, the warmth of his breath tickling her neck.

She laughed again, something so different about him here, out of the palace. As if he could become a man, rather than being a ruler of all he surveyed. She gave a little push on his chest and he let her go. She stood back. Shrugged her top from her shoulders, slowly exposing the exquisite floral bikini top she wore underneath from the clothes she'd been given. His gaze raked over her, jaw tight, arousal straining at his zipper.

'*Dio. Sei così bella.*'

She didn't know what that meant but it sounded like a

worship, a benediction. Yet he stood there, fully clothed,
simply watching her set the pace.

'Where's the reciprocation?'

The corner of his mouth curled into a heated smile.

'Come here,' he said, the voice all command that sent
a shiver of longing through her. She loved this of him, the
demanding, passionate man. All the while knowing that
if she said no, if she took a step back, he'd wait for her.

'Still rule number one?'

He raised an imperious eyebrow, but a smile teased
his mouth. She walked forward into his embrace, his lips
sinking onto her own. She never failed to be surprised
at how such a seemingly hard man could be all softness
when he held her. As if the fact he had a human side was
their secret.

'I'm not being a good host. It's time I showed you the
stateroom.'

Alessio swung her into his arms and strode down the
deck like a man bent on completing a mission—that of
making her cry his name to the room.

Alessio woke to the lull of slapping water on the side of the
yacht. The gentle sway of the ocean. For the first time in
an age, he was at some kind of peace. Sleepy, sated. Barely
caring whether he moved all day. There was one reason for
this newfound satisfaction—a person. He reached to the
side of the bed for Hannah and brushed only the warmth
of empty sheets. Not long gone, then. He lay for a moment,
listening for her, but there was no sound, so he rolled over
and sat up, scraping his hand through his hair.

She was curled on a sofa opposite the bed at the other
side of the room. Feet tucked under her. Drawing on a
sketch pad on her lap with a stick of charcoal.

'You're naked,' he said. The sight of her perfect skin

made the blood race down low. Would he ever get enough of her? He feared not.

She glanced up at him, the merest of smiles touching her well-kissed lips.

'Rule number two, remember?'

He lounged back on the bed. 'And you did what I said. Rule number one. It's a miracle.'

She snorted, such a cute sound, as she peered up at him again, then returned to the page before her. Sketching, rubbing at the paper with her fingers. 'I think I liked you better when you were asleep.'

'I don't believe you,' he said, his body heating each time her insightful gaze returned to him. Arousal, heavy and low, snaked through him again. This attraction, it overtook everything, an overwhelming need only Hannah could satisfy. 'You like me very much when I'm awake.'

He didn't hide how much she affected him. He'd not hold anything back from her. The freedom of such a short time frame meant he didn't have to. Yet the realisation of how little time they had left stung like a forgotten wound exposed to seawater. A surprising and unwelcome jolt. He ignored it. There were better ways of using their day than musing over things like that. He patted the bed next to him. 'Come here.'

'Does your ego need stroking?'

An insistent pulse of desire kept beating its demanding tempo. 'Something needs stroking.'

She didn't even look up at him, her focus all on the page, a slight frown creasing her brow. 'No. I haven't been doing enough sketching. You keep distracting me.'

Hannah being more interested in what was on the piece of paper in front of her than in the real man put him in his place, firmly rooted in a world where he was not the most desirable, sought-after person. It made him feel normal, feel *real*.

A blessed relief.

'Can I see what you're doing?'

'You get the final painting. Everything else is mine. Just lie back and enjoy it. Everyone needs to stop some time.' She looked up at him, that frown still present, her face a study of intensity, making him believe she saw all of him. His sins, his flaws. There was no hiding them with her. And it made him curious.

'What do you see when you look at me?'

'Do you really want to know?'

'I asked the question.'

She put down her charcoal. Placed her hand flat on the page in front of her so her drawing was hidden.

'You like to think you begin and end as Prince of Lasserno. That there's nothing else. But you're more.'

Inside of him, something clenched. Almost like a warning, but she'd piqued his interest now.

'Tell me.'

'Someone who works hard. Too hard.' A shaft of sunlight filtered through the cabin window, painting her pale skin in its warm glow. She looked a picture of perfection sitting there. Alessio didn't want the moment to end. He shrugged.

'It's all part of the job description. My father didn't work hard enough. Saw life as a prince for only what he could get from it. He almost drove Lasserno into ruin.' A tightness rose inside again. Of things unfinished, of work yet to do. It was relentless, exhausting. Never-ending. A needling sensation interrupted the moment. He raised his left wrist, but his watch wasn't there.

'I've put it away for a few days. You need to relax. You'll have plenty of time to save the country. Years of it, in fact.'

The certainty carried in her voice, as if there was no doubt. When, deep down, he doubted himself often. 'Thank you for your confidence. What else do you see?'

She smiled again, a beautiful thing which lit up the room better than the late-morning light.

'Fishing for compliments?'

'Wanting to know how well you know your subject.'

She brought her hand to her mouth. Tapped her lips with her index finger.

'You appear cold, aloof, but you're not. That's the Prince of Lasserno's costume, what you allow the world to see, but it's not real. You care, deeply, for your country and your people, but you refuse to show it to anyone. As if you're not the man, but you *are* the crown. Except there's a human heart beating in your chest. But some days, I think you wish there wasn't. Because being human is messy and ugly and imperfect. It's about desire and need and feelings, and that's not who you want to be. The trouble is, that's exactly who you are.'

Each word hit him like an arrow shot straight, finding its truest and most damaging place. She saw him too well, and her insights caused his heart to race, his chest to constrict.

Others only saw what they assumed was the truth. He could control the narrative with them. Like acting, putting on a show. Right now, Hannah was all risk. Huge reward, but the risk terrified him most of all. She gave him the tantalising glimpse of a life without meticulous attention to duty, and that was a terrible temptation.

'I think that you're worried if you show people the real you, they won't love you. The thing is, they'd love you even more if you would be yourself. Because you're a good man.'

He didn't want to talk now, but he couldn't move. It was as though he was pinned to the bed, frozen in place. He couldn't take this attention on him. He didn't know why he had asked the question of her, because he should have known she'd see things he hadn't wanted others to see.

'Do you want to know what I see in you?' he asked, trying to deflect from himself because the spotlight burned too brightly when it focused on the truth.

'Not really.' She closed her notepad, sat up straighter. So perfect and relaxed in her nakedness.

'Why is that, Hannah?'

She hid herself as well. They both wore costumes, even now pretending to be something they weren't.

'I'm not that interesting.'

'I disagree. Rule number one, remember.'

She rolled her eyes. 'Yes, Your Highness.'

As he was a prince, people didn't mock or tease him. Or joke with him much at all. Stefano was the only person who did, but he'd been a friend for years. Alessio found himself enjoying it from her. The irreverence. The freedom for them both to...*be*.

'You talk about me hiding myself? You do it too. You're a passionate woman when it comes to your art. But you deny that part of yourself, forgetting what you're like in my arms. In bed.'

'And what about you?' Hannah said. 'Wanting to marry someone you barely know and don't love. Better not to marry at all.'

He didn't want to think of marriage, matchmakers, or perfect princesses right now, but they were the reality he couldn't escape. A shortlist of candidates was on his desk, whom he would meet...when Hannah left.

'I have a dynasty to preserve.'

'What if your precious yet-to-be-found princess falls in love with you and you don't love her? Where will you be then? You're condemning someone to a life that's unfair.'

'She'll know what to expect.'

'Or are you afraid of forming a real attachment? That's when you have most to lose.'

Her words hit sharp and true. He couldn't let them go

unanswered. He sat up, the sheet falling from his torso. Hannah's cheeks pinked, but she didn't look away.

'Says the woman who claims she's not interested in love. That her art is enough.'

'At least I'm not trying to draw anyone else into it. This is my life. I'll live it how I see fit.'

She stood and sauntered to him, beautifully naked, the rolling sway of her hips and tight nipples, the slight flush on her chest were telling him what she had in mind. Distraction. And he didn't care because her kind of distraction was the most delicious of all. Let them both drown in it, forgetting everything else.

'You're so perfect in everything you do. Even now, lying in this bed. As if you're artfully displayed. It makes me wonder if you know how to be anything less. Makes me want to mess you up.'

'I invite you to try.'

There was something about her that warned of danger. Like an impending storm, dark and brooding, hovering on the horizon. The bed dipped as she sat on the edge close to him, her fingers blackened from the charcoal she'd smudged across her page. Hannah reached out with one hand to his chest and smeared her fingers across his flesh, leaving dark stripes there. The smile on her face was pure wickedness. 'How does that feel, Your Highness?'

'Like you're not trying hard enough.'

Her pupils flared as she rose to his challenge and climbed over him, straddling his body. Rocking on the hardness between his thighs. He sat forward to wrap his arms around her but she planted her hands flat on his chest and pushed. He fell back, enjoying her new assertion far too much. Hannah took his face in her hands, rubbed her thumbs over his cheeks. He didn't need to see in the mirror to know that she was marking him with the charcoal on her fingers. As if she were claiming ownership. His blood rang in a furious roar as he enjoyed her possession, as if with each stroke she were writing *mine* on his skin. She leaned forward, her lips touching his. Her mouth open, lush. Claiming him. He let her. In this fantasy, for these few days they could be anything they desired. He took what she gave, his hands at her hips as she moved against him. The sheet between them an interruption, a distraction, but necessary. How he wanted to slide into her with no protection, forget they were the Prince and his artist.

She broke the kiss and he almost thrust his hands into her hair and dragged her to him once more, but the way she leaned back with a subtle smile on her lips suggested she was admiring her handiwork.

'Condom,' she said, as she cupped his jaw and traced her thumb almost lovingly in another stripe along his cheek.

He didn't need to be asked twice, reaching to the bedside table where he'd left a number rather than fumble for a packet and interrupt these fleeting moments. Hannah sat back as he grabbed a sliver of foil, tore it open.

'You're going to have to move,' he said. His hands trembled with the desire to be inside her. She shifted back as he shoved down the sheet and rolled the protection in place. All the while she watched him, her fascination with his body addictive, her attention on him complete.

She placed her hand on his chest again. 'Now lie back and relax.'

He almost laughed. How could he relax when he was wound so tight he wanted to snap? His thighs shook. The whole of him quivered with barely restrained desire. It was like nothing he had ever experienced. She positioned herself over him and lowered slowly. He watched her body take him, the shock of the feeling, coupled with the vision, electric. Her head thrown back, hair tumbling over her shoulders, nipples tight and beading with arousal. Such an erotic picture she painted for him. Hannah rode his body as he thrust up into her. Lost in her heat. The sounds she made. Her pure, erotic abandon had the tight, bright sting of arousal crack and shatter with one hard, sharp thrust and shout. Then Hannah tightened around him and broke as well, falling forward onto his heaving chest as he wrapped his arms round her.

'You're well messed-up now,' she said with a shaky laugh, which told him she was probably *well messed-up* herself. And there was nothing he could say or do because she was right. The problem was, he might never wish to go back to his tidy, perfect, righteous life, ever again.

CHAPTER TEN

Two nights and three days of bliss and it was now over.

Hannah sat in the front of an anonymous-looking grey car with Alessio at the wheel. They'd spent the early morning swimming in the deep, cobalt waters of the Mediterranean. Avoiding the inevitable. Pretending the world couldn't touch them. It touched them now. Everything tightening, tensing.

As they drove towards the outskirts of Lasserno's capital, where they would return to the palace, Alessio began to change the most. It was like watching the ground freeze over by degrees. As if the cold chill of winter were creeping up on them, slowly and relentlessly. Where once he'd been loose and relaxed, all of him seemed to be on high alert. Their easy conversation on the yacht dried away, his grip on the steering wheel almost white-knuckled.

She settled back and tried to relax into the seat. The fantasy of the weekend was well and truly over, those few days where they ate, slept, made love, soon to be but a precious memory. She'd thought this would be enough, that she'd be unaffected by it all. But what she hadn't banked on was how much changed when you got to see a real person. And Alessio had become real to her. Not a prince like he was on paper but a magnificent, kind, self-deprecating man who could make her laugh and would soon make her cry, of that she had no doubt.

She wanted to cry for him now. She didn't know how he'd marry some princess in a cold, practical relationship, when their own days had been full to the brim with passion. She couldn't see him as surviving with anything less than what they had had. She could barely take in any air at those thoughts. Of Alessio married, with children. Without her. The idea of him in any other woman's arms thrust through her with all the brutality of a sword to the heart. She looked over at him. His jaw was set, as though he was steeling himself for a life he didn't want.

As if he knew she was looking at him, Alessio turned his head a fraction. 'You've had a touch of the sun. Your skin's pink.'

She shrugged, blinking away the burn in her eyes. His concern and notice could undo her, and she wasn't sure there was thread enough in the world to stitch herself together again. 'I'll be fine. It's a little sunburn.'

'I should have paid more attention.' She couldn't see his eyes, hidden behind sunglasses as they were, but his voice was filled with care. 'Remembered the sunscreen. Your beautiful skin is so pale.'

'Too much time indoors, painting.' She'd never felt like that before, but there'd been a blissful sense of freedom to being in the sunshine, the breeze in her hair. Something other than standing in her studio surrounded by solvent and paints. The same way she'd forgotten the joy of being on horseback, not practising her showjumping, just the pleasure of the ride. All the small things she'd shoved away from herself over the years. Perhaps when she returned home, she could buy a little horse. Take some time to ride again. If she could afford to, because even with Alessio's commission, funds would still be tight. But there was a kernel of hope there, for something more, even if she couldn't have him.

Hannah let out a slow, even breath. She'd not be here much longer and time seemed to be speeding up and careening away.

'I'd like to do a bit of sightseeing in the capital before I leave. I should get a souvenir for Sue.'

She had many things to thank her agent for. Many things to curse her for as well, with this commission. It had shown her life had possibilities again, whilst also snatching them away.

'I'll arrange security for you. A list of places to go.'

It sounded as if he was making himself responsible for her, and that was something she didn't need when they should be pulling apart rather than meshing even further.

'I hardly think I'll have a problem buying a snow globe or something similar. Who'd be interested in me?'

His hands flexed on the steering wheel, though his focus remained resolutely on the road ahead.

'I want you to be safe. I want that for you.'

The words were loaded because she was sure he meant far more. Hannah squashed down the lick of heat running through her. He was a good man. He cared. The way he did with the children at the hospital, that was all. It meant nothing more.

It couldn't.

He was not safe, not for her. Not ever. With him, she found herself wanting things she'd not contemplated for years, and those things could crack her in two. Because love meant leaving the door open to your own destruction and inviting the destroyer in. She could never give her whole heart because then she'd lose all over again, and she wasn't sure she'd survive it when she barely had last time.

'I'd like to go on my own. Having security would be strange and take the fun away from things. But I'll take a list of places to go. Thank you.'

'If I could have come with—'

'You're the Prince of Lasserno.' She put him back in that box where he should remain. Would even tie it with a tight, bright gold ribbon to keep him firmly back in place. 'You can't just go sightseeing with some random tourist.'

'You're not a random tourist, Hannah.' His voice was soft. The cabin of the car filled with the weight of things unsaid. Of how much more this, between them, had become.

'I'm sure you'll have too much to do.'

Alessio checked his watch, now firmly back on his wrist as if it had never left. 'Always. I may have a parliament for advice, but in the end, this is an absolute monarchy. There is only me.'

There is only me.

He'd never let anyone in, and it struck her as sad and exhausting.

The roads were busier as they approached the capital but the run to the palace seemed clear. As she sat staring at the castle looming on the horizon the roar of a motorcycle came from behind, louder, closing in. Then it was right there. At the passenger side. Two people, one driving, one pillion. Something in their hand. Camera. Trying to shove it against the window of the car. A flash.

She reflexively held up her hand against the tinted glass, her heart pounding a sickening tempo. Another flash. Alessio hissed something through his teeth. She didn't need to understand Italian to know he swore. He grabbed the brim of his cap and pulled it lower. Hannah wore nothing on her head but did have sunglasses. She pushed them up her nose, not that it would make much difference.

'In the glove compartment there's a cap. Put it on. Pull the sun visor down.'

She did as he said. The motorcycle sped ahead while the

passenger turned, trying to get photos through the windscreen. A shrill tone rang out through the car. Alessio's phone. He answered hands-free and a terse voice filled the interior, speaking rapid Italian. Stefano.

She couldn't understand what they said, but the fury in Alessio's voice, the tight, cold rage, chilled the car by degrees. She wrapped her arms round herself as she took in the importance of what was happening. But what did the press know? It could be he'd taken her out sightseeing as he'd suggested, the Prince showing a guest around his country. That was easily enough explained, wasn't it?

The call disconnected. Silence filled the car apart from Alessio's hard, jagged breaths.

'I'm sorry,' she said, because what more was there to say? 'It might not be that bad.'

'It is *that bad*.' His grip tightened on the wheel again, his mouth a thin, hard line. 'They are at the palace. Every entrance, though the western gate apparently has fewer.'

'Can we—?'

'Not now.' He took one hand from the tight grip of the wheel and dragged it over his face.

She'd been royally dismissed. Experienced it in the sharp cut of his voice. In the way all of the warmth had left him, and he'd turned into Lasserno's ruler once more. Another motorcycle joined the first. Alessio kept the speed steady and didn't try to outrun them, for which she was thankful. She stopped looking at the road in front and instead stared down at her lap, her fingers twisting in the soft fabric of her dress. Maybe no one would know who she was, but a sick feeling of bile rose in her throat. Her quiet, anonymous life in the country was likely to be shattered. The protection of those walls she'd built around herself—her art, her peace—all crumbling away. The palace loomed large ahead, and she saw it now like a kind of prison. They didn't approach from the front, or from the entrance they'd sneaked out of only three blissful days earlier, but a side entrance where palace guards stood, holding back a throng of photographers jostling for position. If this was the western gate, she'd hate to see what the others were like.

The car pushed through into a large courtyard. Alessio stopped, switched off the engine. Sat for a few moments then turned to her. She couldn't see his eyes behind the sunglasses but the whole atmosphere inside the car felt accusatory. As if somehow, she was to blame for this. Then he opened the door, thrusting it wide as he launched himself from the car and slammed it shut behind him.

Hannah took off her cap to put it back in the glove compartment and grabbed her handbag before following, running to keep up as Alessio barely broke his stride, his staff bowing as he passed, looking at her with some curiosity.

She didn't know how long they walked through what appeared to be service corridors, until they reached a vast, familiar hall and a door she immediately recognised. Alessio's office. Inside, Stefano stood by one of the mullioned windows, speaking rapid-fire on the phone. When they entered, he hung up. Alessio tore off his sunglasses and cap, tossed them on his desk. He and Stefano exchanged a look—Stefano's all sympathy, Alessio's barely concealed fury.

'What's being said?'

'They know about the hospital visits. That's been online already.'

'The families?'

'Are being protected. They won't talk. You know that.'

Alessio's head dropped. He stared at the carpet as if a solution could be divined there. All the while, Hannah realised she was superfluous. And she didn't know what to do. Stand. Sit. Pace. Everyone in this room was still.

Her, Alessio, Stefano. Like chess pieces waiting for the first move.

'They're using the sick children to make a story about me.'

'It's not a bad thing, since it's a good story. As I've said before.'

'What about this?' Alessio waved his hands between him and Hannah, as if she were nothing. His dismissal sliced sharp and fresh like a paper cut.

Stefano deigned to look at her then. Nice to know she existed. She couldn't tell what he was thinking, everything about him inscrutable in those moments. But he seemed paler, his eyes tight. No tie, the top button of his shirt undone.

'The speculation online is intense, but only in the less reputable media…for now. The photographs of you in the car will break soon enough. Who knows what they'll say? My staff won't talk, if that's your concern.'

'They never have before. I have *no* concerns there.'

'I have a team considering the problem.' Stefano looked at her again and in the deep pit of her stomach she knew *she* was the problem here. Something to be dealt with. Not a person with fears of her own. 'I'll see them now, on how we manage things going forward.'

He left the room and Alessio walked to the window, looked out over Lasserno. His country. The only thing he desired or needed, she was coming to realise.

'Never complain, never explain,' she said.

He wheeled round, all of him so hard and tense it was as if one more push and he might snap. She wanted to do something. Reach out. Comfort. Say it would all be okay. But she knew some things would never be okay again, for either of them.

'What?'

'The British Royal family. That's what they do.'

'Trust me.' He began to pace the room in that familiar way of his, as if he needed to expend energy. 'I won't be giving statements.'

'How did the press find out?'

He raised one coal-dark eyebrow at her, the burnt umber gaze of his so heated only hours ago, now cold and forbidding like some bottomless, muddy pool. 'How, indeed?'

'You think...me?'

He looked so out of place in this moment, in his disarray. Wearing casual clothes and not the suit he donned as his usual armour. Surrounded by his ancestors glaring down from their lofty height on the walls, as if the weekend of humanity he'd stolen was some kind of disgrace.

'I trust everyone else around me. But this story is a familiar one.'

It dawned on her then, what he wouldn't say out loud. He didn't trust *her*. 'It might be an annoyance for your private life, but have you ever thought how this debacle could affect me?'

He stopped his pacing. Dead.

'You?'

Said as if he'd only just realised she was a person who might have thoughts and feelings about this too. She threw up her hands and began pacing then. As if Alessio's will to constantly be on the move had infected her.

'No, clearly you haven't thought about me at all. Other than to accuse me.'

'I've accused you of nothing.'

The *yet* hung unsaid.

'I sign non-disclosure agreements with all of my clients. My word about what I discover is absolute. Would any of them trust me if they thought I would spill my secrets to the press? No. Sure, I could paint people, but it would never be the same. It would destroy my process. Ruin *everything*.'

The corner of his mouth rose in something like a sneer. Not quite contempt, but close enough.

'You're financially distressed. Your uncle mismanaged your inheritance. A tell-all about me would fill your bank account,' Alessio hissed, cold, cruel and furious.

She stopped then, as if those words had stripped the will to move right out of her. There was such accusation in his gaze. It was as though he was a brittle shell filled with nothing but disdain.

'You honestly believe I would talk about this, us…' she waved between them as he had done, only this had meant something to her '…to the press? What kind of world do you live in?'

'Look around you.' He spread his arms wide, like some sacrifice. 'I live in the real world! Where people want what they can't have and take what they can.'

His words cracked her, cleaving her in two. She grabbed on to the back of an armchair and gripped the silken fabric tight in case the halves of her fell to the floor. 'If this is the real world then I don't want any part of it.'

'Luckily for you, you shall have none.'

A reminder once again she was being firmly put in her place. A place she'd never sought to leave, until the weekend just past. 'I know.'

'Do you? I'm glad to hear it, since you'll leave today. Within the hour. I'll have your things sent to you. My jet—'

She shook her head. Let go of the armchair's support. She needed none. She'd lived on her own terms almost since the day her parents had died. She'd do it again. As for now, she needed to get away from him, from his life and the trappings of it. Get back to the comfort and safety of her home and her relative anonymity. She didn't want sorrowful looks from royal flight attendants as she wept into a cup of tea.

Because she'd cry, but not in front of him.

'I'll fly on some airline.'

He shook his head. 'You think the press in Lasserno are bad? They're kittens compared to what you're walking into. How will you drive home, on narrow country roads being chased by motorcycles? Cars? I think not.'

If he were concerned he might have looked stricken, but that wasn't what was happening here. He didn't care about her. He never really had. His reputation was his only interest and everything else was peripheral. But there was one thing they needed to address: what she was being paid to do, since she was just an employee now.

'Your portrait.'

Something about him changed then. Alessio seemed to straighten, stand taller. Even if you didn't know it, seeing him in this moment you'd realise he was ruler of all he surveyed. Uncompromising and absolute.

'I want no portrait. Every time anyone looks at the painting, they'll speculate about what *you* saw and exactly how much. It can *never* be what I wanted it to be, a statement of intent. I'll find someone else. But don't fear. You'll be paid for your time.'

There was the final blow, his words like a kick to the stomach. It was as if for a second time her world had been taken from her. All of this, here, had been for nothing.

If she weren't made of stronger stuff, she might bend in two. But she'd survived the death of her parents and her horse, the rejection of her boyfriend, the dishonesty of her uncle. She could survive Alessio Arcuri. And she'd show him.

'You'll pay me…for my *time*. My…services rendered. What a fine way to make a woman feel cheap.' She took a deep breath, looked him straight in the eye so he could see how strong she really was, and just how much he'd meant to her until this. 'I don't want to be paid. I want nothing from you. So go and find your perfect princess. I hear royal weddings and babies are big news. They'll erase any rumours about me from your life.'

She turned her back on him, needing to get out and get away. Wanting to run but carrying herself with all the dignity she deserved, because she wasn't at fault, even though this whole place seemed intent on blaming her. Instead, she injected steel into her spine and walked to the door with her head held high. Walked away from him. As she reached out for the door handle, she hesitated. Not turning, because she didn't want to see Alessio ever again. Seeing him might remind her of what she'd lost. What she never really had in the first place.

'Thank you, Your Highness, for making our parting so much easier.'

CHAPTER ELEVEN

ALESSIO STARED AT the broken-apart travelling crate. The wood was scattered about the floor of his office after he'd cracked it apart with the crowbar he'd asked his staff to deliver here. That infernal wooden case had taunted him from the moment it had been delivered a few days before. No note, no explanation. A return address for Ms Hannah Barrington the only suggestion of what it contained.

A portrait. One he didn't want, but one he got anyway.

And *this* portrait. He stood back. This wasn't a painting to be hung in a throne room. It was deeply, achingly personal and he had no idea what to do with it. Because as he looked at the picture, what he saw was not the man he stared at in the mirror every morning but another self. Real. A better version of him.

There was no elegant quality to the brushstrokes. They slashed across the canvas with a terrifying brutality. *He* was the sole focus of the artist's gaze. Sitting side-on, with his head turned to the painter. White shirt slightly unkempt, open at the neck. Hair unruly as if he'd rolled out of bed and raked his hands through it, sat in a chair and looked at the person holding the brush. Hannah. His fingers were steepled, contemplating her. Eyes intense and focused, fixed on one woman, as if he would never look away. Corners of his lips tilted in the merest of smiles in a moment where it seemed some secret had been told, which only the painter and the subject knew.

This was a picture for a private space, for a bedroom, where the intimacies it spoke of could be understood only by the people who saw it each day.

From the packing had also fallen two small spiral sketchbooks, those she'd carried around with her. He flicked through them. There was the small landscape in watercolour pencil she'd done when she'd first arrived. The view from her window. The rest were sketches of him. His hands, his eyes. Lips. Rough outlines of him stalking the floor. Smiling. Naked in bed on Stefano's yacht. His life, the man, in black, white and grey. In the beginning, he recognised the person in those pictures. Cold, aloof. Remote from everything around him. As they progressed, Hannah had seen him in ways he no longer saw himself, seen the tiny glimpses of happiness. And then those when they were together, alone. In them, he was unrecognisable.

A man changed.

He glanced at the desk, where a folder lay: his shortlist of princesses. They were everything he'd asked for. Bright, beautiful, intelligent women from royalty who understood the job they'd be asked to do. He'd been to dinner with a few and each time he had, every part of him rebelled. Spending even a second with a woman who was not Hannah felt like a betrayal.

Because no matter how he'd tried to forget her, he couldn't. Work didn't help. Riding Apollo didn't help. Nothing did. Her touch, her laugh, the scent of her like autumn apples…all embedded in his memory. And now he had the portrait, which hinted at something he dared not name because of what he'd done to her.

He loathed how she'd looked at him on her last day here. As if he'd warped something perfect, to make it ugly. Taking his fears and frustrations out on her, when she was the victim. Because she wasn't the perpetrator, of that he was sure. He had all the power. She was the one with everything to lose. A rumoured affair with his artist had risen as a moment of brief interest in a world of many such events and faded away. All the while she'd maintained a dignified silence. His father might have laughed at the evidence of his son's human failings, though to Alessio those taunts were now meaningless. All he'd been obsessed by was its effect on her, trawling her name in the daily international press, but she was a secondary character in a story already forgotten by everyone except him.

The door of his palace office opened, and Stefano walked in. Hesitated beside the picture still half in its packing case. Nudged the crowbar discarded on the carpet beside it with the toe of his shoe.

'I thought you'd send it back or put it away without looking at it.'

He'd wanted to. The sheer terror of what Hannah might have painted had stopped him breaking open the picture for days. But he'd needed to exorcise her, and he thought, by finally confronting the portrait, that he would. He hadn't, and in fact it had made things worse.

'It's only a painting.' The lie stuck in his throat. It was more than that. So much more. A mirror to possibilities he'd rejected in a way that couldn't easily be repaired.

'If you say so.'

His friend looked drawn and tired. As if he carried a burden too heavy for one man. No enthusiasm left in him. Stefano hadn't been the same since Hannah had left the palace. Alessio thought it was managing the press fallout, the work since. He began to realise how much he missed, and how this might be something more.

'What do you say?' Alessio asked.

'I say we've both made terrible mistakes, and now it's time to face them.'

Something about the weight of those words carried a warning that things might never be the same again. 'I don't know what you mean.'

'You're not a stupid man, my friend. I don't need to point out your grave error. As for mine…' Stefano handed Alessio an envelope. 'My resignation.'

A terrible cold settled over Alessio, even in the middle of Lasserno's glorious summer. As if everything were changing and he would be the ultimate loser. Stefano stood back. Formal. Aloof. An employee and nothing more. Alessio wouldn't accept it. Right now, things needed to stay the same.

'No. Whatever the problem is, I'll fix it. Do you need a holiday? A pay rise?'

Stefano laughed. There was no humour in the tone. It sounded like a mockery of all things happy. 'Ever the Prince. There are some things you can't repair with money or power.'

'Why are you doing this?'

Stefano didn't answer. He turned, walked towards Hannah's painting. Alessio wanted to hide it. Keep it to himself. Such a deeply private piece left him vulnerable, as though everything about him was set to be exposed, his darkest hopes and dreams, which only Hannah knew.

'She's in love with you,' Stefano said.

'What?' A bright burst of something perfect, like hope, tore through him. A cruel sensation when he had nothing to hope for after what he'd done.

'As I said, you're not a stupid man. *Look* at the picture.' Stefano pointed at it, his finger stabbing the air. 'What you need in your life, Alessio, is someone to see you like *that*. The man behind the mask of the prince. You also need someone in your life you can look at as you looked at Hannah in that very moment.'

Inside he *knew*. This was a picture painted by someone

who saw the soul of another person. That didn't come simply by fine observation. It was more. Hannah had quietly given him her heart somewhere in the two weeks they'd been together. He'd selfishly taken it, and cruelly rejected it when she'd asked for nothing in return but his respect.

The problem was, he'd given her his heart as well, which was why everything seemed broken. Because she'd taken it back to England when she'd gone, and now he was left only half a man.

'Is *this* why you're resigning?'

Stefano slowly shook his head, as if the movement was too wearying to bear.

'I'm resigning because, whilst you *might* be able to repair your great error, I can't repair mine. You want to know who leaked to the press? I did.'

Alessio dropped into the chair behind his desk. He had no power to move, like a child's toy whose batteries had gone dead.

'You threw Hannah and me to those leeches?' A wicked fire lit inside, the burn threatening to overwhelm him. He clenched his fists. If he hadn't known Stefano his whole life he might have thrown punches in this moment. But there was so much he'd missed with Hannah, what hadn't he seen with his oldest friend?

Stefano shoved his hands in the pockets of his trousers. Dropped his head. 'Only about your visit to the hospital. What I failed to recognise is that small piece of information would start press interest about what else you might be doing in secret. *That's* what led to them discovering about you and Hannah. And I'll never forgive myself for it.'

It was as if the floor fell out beneath him. Alessio gripped the arms of his chair to hold himself stable when nothing in his life was any more.

'*Dio!* Stefano. Why?'

'You hide all of yourself. What you present to the world is a version of who you think everyone should see. Yet that image didn't comfort the people of Lasserno. It made them fear they were getting someone who didn't care for them at all, and that opinion was bleeding into the press. I thought a small glimpse of the private man would help show people who you truly are. And that it would allow you to see past the constraints you impose upon yourself, to the *possibilities*. Instead I caused greater harm.'

Alessio nodded. What more could he do? He'd lost everything. Hannah. His best friend. He couldn't fathom Stefano's betrayal. He couldn't forgive himself for what he'd done to Hannah, driven by fear of finding something real.

'You need a person you can trust in this position. I've arranged for someone temporary to take my place. There were a few good candidates in the palace.'

'That's…acceptable.' Alessio didn't know what more to say. His world crumbled around him with Stefano the last brick to fall.

His friend walked towards the door of the office for the last time. Just as Hannah had walked away only months before.

'My family has served yours for centuries. But you must believe this has never been work for me. It's been my pleasure as your friend.'

He then stopped…hesitated with his hand still resting on the doorknob.

'I have some advice. From Machiavelli. *"Any man who tries to be good all the time is bound to come to ruin among the great number who are not good."* Allow yourself some imperfections. You have a chance to make things right. I've run out of mine.'

Stefano gave a final bow and shut the door. And for the first time in his life Alessio felt completely alone.

* * *

Hannah stood in her studio, the window opening wide onto the sunny garden beyond. This place had once been her oasis of peace, where she could lose herself. Now it seemed more like a prison. She flopped into the threadbare sofa in a dusty corner, cup of tea in hand, body sluggish with a tiredness that hadn't seemed to have left her since she'd returned home. Self-inflicted to be sure, but it was as though she'd never feel awake again, this pressing lassitude which had stolen over her.

From the moment she'd walked into this space on returning from Lasserno she'd begun to work, grabbing a canvas and painting with a ferocity which shut everything out. She'd worked all day and through the nights. Barely sleeping or eating till she'd finished Alessio's portrait. Pouring all her heart and most of her soul into the picture to get one man out of her life. The tears and the pain worked through her fingers onto the canvas, then she'd let it go.

Or that was what was supposed to have happened. In the past, each time she'd finished a portrait had been like a great cleansing. She'd send the picture on its way and leave its subject behind as a fond memory whilst she started afresh.

Not this time. The ache of loss remained like a wound unhealed, as if the bleeding out would never stop. Hannah realised what it was now. All that time she'd spent shielding herself from the pain of love and her heart had gone and fallen in love anyway. At least she'd learned something. Suffering this kind of pain wouldn't break her. Even though the colours of the world didn't seem right, as if everything were sepia-toned, she was still standing. One day she might even be able to look back to a time when for a few fantasy moments she was made to believe she could be a princess.

She hadn't been treated like a princess in the end, though. That Alessio believed she might betray what they'd shared had shredded what remained of her heart. It told Hannah that, whilst what had happened was of great moment to her, to Alessio it meant nothing. It can't have, or he would never have thought she'd talk to the press.

Sure, they'd sniffed around when she returned to the UK, offering large sums for an exclusive. It would have solved all her financial woes, just as he'd accused. But the idea of betraying those precious moments with Alessio made her sick to the stomach.

And yet, some money had arrived in her account. Whilst she'd refused it back in Lasserno, Sue had been more circumspect when contacted by the palace. Now there were funds enough to keep the sharks at bay. It might not refill the coffers her uncle had raided, but it would do. Her uncle's assets were being sold to help pay his debts, and that would help too. She could rebuild. She had her art. Things would be fine. Truly fine.

If only she could plug the Alessio-sized hole in her heart.

She stared at the blank canvas on her easel, one she had no inspiration for. At least, not for the intended subject. Another consumed all her interest. A man with black hair and umber eyes and a glance which could set her aflame. If she picked up a pencil now she'd be able to perfectly reproduce the crinkles at the corners of his eyes when he smiled, the sensual curve of his lips when he looked at her. It was as if she would always be able to draw him. He was embedded inside her. Yet a prince had no part in her life. She went to the window. Breathed the warm air. Tried reminding herself that these simple things were what made her happy. One day her heart *would* believe her head, but not today.

The tinkle of the doorbell woke Hannah from her inertia. She'd had a few visitors since she'd returned here. Kind people in the village bringing jams, biscuits and sympathy. Probably seeking gossip, but she gave them none and the small tokens had helped.

She made her way to the front door. Pulled a band from the pocket of her jeans and raked her hair into an untidy knot on her head. Steeled herself for a visitor she didn't really want. She'd had a spyhole installed at the suggestion of the local constable when some of the press had become more insistent. Out of caution she peeked through.

Alessio.

She grabbed on to the door jamb to hold herself upright, her heart rate spiking at the thrill of seeing him again, even through the dim fisheye glass. She'd tried telling herself over and over he didn't matter but her heart now called her out as a liar. Hannah froze. Open the door? Ignore it? Tell him to go away? She stood back, trying to steady her rapid breathing, and jumped when the bell gave another short, sharp burst. In that moment she acted on impulse, turning the key and wrenching at the door.

He came into view in a dizzying rush, like the swoop of a roller coaster. More beautiful than she remembered, but then Alessio had always seemed hyper-real to her. He wore an immaculate blue suit, pristine white shirt, bold viridian tie. Nothing at all conciliatory about him, clothed in his armour of choice, as if ready for battle. The only thing about him that wasn't perfect was the stubble on his jaw of a day or two unshaven. The contrast between that casual aberration and the rest of him made her treacherous little heart flutter like the butterflies around the hollyhocks in her garden.

'Hannah.'

The way he said her name… It tumbled from his lips as if the syllables hurt to speak them. As if it had so much meaning. She wanted to mean something to him, but it was a fool's game she had no time to play. She knew her place, and needed to remind herself of it, so she dropped herself into a deep curtsey. 'Your Highness.'

He winced. 'There's no need. Not after—'

'Of course there's a need. What did your dossier say? *"The first time you meet His Royal Highness in the day, you shall curtsey."*'

'We're not in the palace.'

'No, we're definitely not.' She gripped the door, focused on the cut of the wood into her palm. Better that than focusing on the pain in what remained of her heart. 'Did you come looking for more horses? Because there are none here.'

'I'm looking for something, but not horses.'

'And no private secretary to act as a shield between you and me. What a risk-taker you are. How people might talk.'

He dropped his head, looking at the doorstep. To the worn doormat, the faded "Welcome" she'd meant to replace but never seemed to find the time.

'Any risk to me here is deserved. May I come inside?'

She didn't want him here and craved him all the same, the emotions confused and jumbled in a way she couldn't sort out. Curdling in her stomach like an ill-chosen meal.

'What are you doing here?'

'I need to…talk.'

'I'm not sure I need to listen.'

He shoved his hands in the pockets of his trousers. 'I deserve that. But I'd still like you to hear what I have to say. Please.'

She studied him now, in a way she hadn't allowed herself only moments before. Part curiosity, part need. Those lines around his eyes that creased when he smiled appeared more pronounced, though the look wasn't a happy one. There were dark smudges underneath his eyes as if she'd run her charcoal-covered fingers there. That thought was a reminder of a blissful afternoon on Stefano's yacht when everything had seemed so perfect. But she shouldn't reminisce about those few days—they were long gone. Still, listening didn't cost her much and might give them both some closure, far enough away from their tortured last day. She stepped back and allowed him in. He crowded out the small entry foyer.

'Come to the studio.'

That was her war room, where she usually felt competent and safe. Though everything seemed a risk to her right now. Once again, Alessio was her greatest danger, and yet she still wanted to poke her fingers into the fire and be burned. But she'd remind them both of her place in his life.

'I should thank you for the payment, even though you went against my wishes.'

'I took two weeks of your time. It was the least I could do.'

The least he could do... The pain of that morning roared back in a rush and she couldn't hold it in. She didn't care any more, striding right up to him, invading his space. Wanting to push him away and hold on tight, all at the same time. The burn of tears pricked at her eyes, but she was *done* crying. Too many tears had been shed over him already.

She planted her hands on her hips. Better than reaching out to touch.

'I would have walked away, at the end of it all. After those two weeks, I would have stepped onto a plane and you would never have heard from me again.' As much as her heart had rebelled at the time, it was what she would have done because he was looking for someone other than her. Because she loved him and that was what you were supposed to do when you loved something: you set it free. 'But you cheapened *everything*. Turned something beautiful into something dirty.'

'I know. Only one of us was acting like an adult that day. I hurt you intentionally.'

She bit on her lower lip, hoping the sting might take her mind off the pain his admission caused.

'Is that what this is, a kind of sorry? You didn't need to fly all the way here. You could have sent a card. *My deepest apologies for being a jerk.* Maybe some flowers as a final kind of blow-off.'

Alessio stood there. Immaculate. Impassive. Taking what she gave. Even though he appeared a little careworn, it only added to his underlying appeal.

'I'll never forgive myself for how I treated you. I was afraid of what I felt but the coward in me chose to believe I meant no more to you than the money I could provide. That's *my* issue. I shouldn't have cheapened the most treasured time of my life because of fear, when the perpetrator of the press leak was closer to home.'

'Who talked?' Alessio trusted everyone in the palace. He had assured her that what they had could be kept secret. And yet someone had betrayed him. It had to hurt for a man like Alessio, that misplaced confidence. She saw the cracks in his façade then, not only the two-day growth and tired eyes, but also his slightly paler skin. The tightness around his mouth. All of him looking older and more deeply etched than before.

'Stefano.'

It was as if a rock had settled in the pit of her stomach. She almost reached out to him, to comfort. But Alessio hadn't wanted her before, and if he pushed her away again she might never recover. There were some memories she wouldn't allow to become any more tainted.

'I'm sorry.' She meant it. She understood betrayal from someone she should have been able to trust too. 'Did he say why?'

Alessio might have been cruel to her but she wouldn't be

the same to him. She was better than that. He walked over to the battered table holding her paint, brushes and palette.

'His intentions were good, but misplaced. And yet I can't find it in my heart to blame him.' He mindlessly sorted through the tubes of paint. Picked one up. 'Alizarin Crimson. The colour of righteous anger.'

He might have smiled then. Something about him seemed to lighten for a moment, the hint of his lips turning up at the corners. It softened him, like a dry brush smudging over the sharp edges of a painted line.

'You remembered,' she said. A door inside her that should have been locked tight opened a fraction. But they wanted different things, didn't they? He'd told her from the beginning. Yet her silly heart simply craved to beat to a singular rhythm.

Alessio's.

'I remember everything. I can't forget. But I'm not good at the words for this.' He took off his coat, tossed it on the worn couch. Loosened his tie, as if he was going into a battle of another kind. An emotional one. 'I don't know how to be anything other than the Prince of Lasserno. It's all I was trained for. Then I received the portrait and drawings. And I finally saw myself through your eyes. I want to be *that* man. The one in the picture. I want to be that man, for you.'

Everything stopped. The silence, as if the universe waited and yet she couldn't quite fathom the words.

'What are you saying?'

'Do I have a chance to make this right?'

All colour in the world flooded back in a rush, as though things were too bright, too real. But the threat of his words crept up like some choking vine round her throat. That this couldn't work, that dreams didn't come true. Yet when she looked at him, all she saw on his face was hope. And her choice became clear. Saying no meant fear had won. Hannah was tired of losing that battle. She'd been afraid for long enough. It meant there was only one answer to give. So she let that hope fill her and overflow as she prepared to say one simple word.

'Yes.'

Yes. That single syllable went off like a bomb in Alessio's head, shattering everything. A chance. A fragile chance to repair what he'd broken. Build anew. She stood before him like a warrior. Tall. Proud. Putting him to shame. In her worn jeans with rips at the knees that perhaps hung a bit more loosely than the last time he'd seen her in them. Her hair in a messy topknot, strands falling about her face. Her green eyes flashing bright and vibrant, a warning to him that nothing here was certain. And yet he knew today was about laying his soul bare for her to trample on as she saw fit, even if it meant he lost the precious chance she'd granted him. Now was the time to be brave. As brave as her.

'I love you, Hannah.' Those words ground out of him, though easier than expected because they were his deepest truth. The root of all things good in his life. Her eyes widened a fraction, her hands clenched. He didn't know what those things meant, but he carried on regardless. She deserved these words; she should have nothing less. 'From the moment I saw you here I knew you were a danger to me, so to ruin any chance with you I was unspeakably cruel. But that doesn't change the *real* truth. There is only you.'

Her eyes gleamed a little brighter. Tears? What he wouldn't give to hold her, to tell her it would all be okay, but he couldn't, because he was the cause of her suffering.

'What about your perfect princess?'

'I've spent too long setting standards of perfection that were impossible for me to meet. I don't want some perfect princess. I need the woman who captured my heart.'

She turned and walked to the window, staring outside into the rambling cottage garden, bright and beautiful in the English summer. Her hand reached up to her face, swiping at it.

'You hurt me. Claiming you now love me isn't a free pass.' Her voice was almost a whisper. The ache in it clawed at him, his own pain at what he'd done to her well deserved. His cross to bear. Alessio walked towards her, close enough to comfort if she eventually accepted it, far enough to give her the space she obviously needed.

'I know. All I've ever seen of love is that it brings pain. It seemed to be a poisoned thing. What I failed to realise is the great joy it can bring as well. I want to repair what I've done here, even if you can't love me back.'

Her shoulders hunched. She wrapped her arms round herself, as if she were trying to hold all the pain in. He hated that he'd done this. Failed the person he cared for the most.

'The problem is I can't *stop* loving you.'

He shut his eyes, giving a quiet thank-you to the heavens. It was as if everything that had been knotted up tight began to loosen. She loved him. She *still* loved him. His responsibility now was even greater than before. To honour her the way he should have from the beginning.

'I want to take the pain away by loving you back. Fiercely and for ever.'

Hannah turned, her eyes pink-rimmed. It was all he could do not to reach out and hold her, but he didn't have permission for that, not yet. She held out her hands in front of her, looked down at them. Splayed her fingers. The light from the window behind bathed her in an ethereal glow. She looked like a beautifully flawed angel.

'I'm pretty sure princesses don't have paint-stained hands.'

He feared he'd been the one to make her unsure about

this, about herself, when he'd witnessed her being more regal than most royalty he'd ever met. Being a mere princess was beneath her. If he could make her a queen, he would.

'A princess can have whatever she wants. What *I* want is the artist who painted the portrait of the man now hanging in my bedroom. The man I should have aspired to be all these years. Not a prince, but a man in love. That love is what makes me a better person. There is no one other than you, Hannah. There never will be. The question is whether you want me for ever in return. And I'm prepared to wait. However long it takes.'

She looked up at him, eyes wide and sad and yet still tinged with hope, because it was all either of them had left. Hope that each would take a chance on the other, to build something towering and great, that could withstand anything life threw at them.

'What if however long is right now?'

He couldn't help the smile that broke out on his face, the fire of blazing happiness that lit inside. That she wanted him, that he was enough. The weight of the world rose from his shoulders. A lightening in his soul.

'Then I'll immediately accept whatever you allow. I don't expect your trust, perhaps not for years. But I'll fight for it each day. For you to be by my side. As my wife, my princess, my artist, my *everything*. You already own all my heart. Let me give you my whole world.'

She took a step towards him. 'You have my trust now. I'm not risking my heart for just anyone.'

Alessio opened his arms and Hannah walked right into them. He tightened them round her, soaking in her warmth, relishing in the feel of her body against his. His love. His heart. His home. She tilted her head up, her lips parted. He dropped his mouth to hers, the kiss coaxing, loving, saying in his gentle way what he had trouble verbalising. That he loved her more than words could ever express.

'It's no risk, *bella*.' That was his vow and promise, from this moment forward. 'I will cherish and care for your precious heart for ever.'

EPILOGUE

ALESSIO STROLLED THROUGH the doorway of the pavilion where Hannah now had her studio. The afternoon sun filtered like a patchwork through the windows, warming the space. She didn't look up at him as he entered. He loved that about her…her absolute focus when absorbed by her art.

No words were necessary to describe the love they shared, even in those moments. As she'd begun painting his coronation portrait he'd sat for her, stretches of blissful silence where he could watch her work. The concentration. She had it now, a tiny frown plaguing her forehead, as if something about the canvas troubled her. Something about him, since she was still working on his picture.

'I worry about you down here—it's too far from the palace.'

Her frown melted away. She looked up at him and smiled. The joy in it, seeing him, could light up his darkest places. When fear threatened, that he wouldn't be enough to guide the country through what was ahead of it, she could chase it away with the tilt of her perfect lips. With Hannah, there was no room for anything other than courage, love and trust.

'Don't be ridiculous. It's only a short stroll and the light's perfect.' She rose from the stool on which she'd been sitting and placed her hands on the small of her back, arching in a stretch. The soft fabric of her dress moulded to show off her rounded belly. Four months along and the pregnancy news in his country had reached fever pitch, with speculation over whether the baby would be a boy or a girl and bets being taken. Not even he and Hannah knew. Not yet. They wanted to keep some surprises, and to them it didn't matter. Either a little prince or princess would fill them with even more happiness, if that were possible.

He welcomed every moment of the bliss Hannah had brought to his life. A flood of warmth coursed over him. Love, pride. A whole mix that filled every day. He walked towards her, slowly, because she'd banned him from seeing his portrait until she was satisfied with it. He wondered if she ever would be.

'May I look now?' he asked.

'I think it's done.' That little frown was back again. He wanted to wipe it away, but at least the only time she ever seemed uncertain now was with her art. Not about his love, or her role. Never those things. He adored her; his people adored her. The murals she had designed and helped paint at the children's hospital had cemented Lasserno's love for its new Princess.

Even his father had given public praise for Alessio's choice of bride. Not that Alessio cared, but Hannah and her pregnancy had opened a door to communication that months ago would have seemed insurmountable. Perhaps miracles could happen. Alessio hadn't put any faith in them till Hannah's presence in his life made him believe anything was possible, including a truce with his father.

'What are you waiting for?' Hannah asked. Alessio shook himself out of his introspection. He walked round the canvas on the easel in the middle of the room and saw himself. It was like looking in a mirror. In this picture he sat in his office, surrounded by his ancestors. A magnificent representation of the Prince he'd once striven to be.

His honours and regalia pinned to his military jacket. He didn't care for any of it.

The only honours he craved now were Hannah's.

'He seems almost forbidding. Unlike your other portrait.'

Strange how his perceptions of what his country needed from him had changed with Hannah's presence in his life, all the hard edges of himself burnished smooth by the love she brought to him. Love he wasn't afraid of any more. Her love made him strong, not weak.

'The first portrait is of the private man. The one only I'm privileged to see. I'll keep him all for myself. This one is the Prince your country needs. Strong. Eternal. The greatest prince Lasserno will ever have.'

That praise filled him. Her love, and how freely she gave it, was boundless. He swooped her up, swung her into his arms. She shrieked, and then started giggling.

'What are you doing?'

'Taking this somewhere more comfortable.'

He moved to the seating area he'd installed in this place. Nothing wanting, for her at least. Every comfort available to her. If this was to be her studio, it had to be perfect. Given the time she spent down here, he hoped it was.

He placed her gently on the large, soft sofa in the corner. Knelt in front of her. Kissed her pregnant belly. Her hand moved to his head, stroked through his hair. He shut his eyes and savoured her touch. One quiet moment of perfection in an otherwise long day. There had been so many small moments like this and Alessio relished each one.

When he opened his eyes Hannah's head tilted to the side, as if she were trying to peer inside him. He could hold no secrets. She owned them all.

'Have you spoken to Stefano?'

Ah. The one wound that remained unhealed. The only ache that hadn't gone away. Being more open with the media now, Alessio saw what Stefano had tried to do. Lasserno *was* happier when shown their leader openly caring. In that way, he'd been right.

'I've tried.'

'You're writing him missives, aren't you?'

Hannah knew him too well. In some things, change came slowly. 'He may not want to speak to the man, but he *will* answer to his Prince. His family always has. It's treasonous to do otherwise.'

'Allow him his pride. He'll answer when the time's right. Anyway, I don't answer you a lot of the time. Am I committing treason too?' Her lips curled into a sultry smile.

'That's to my benefit. You remind me I'm only human, and that's all I have to be.'

Hannah's hand drifted to her belly and all he could see was their future, bright and brilliant.

'I love the human side,' she said.

Alessio trailed his fingers up her legs and she shivered under his touch, goosebumps peppering her skin. 'I love it when you're wearing a skirt.'

'I know.' Her legs parted and his hands drifted higher, his thumbs circling on her inner thighs, her body pliant as it sank into the softness of the sofa.

'I love it even better when you're wearing nothing at all,' he said.

'Rule number two, I seem to remember.'

'What about rule number one?'

She rolled her eyes. 'I didn't promise to obey you when we married. But I did promise to love you.'

Alessio laughed. There was so much laughter in his life now. Hannah brought it into every day. Yes, there was plenty of work too, but there was still play. She could infuse even the difficult times with a sense of fun.

'I love *you*,' he said. Those three words never seemed

enough for the bone-deep sentiment they carried. He was aware of the privilege and the trust she'd shown him by saying *yes*. Alessio ensured she knew it every day, so there could be no doubt she'd made the right choice in choosing him.

She cupped his face and the look she gave him could have cut him off at the knees, so it was good that he was kneeling right now. Her eyes were soft, brimming with emotion. So much emotion. He could constantly worship her…it was no trial at all.

'I love you even more.'

He took her hand, running his thumb over her wedding ring and her engagement ring. The ring, which he'd had made especially for her. Their love was so bright and new he wanted gems to reflect that truth. Reflect her. A large emerald the colour of her eyes, flanked by two rubies, the colour of his endless love.

'Never doubt my feelings.'

'I never do.'

He smiled again, slipped his hands into the warm silk of her hair. Alessio relished the lifetime of these moments ahead of them. A future which held her in it was one to anticipate and cherish. Then he dropped his mouth to hers. Kissed her welcoming lips. And spent the afternoon in this pavilion, once built to love, proving their words to be true.

* * * * *

COMING SOON!

MILLS & BOON

THE HEART OF ROMANCE

A ROMANCE FOR EVERY READER

MODERN

Prepare to be swept off your feet by sophisticated, sexy and seductive heroes, in some of the world's most glamourous and romantic locations, where power and passion collide.

HISTORICAL

Escape with historical heroes from time gone by. Whether your passion is for wicked Regency Rakes, muscled Vikings or rugged Highlanders, awaken the romance of the past.

MEDICAL

Set your pulse racing with dedicated, delectable doctors in the high-pressure world of medicine, where emotions run high and passion, comfort and love are the best medicine.

True Love

Celebrate true love with tender stories of heartfelt romance, from the rush of falling in love to the joy a new baby can bring, and a focus on the emotional heart of a relationship.

Desire

Indulge in secrets and scandal, intense drama and plenty of sizzling hot action with powerful and passionate heroes who have it all: wealth, status, good looks…everything but the right woman.

HEROES

Experience all the excitement of a gripping thriller, with an intense romance at its heart. Resourceful, true-to-life women and strong, fearless men face danger and desire - a killer combination!

To see which titles are coming soon, please visit
millsandboon.co.uk/nextmonth

MILLS & BOON

Coming next month

THE SICILIAN'S FORGOTTEN WIFE
Caitlin Crews

"I wish only to kiss my wife," Cenzo growled. "On this, the first day of the rest of our life together."

"You don't want to kiss me," she threw at him, and he thought the way she trembled now was her temper taking hold. "You want to start what you think will be my downward spiral, until all I can do is fling myself prostrate before you and cringe about at your feet. Guess what? I would rather die."

"Let us test that theory," he suggested, and kissed her.

And this time, it had nothing at all to do with punishment. Though it was no less a claiming.

This time, it was a seduction.

Pleasure and dark promise.

He took her face in his hands, and he tasted her as he wanted at last. He teased her lips until she sighed, melting against him, and opened to let him in.

He kissed her and he kissed her, until all that fury, all that need, hummed there between them. He kissed her, losing himself in the sheer wonder of her taste and the way that sweet sea scent of hers teased at him, as if she was bewitching him despite his best efforts to seize control.

Cenzo kissed her like a man drowning and she met each thrust of his tongue, then moved closer as if she was as greedy as he was.

As if she knew how much he wanted her and wanted him, too, with that very same intensity.

And there were so many things he wanted to do with her. But kissing her felt like a gift, like sheer magic, and for once in his life, Cenzo lost track of his own ulterior motives. His own grand plan.

There was only her taste. Her heat.

Her hair that he gripped in his hands, and the way she pressed against him.

There was only Josselyn. His wife.

He kissed her again and again, and then he shifted, meaning to lift her in his arms—

But she pushed away from him, enough to brace herself against his chest. He found his hands on her upper arms.

"I agreed to marry you," she managed to pant out at him, her lips faintly swollen and her brown eyes wild. "I refuse to be a pawn in your game."

"You can be any piece on the board that you like," he replied, trying to gather himself. "But it will still be my board, Josselyn."

He let her go, lifting up his hands theatrically. "By all means, little wife. Run and hide if that makes you feel more powerful."

He kept his hands in the air, his mock surrender, and laughed at her as he stepped back.

Because he'd forgotten, entirely, that they stood on those narrow stairs.

It was his own mocking laughter that stayed with him as he fell, a seeming slow-motion slide backward when his foot encountered only air. He saw her face as the world fell out from beneath him.

Continue reading
THE SICILIAN'S FORGOTTEN WIFE
Caitlin Crews

Available next month
www.millsandboon.co.uk

LET'S TALK
Romance

For exclusive extracts, competitions
and special offers, find us online:

- **f** facebook.com/millsandboon
- **🐦** @MillsandBoon
- **📷** @MillsandBoonUK

Get in touch on 01413 063232

For all the latest titles coming soon, visit
millsandboon.co.uk/nextmonth

MILLS & BOON
Desire

Indulge in secrets and scandal, intense drama and plenty of sizzling hot action with powerful and passionate heroes who have it all: wealth, status, good looks…everything but the right woman.

MILLS & BOON
HEROES
At Your Service

Experience all the excitement of a gripping thriller, with an intense romance at its heart. Resourceful, true-to-life women and strong, fearless men face danger and desire - a killer combination!